TEXAR'S REVENGE:

OR,

North Against South.

(NORD CONTRE SUD.)

A TALE OF THE AMERICAN CIVIL WAR.

(COMPLETE IN ONE VOLUME.)

PART I.

BURBANK, THE NORTHERNER.

BY

JULES VERNE,

AUTHOR OF "ROUND THE WORLD IN EIGHTY DAYS," ETC., ETC., ETC

ILLUSTRATED.

Fredonia Books
Amsterdam, the Netherlands

Texar's Revenge:
North Against South
A Tales of the American Civil War

by
Jules Verne

ISBN: 1-4101-0064-2

Reprinted from the 1888 edition

Fredonia Books
Amsterdam, The Netherlands
http://www.fredoniabooks.com

In order to make original editions of historical works available to scholars at an economical price, this facsimile of the original edition of 1888 is reproduced from the best available copy and has been digitally enhanced to improve legibility, but the text remains unaltered to retain historical authenticity.

TEXAR'S REVENGE;

OR,

North Against South.

(NORD CONTRE SUD.)

PART I.

TEXAR, THE SOUTHERNER.

CONTENTS.

CONTENTS.

CHAPTER XI.

NORTH AND SOUTH.

Part I.

BURBANK THE NORTHERNER.

CHAPTER I.

ON BOARD THE "SHANNON."

FLORIDA was annexed to the American federation in 1819; it was organized into a state a few years afterwards. By the annexation the area of the republic was increased by some 67,000 square miles. But the star of Florida shines with second-rate brilliancy in that constellation of thirty-eight which spangle the banner of the United States of America.

Florida, throughout, is a low, narrow tongue of land, and its rivers, with one exception—the St. John's—owing to the narrowness of the country, are of no importance. From such a slight rise, there is not sufficient fall for the watercourses to be of any rapidity ; there are no mountains, only a few lines of "bluffs" or low hills such as are numerous in the central and southern regions of the Union. In form the peninsula is not unlike the tail of a beaver dipping into the ocean between the Atlantic on the east and the Gulf of Mexico on the west.

Florida's nearest neighbour to the north is Georgia, the frontier running a little above the isthmus which joins the peninsula to the continent.

Florida seems to be a country apart, with its people half Spaniards, half Americans, and its Seminole Indians so

different to their congeners in the west.   In the south it is
arid, sandy, almost entirely bordered by sand-hills formed
by successive irruptions of the Atlantic ; but in the north
its plains are of marvellous fertility.   Its name is justified,
to the letter.   The flora is superb, vigorous, and of exuberant variety, more especially in that portion watered by
the St. John's.   This river is a broad stream flowing from
south to north, over a course of some two hundred and
fifty miles, of which one hundred and seventeen, up to Lake
George, are navigable.   The rivers flowing east and west
have no room for length ; but the St. John's, from its central
course to the north, suffers from no such hindrance, and
numerous branches run into it or rather into the multi-
tudinous creeks along its banks.   The St. John's is in fact
the chief artery of the country, which receives its life from
its waters, for water is the blood of the earth.

It was the 7th of February, 1862.   The steamboat
Shannon was running down the St. John's.   At four o'clock
in the afternoon she was due at Picolata, after calling at
the piers higher up the river, and the forts in St. John's
and Putnam counties.   A few miles beyond she would
enter Duval county, which is bordered by Nassau county
and cut off from it by the river bearing that name.

Picolata itself is not of much importance, but its neighbourhood is rich in indigo plantations, sugar plantations,
rice fields, cotton fields, and vast cypress groves.   For
some distance round the population is numerous, and it is
an important centre for trade and travellers.   It is the
landing-place for St. Augustine, one of the chief towns of
eastern Florida, situated some dozen miles away on that
part of the sea-coast sheltered by the long island of Anastasia.   An almost straight road leads from the river port
to the town.

On the pier at Picolata there are to day many more
travellers than usual.   Some speedy vehicles known as
stages, each seating eight persons, drawn by four or six
mules galloping like mad along the road across the marsh,
had brought them from St. Augustine.   It was important
for them not to miss the steamboat ; to do so would be to

risk a delay of at least forty-eight hours in getting back to the towns and villages down the river. For the *Shannon* made only one passage up or down each day, and she was the only means of transport. It was therefore necessary to be at Picolata when she called ; and the vehicles had unloaded their passengers an hour before she was due.

There were about fifty men on the gangway at Picolata. While they waited they were talking excitedly. They had divided into two groups not at all anxious to mix with each other. What had brought them from St. Augustine ? Was it some serious matter, some political contest ? It was obvious that there was no chance of their agreeing. Enemies they had come and enemies they would return. That could be seen clearly enough from the angry looks they exchanged, from the marked division between the groups, from several ill-sounding words whose defiant meaning no one could mistake.

A prolonged whistling began to be heard above stream.

The *Shannon* soon appeared at the bend of the right bank half a mile above Picolata. Thick clouds of smoke escaped from her two funnels, and crowned the large trees which the sea breeze was shaking on the opposite bank. The moving mass grew larger rapidly. The tide had just turned ; and the current, which for three or four hours had been against her, was now in her favour and taking the waters of the St. John's towards the sea.

At length the bell was heard. The wheels going astern stopped the *Shannon*, and her hawsers brought her alongside the pier.

The passengers went on board somewhat hastily. One of the groups went first ; the other did not move. It looked as though they were waiting for one or several travellers who ran a chance of being late. Two or three men went up the pier to the place where the road from St. Augustine came in ; and then they looked towards the east, evidently with impatience.

And not without reason ; for the captain of the *Shannon*, who was on the bridge, shouted to them,—

"Now then ! come on !"

"In a minute or two," answered one of the men in the group that remained on the gangway.

"I can't wait, gentlemen."

"A few minutes!"

"No! not one!"

"Only a moment!"

"Impossible! The tide is running out, and I may have no water over the bar at Jacksonville."

"And besides," said one of those on board, "there is no reason why we should put up with their fancies."

"That is what I think, Mr. Burbank," said the captain. "Duty first. Now then, gentlemen, come on board; I am off."

And the sailors began to push away the steamboat from the pier, while sonorous jets escaped from the steam-whistle. A shout stopped the manœuvre.

"There is Texar! There is Texar!"

A carriage came rattling along at full speed and dashed round the turning up to the pier. The four mules, which formed the team, stopped at the gate. A man got down. Those of his companions who had gone up the road rejoined him at a run. Then all of them went on board the boat.

"A moment more, Texar, and you could not have gone. That would have been awkward for you," said one of the group.

"Yes! It would have been two days before you got back to—where?—We shall know when you choose to tell us!" added another.

"And if the captain had listened to that rascal Burbank," said a third, "the *Shannon* would have been a quarter of a mile down stream by now."

Texar had just stepped on to the fore leck-house, accompanied by his friends. He contented himself with a look at James Burbank from where he was only separated from him by the bridge. Although he said not a word, the look he gave was sufficient to show the implacable hatred that existed between the two men. Burbank looked Texar straight in the face, turned his back on him, and went to sit on the after deck-house, where his friends had already seated themselves.

"Burbank is not happy!" said one of Texar's companions. "And no wonder! He lost by his lies, and the recorder did justice to his false witness—"

"But not to himself," interrupted Texar, "and that justice I will undertake."

The *Shannon* had slacked off the hawsers. Her bow pushed off by the long poles, took the line of the current, and driven by her powerful wheels, helped by the ebbing tide, she glided rapidly between the banks of the St. John's.

American river steamboats are well known. They are many-storied houses crowned with wide terraces, and dominated by the two funnels and the flagstaffs which support the ironwork of the awnings. On the Hudson as on the Mississippi, these steamboats are floating palaces, and can hold the population of a small town. But there was no need for such grandeur on the St. John's. The *Shannon* was only a floating hotel, although in its interior and exterior arrangements it was similar to the *Kentucky* and the *Dean Richmond*.

The weather was magnificent. The very blue sky was spotted with light freckles of vapour that thinned off towards the horizon. In the thirtieth parallel of latitude the month of February is almost as warm in the New World as it is in the old on the confines of the Sahara ; but a gentle breeze blown in from the sea tempers its excess.

Most of the passengers on the *Shannon* stopped on the deck-house to breathe the fresh air that the wind brought them from riverside forests. The slanting rays of the sun could not reach them beneath the awnings which were shaken like punkahs by the speed of the steamboat.

Texar and the five or six companions who had embarked with him, had thought well to go below to one of the boxes in the dining-room. There, with throats seasoned to the strongest drinks of American bars, they tossed off whole glasses of gin and Bourbon whiskey. They were indeed a rough lot, rude in habit and speech, wearing more leather

than cloth, and more accustomed to live in the woods than
in cities. Texar appeared to have some right of superiority
over them, due, doubtless, to the energy of his character as
well as to his position and means. When Texar did not
talk, his comrades remained silent and spent the time in
drinking.

Texar, after carelessly running his eye over one of the
newspapers which littered the dining-room tables, had
just thrown it aside, saying,—

"That is all old news."

"I believe you," said one of his companions, "the paper
is three days old."

"And a good many things happen in three days," added
another.

"What is the latest about the war?" asked Texar.

"As far as we are concerned, the latest is that the
Federals are preparing an expedition against Florida, and
that means we may expect an invasion of northerners!"

"Is that true?"

"I don't know, but I heard of it at Savannah, and I
heard of it again at St. Augustine."

"Well, let these Federals come!" exclaimed Texar,
striking his fist on the table so as to make the glasses and
bottles shake. "Yes! let them come! and we shall see
if the Florida slave-owners will allow themselves to be
robbed by the abolitionist thieves."

Texar's reply will have told two things to those readers
who are unacquainted with what was then happening in
America. First, that the war of Secession, declared really
by the gun fired on Fort Sumter on the 11th April, 1861,
was then in its most critical phase, for it had extended
almost to the farthest limits of the Southern States; and
secondly, that Texar, a supporter of slavery, made common
cause with the immense majority of the people in the slave
states. On board the *Shannon* were representatives of both
parties. One—to use the different appellations bestowed on
them during the long struggle—consisting of northerners,
anti-slavery men, abolitionists or federals; the other of
southerners, slavery men, secessionists or confederates.

An hour afterwards Texar and his comrades, having had quite enough to drink, appeared on the upper deck of the *Shannon*. She had already passed Trent Creek and Six Mile Creek on the right bank, Trent Creek coming in from a vast cypress grove, Six Mile Creek bringing its waters down from the Twelve Mile Marsh, of which the name tells the extent The steamboat's course lay between borders of magnificent trees, tulip-trees, magnolias, pines, cypresses, yuccas, and many others, whose trunks were hidden by the wild undergrowth of azaleas and serpentarias. Occasionally, at the mouths of the creeks leading up to the marshy plains of St. John and Duval counties, a strong odour of musk impregnated the atmosphere, coming not from the shrubs, whose emanations are so penetrating in this climate, but from the alligators hurrying under the bushes at the noisy passage of the *Shannon*. Then there were birds of all sorts, woodpeckers, herons, jacamars, bitterns, white-headed pigeons, mocking-birds, and a hundred others differing in form and plumage, while the cat-bird reproduced all the sounds of the forest with his ventriloquial voice.

As Texar mounted the last of the steps on to the upper deck, a woman met him on her way down to the interior of the saloon. When she found herself face to face with him, she stepped back. She was a half-breed in the service of the Burbank family ; her first movement had been one of unconquerable repulsion at finding herself suddenly face to face with the declared enemy of her master.

Texar gave her an evil look as she stepped back, and then shrugging his shoulders, he joined his companions.

"Yes, it is Zermah," he said, "one of the slaves of Mr. James Burbank, who says he does not approve of slavery."

Zermah made no reply. When the way to the saloon was clear, she went down it without turning to take any notice of the observation.

Texar strolled towards the bow of the steamboat ; there

after lighting a cigar, he apparently dismissed from his notice the friends who had followed him, and began to watch with some attention the left bank of the St. John's along the border of Putnam county.

Meanwhile, on the after-deck of the *Shannon*, the conversation had run on the war. When Zermah went, Burbank had remained with two of his friends, who had accompanied him to St. Augustine. One was his brother-in-law, Edward Carrol, the other was Mr. Walter Stannard, a Floridan living at Jacksonville. They were talking with considerable animation of the sanguinary strife of which the issue was a question of life or death to the United States. But, as we shall see, Burbank's opinion of the issue differed considerably from Texar's.

"I am anxious," said he, "to get back to Camdless Bay. We have been two days away. Perhaps some news of the war has arrived. Perhaps Dupont and Sherman are now masters of Port Royal and the islands of South Carolina."

"Anyhow, it will not be long before they are," said Carrol, "and I shall be much astonished if President Lincoln does not carry the war into Florida."

"And it will not be before it is time!" said Burbank. "It is quite time that the will of the Union should be imposed on these southerners of Georgia and Florida, who fancy they are too far off to be reached! See to what a degree of insolence vagabonds like Texar are led! He feels that he is supported by the slaveholders, and excites them against us northerners, whose position, which gets more and more difficult every day, lays us open to the back-wash of the war."

"You are right, James," said Edward Carrol. "It is of consequence that Florida should return as soon as possible to the authority of the Washington Government. If the Federal army does not come quickly we shall have to abandon our plantations."

"It may be only a question of days, Burbank," said Stannard. "When I left Jacksonville the day before yesterday, people were getting uneasy at the news of

Commodore Dupont's supposed plans for opening up the
St. John's, and that would give a pretext for threatening
those who do not think with the slave-owners. I am
afraid that a rising would turn out the authorities of the
town in favour of fellows of the worst description."

"I should not be surprised if it did," said Burbank.
"We shall have a bad time of it till the Federal army
comes ; but it cannot be helped."

"What can we do?" asked Walter Stannard. "Supposing there exist at Jacksonville and other places a few
brave colonists who think as we do on this slave questions
they are not strong enough to withstand the Secessionists.
We can only reckon for safety on the arrival of the
Federals, and wish that when intervention is decided on it
will take place without delay."

"Yes. Would they were here," exclaimed Burbank, "to
deliver us from these blackguards ! "

And we shall soon see that these Northerners, who, on
account of family or other interests, were obliged to live
amid a slave-holding population and conform to the
usages of the country, were fully justified in their fears and
the language they held concerning them.

The news discussed by Burbank and his friends was
true. The Federal Government was preparing an expedition for the subjugation of Florida ; not so much, however, for the military occupation of the State as the closing
of the outlets against the blockade-runners, who took away
local productions and brought in arms and munitions of
war. It was in consequence of this blockade that the
Shannon no longer plied up the southern coast of
Georgia, which was then in the power of the Northern
generals. For prudential reasons she stopped a little
beyond the mouth of the St. John's, towards the north of
Amelia Island, at the port of Fernandina, the terminus of
the Cedar Keys railway, which crosses the Florida peninsula obliquely to the Gulf of Mexico. Higher than
Amelia Island and the river St. Mary the *Shannon*
would have risked capture from the Federal cruisers
which were constantly on the coast.

2

It follows that the passengers were chiefly Floridans, whose business did not require their crossing the frontier. All of them were dwellers in the towns or villages on the St. John's and its affluents, and for the most part lived at St. Augustine or Jacksonville. At the different places they landed, and embarked either by the gangways from the wharves, or by piers built out in the English fashion.

One of the passengers intended, however, to quit the steamer in mid-stream. His plan was to leave her at a part of the river where there was no wharf or pier, nor village, nor isolated house, nor even a hunting or fishing hut in sight.

The passenger was Texar.

About six o'clock the *Shannon* gave three sharp screams from her steam whistle. Her wheels were almost immediately stopped, and she began to drift along with the stream, which hereabouts runs slowly. She was then off the entrance to Black Creek.

This creek is a deep gash in the left bank, into which flows a small river of the same name, which runs by the foot of Fort Heilman, almost on the boundary between Putnam and Duval counties. Its narrow opening is entirely hidden beneath an arch of boughs and foliage matted together, as close as the woof of some close tissue. This gloomy lagoon was almost unknown to the people of the country. No one knew that Texar had there his dwelling. The opening of the creek seemed in no way to break into the line of bank, and as night was falling rapidly, it would require a very skilful boatman to take a boat into such a place.

At the first whistle of the *Shannon*, a shout had come in answer—three times. A light burning among the trees on the bank was put in motion, showing that a canoe was coming out to meet the steamer.

It was only a skiff—a little bark boat, driven by one paddle. Soon the skiff was half a cable-length from the *Shannon*.

Texar stepped up to the front of the fore-deck and making a speaking-trumpet with his hands, shouted,—

"Ahoy !"

"Ahoy !" came back in answer.

"Is that you, Squambo ?"

"Yes, master !"

"Come alongside."

The skiff came alongside. By the light of the lantern attached to its bow, the man. could be seen who was paddling it. He was an Indian, black-headed, naked to the waist, and sturdily built, to judge from the torso revealed in the fitful light.

Texar returned towards his companions and shook hands with them, bidding them a significant *au revoir*. Then giving a threatening look towards Mr. Burbank, he descended the ladder from the sponson, and stepped into the skiff. In a few turns of the paddle-wheels the steamer was out of sight, and no one on board could suspect that the little craft was about to vanish under the dark thickets on the bank.

"One scoundrel the less on board," said Carrol, without caring if he were heard by Texar's companions.

"Yes," said James Burbank, "and at the same time, a dangerous scoundrel. I have no doubt of it myself, although he has always been able to escape conviction."

"Anyway," said Stannard, "if a crime is committed to-night in the neighbourhood of Jacksonville, they cannot accuse him, for he has left the *Shannon*."

"I don't know that," said Burbank, "if they told me he had been stealing or assassinating this very moment fifty miles off in the north of Florida, I should not be surprised. And if he managed to prove that he was not the author of the crime, I should not be surprised after what has happened. But it is not worth while to worry ourselves about such a man. You are going back to Jacksonville, Stannard ?"

"To-night."

"Is your daughter expecting you ?"

"Yes, I am going to meet her."

PART I

"I understand," said Burbank; "and when are you coming to Camdless Bay?"

"In a day or so."

"Then come as soon as you can, my dear fellow. We are on the eve of very important events, and matters will get worse as the Federal troops come nearer. And I fancy your daughter Alice and you would be in greater safety at Castle House than in the town, where the Southerners are capable of any excess."

"Am I not a Southerner, Burbank?"

"Certainly, but you think and act as if you belonged to the North."

An hour afterwards the *Shannon*, carried along by the ebb which became stronger and stronger, passed the little village of Mandarin, placed on its green hill. Then five or six miles farther she stopped on the right bank of the river. A quay had been built there for ships to load and discharge at. A little above was an elegant pier, with a light wooden bridge suspended from two chains. This was the landing-place for Camdless Bay.

At the end of the pier were two blacks with lanterns, for the night was now very dark.

Burbank took leave of Stannard, and followed by Edward Carrol stepped off on to the pier.

Behind him went the half-breed Zermah, who answered from a distance to a child's voice.

"I am here, Dy! I am here!"

"And father?"

"Father is here too!"

The lights receded, and the *Shannon* continued her voyage, crossing obliquely to the left bank.

Three miles beyond Camdless Bay, on the other side of the river, she stopped at the pier of Jacksonville to put ashore most of her passengers.

There Walter Stannard went off with three or four of the men whom Texar had left an hour and a half before. Only half a dozen passengers were left on board, some for Pablo, a little town near the lighthouse at the mouth of the St.

John's, others for Talbot Island, off the coast at the opening of the channels of the same name, and others for the port of Fernandina.

The *Shannon* continued to beat the waters of the river, and cleared the bar without accident. An hour afterwards she disappeared at the turn of Trout Creek, where the St. John's mingles its already rough waters with the waves of the ocean.

CHAPTER II.

CAMDLESS BAY.

CAMDLESS BAY was the name of the plantation that belonged to James Burbank. There he lived with his family. The name of Camdless comes from one of the creeks of the St. John's, which runs in a little above Jacksonville, and on the opposite side of the river. Communication with the city was thus easy. A good boat, a north or south wind, and the ebb for going and the flood for returning, and in an hour the three miles could be sailed between Camdless Bay and the chief town of Duval county.

Burbank owned one of the finest properties in the country. He was rich himself, and his family was rich, and in addition to the Florida estate he held important landed property in the state of New Jersey, which adjoins the state of New York.

The site on the right bank of the St. John's had been very happily chosen for the foundation of a wealthy establishment. To its natural conveniences man had little to add. The land itself was adapted for all the requirements of extensive works, and the plantation of Camdless Bay, managed by an intelligent man, active and in the prime of life, well helped by his staff, and with no want of capital, was in a most flourishing state.

The plantation was twelve miles round, and had an area of four thousand acres. There were larger plantations in the Southern States, but there were none better managed. Dwelling-house, outbuildings, stables, cattle-sheds, huts for the slaves, farm-buildings, stores for the products of the soil, yards for handling them. workshops and mills, rail-

ways converging to the landing-place and carriage roads,—
everything was marvellously arranged from a practical
point of view ; that it was a Northerner who had con-
ceived, organized, and executed these works could be seen
at the first glance. It was only plantations of the first
class in Virginia or the Carolinas that could rival Camdless
Bay. Besides, the ground consisted of " high hummocks,"
adapted for the culture of cereals, " low hummocks,"
specially fitted for coffee-shrubs and cocoa-trees, and
marshes, or salt savannahs, where rice and sugar-cane
fields could flourish.

It is well known that the cotton of Georgia and Florida
is the most appreciated in the different markets of Europe
and America, owing to the length and quality of its fibres,
and the cotton-fields, with their plants in long, regularly-
spaced lines, their leaves of tender green and their yellow
flowers, were among the chief sources of revenue. At
harvest-time these fields, for an acre or an acre and a half,
would be covered with huts in which lived the slaves,
women and children, whose duty it was to collect the
capsules and take out the tufts—a very delicate operation,
for the fibres must not be disturbed. The cotton, dried in
the sun, was cleaned in a mill by means of toothed wheels
and rollers, squeezed in a hydraulic press, done up in bales,
hooped with iron, and so packed for exportation ; and
sailing-ships or steamers could load alongside the wharf at
Camdless Bay.

James Burbank also devoted much attention to large
fields of coffee-shrubs and sugar-canes. Here were plantations of from a thousand to twelve hundred trees, from
fifteen to twenty feet high, resembling Spanish jasmine
in their flowers, and with fruits as big as a cherry containing the two grains, which it was only necessary to
extract and dry. There were large fields, we might say
marshes, bristling with thousands of those long reeds, nine
to eighteen feet high, with their crests shaking like the
plumes of a troop of cavalry on the march. This crop,
which was the subject of special care at Camdless Bay,
yielded the sugar in the form of a liquor, which the refinery

transformed into refined sugar, and then, as derived products
the syrups used in the manufacture of tafia and rum, and
cane wine, a mixture of saccharine liquor with pineapple
and orange juice. Although the crop was less important
than that from the cotton, the cultivation was there a very
profitable one. A few enclosures of cocoa-trees, fields of
maize, yams, potatoes, tobacco, and two or three hundred
acres under rice, brought in a large amount of additional
profit.

But James Burbank had another enterprise on hand
which produced at least equal profit to that of the cotton
industry. This was the clearing of the forest which covered
much of the estate. To say nothing of the products
of the cinnamons, pears, oranges, citrons, olives, figs,
mangoes, and bread fruits, or of all the fruit trees of
Europe acclimatized so splendidly in Florida, the forests
were regularly and constantly thinned. And great was
the value of the logwoods, gazumas or Mexican elms, now
used for so many purposes, baobabs, coral woods, with
twigs and flowers as red as blood, buckeyes, a kind of
yellow-flowered chestnut, black walnuts, oaks, southern
pines, which yield such admirable specimens for the car-
penter and shipwright, pachiriers whose seeds the sun at
noon explodes like so many petards, parasol pines, tulip-
trees, firs, cedars, and above all cypresses, the most widely
extended tree in the peninsula, with its forests from sixty
to a hundred miles in length. James Burbank had erected
several sawmills in different parts of the plantation. Dams
had been placed in several of the tributaries of the St.
John's, and the peaceful streams broken into falls, which
gave the mechanical power required to produce the beams,
joists and planks of which the ships each year took entire
cargoes.

There was, besides, a considerable stretch of prairie, on
which flourished the horses, mules, and cattle in numbers
enough to supply every agricultural want.

There are birds of all species in the woods or on the
fields or plains of every part of Florida, and it can be
imagined how they swarmed at Camdless Bay. Above

the trees soared the white-headed eagles with great spread of wing, whose shrill call resembles the fanfare of a cracked trumpet, vultures of extraordinary ferocity, giant bitterns, with a pointed beak like a bayonet. On the banks of the river among the reeds and beneath the interlacement of gigantic bamboos were flamingoes, pink or scarlet, white ibises looking as if they had been stolen from some Egyptian monolith, pelicans of colossal stature, myriads of terns, sea-swallows of all kinds, crab-catchers with tuft and green pelisse, purple-plumaged curlews, with brown down spotted with white, jacamars, kingfishers with golden reflections, a whole world of divers, waterhens, widgeons of the whistling species, quails, plovers, to say nothing of the petrels, puffins, scissorbeaks, seacrows, gulls, and tropic-birds which the wind would bring into the St. John's, and occasionally even flying-fish, beloved of epicures. On the prairies swarmed snipe, woodcock, curlews, marbled godwits, sultan-fowls with plumage of red, blue, green, yellow and white, like a flying palette, partridges, and white-headed, red-winged pigeons ; among the eatable quadrupeds, grey squirrels, long-tailed rabbits, half-way between the hare and rabbit of Europe, and herds of deer, and besides these, racoons, turtle, ichneumons, and unfortunately a good many serpents of venomous species. Such was the repre-sentation of the animal kingdom at Camdless Bay, without reckoning the negroes, male and female, employed on the plantation. And if these were human beings, what excuse was there for the monstrous custom of slavery, by which they were bought and sold like cattle ?

How was it that James Burbank, a partisan of the anti-slavery cause, a Northerner, hoping for the triumph of the North, had not been able to free the slaves on his planta-tion ? Would he hesitate to do it when circumstances became favourable ? Certainly not ! And it was now only a question of weeks, of days perhaps, before the Federal army, which already occupied the outposts, would advance into Florida.

Already Burbank had done all he could to improve the lot of his slaves. There were about seven hundred blacks.

of both sexes, properly lodged in the large barracoons, well looked after and kindly treated, and worked well within their powers. The overseer had orders to treat them all with justice and consideration ; and the duties were done none the worse for corporal punishment having for some time been abandoned at Camdless Bay. This was a striking contrast with the custom of the generality of Floridan plantations, and the system was not looked on with favour by James Burbank's neighbours. And, as may be imagined, this made matters somewhat embarrassing, particularly now the fortune of arms had come to the solution of the slavery question.

The slaves dwelt in healthy, comfortable huts. Grouped in fifties, these huts formed a dozen villages, otherwise called barracoons, by the side of a running stream. There the blacks lived with their wives and children. Each family was as much as possible employed in the same work in the fields, the forests or the workshops, so that its members were not scattered during working hours. At the head of these villages was a sub-overseer, acting as mayor practically, with his head-quarters in the private grounds of Camdless Bay. These grounds were enclosed by a high palisade, of which the pointed stakes rose verti-cally, half-hidden beneath the verdure of the exuberant vegetation. Inside the palisade rose the private house of the Burbank family. Half house and half castle, it had appropriately been called Castle House.

For many years Camdless Bay had belonged to the ancestors of James Burbank. When there was a fear of Indian depredations, the owners had fortified the principal house. The time was not very distant when General Jessup defended Florida against the Seminoles. The colonists had suffered much from these nomads. Not only did the Indians rob them, but they added murder to the burning of their homes. Even the towns were threatened with invasion and pillage. In many a spot rose the ruins that the bloodthirsty Indians left smoking behind them. Less than fifty miles from Camdless Bay there was still to be seen " the house of blood " in which Mr. Motte and his wife and three daughters had been scalped and massacred by the Seminoles. But the war of extermination between the white man and the red man is practically over; the Seminoles were conquered, and sought refuge to the west of the Mississippi. People spoke of them no more, though a few bands still roamed among the marshes of Southern Florida.

It will therefore be understood that the houses of the colonists were built so as to defy a sudden attack of the Indians, and hold out until the arrival of battalions of volunteers, enrolled in the towns or neighbouring villages. And on this plan Castle House had been designed.

It stood on a slight rise of the ground, in the centre of a small park of about three acres, situated a few hundred yards from the St. John's. A rather deep watercourse ran round the park, and the palisading on its inner bank completed the defence. The only entrance was by a little bridge thrown across the circular moat. Behind the rise, a mass of beautiful trees covered the slopes of the park. An avenue of young bamboos, with the stems crossing in pointed arches, formed a long nave, leading from the lawn to the landing-place. Beyond, among the trees, were green lawns and wide paths with white borders, ending in a sandy terrace along the principal front of Castle House.

The castle was irregularly built, and offered much of the unexpected in its grouping and of the capricious in its details. But should its assailants ever break through the park palisades, it would remain defensible, and could maintain a siege of some hours. Its windows on the ground-floor were protected by iron bars. The main door in the front face was as strong as a portcullis. At certain points along the walls, which were built of a sort of marble, were a few turrets, which rendered the defence easier, as they allowed of the aggressors being taken in flank. In short, with its openings reduced to such only as were strictly necessary, the central tower, on which flew the standard of the United States, its lines of battlements along some of the ridges, the slope of its wall at the foot, its high roof, many pinnacles, the thickness of its inner walls, which here and there were loopholed, the place resembled a fortress much more than a dwelling house.

As we have said, it had been necessary to build it so for the security of its inhabitants at the time of the Indian troubles in Florida. There was even in existence a sort of subterranean tunnel which, after passing under the palisade and circular moat, put Castle House in communication with a little creek of the St. John's called Marine Creek. This tunnel could serve as a means of secret escape in case of extreme danger.

At the time in question, the Seminoles, having been driven out of the peninsula twenty years before, were no longer to be feared. But who could say what was reserved for the future ? and might not the danger James Burbank had no reason to fear from the Indians, come from his compatriots ? Was he not an isolated Northerner at the end of the Southern States, exposed to all the changes of a civil war, which had been hitherto most sanguinary and fertile in reprisals ?

But the necessity of providing for the safety of Castle House had in no way interfered with its interior comfort. The rooms were large and luxuriantly and superbly furnished. The Burbank family were blessed with every comfort and every satisfaction fortune can give when it is united to artistic feeling on the part of its possessor.

Behind the house, in the private park, were splendid gardens, extending to the palisade. The stakes were hidden beneath climbing shrubs and passion-flowers, amid which humming-birds hopped in myriads. Orange-trees, olive-trees, fig-trees, pomegranate-trees, and pontederias with blue bouquets, and magnolias with calices of old ivory perfuming the air, palm-trees waving their fans in the breeze, garlands of violet-shaded coboeas, clumps of green rosetted tupeas, yuccas with their sharp clicking sabres, rosy rhododendrons, clumps of myrtle and shaddocks—in fact everything produced by the flora of a zone which touches the Tropics and could be gathered in its parterres to perfume the air or please the eye.

At the extremity of the palisading, under the cypresses and baobabs, were the stables, coachhouses, kennels, dairy, and poultry-yard. Under the thick foliage of these fine trees, impenetrable by the sun, the domestic animals had nothing to fear from the heat of summer, and the running water brought in from the streams close by gave an agreeable and healthy freshness to all.

This private domain was, it will be seen, a marvellously well-arranged nook in the centre of James Burbank's establishment. No rattle from the cotton-mills, roar from the saw-mills, ring of the axes on the tree-trunks, nor any of the sounds which are inseparable from such an important concern, could be heard beyond the palisades.

The thousands of birds of the Floridan fauna would pass and flutter from tree to tree. But these winged songsters, whose plumage rivalled the brilliancy of the flowers, were as welcome as the perfumes which the breeze bore with it as it swept over the neighbouring woods and prairies.

Such was Camdless Bay, the plantation of James Burbank, one of the richest in eastern Florida.

CHAPTER III.

THE WAR OF SECESSION.

AND now for a few words on the war of secession, with which this history is intimately connected.

And in the first place let this be understood, as has been well said, in his remarkable "History of the Civil War in America," by the Comte de Paris, who was formerly one of General McClellan's aide-de-camps, this war was not caused by any question of tariffs, nor of a difference of origin between the North and the South. The Anglo-Saxon race reigns over the whole territory of the United States. The commercial question was never entertained in this terrible fratricidal strife. "It was slavery, which, prospering in one half of the Republic and abolished in the other, created two hostile societies. It had profoundly modified the manners of those where it prevailed, while leaving untouched the outward forms of government. It was not the pretext or the occasion, but the cause, and the only cause, of the antagonism which inevitably resulted in civil war."

In the slave states there were three classes. The lowest consisted of four millions of enslaved negroes, a third of the population. The highest was the caste of the slave-holders, comparatively uneducated, rich, scornful, who kept the direction of public affairs completely in their hands. Between these classes was the lower class of whites, turbulent, idle and miserable, ardent advocates for the maintenance of slavery for fear of seeing the freed negroes elevated to their level.

The Northerners had against them not only the rich proprietors, but also those whites who lived, especially in the country, among the slave population. The strife was consequently frightful. In families such dissensions were produced that brothers fought against each other, some under the Federal, some under the Confederate flag. But a great nation could not hesitate to destroy slavery to its roots. In the last century the illustrious Franklin had demanded its abolition. In 1807 Jefferson had recommended Congress to "prohibit a traffic of which the morality, honour, and dearest interests of the country had long required the disappearance." The North was therefore in the right to march against the South and subdue it. And to follow that with a closer union between the elements of the Republic, and the destruction of that fatal, threatening illusion that the citizen owed obedience first to his own state, and in the second place to the federation.

It was in Florida that the first question as to slavery had arisen. At the commencement of the century a half-breed Indian chief, named Osceola, had for his wife a maroon slave born in the marshy part of Florida known as the Everglades. One day the woman was recaptured as a slave and taken away by force. Osceola raised the Indians, began an anti-slavery campaign, and was taken prisoner and died in his prison. But the war continued, and, says the historian Thomas Higginson, "the money it cost was three times as much as that paid to Spain for the purchase of Florida."

And now for the beginnings of the war of secession, and the state of affairs in the month of February, 1862, when James Burbank and his family were to experience such terrible counterblows that it has appeared interesting to us to make them the subject of this history.

On the 16th October, 1859, the heroic Captain John Brown, at the head of a small band of fugitive slaves, had seized on Harper's Ferry in Virginia. His object was to free the men of colour. He proclaimed it loudly. Beaten by the militia, he was taken prisoner, condemned to death, and hanged at Charleston on the 2nd of December, 1859, with six of his companions.

On the 20th of December, 1860, a convention assembled

in South Carolina and adopted with enthusiasm the proposal of secession. The following year, on the 4th of
March, 1861, Abraham Lincoln was elected President of
the Republic. The Southern States regarded his election
as a menace to the institution of slavery. On the 11th of
April, Fort Sumter, one of the forts defending Charleston
harbour, fell into the power of the Southerners commanded
by General Beauregard. North Carolina, Virginia, Arkansas, and Tennessee at once threw in their lot with the
Separatists.

Seventy-five thousand volunteers were raised by the
Federal Government. At the outset Washington, the
capital of the United States of America, was prepared
against a sudden attack, the arsenals of the North which
were empty were revictualled—those of the South had
been well provisioned by President Buchanan. War
material was got together with extraordinary effort. Then
Abraham Lincoln declared the Southern ports in a state
of blockade.

Active hostilities broke out in Virginia. McClellan
repulsed the rebels in the west ; but on the 21st of July,
at Bull Run, the Federal troops, under the orders of
MacDowell, were routed, and fled to Washington. The
Southerners feared no longer for the safety of Richmond,
but the Northerners had much to fear for the capital of
the American Republic. A few months afterwards, the
Federals were again defeated at Bull's Bluff. These
misfortunes were compensated for by the expeditions
that put into the hands of the Unionists Fort Hatteras
and Port Royal Harbour, which the Separatists never
retook. At the end of 1861, the command-in-chief of
the armies of the Union was given to Major-General
George McClellan.

During this year the Confederate corsairs swept the
seas of both worlds. They were welcomed in the ports
of France, England, Spain, and Portugal—a great mistake which, by giving the Secessionists the rights of
belligerents, resulted in encouraging and prolonging the
civil war.

The naval events, which caused so much stir, were the appearance of the *Sumter* and her famous Captain Semmes ; the appearance of the ram *Manassas ;* on the 12th of October the sea-fight at the mouth of the Mississippi ; on the 8th of November, the stoppage of the *Trent*, an English ship, on which Captain Wilkes captured the Confederate envoys—and which nearly brought on a war between Great Britain and the States.

Meanwhile Abolitionists and Slaveholders were engaged in sanguinary combats, with alternating success and defeat in the State of Missouri. One of the chief generals of the North, Lyon, was killed, and this necessitated the retreat of the Federals to Rolla, and the march of Price and his Confederates towards the North. There was a fight at Frederictown on the 21st of October, and at Springfield on the 25th, and on the 27th, Fremont occupied the latter town with his Federals. On the 19th of December, the fight at Belmont between Grant and Polk was indecisive. At length winter, which is always severe in North America, put an end to the operations.

In the first months of the year 1862, truly prodigious efforts were made by both sides.

In the North, Congress voted a levy of 500,000 volunteers—there were a million before the end of the struggle —and sanctioned a loan of 500 millions of dollars. Huge armies were created, the chief being that of the Potomac. Their generals were Banks, Butler, Sherman, McClellan, Meade, Thomas, Kearny, Halleck, to mention only the most famous. Infantry, cavalry, artillery, engineers, were formed and organized. War material was manufactured at express speed, Minie and Colt carbines, rifled cannon on the Parrott and Rodman systems, smoothbore cannon and Dahlgren columbiads, howitzers, revolver-cannons, siege artillery, and shrapnel shell. They organized army telegraphs and army balloons, the reporting service of the large newspapers, the transport service employing 20,000 carts, drawn by 84,000 mules. Provisions of all kinds were

3

got in under the direction of the chief of the commissariat. New ships of the ram type were built on the plan of Colonel Ellet, and armoured gunboats were built on the plan of Commodore Foote, to make their first appearance in maritime war.

In the South equal zeal was shown. The cannon foundries of New Orleans and Memphis, and the forges of Tredegar, near Richmond, turned out their Parrotts and Rodmans. But that was not enough. The Confederate Government sent across to Europe. Liège and Birmingham sent shiploads of arms, and cannon on the Armstrong and Whitworth systems. Blockade-runners brought the war material into the ports, and took away cotton in exchange. Then the army was organized. Its generals were Johnston, Lee, Beauregard, Jackson, Crittenden, Floyd, and Pillow. Irregular troops, militia and guerillas, were raised in addition to the four hundred thousand volunteers enrolled for three years at the most, or one year at the least, voted by the Secessionist Congress on the 8th of August.

The preparations did not hinder the strife from beginning before the winter was half over. Of the slaveholding territory, the Federal Government occupied only Maryland, Western Virginia, some part of Kentucky, most part of Missouri, and a few points on the sea coast.

Hostilities first broke out again in the east of Kentucky. On the 7th of January, Garfield fought the Confederates at Middle Creek, and on the 25th they were beaten again at Logan Cross or Mill Springs. On the 2nd of February Grant embarked with two divisions on some of the large Tennessee steamboats, to support Foote's cuirassed flotilla. On the 6th, Fort Henry fell into his power. Thus was broken a link of the chain " on which," said the historian of this civil war, " rested the whole system of his adversary Johnston's defence." Cumberland and the capital of Tennessee were thus threatened, and were within easy reach of the Federal troops ; and Johnston endeavoured to concentrate on Fort Donelson, so as to regain a surer base for the defensive.

At this time, another expedition, consisting of six thousand men, under the orders of Burnside, and a flotilla of twenty-four armed steamers and fifty transports, descended the Chesapeake and assembled in Hampton Roads on the 12th of January. In face of violent storms it started on the 24th of January for Pimlico Sound, to capture Roanoke Island, and reduce the coast of North Carolina. But the island was fortified. On the west the channel was defended by a barrier of sunken ships. Batteries and field works made access difficult. Five or six thousand men with a flotilla of seven gunboats, were ready to withstand any attempt at landing. Nevertheless, notwithstanding the bravery of the defenders, on the 7th and 8th of February the island surrendered to Burnside, with twenty guns and more than two thousand prisoners Next day the Federals were masters of Elizabeth City and the coast of Albemarle Sound, that is to say, the north of this inland sea.

But to conclude this description of the position of affairs up to the 6th of February, it is necessary to speak of the Confederate general, the old professor of chemistry, Jackson the puritan soldier who defended Virginia. After the recall of Lee to Richmond he commanded the army. He left Winchester on the 13th of January, with his 10,000 men, then he crossed the Alleghanies, to advance on Bath on the Ohio railroad. Defeated by the climate, overwhelmed by the snowstorms, he was forced to return to Winchester, without having attained his object.

And now for that which concerns us more specially, on the southern coast from Carolina to Florida.

During the second half of 1861, the Northerners possessed sufficient swift vessels to police the seas, although they could not catch the famous *Sumter* which in January, 1862, put in at Gibraltar, before beginning her cruise in European waters. The *Jefferson Davis* endeavouring to escape from the Federals had fled to St. Augustine in Florida, and sunk as she entered the channel. Almost at the same time the *Anderson*, one of the cruisers off the Florida coast, captured the privateer *Beauregard*. But in England new ships were fitting out for the fray. It was then that President Lincoln's proclamation extended the blockade, a fictitious

PART I.

blockade of 2800 miles. To watch them only two squadrons were available : one to blockade the Atlantic, the other the Gulf of Mexico.

On the 12th of October, for the first time, the Confederates endeavoured to clear the mouth of the Mississippi with the *Manassas*—the first ship plated with iron used in the war—and a flotilla of fire-ships. The attempt did not succeed, and the corvette *Richmond* escaped from capture, safe and sound, on the 29th of December, though a small steamer, the *Seabird*, carried off a Federal schooner in sight of Fort Monroe.

It was, however, necessary to have a point which could serve as a base of operation for the Atlantic cruisers. The Federal government resolved to seize on Fort Hatteras, which defends the channel of the same name, at that time much used by the blockade runners. Its capture was not easy. It was supported by a square redoubt, called Fort Clarke. A thousand men and the Seventh North Carolina regiment, were entrusted with its defence. The Federal squadron composed of two frigates, three corvettes, a despatch-boat, and two large steamers anchored in the passes on the 27th of August. Commodore Stringham and General Butler were in charge of the attack. The redoubt was taken. Fort Hatteras, after a long resistance, hoisted the white flag, and a base of operations was secured by the Northerners for the rest of the war.

In November the island of Santa Rosa, at the east of Pensacola, on the Gulf of Mexico, a dependency of Florida, fell into the hands of the Federals, notwithstanding the efforts of the Confederates.

The capture of Fort Hatteras not appearing sufficient for the proper conduct of their operations, it was decided to occupy other positions on the coasts of South Carolina, Georgia, and Florida. Two steam frigates, the *Wabash* and *Susquehannah*, three sailing frigates, four corvettes, six gunboats, many despatch-boats, twenty-five colliers laden with provisions, and thirty-two steamers transporting 15,600 men under the orders of General Sherman, were placed under the command of Commodore Dupont. The flotilla mustered on the 25th of October before Fort Monroe. After experiencing a terrible storm off Cape Hatteras, the fleet reached Hilton Head between Charlestown and Savannah, close to Port Royal Harbour, one of the most important in the States, and where General Ripley held command. Forts Walker and Beauregard defended the entrance, about two miles and a half apart ; eight steamers also formed part of the defences, and the bar rendered the harbour almost impregnable to an enemy's fleet.

On the 5th of November, the channel having been buoyed, Dupont entered the harbour after a cannonade, but he was not able to land Sherman's troops. On the 7th, in the afternoon, he attacked Fort Walker and then Fort Beauregard. He overwhelmed them with his storm of shell. The forts were evacuated ; the Federals took possession of them almost without a struggle ; and Sherman occupied the position which was of so much importance for the military operations that were to follow.

This was a blow at the very heart of the Southern States. The neighbouring islands fell one after the other into the power of the Federals, even Tybee Island and Fort Pulaski which commanded the Savannah river. At the end of the year Dupont was master of the five great bays of North Edisto, Saint Helena, Port Royal, Tybee, Warsaw, and all the islands scattered along the coast of Carolina and Georgia. And on the 1st of January, 1862, a final success enabled him to reduce the Confederate works on the banks of the Coosaw.

Such was the situation of the belligerents at the commencement of February, 1862. Such was the progress of the Federals towards the South, when the fleet of Dupont and the troops of Sherman were menacing Florida.

CHAPTER IV.

THE BURBANK FAMILY.

IT was a few minutes past seven when James Burbank and Edward Carrol mounted the steps on which opened the principal door of Castle House, looking towards the St. John's. Zermah, holding the little girl by the hand, walked behind them. They entered the hall, which was a kind of large vestibule with its back rounded into a dome, and containing the double twist of the great staircase which led to the upper floors.

Mrs. Burbank met them, accompanied by Perry, the chief overseer of the plantation.

" No news from Jacksonville ? "

" No."

" No news from Gilbert ? "

" Yes—a letter."

" Heaven be praised ! "

Such were the first questions and answers that passed between Mrs. Burbank and her husband. James Burbank, after kissing his wife and little Dy, opened the letter which was handed to him. It had not been opened in his absence, for, in consideration of the existing state of affairs, Mrs. Burbank thought it best that her husband should be the first to know what it contained.

" This letter did not come by the post ? " asked Burbank.

" No, sir," said Perry, " that would have been too risky."

" Who brought it ? "

" A Georgia man Mr. Gilbert felt he could trust."

" When did it arrive ? "

" Yesterday."

" And the man ? "

" Went away this evening."

" Well paid for his work ? "

" Yes, well paid," said Mrs. Burbank, " but by Gilbert, and he would not take anything from us."

The hall was lighted by two lamps placed on a marble table before a large sofa. James Burbank went and sat at the table, and his wife and daughter sat near him. Edward Carrol, after shaking hands with his sister, had thrown himself into an arm-chair. Zermah and Perry were standing together near the stairs ; both of them were sufficiently of the family for the letter to be read in their presence.

The letter was opened.

" It is dated the 3rd of February," said James Burbank.

" Four days after date ! " said Carrol, " that is a long time under the circumstances."

" Read it, papa, read it," said the little girl, with a very natural impatience at her age.

" This is what it says,—

" On board the *Wabash*, at the anchorage of Edisto.
            " 3rd February, 1862.

" DEAR FATHER,—I begin by sending my love to my mother, my little sister and yourself, not forgetting Uncle Carrol, and to omit nothing, I send Zermah all the remembrances of her husband, my brave and devoted Mars. We are going on as well as possible, and should very much like to be with you. It will not be long before we are, notwithstanding Mr. Perry, who, on seeing the progress of the North, must be much concerned—obstinate slave-owner as he is, the worthy overseer ! "

" That is one for you, Perry," said Carrol.

" Every man is welcome to his ideas," said Perry, in the tone of a man who had no intention of giving up his own.

Burbank continued,—

" This letter will reach you by a man I can depend on. You will have heard that Commodore Dupont's squadron has gained possession of Port Royal Harbour and the neighbouring islands. The North is gradually beating the South, and it is very likely that the Federal Government will occupy the chief ports of Florida. They are talking of an expedition under Dupont and Sherman at the end of the month. This is very probable, and we shall occupy the bay of St. Andrew's, whence we shall advance into Florida. I am in a hurry to get there, dear father, and particularly with our victorious flotilla. The situation of my people among the slave-holding population, makes me very anxious ; but the time is coming when triumph will wait upon the ideas that have always been to the fore at Camdless Bay. If I could get away I should be with you in twenty-four hours ; but that would be too risky for you as well as for me, and you must be patient. In a few months we shall again meet together at Castle House. And now I must end, asking myself if I have forgotten anybody in my message. And I have ! I have forgotten Mr. Stannard and my charming Alice, whom I am longing to see. Give my regards to her father, and to her give more than my regards.

"Respectfully and sincerely yours,

"GILBERT BURBANK."

James Burbank laid the letter on the table, and Mrs. Burbank lifted it to her lips, then little Dy put a sounding kiss on her brother's signature.

"Brave fellow ! " said Edward Carrol.

"And brave man !" added Mrs. Burbank, looking at Zermah, who had clasped the little girl in her arms.

"We must tell Alice," said Mrs. Burbank, "that we have received a letter from Gilbert."

"Yes, I will write to her," said James Burbank. "Besides, in a day or two I must go to Jacksonville and see Stannard. Since Gilbert wrote there may be other news of the proposed expedition. May our Northern friends soon come, and may Florida again be under the Union flag ! Our position here may end in being untenable."

In fact, as the war approached the South, a change took

place in Floridan opinion on the subject which had set the United States at variance. Up to then slavery had not been extensively developed in the old Spanish colony, which had not taken part in the Secession movement with the same ardour as Virginia and the Carolinas. But leaders had sprung up among the slave party, and now these people, ready for outbreak at any moment, having everything to gain by disturbances, were in the majority among the authorities of St. Augustine, and principally of Jacksonville, where their supporters were the vilest of the populace. Hence the position of James Burbank, whose birth and ideas we know, had become an anxious one.

Twenty years before, James Burbank had left New Jersey, where he still possessed some property, and came to Camdless Bay with his wife and his son, then four years old. We know how the plantation had prospered, thanks to his own intelligent labours and the assistance of his brother-in-law, Edward Carrol. He had taken a great liking to the vast establishment which had been handed down to him by his ancestors. Here was born his second child, little Dy, fifteen years after he had fixed his home in the South.

He was then forty-six years old, of strong constitution, accustomed to work, and never sparing himself. We know he was of energetic character; firmly attached to his opinions, he did his utmost to let them be widely known. He was tall and slightly grey; his face had a somewhat severe but frank and encouraging look. With the goatee of the Americans of the North, without whiskers or moustache, he was a typical New England Yankee. Throughout the plantation he was liked, for he was kind, and he was obeyed, for he was just. His blacks were devoted to him, and he waited not without impatience for circumstances to permit of his giving them their liberty. His brother-in-law was about the same age, and took charge chiefly of the accounts of Camdless Bay. Carrol was quite at one with him in everything, and shared in his view of the slave question.

Mr. Perry, the overseer, was the only one of a different

opinion in this little world of Camdless Bay. Let it not be thought that this worthy man ill-treated the slaves. Far from it. He even tried to make them as happy as their condition allowed him.

" But," said he, "there are warm countries in which work on the land can only be done by blacks, and blacks who are not slaves are no longer blacks ! "

Such was his theory, which he discussed on every occasion that offered. But he was in no way disconcerted at the fortune of war which favoured the anti-slavery cause. He was, in short, an excellent fellow, and a brave one too, and when James Burbank and Edward Carrol had joined the militia, known as "the minute men," from being ready to start at any minute, he had gallantly joined them in their last struggle with the Seminoles.

Mrs. Burbank was at this time thirty-nine years of age. She was still very handsome. Her daughter would one day resemble her. James Burbank had found in her a loving, affectionate companion, to whom he owed most of the happiness of his life. The unselfish woman lived but for her husband and her children, whom she adored, and for whose safety she felt the keenest apprehension now that circumstances had brought the civil war into Florida. Diana, or rather Dy, as she was familiarly called, a child of six, quick, loving, and happy, lived at Castle House with her mother, but Gilbert was away, his absence causing continued anxiety, which Mrs. Burbank could not always dissimulate.

Gilbert was then in his twenty-fifth year, and in him were conspicuous the moral qualities of his father, with a little less stiffness, and the same physical qualities, with a little more grace and charm. A bold companion, skilled in all bodily exercises, he was as accomplished as a horseman as he was as a seaman and hunter. To the great alarm of his mother, the huge forests and marshes of Duval county had often been the scene of his exploits, as had the creeks and passes of the St. John's up to its furthest mouth at Pablo. Gilbert felt himself fully trained for the work of a soldier when the first shots were fired in the war. He considered that his duty called him to the Federal troops, and he did not hesitate. He asked to be allowed to go. Great was the grief he thus caused his mother, and great was the danger to all, but James Burbank did not dream for a moment of refusing his son's request. He thought, like him, that it was a duty, and everything must give place to duty.

Gilbert, then, set out for the North ; but his departure was kept as secret as possible. If it was known at Jacksonville that James Burbank's son had entered the Northern service, reprisals would at once have been taken on Camdless Bay. The young man had been given letters of introduction to his father's friends in New Jersey. He had always shown a taste for the sea, and his friends had had no difficulty in procuring him an appointment in the Federal navy. Promotion was rapid in those days, and as Gilbert was not one of those who remained in the rear, he soon got on. The Washington Government had its eyes on this young man who in the position he found his family, did not hesitate to offer his services. Gilbert distinguished himself at the attack of Fort Sumter. He was on the *Richmond* when that ship was rammed by the *Manassas* at the mouth of the Mississippi, and contributed largely to recapture her. After this affair he was made an ensign, although he had not been through the naval school at Annapolis any more than many of the other officers who had been transferred from the mercantile marine. In his new capacity he joined the squadron of Commodore Dupont, and assisted at the brilliant attack on Fort Hatteras and the capture of the Seas Islands. During the last few weeks he had been a lieutenant on one of Dupont's gunboats which were about to force the mouths of the St. John's.

Gilbert himself longed for an early termination of the war. He loved and was loved ; and when his service was over, he would return to Camdless Bay and marry the daughter of one of his father's best friends.

Mr. Stannard did not belong to the class of Floridan planters, A widower, and a man of fortune, he had devoted

himself entirely to the education of his daughter. He
lived at Jacksonville, so that to get to Camdless Bay he
had only to go up three or four miles of the river. For
fifteen years not a week had passed without his visiting
the Burbanks. It might almost be said that Gilbert and
Alice were brought up together, and a marriage that had
been planned for years had now been decided on, which
would bring happiness to both. Although Walter Stannard
was a native of the South, he was an anti-slavery man, as
were several others of his Floridan fellow-citizens; but
these were not numerous enough to withstand the majority
of the inhabitants of Jacksonville, whose opinions daily
tended more and more in favour of the Separatist movement. Stannard and his friends began consequently to
be looked upon unfavourably by the leaders of the county,
and especially by the small whites and populace, who were
ready for any excess.

Walter Stannard was born at New Orleans. Mrs.
Stannard was a Frenchwoman; she had died young, and
left to her daughter those noble qualities which are
peculiar to French blood. When Gilbert went away,
Alice had shown an energy that had given Mrs. Burbank
much comfort and support. Although she loved Gilbert
as she herself was loved, she invariably told his mother
that it was his duty to go and fight for the good cause, to
fight for the freedom of a race, and, in short, for liberty.
She was then nineteen; fair, with eyes almost blue, of
warm complexion, elegant figure, and distinguished
features. She might be a little serious, but so mobile was
her expression, that the least smile would light up her
beautiful face.

The Burbank family would not be known in all its most
faithful members, if we omitted to say something of its
two servants, Mars and Zermah.

As we have seen from his letter, Gilbert had not gone
away alone. Mars, the husband of Zermah, had accompanied him. He could not have found a more devoted
companion than this slave from Camdless Bay, who had
become free by setting foot on anti-slavery soil. But to

Mars, Gilbert was always "the young master," and he would not leave him, although the Federal Government had already formed regiments of negroes, where he would have found a place.

Mars and Zermah were not of the negro race by birth. They were half-breeds. Zermah's brother was that heroic slave, Robert Small, who, four months later, captured from the Confederates in the very bay of Charleston, a steamer with two guns, which he took over to the Federal fleet.

The marriage of Zermah and Mars was a happy one; which more than once, during its first years, the odious traffic in slaves had threatened to break. It was at the moment when they were about to be separated by the fortune of the auction-room, that they came to Camdless Bay.

These were the circumstances.

Zermah was thirty-one years old, Mars thirty-five. Seven years before, they had been married when they belonged to a Mr. Tickborn, whose plantation was on the river, twenty miles above Camdless Bay. For some years Tickborn had had business transactions with Texar, who was often a welcome visitor to the plantation. There was nothing surprising in this, for Tickborn was not thought much of in the county. His abilities were not very brilliant; and, his affairs not prospering, he was obliged to put up a lot of his slaves for sale.

At this very time Zermah, who was very badly treated like all the rest on Tickborn's plantation, brought a baby into the world, which was immediately taken away from her, for while she was in prison for a crime of which she was innocent, her baby died in her arms. It may be guessed what was the grief of Zermah, and the anger of Mars. But what could they do against a master to whom belonged their flesh, living or dead, because he had bought it?

To this sorrow another no less terrible was added. The day after their child died, Mars and Zermah were packed off to the auctioneer, and threatened with separation

Yes! The consolation of finding themselves together under a new master was denied them. A man presented himself who offered to buy Zermah, and Zermah alone, although he did not own a plantation. This man was Texar. His friend Tickborn was about to sign the agreement when, at the last moment, another bidder appeared on the scene and offered a higher price. This was James Burbank, who happened to be at the sale, and was touched at the fate of the unhappy half-breed, praying in vain that she should not be separated from her husband.

Burbank was in want of a nurse for his little girl, and learning that one of Tickborn's slaves had just lost her child, he came to look at her ; but, touched by Zermah's tears, he did not hesitate to offer for herself and husband a price that exceeded all that had been bid up to then.

Texar knew James Burbank. He had been several times warned off his plantation as a suspicious person. And from this arose the hatred which Texar had vowed to all the family of Camdless Bay. Texar tried to bid against the rich planter. It was in vain. He grew obstinate. He rose to double the price that Tickborn had asked for the half-breed and her husband. This made Burbank pay very dearly for them—but he got them.

And so, not only were Zermah and Mars not separated from each other, but they had entered the service of the best of the planters in Florida. Six years afterwards, Zermah was still in all the maturity of her half-breed beauty. Of energetic character, heartily devoted to her master, she had more than once had occasion —and would soon have occasion again—to prove her fidelity. Mars was worthy of the wife to whom the charitable act of James Burbank had for ever attached him. He was a remarkable specimen of those Africans in whom there is a large proportion of Creole blood. Tall, stout, courageous to a fault, he served his new master well.

These two new servants were not treated like slaves. They had soon become appreciated for their kindness

and intelligence. Mars was specially occupied in looking after young Gilbert ; Zermah was Diana's nurse. In such positions they were bound to be admitted to a certain intimacy with the family.

Zermah always felt a mother's love for the little girl, the love she could not bear the child she had lost. Dy returned it, and the filial affection of the one responded to the maternal cares of the other, and Mrs. Burbank was as friendly to Zermah as she was grateful.

The same feeling existed between Gilbert and Mars. Active and strong, the half-breed had made his young master an expert in all manly exercises, and James Burbank could only congratulate himself at having found him for his son.

Never had Zermah and Mars been so happy, and that after leaving the hands of Tickborn and nearly falling into those of Texar. They were never to forget it.

CHAPTER V.

BLACK CREEK.

AT dawn, the morning after the *Shannon's* journey down the St. John's, a man was walking on the bank of one of the islets at the bottom of the lagoon of Black Creek. It was Texar. A few steps away was an Indian sitting in the skiff which had met the steamer. It was Squambo.

After walking up and down for a minute or two, Texar stopped under a magnolia-tree, drew down one of the lower branches and picked off a leaf and its stem. Then he drew from his note-book a short letter, containing only three or four words written in ink. He rolled up the letter and stuffed it into one of the lower veins of the leaf. This was done so cleverly that the leaf lost nothing of its usual look.

" Squambo ! " said Texar.

" Master ! " replied the Indian.

" Go—you know where ! "

Squambo took the leaf, put it in the bow of the skiff, sat down in the stern, paddled himself off, turned the extreme point of the islet, and entered the tortuous passage under the thick bower of trees.

The lagoon is cut up into a labyrinth of channels, among which only a man thoroughly conversant with the tangled network of black waters could find his way.

However, Squambo did not hesitate. Where no one could see an outlet he boldly entered with his skiff. The lower branches that he lifted up fell behind him, and left no trace of anything having passed beneath them. Along winding channels, no larger than drains, he paddled his canoe. Quite a world of aquatic birds flew up at his approach. Slimy eels, with suspicious heads, slipped under the roots which emerged from the water. Squambo cared for none of these things, no more than he did for the sleeping caymans, which he could wake by striking them as they lay on their beds of mud. He kept on without a stoppage, and when he had no room to paddle, he pushed himself along as if with a boat-hook.

Although it was now broad daylight, and the heavy night mist had begun to evaporate under the first rays of the sun, nothing could be seen of it beneath this impenetrable roof of verdure. Even in the noonday sun no ray of light could pierce it. All was shrouded in semi-obscurity, which suited well the crawling creatures that swarmed in its black waters, and the thousands of aquatic plants that floated on their surface.

For half an hour Squambo advanced from one island to another. When he stopped, it was because his skiff had reached one of the last branches of the creek.

At this spot, where the marshy part of the creek ended, the trees were less crowded and intergrown, and the light of day found admittance. Beyond was a vast prairie bordered with forest, but slightly above the level of the St. John's. The foot, in treading on the marshy ground, gave the same sensation as if treading on an elastic mattress. A few sassafras bushes, with slender leaves and violet berries dotted the surface with their capricious zigzags.

After mooring his canoe to one of the twigs on the bank, Squambo jumped ashore. The night mist was drying off, the prairie, quite deserted, was gradually rising from the fog. Among a group of five or six trees close by was a magnolia of moderate height.

The Indian stepped towards this tree. He reached it in a few minutes, and drew down one of the lower branches. To its end he fixed the leaf that Texar had given him, then the bough, left to itself, sprung up, and the leaf was lost in the foliage.

Squambo returned to his skiff, and then paddled back to the islet where his master awaited him.

Black Creek is so called from the colour of its waters,

4

and covers an area of about six hundred acres. Fed by
the St. John's, it is a sort of archipelago quite impenetrable to those who do not know its infinite windings. A
hundred islands dot its surface ; no bridges or causeways
join them. A few high branches interlace above the thousands of channels that separate but do not form easy communication lines between the different points of the lagoon.

One of these islands, nearly in the centre of the system,
is the most important, on account of its size—some twenty
acres—and its elevation, five or six feet above the mean
tide of the St. John's.

At some distant period, this island had served as the
site of a fortress, a sort of blockhouse, now abandoned
—at least, in a military sense. Its palisades, half ruined
by rot, still stood beneath the large trees, magnolias,
cypresses, oaks, black walnuts, and austral pines, interlaced
by festoons of cobœas and other endless creepers.

Beyond the outer ring the eye could make out under
the heap of verdure the geometrical lines of the little
fortress, or rather the outpost, which had never been
intended to hold more than a score of men. Narrow
loopholes peeped out of the wooden walls. Turfed roofs
covered them with a carapace of earth. Inside were a
few rooms arranged round a central apartment, containing a store of provisions and munitions. To enter the
fortress, it was necessary to get through the palisades at
the narrow postern, then to cross the yard, planted with a
few trees, and mount a few steps built up of boards.
These led to the only door giving admittance to the
interior, and was merely an embrasure that had been altered
to suit the purpose.

Such was the usual retreat of Texar—a retreat which
nobody knew. There, hidden from all eyes, he lived with
this Squambo, who was devoted to a master of whom
he did not think much, and with five or six slaves, who
thought even less of him.

This islet of Black Creek was, it will be seen, some distance from the wealthy establishments on each side of the

river. There was barely a living on it for Texar and his companions, whose wants were not great. A few domestic animals, half a dozen acres planted with potatoes, yams, cucumbers, twenty fruit-trees, almost in their wild state, —that was all, without counting what the hunter could find in the neighbouring forests, or the fisherman in the lagoon, which never failed to yield its harvest. But, doubtless, the dwellers at Black Creek had other resources, of which only Texar and Squambo knew the secret.

The safety of the blockhouse was almost assured by its situation in such an inaccessible spot. Besides, who would seek to attack it, and why? In any case, any suspicious approach would be signalled at once by the dogs of the island, two of those ferocious bloodhounds imported from the Caribbees, formerly employed by the Spaniards to hunt down the negroes.

Such was Texar's dwelling, and it was worthy of him. Now for Texar himself.

Texar was then about thirty-five. He was of medium height, and of vigorous constitution, hardened by the adventurous life in the open air which had always been his. A Spaniard by birth, he did not hide his origin. His hair was black and coarse, his eyebrows thick, his eyes greenish, his mouth large, with thin indrawn lips, as if it had been made by a sabre-stroke, his nose short, and his nostrils like those of a wild beast. His whole physiognomy denoted craft and violence. He had formerly grown his full beard; but for the last two years, after it had been half burnt in some affair that no one knew anything about, he had shaved it off, and the cruelty of his features was rendered all the more apparent.

Twelve years before, this adventurer had come to settle in Florida in this abandoned blockhouse, the possession of which nobody thought of disputing. Whence came he? Nobody knew. What had been his former life? It was said, and rightly so, that he had been a slave-dealer, and had sold his cargoes of blacks in the ports of Georgia and the Carolinas. Had he made a fortune in this odious trade?

PART I.

It did not seem like it. And, in fact, his reputation was of the slightest even in a country where men of his sort are numerous.

Nevertheless, if Texar was better known than respected, that did not prevent his exercising a real influence in the county, and particularly at Jacksonville, although it was, it is true, among the least reputable inhabitants. He often went to the chief town on business, which he never spoke about, and had made a number of friends among the small whites and more objectionable people of the place. This we have seen when he was returning to St. Augustine with his companions. His influence extended to a few planters on the St. John's, whom he sometimes visited, though they never visited him, for no one knew of his retreat at Black Creek.

Sport was a natural pretext for this intercourse, which established itself without difficulty among people of the same habits and tastes. This influence had grown during the last few years, owing to the opinions which Texar ardently defended. The slave question had hardly brought about the division between the United States, than the Spaniard had posed as the most obstinate and determined of slavery partisans. It should be understood that he had little real interest in the matter, for his slaves only amounted to half a dozen. It was the principle he sought to defend. By what means ? By an appeal to the most hateful passions, by exciting the cupidity of the populace, by urging them to pillage, incendiarism, even to murder, against the inhabitants or planters who shared in the ideas of the Northerners. And now this dangerous adventurer was seeking to supersede the civil authorities of Jacksonville, men of moderate opinions and high character, by the most furious of his partisans. By becoming master of the county, he would have a free field for the exercise of his personal vengeance.

It will be understood from this, why James Burbank and other planters had not neglected to keep an eye on the proceedings of such a man, whose evil instincts had already made him formidable ; and why the hate on one side and defiance on the other had been augmented by the approaching events.

Besides, there was much in the past life of Texar after he had retired from trade which was suspicious. During the last outbreak of the Seminoles, everything seemed to prove that he had a secret understanding with them. Had he told them what blows to strike, what plantations to attack ? Had he helped them in their ambushes and surprises ? There was a strong suspicion that this was the case, and the magistrates had issued a warrant against the Spaniard, and brought him to trial. But Texar had pleaded an alibi, a plan of defence of which he again availed himself later on ; and it was proved he could not have taken part in the attack on a farm in Duval county, when at the same moment he was at Savannah, in the State of Georgia, about forty miles to the north.

During the following years there were many serious robberies, sometimes from plantations, sometimes from travellers. Was Texar an author or accomplice in these crimes ? Suspicions were strong, but as there was no proof, nothing could be done.

At last an opportunity offered which seemed to bring this hitherto unseizable malefactor within reach of the law ; and this was the affair for which he had the day before been brought before the court at St. Augustine.

Eight days before, James Burbank, Carrol, and Stannard were returning from visiting a plantation not far from Camdless Bay, when about seven o'clock in the evening, as night was falling, they heard cries of distress. They came to the spot whence the cries proceeded, and found themselves in front of the buildings of an isolated farm. The buildings were on fire. The farm had been previously pillaged by half-a-dozen men who had just dispersed. The authors of the crime were not far off. Two of them could be seen running away through the woods.

James Burbank and his friends courageously started in pursuit, and the chase took them towards Camdless Bay.

It was in vain. The incendiaries escaped in the woods. But Burbank, Carrol, and Stannard had recognized one of them. It was the Spaniard.

And more than this—and corroborating the proof—at the instant this individual had disappeared on the boundary of Camdless Bay, Zermah, who was passing, had been knocked aside by him. And she, like the others, recognized him as Texar, running at full speed.

It is easy to imagine that such an affair would make considerable stir in the county. A robbery, followed by incendiarism, was a most serious crime where the plantations were spread over a large extent of country. Burbank brought a formal accusation against Texar, and the authorities took proceedings.

The Spaniard was brought to St. Augustine before the Recorder, and then, when confronted by the witnesses, James Burbank, Walter Stannard, Edward Carrol, and Zermah, was unanimously recognized as the man who was running away from the fire. There could be no mistake as far as they were concerned. Texar was one of the authors of the crime.

The Spaniard, for his defence, brought a number of witnesses to St. Augustine. They declared that on the evening in question they were with Texar at Jacksonville, in the tienda of Torilla, a sufficiently ill-famed drinking-shop in those parts. Texar had not left them all the evening. And that there could be no mistake about this, at the very time the crime was committed, the Spaniard had had a dispute with one of them which had ended in blows and threats, for which legal proceedings would probably be taken.

At this evidence, which was beyond suspicion—for some of the witnesses were strangers to Texar—the magistrate at St. Augustine could only close the inquiry and allow the defendant his expenses.

The alibi had thus been once more fully established to the advantage of this strange individual

It was after this affair, and in company with his witnesses' that Texar had returned to St. Augustine on the evening of the 7th of February. We have seen how he conducted himself on board the *Shannon* while the steamer descended the river. Then, on the skiff brought to meet him by Squambo, he had regained the abandoned blockhouse.

Squambo was a Seminole, intelligent and crafty, and had become the confidant of Texar, who had taken him into his service immediately after the last expedition of the Indians with which his name had been mixed up.

The Spaniard had resolved to revenge himself on James Burbank by all possible means. Amid the many conjunctions that the war daily gave rise to, if Texar could upset the authorities of Jacksonville he could make himself formidable to Camdless Bay. James Burbank was of such energetic and determined character that he had no fear of such a man, but Mrs. Burbank had only too many reasons to tremble for her husband and her family.

And all the more would she have been anxious had she known that Texar suspected Gilbert Burbank of having joined the Northern army. How had he learnt this, for the departure had been secret? Probably from his spies.

If Texar thought that James Burbank's son was in the Federal ships under the orders of Dupont, would he not probably devise some trap for the young lieutenant? Yes! And if he could entice him on to Floridan territory and capture him, we can imagine what would be his fate at the hands of these Southerners, exasperated at the progress of the Northern arms.

Such was the state of affairs when this story begins. Such was the position of the Federals on the maritime frontier of Florida, of the Burbanks in Duval county, and of Texar not only at Jacksonville but throughout the slave territories. If the Spaniard could gain his ends, if the authorities could be replaced by his partisans, it would be easy for him to send forth on Camdless Bay a populace maddened against the Abolitionists.

About an hour after Squambo had left Texar, he

returned. He drew his skiff to the bank, entered the palisades, and mounted the steps into the blockhouse.

"Is it done?" asked Texar.

"It is done, master."

"And—nothing?"

"Nothing."

CHAPTER VI.

JACKSONVILLE.

"YES, Zermah, yes, you were created and placed in the world to be a slave!" said the overseer, mounting his favourite hobby. "Yes! a slave, and never to be a free creature."

"That is not my opinion," replied Zermah calmly, without the least animation, so many had been these discussions with the overseer of Camdless Bay.

"It is possible, Zermah! But in any case you will in the long run come over to the opinion that no equality can exist between the whites and the blacks."

"It already exists, Mr. Perry, and it has always existed."

"You are mistaken, Zermah, and the proof is that the whites are ten times, twenty times—what am I talking about?—a hundred times more numerous on the earth than the blacks?"

"And it is on that account that they have made slaves of them," answered Zermah, "they had the strength and they abused it. But if the blacks had been in the majority, the whites would have been the slaves! Or rather they would not, for the blacks would have shown more justice, and certainly less cruelty."

Do not let it be supposed that this conversation hindered Zermah and the overseer from remaining on good terms with each other. At the moment they had nothing else to do but talk. They might, perhaps, have chosen a more useful subject of conversation, and they doubtless would have done so had it not been for the overseer's mania for continually discussing the slave question.

The two were seated in the stern of one of the Camdless

Bay boats, worked by four men from the plantation. They were crossing the river, taking advantage of the ebbing tide, on their way to Jacksonville. The overseer had some of Mr. Burbank's business matters to attend to, and Zermah was going to buy a few things for little Dy.

It was the 10th of February. Three days before James Burbank had returned to Castle House, and Texar to Black Creek after the affair at St. Augustine.

The day before Mr. Stannard had heard from Camdless Bay, about the last letter from Gilbert. The news did not arrive any too soon for Alice, whose life had been one of continual anxiety since the outbreak of the war.

The boat under her lateen-sail slipped along swiftly. In a quarter of an hour she reached Jacksonville. The overseer had, therefore, little time to develop his pet theory, but he made the best of it.

"No, Zermah," said he. "No! If the blacks had been in the majority, it would have made no difference. And I tell you this, that whatever may be the result of the war, we shall certainly go back to slavery, for slaves are necessary to work the plantations."

"Mr. Burbank does not think so, as you know," said Zermah.

"I know, but I think Mr. Burbank is wrong notwithstanding the respect I have for him. A black ought to be part of the estate in the same way as the animals and implements. If a horse could go away when it chose, if a plough could change hands when it pleased, no work would be possible. Let Mr. Burbank emancipate his slaves, and you will see what will become of Camdless Bay."

"He would have done so already," said Zermah, "if circumstances had allowed him to do so. And would you like to know what will happen when the emancipation of the slaves is proclaimed at Camdless Bay? Not a single black will leave the plantation, and nothing will be changed, except the right to treat them as beasts. And, as you have never exercised that right, Camdless Bay will remain as it was."

"Do you consider you have converted me to your ideas?" asked the overseer.

"Not in the least. It would be useless to do so, and for a very simple reason."

"What is that?"

"That at the bottom you think just the same as Mr. Burbank, Mr. Carrol, Mr. Stannard, and every one else who has a generous heart and a just mind."

"Never, Zermah, never! And I even affirm that what I say is in the best interests of the blacks. If you leave them to themselves they will perish, and the race will soon disappear."

"I know nothing about that, Mr. Perry. But anyhow, better the race should disappear than be condemned to the perpetual degradation of slavery."

The overseer would have replied, for he had by no means reached the end of his arguments; but the sail was taken in and the boat ran alongside the pier, there to await the return of Zermah and the overseer, who landed at once and set off about their business.

Jacksonville is situated on the left bank of the St. John's, at the end of a somewhat low plain, surrounded by an horizon of magnificent forests, which form an ever-verdant frame. Fields of maize and sugar-cane and rice, particularly by the river side, occupy a part of the plain.

Twelve years ago Jacksonville was but a big village, with a suburb, where the black population lived in huts built of mud and reeds. At the time of our story the village was becoming a town. Its houses were becoming more comfortable, its streets better planned and better kept, and the number of its inhabitants doubled. And the year before the chief town of Duval county had gained considerably by being united by railway to Tallahassee, which is the capital of Florida.

The overseer and Zermah noticed that there was a good deal of excitement in the town. Some hundreds of the inhabitants, Southerners of American birth, and mulattoes and half-breeds of Spanish origin, were waiting for the arrival of the steamboat, of which the smoke was in sight

down stream over a low point of the St. John's. Some
even, in order to reach the vessel more quickly, had started
towards her in rowing-boats, and others had gone off in a
few of those one-masted dogger-boats which are so common
at Jacksonville.

There had been serious news from the war the evening
before. The scheme of operations hinted at in Gilbert
Burbank's letter had become partly known. It had been
ascertained that Commodore Dupont's flotilla was getting
ready for sea, and that General Sherman was to take his
troops on board. Where was the expedition going?
They could not say for certain, but everything pointed
to the St. John's and the coast of Florida as being its
object.

When the steamer, which came from Fernandina, had
stopped at Jacksonville, her passengers could only confirm
that news. They even added that Commodore Dupont
would probably anchor in St. Andrew's Bay, while waiting
for a favourable moment to force the passes at Amelia
Island and the estuary of the St. John's.

Immediately the mob swarmed up into the town, putting
to noisy flight the flock of urubus which do the scavengering
of the streets. Shouts arose, "Down with the Northerners!
Death to the Northerners!" Such were the cries that
Texar's friends started to further excite the already excited
population. The crowd gathered in front of the court-
house, the police-office, and the episcopal church. The
authorities would have more trouble in quieting the outbreak, particularly as Jacksonville, as we have already
remarked, was divided on this slave question. And in
times of trouble, the noisiest and the hastiest make the
law, and the moderate men eventually submit to their
domination.

Naturally in the taverns and tiendas the shouts were the
loudest. There it was that the plans were formed for
offering an indomitable resistance to the invasion.

"Let us send the militia to Fernandina," said one.

"Let us sink some ships in the channel of the St.
John's," said another.

" Let us run up some earthworks round the city, and get
the guns for them," said another.

" Let us send for help by the railway from Fernandina
to Keys."

" Let us put out the light at Pablo, and so prevent the
enemy's fleet getting in at night."

" Let us put down torpedoes in the river."

The torpedo was almost a new thing in the American
war, and although they were not too well acquainted with
the way to manage it, they were evidently longing to
use it.

" Above all," said one of the most excited orators at the
tienda of Torillo, " we should send to gaol all the Northerners in the town, and all those Southerners who think
with them."

It would have been very strange if somebody had not
brought forward this proposition, the *ultima ratio* of
sectaries everywhere. And, of course, it was received
with cheers. Luckily for the honest people of Jacksonville the magistrates were to hesitate some time before
giving in to this popular prayer.

As she passed through the streets, Zermah took careful
notice of what was going on, so as to tell her master. He
would be seriously affected by the movement. If violent
measures were taken, such measures would not stop at the
town. They would extend beyond it to the plantations
in the county. Camdless Bay would be one of the first
to be visited. Hence the half-breed, in order to obtain
more precise information, called at Mr. Stannard's house a
little way out of the town.

This was a charming, comfortable dwelling, agreeably
situated in a sort of green oasis which the clearing-axe had
left in a corner of the plain. Under Alice's care the inside
as well as the outside of the house was excellently looked
after.

Zermah was received with great cordiality. At first
Alice spoke to her about Gilbert's letter, and Zermah was
able to tell her almost his very words.

" Yes," said Alice, " he is not far off now. But under

what circumstances will he come back to Florida? And
what dangers may there not be for him before the expedition is over!"

"Dangers, Alice," said Mr. Stannard. "Do not be nervous.
Gilbert faced greater when cruising off the coast of Georgia
and in that Port Royal affair. I do not think Florida's
resistance will be very terrible or very long. What can we
do with this St. John's, which will let the gunboats into the
very heart of the country? All defence seems to me difficult, if not impossible."

"May what you say be true," said Alice, "and may
heaven grant that the war will soon be over!"

"It will only end by wiping out the South," replied Mr.
Stannard. "That will take a long time, I am afraid; and
Jefferson Davis and his Generals—Lee, Johnston, and
Beauregard—will hold out for some time in the centre.
The Federals will not have an easy triumph over the Con-
federates. But as to Florida, that can easily be captured;
unfortunately its possession will not ensure the final
victory."

"It is to be hoped that Gilbert will not be imprudent,"
said Alice, joining her hands. "If he yields to the wish to
see his family for a few hours when he is so near them—"

"And seeing you, Miss Alice," said Zurmah, "for are
you not already one of the family?"

"Yes, Zermah, in heart."

"No, Alice, there is nothing to be afraid of," said Mr.
Stannard. "Gilbert is too sensible to run any risk when
Commodore Dupont could occupy Florida in a few days;
there would be no excuse for the foolhardiness of coming
here until the Federals are masters."

"Particularly now that people are more than ever ready
to break out into violence," answered Zermah.

"The town, this morning," said Mr. Stannard, "is in a
very excited state. I saw who are the ringleaders, and I
heard them. Texar is with them, and is urging them on
and exciting them. The scoundrels will end by raising
the lower classes not only against the magistrates, but
against all who do not agree with them."

"Do you not think, Mr. Stannard," said Zermah, "that it would be better for you to leave Jacksonville—at all events for a short time. It would be wisest not to come back till after the coming of the Federal troops. Mr. Burbank told me to tell you that he would be glad to see you and Miss Alice at Castle House."

"Yes, I know," said Mr. Stannard. "I have not forgotten Mr. Burbank's offer. But is Castle House any safer than Jacksonville? If these adventurers become masters here, will they not spread over the country, and will the plantations escape their ravages?"

"Mr. Stannard," said Zermah, "it seems to me that if there is any danger it would be better to be together."

"Zermah is right, father. It would be better for us all to be at Camdless Bay."

"Certainly, Alice," said Mr. Stannard. "I am not going to refuse Burbank's invitation; but I don't think the danger is so pressing. Zermah can tell our friends that it will take me a few days more to put things in order, and then we will avail ourselves of the hospitality of Castle House."

"And when Mr. Gilbert arrives," said Zermah, "he will at least find there all he loves."

Leaving Mr. Stannard and his daughter, Zermah made her way through the crowd, which grew more and more excited, and regained the pier, where the overseer was waiting for her. They got into the boat, and Mr. Perry resumed the usual conversation at the very point he had left it.

In saying that the danger was not imminent Mr. Stannard was mistaken. Jacksonville was to have immediate experience of the effects of the war.

The Federal Government acted throughout with much circumspection; they proceeded step by step. Two years after the outbreak of hostilities, Abraham Lincoln had still to proclaim the abolition of slavery throughout the whole territory. Many months were still to elapse before the president's message proposed to solve the slave question by gradually buying out and emancipating the blacks, before the vote was passed of 200,000*l*., with the authority, by way of indemnity, to give 60*l*. for every slave freed.   If some of the Northern generals had been authorized to suppress slavery in the counties invaded by their armies, they had, up to then, disavowed it.   Opinions were not unanimous on the subject, and there were several Unionist chiefs reported to be against the measure, as being neither logical nor opportune.

Meanwhile the war dragged on, and much to the disadvantage of the Confederates.   General Price, on the 13th of February, had had to evacuate Arkansas with his contingent of Missouri militia.

We have seen that Fort Henry was captured and occupied by the Federals.   Now they were attacking Fort Donelson, which was defended by powerful artillery and covered by three miles of works, embracing the little town of Dover.   Notwithstanding the cold and the snow, the fort, attacked on the land by the 15,000 men under General Grant and on the water by the gunboats of Commodore Foote, surrendered on the 14th of February, with an entire division of men and materials of war.

This was a serious check for the Confederates.   The effect produced by the defeat was immense.   As an immediate consequence came the retreat of General Johnston, who had to abandon the important town of Nashville on the Cumberland.   The inhabitants were seized with panic, and left it as soon as he had gone, and a few days afterwards the same thing happened at Columbus.   The whole State of Kentucky was thus in Federal hands.

We can easily imagine with what feelings of anger and ideas of revenge these events were received in Florida. The authorities were powerless to arrest the agitation, which spread to the most distant villages in the counties. The danger hourly increased for those who did not share in the opinions of the Southerners and join in the plans of resistance against the Federal troops.   At Tallahassee and St. Augustine there were troubles which were easily put down ; but at Jacksonville the rising of the populace threatened to degenerate into acts of unqualified violence.

The position at Camdless Bay became more and more disquieting. With his men so thoroughly devoted to him, James Burbank might perhaps hold out for a time, although it was then very difficult to procure arms and ammunition in sufficient quantities. At Jacksonville, Mr. Stannard was in great danger of losing his house, his daughter, and all he possessed. James Burbank knowing how he was placed, wrote him letter after letter. He sent many messengers asking him to come to Castle House without delay. There he would be in comparative safety, and if he had to find another retreat, if he had to take refuge in the interior until the Federals had quieted the country by their presence, it would be easier for him to do so.

Mr. Stannard at last resolved to leave Jacksonville and take refuge at Camdless Bay. He started on the morning of the 23rd, with as much secrecy as possible, and without informing any one of his plans. A boat waited for him at a little creek about a mile up the St. John's. Alice and he reached it in safety, crossed the river, and landed at the Camdless Bay pier, where the Burbanks were waiting for them.

It is easy to imagine their reception. Was not Alice already Mrs. Burbank's daughter? Now they were reunited. The dark days that were coming would be passed together in greater safety and less anxiety.

It was indeed time to leave Jacksonville. The next day Mr. Stannard's house was attacked by a lot of scoundrels, who marked their violence under a show of local patriotism. The authorities had great difficulty in saving the house from pillage, and in protecting some other houses belonging to honest citizens who did not share in the opinions of the mob. Evidently the hour was coming when the magistrates would be replaced by the chiefs of the rioters, who were doing their best to increase the excitement.

As Mr. Stannard had told Zermah, Texar had left his unknown retreat and was in Jacksonville among his habitual companions, who had been recruited from the very worst of the population, drawn from the plantations up the river. These scoundrels had resolved that they would have their

5

way in the towns as they had had it in the country. They corresponded with their adherents in the different counties of Florida, and by keeping the question of slavery well to the front, gained in numbers every day. In a short time at Jacksonville, as at St. Augustine, the vagabonds, adventurers, and backwoodsmen who had come crowding in, would become the masters and have the military and civil power in their hands. The militia and regular troops would hasten to make common cause with them, as has often happened in times of trouble when violence is the order of the day.

James Burbank was fully aware of what was passing. Many of his confidential agents, on whom he could depend, kept him informed of what was taking place at Jacksonville. He knew that Texar had reappeared there, and that his detestable influence had extended over the whole of the lower population which, like him, was of Spanish origin. Such a man at the head of affairs was a direct menace to Camdless Bay. And so Burbank was making ready for either resistance, if it were possible, or retreat if it became necessary to abandon Castle House to fire and pillage. Above all things to provide for the safety of his family and friends was his first and constant care.

During these days Zermah's devotion knew no bounds. At all hours she watched the boundaries of the plantation, particularly on the river side. A few slaves, chosen from among the most intelligent and best, lived day and night at posts which had been assigned to them. Any attempt against the estate would have been reported immediately. The Burbanks would not be taken unawares, without having time to take refuge in Castle House.

But James Burbank need not have been so anxious about a direct strong-handed attack. So long as the authority was not in the hands of Texar and his people there was no abandonment of official form. Under the pressure of public opinion the magistrates were brought to decide on a measure that would give a sort of satisfaction to the slavery partisans, who were so incensed against the North.

Burbank was the most important of the Florida planters, the richest of those who were known to hold liberal opinions. It was he who was first thought of to give an explanation of his personal ideas on enfranchisement in the midst of a slaveholding country.

In the evening of the 26th an orderly from Jacksonville arrived at Camdless Bay, and handed in a letter addressed to him. This is what the envelope contained:—

"Mr. James Burbank is ordered to present himself in person to-morrow, the 27th February, at eleven o'clock in the morning, at the Court of Justice before the authorities of Jacksonville."

That was all.

CHAPTER VII.

BEFORE THE COURT.

IF this was not the clap of thunder, it was the lightning flash that preceded it.

If James Burbank was not shaken by it, what were the feelings of his family? Why should the owner of Camdless Bay be summoned to Jacksonville? It was indeed a summons, not an invitation, to appear before the authorities. What were they going to do? Was this the beginning of some prosecution against him? Was it his liberty or his life that was in danger? If he obeyed—if he left Castle House—would they let him come back? If he did not obey, would they use force to bring him? And in that case to what dangers, to what violence, would his people be exposed?

"You shall not go, James."

It was Mrs. Burbank, who spoke in the name of all.

"No, Mr. Burbank," said Alice. "You must not think of leaving us—"

"To put yourself in the power of such people," added Carrol.

Burbank did not answer. When he first read the curt order to appear he had become so angry that he could scarcely restrain himself. What had happened to make the magistrates so daring? Had Texar's companions and partisans found their way into office? Had they procured the dismissal of the authorities who had hitherto acted with some moderation? No. Overseer Perry had returned in the afternoon from Jacksonville and brought no such news.

"Could it be some event of the war?" said Mr. Stannard; "some advantage gained by the Southerners which has led them to attack us?"

"I am afraid that must be it," said Edward Carrol. "If the North has experienced some check, these scoundrels will fancy they are no more in danger from Commodore Dupont, and are capable of proceeding to any excess."

"They say that in Texas," said Mr. Stannard, "the Federal troops have had to retire before the militia, and re-cross the Rio Grande, after a severe defeat at Valverde. At least, that is what I was told by a Jacksonville man I met about an hour ago."

"Evidently that is what has made these fellows so bold," said Carrol.

"Then Sherman's army and Dupont's flotilla will not come!" exclaimed Mrs. Burbank.

"It is only the 26th of February," said Alice, "and, according to Gilbert's letter, the Federal ships will not be ready for sea before the 28th."

"Then you want the time to get down to the mouths of the St. John's," added Mr. Stannard, "to force the passes clear the bar, and make a descent on Jacksonville. That will take ten days."

"Ten days?" said Alice.

"Ten days!" added Mrs. Burbank. "And before then what may not happen to us?"

James Burbank took no part in the conversation. He was thinking. He was asking himself what he was to do. To refuse to obey was to see the whole populace of Jacksonville advance on Camdless Bay with the open or tacit approval of the authorities. How great would then be the danger to his family! Better risk his own safety than theirs. If his life or liberty were in peril, better that the peril should threaten him alone.

Mrs. Burbank looked at her husband with the keenes anxiety. She felt that he was fighting a battle with him self. She hesitated to question him. Neither Alice, no Stannard, nor Carrol dare ask him what his answer was to be. It was little Dy who, unconsciously, no doubt, made herself the mouthpiece of the family. She had gone near her father, who took her on his knee.

"Father!" said she.

"What is it, dear?"

"Are you going to those wicked people who want to do you such harm?"

"Yes. I will go."

"James!" exclaimed Mrs. Burbank.

"I must; it is my duty. I will go!"

James Burbank had spoken so resolutely that it was useless to say anything against his determination. He had evidently thought over all the consequences. His wife went and sat beside him, and put her arms round him, but she said nothing. And what could she say?

"My friends," said Burbank, "it is possible that we are exaggerating the importance of this arbitrary act. What can they say against me? Nothing, as they know well. Accuse me of my opinions? My opinions are my own. I have never hidden them from my adversaries; and, as long as I live, I shall not hesitate to proclaim them to their face."

"We will go with you, James!" said Carrol.

"Yes," added Stannard. "We will not let you go to Jacksonville alone."

"No, my friends," answered Burbank. "To me alone comes the order to appear before the magistrates, and I alone will go. I may be kept there for some days. It is, therefore, better that you stay at Camdless Bay. To you I entrust my family during my absence."

"And you are really going?" said Dy.

"Yes, my little daughter," said Burbank playfully; "but if I do not lunch with you to-morrow I will come back to dinner, and we'll pass the evening together. Now, tell me if, while I am at Jacksonville, there is anything I can buy you? What can I do to please you? What shall I bring you?"

"Bring yourself, father," said the child; and at this expression of what all felt, the family separated, after Burbank had taken such measures of security as the occasion required.

The night passed without an alarm. In the morning Burbank was awake with the dawn, and was soon on his way down the avenue of bamboos leading to the pier. There he gave orders for a boat to be ready at eight o'clock to take him across the river.

As he returned to Castle House from the pier he was met by Zermah.

"Master," she said, "your mind is made up? You are going to Jacksonville?"

"Yes, Zermah, and in the interest of all. You understand, do you not?"

"Yes, master. A refusal on your part would bring Texar's mob on Camdless Bay."

"And that is a serious danger which must be avoided at all cost," said Burbank.

"Do you wish me to go with you?"

"On the contrary, I wish you to remain on the plantation. It is necessary that you should be near my wife, near my child, in case any danger should threaten them before my return."

"I will not leave them."

"You have no news?"

"No! It is true, however, that suspicious characters are prowling around the plantation. They have been watched. Last night two or three boats crossed the river. Do they think that Mr. Gilbert is with the Federals under Commodore Dupont, and is coming secretly to Camdless Bay?"

"My brave boy!" said Burbank. "No! he is too sensible to be so rash."

"I am afraid Texar has some suspicion on the subject. They tell me his influence gets greater every day. When you are at Jacksonville beware of Texar, master—"

"Yes, Zermah, as of a poisonous reptile! But I am on my guard. While I am away, if he makes any attempt against Castle House—"

"Never fear, master, for yourself; and never fear for us. Your slaves will defend the plantation, and, if necessary, will die to the last man. They are devoted to you. They love you. I know what they think, what they say, what they will do. There have been people here from other plantations to raise them against you, but they will not listen to them. They are all one family with yours, and you can depend upon them."

" I know it, Zermah, and I trust to them."

Burbank returned to the house. The moment came ; he bid farewell to his wife, his daughter, and Alice. He promised them to do nothing to provoke the magistrates to violence. He would be sure to come back that night. He bid everybody good-bye and left them. Certainly James Burbank had much to fear for himself; but there was much to be feared for those he left at Castle House.

Stannard and Carrol went with him to the landing-place at the end of the avenue. There he gave them his last instructions ; and with a beautiful breeze from the south-west, the boat rapidly left the pier of Camdless Bay.

An hour afterwards, about ten o'clock, Burbank landed at Jacksonville. The quay was then deserted. There were only a few sailors discharging the cargoes of the dogger-boats. He was not recognized ; his arrival was not announced at all, and he was able to cross to the end of the harbour and call on one of his friends, Mr. Harvey.

Mr. Harvey was much surprised and uneasy at seeing him. He had not thought that he would have obeyed the order to present himself at the court. In the town it was not thought that he would. As to who had been the cause of the order being given, Mr. Harvey did not know. Probably, with a view to satisfy public opinion, the magistrates were going to ask him to explain his conduct since the beginning of the war, particularly with regard to his slaves. Perhaps they were going to keep the richest Federal farmer in Florida as a hostage. Would it not have been better to have stopped at Camdless Bay ? So thought Mr. Harvey. Could he not go back as nobody knew he had come ?

Burbank had not come merely to go back again. He wished to know what it was all about, and he would know.

Some very interesting questions as to the state of affairs generally were then put by him to his correspondent.

Had the authorities been replaced by the ringleaders of the mob?

Not yet, but their position had become precarious.

Had the Spaniard Texar any hand in the popular movement that was about to take place?

Yes. He was looked upon as the leader of the advanced slave-holding party in Florida. He and his companions would probably soon be masters of the town.

Had the last news from the war been confirmed?

It had been. The organization of the Southern States had just been completed. On the 22nd of February the Government had been definitely formed, with Jefferson Davis as President and Stephens as Vice-President, and they had been invested with power for six years. Congress, composed of two houses, had assembled at Richmond. Jefferson Davis, three days before, had asked for compulsory service. Since then the Confederates had had a few successes of no great importance. On the 24th, an important detachment of McClellan's had crossed the Upper Potomac, and the Southerners had consequently evacuated Columbus. A great battle was imminent on the Mississippi between them and the army of General Grant.

And how about the squadron that Dupont was to bring to the mouths of the St. John's?

Rumours were afloat that in ten days it would attempt to force the passes. If Texar and his partisans were meditating an outbreak to get the town into their hands, no time was to be lost.

Such was the state of affairs at Jacksonville; and who could tell if the Burbank incident would not hasten the catastrophe?

When the time came for him to appear James Burbank left his friend's house and walked to the Courts of Justice. There was much excitement in the streets. The people were crowding towards the courts. It seemed as though the case, though it might be of little importance in itself,

would bring about a rising that might have deplorable
consequences.

The square was full of people, mostly of the poorer
whites, half-breeds, and negroes. Naturally they were
noisy. If those who could obtain admission to the court
were few, a good many of Texar's partisans would nevertheless be there. With them would be a sprinkling of
law-abiding citizens opposed to such an act of injustice,
but it would be difficult for them to withstand the party
bent on removing the authorities of Jacksonville.

As soon as Burbank appeared in the square he was
recognized. A loud shouting arose ; and it was not in his
favour. A few courageous citizens surrounded him, having
no intention that an honourable and much-respected man
should be exposed to the brutalities of the mob. In
obeying the summons he had received Burbank had shown
his dignity and decision of character, and his doing so
was worthy of recognition. He was therefore able to
make his way across the square. He reached the door of
the court, entered, and stopped at the bar to which he had
been so unjustly summoned.

The chief magistrate of the town and his assistants
were already on the bench. They were moderate, reasonable men. The menaces and recriminations to which they
had been subject ever since the outbreak of the war may
be imagined. To remain at their posts required no little
courage and energy. It was only because the slave question caused less excitement in Florida than in the other
states of the South that they had been able to withstand
the attacks of the turbulent party. Secessionist ideas
were, however, making way ; and with them the influence
of the lower classes and adventurous vagabonds daily increased ; and it was to satisfy public opinion, to a certain
extent under the pressure of the more violent agitators,
that the magistrates had decided to summon James Burbank, on information given by one of their leaders—the
Spaniard Texar.

The murmur—of approbation from one side, of disapprobation from another—which greeted the proprietor of

Camdless Bay as he entered the court soon subsided. Erect, with the dauntless look of a man that had never failed, he did not even wait for the magistrate to ask him the usual questions, but in a firm voice he said,—

"You asked for James Burbank. James Burbank is before you."

After the first formalities, to which Burbank answered very briefly, he said, " Of what am I accused ? "

"Of opposing by word, and probably by deed, such ideas and hopes as are now held by the majority in Florida."

"And who is my accuser ? "

"I am."

It was Texar. Burbank recognized his voice. He did not even turn his head ; he contented himself with shrugging his shoulders in token of his contempt for his accuser.

On the other hand, Texar's partisans encouraged their leader by voice and gesture.

"And in the first place," said he, " I tell James Burbank to his face that he is a Northerner! His presence at Jacksonville, in a Confederate State, is a standing insult. He is a Northerner at heart and by birth ; why has he not gone back to the North ? "

" I am in Florida," replied Burbank, "because it suits me to be there. I have lived in the county for twenty years. If I was not born in it you know at least where I came from ; and that is more than you can say for those whose past is unknown, and who live not in the light of day, and whose private life ought to be inquired into much more than mine."

Although this was a direct attack on Texar, he made no sign.

" What next ? " asked Burbank.

" Next," said the Spaniard, "when the country has risen for the maintenance of slavery, and is ready to shed its blood to repulse the Federal troops, I accuse James Burbank of being an anti-slavery man, and the head of an anti-slavery propaganda."

"James Burbank," said the magistrate, "in the circumstances in which we are placed, you will understand that
this charge is of exceptional gravity. I shall be glad to
have your answer."

"Sir," said Burbank, "my answer is very simple. I
have assisted in no propaganda, nor do I intend doing so.
The charge is false. As to my opinions on slavery, if I
am permitted to refer to them here, I may say that I am
an abolitionist ! I deplore the strife that is raging between
the South and the North. I am afraid that the South is
marching to inevitable disaster, and it is in her own
interest that I wish to see her on another road instead of
engaging in a war against common sense. You will remember some day that those who spoke to you as I am
speaking were in the right. When the time has come for
a change, for a step in moral progress, it is foolish to withstand it. The separation of the North from the South
would be a crime against the American country. Neither
reason, nor justice, nor force is on your side, and the
crime will never be accomplished."

These words were received with a few shouts of approval, speedily drowned in more noisy demonstrations.
The majority were not prepared to accept them.

When the magistrate had obtained silence in the court
James Burbank continued :—

"And now," said he, "I am ready for more precise
charges, as to facts, be it understood, and I will reply to
them when you tell me what they are."

The magistrates were much embarrassed by this digni-
fied bearing. They knew of no fact that could be charged
against Mr. Burbank. Their object had been to let the
charges be made and let them be proved, if proofs existed.

Texar saw that he must explain in greater detail or he
would fail.

"Be it so," said he. "But it is not my notion of what is
best to invoke freedom of opinion on the slave question
when the country has risen in support of the clause. But
if James Burbank has the right to think as he likes on the
subject—if it is true that he abstains from making converts

to his ideas, at least he might abstain from corresponding with the enemy at the gates of Florida."

This accusation of complicity with the Federals was a very serious one at that time, and hence the thrill of excitement that ran through the audience. It was, however, still vague, and had to be proved.

" You pretend that I correspond with the enemy ?"

" Yes," said Texar.

" Prove it. I should like you to."

"Very well," said Texar. "About three weeks ago a messenger to James Burbank left the Federal army, or rather, the flotilla of Commodore Dupont. The man came to Camdless Bay, and he was followed from the time he left the plantation till he re-crossed the frontier. Do you deny that ?"

Evidently this was the messenger who had brought the young lieutenant's letter. Texar's spies had not been deceived. This time the charge was definite, and Burbank's reply was anxiously waited for.

He did not hesitate to tell them what was only the truth.

" Yes," said he, " a man did come about that time to Camdless Bay, but the man was only a messenger. He did not belong to the Federal army, and he simply brought a letter from my son—"

" From your son," interrupted Texar ; "from your son, who, if we are correctly informed, is in the Unionist service, who is, perhaps, in the van of the invaders now on the march to Florida."

The vehemence with which Texar pronounced these words made a strong impression on the people in the court. If James Burbank, after admitting that he had received a letter from his son, admitted that Gilbert was in the Federal army, how could he get over the charge of being in communication with the enemies of the South?

"Will you reply to the evidence against your son ?" asked the magistrate.

"No, sir," replied Burbank, "I have nothing to say in the matter. There is no charge against my son that I know of. I alone am accused of holding communication with the Federal army, and I deny it, and I defy this man who attacks me on account of his own personal hatred towards me to bring forward a single proof."

"He admits, then, that his son is now fighting against the Confederates!" exclaimed Texar.

"I admit nothing," said Burbank. "It is for you to prove the charge you bring against me."

"Good! I will prove it," replied Texar. "In a few days I shall be in possession of the proof you ask, and when I have it—"

"When you have it," replied the magistrate, "we can take it into consideration. Until then, I do not see what charges Mr. Burbank has to answer."

In deciding in this way the magistrate acted like an honest man. He was right undoubtedly; unfortunately he was wrong to be right with a public so prejudiced against the planter of Camdless Bay. And then followed an ominous murmuring, and even protesting, on the part of Texar's companions. The Spaniard saw how things were going, and abandoning the charges against Gilbert Burbank, returned to those against his father.

"Yes," he said, "I will prove all that I have advanced with regard to James Burbank's being in communication with the enemy preparing to invade Florida. Meanwhile, the opinions he publicly professes—opinions so dangerous for the cause of slavery—constitute a public danger; and, in the name of all the slaveholders who will not submit to the yoke of the North, I demand that he be secured."

"Yes! yes!" exclaimed the partisans of Texar, while some of the audience endeavoured in vain to protest against the unjustifiable proposal.

The magistrate succeeded in quieting the assembly, and then Burbank replied,—

"I shall do all that my strength and my rights allow me to oppose such tyranny. I am an abolitionist. And I have already told you so. But opinion is free, I suppose, in a system of government founded on freedom. Up to now it has not been a crime to be an anti-slavery man, and as I am not a criminal the law is powerless to punish me."

Renewed shouts of approval seemed to show that Burbank was getting the best of it. Texar saw that the time
had come to change his batteries. We need not, therefore,
be surprised when he hurled at Burbank the following
unexpected challenge :—

"Well, if you do not believe in slavery, why do you not
free your own slaves ? "

"I will do so," answered James Burbank. "I will do so
as soon as the time comes."

"Indeed! That means you will do so when the Federal
army is in possession of Florida. You want Sherman's
soldiers and Dupont's sailors to give you courage to act up
to your ideas! That is prudent, but it is cowardly."

"Cowardly!" exclaimed Burbank indignantly, and not
seeing the snare spread for him.

"Yes, cowardly," said Texar. "You dare not put your
ideas into practice! You only want to curry popularity with
the Northerners! You are an abolitionist only for appearance sake; at heart you are a slavery man."

James Burbank drew himself up. He gave his opponent
a long look of scorn. Such hypocrisy was manifestly
absurdly out of keeping with his frank, loyal existence.
In a clear, decided tone, that could be heard by all, he
said :—

"Inhabitants of Jacksonville, from this day forth I shall
not keep a slave. This very day I proclaim the abolition of slavery over the whole plantation of Camdless
Bay."

At first this bold declaration was greeted with cheers.
It had required true courage to do such a thing—courage
more than prudence perhaps. Burbank had allowed his
indignation to get the better of him.

It was evident that his action would compromise the
interests of the other Florida planters, and at once a reaction took place in the court. The applause was silenced
by the vociferations not only of those who were slaveholders
on principle, but of those who till then had been indifferent
on the slavery question.

And Texar's friends would have profited by this reaction

to commit some act of violence on James Burbank if the
Spaniard himself had not restrained them.

"Leave him alone," said he. "Burbank has disarmed
himself. Now he is ours!"

His meaning was immediately understood, and his partisans refrained from any act of violence. He even felt no
misgivings when the magistrates told Burbank he might go
—there was no proof to warrant his incarceration. If the
Spaniard could make good his words later on, and produce
witnesses to show that Burbank was in communication with
the enemy, the magistrates could take action. Until then
Burbank was free.

True, the declaration of enfranchisement relative to
Camdless Bay was made publicly, and might eventually
serve as a pretence on the part of the mob for proceedings
against the authorities of the town.

As he left the court Burbank was followed by a dis-
orderly crowd very evilly disposed towards him, but the
police kept them from assaulting him. There were shouts
and threats, but no acts of violence. Evidently Texar's
influence protected him.

He reached the quay, where his boat was waiting.
There he took leave of his friend Mr. Harvey; and then,
pushing off, he was soon out of range of the vociferations
with which the rabble of Jacksonville saluted him as he
left them.

As the tide was going down, the boat took at least two
hours to get across to Camdless Bay, where the family were
waiting for him. Great was their joy when they saw him
coming back. Many reasons had they had for fearing he
would be kept away from them.

"No," said he to little Dy as he kissed her; "I promised
to come home to dinner, my dear, and you know I never
break my promises."

CHAPTER VIII.

THE LAST SLAVE.

THAT evening James Burbank told his people what had happened at the court. Texar's hateful conduct was revealed. It was at his instigation that the summons had been sent to Camdless Bay. The conduct of the magistrates had been worthy of praise. When the charge of communicating with the Federals had been made they had asked for the proof, and as the proof was not forthcoming Burbank was set at liberty.

With these vague charges Gilbert's name had been mixed up. There could not be much doubt that the young man was with the Northern army. Was not James Burbank's refusal a half-admission that the assertion was true? And consequently great was the fear and anxiety on the part of Mrs. Burbank, and Alice, and all the family. If the son could not be got at would not the rabble of Jacksonville take vengeance on his father? Texar had boasted that in a few days he would produce his proof; and it was not impossible that he could do so. What would have to be done then?

"Poor Gilbert," said Mrs. Burbank, "to know he is so near to Texar, who will stop at nothing to attain his end."

"Could we not let him know what is happening at Jacksonville?" asked Alice.

"Yes," said Mr. Stannard, "we might let him know that the slightest imprudence on his part will have the most deplorable consequences for his and him."

"And how are we to let him know?" asked James Burbank. "There are spies all round the plantation;

6

there can be no doubt of that. The messenger Gilbert sent was watched back to the frontier. Every letter we write may fall into Texar's hands. Every man we send with a verbal message may be arrested on the road. No, my friends, do not try to make matters worse. May heaven send the Federals into Florida without delay! It is time they came now ; the minority of honest people is threatened by the scoundrels of the country."

James Burbank was right. Owing to the watch kept round the plantation it would be very imprudent to hold any communication with Gilbert. And the time was approaching when he and his people would be in safety under the protection of the Federal army.

In fact, it was the very next morning that Commodore Dupont was to start from his anchorage at Edisto. In three days his flotilla would have dropped down the Georgia coast and reached St. Andrew's Bay.

Then James Burbank told his friends of the very serious matter that had happened before the magistrates ; how he had been led to reply to Texar's taunt as to the slaves at Camdless Bay. Strong in his right, strong in his conscience, he had publicly declared the abolition of slavery on his estate. This was what no Southern state had yet allowed to be proclaimed without having been obliged by the fortune of war. He had done it entirely of his own free will.

The declaration was as bold as it was magnanimous. What would be its consequences no one could foresee. Evidently it would not make Burbank's position less hazardous in this slave-holding country. It might, perhaps, provoke some desire of revolt among the slaves on other plantations. That did not matter ! His friends, excited by the grandeur of the action, fully approved of what Burbank had done.

"James." said Mrs. Burbank, "whatever may happen, you did quite right to reply in that way to Texar's odious insinuations."

"We are proud of you, father !" said Alice, giving Mr. Burbank the name for the first time.

"And so, my dear girl," said James Burbank, "when Gilbert and his Federals enter Florida they will not find a single slave at Camdless Bay."

"Thank you, Mr. Burbank," said Zermah. "I thank you for my companions and myself. As far as I am concerned I never felt I was a slave. Your kindness and generosity have always made me seem like as free as I am to-day."

"Quite so, Zermah," said Mrs. Burbank. "Slave or free, we shall love you none the less."

Zermah vainly tried to hide her emotion. She took Dy in her arms and clasped her to her bosom.

Carrol and Stannard cordially shook hands with Burbank to show how they applauded his deed of daring— and justice.

Evidently the Burbank family in their generous enthusiasm forgot all about the complications to which the act might give rise.

No one at Camdless Bay would think of blaming James Burbank, unless perhaps Mr. Perry, the overseer, when he heard what had taken place. But he was away on duty and would not be back till late at night.

When the family gathering broke up, Mr. Burbank told them that next morning he would give the slaves their liberty.

"We will be with you, James," said Mrs. Burbank, "when you tell them they are free."

"Yes, so will all of us," said Carrol.

"And me, too!" said little Dy.

"Yes, my dear; you too."

"Zermah," said the little girl, "are you going to leave us now?"

"No, my child!" said Zermah. "No, I will never leave you!"

In the morning, the first person Mr. Burbank met in the private garden was Perry the overseer. As the secret had been kept, he had heard nothing about it. He soon heard it from the lips of his master—much to his amazement.

"Oh Mr. James! oh, Mr. James!"

PART I.

The worthy man was quite astounded, and other words failed him.

"But that ought not to surprise you, Perry," said Burbank. "I am only anticipating matters. You know that the enfranchisement of the blacks is an act imposed on every State that is careful of its dignity."

"Its dignity, Mr. James! What sort of a thing is this dignity?"

"You do not understand the word 'dignity,' Perry? Well, careful of its interests."

"Its interests—its interests, Mr. James! You say careful of its interests!"

"Certainly, and the future will show you I am right."

"But where are we to get the labour for the plantation, Mr. Burbank?"

"Amongst the blacks, Perry."

"But if the blacks are free not to work they will not work."

"They will work; and, what is more, work with more zeal and more pleasure, for their condition will be better."

"But your blacks, Mr. James! Your blacks will begin by leaving you."

"I shall be much astonished if a single one does anything of the sort."

"But I am no longer overseer of the slaves at Camdless Bay."

"No, but you are overseer at Camdless Bay; and I do not suppose your position will be any the worse for commanding free men instead of slaves."

"But—"

"My dear Perry, I warn you that I have an answer for all your buts. Look after what you have to do regarding a measure which you cannot prevent, and of which all my family approve."

"And do the blacks know nothing about it?"

"Not yet," said Burbank; "and do not say anything about it to them. They shall be told it to-day. You can assemble them in the park at three o'clock this afternoon, and tell them I have a communication to make to them."

Then the overseer retired with many a gesture of astonishment.

"Blacks who are not slaves! Blacks who will work for themselves! Blacks who will have to look after their own wants! It is a regular capsize of the social order! It is the upsetting of all human law! It is against nature—yes, against nature!"

During the morning Burbank, Stannard, and Carrol went out in the break to visit the northern boundary of the plantation. The slaves were busy at their usual work in the fields of rice and coffee-shrubs and sugar-canes. There was the same bustle going on in the workshops and saw-mills. The secret had been well kept. No communication had been established between Jacksonville and Camdless Bay. These who were so directly interested knew nothing of James Burbank's project.

In driving along the boundary of the estate Burbank and his friends wished to assure themselves that the neighbourhood of the plantation presented nothing suspicious. After yesterday's declaration, it was to be feared that some of the Jacksonville mob or the people of the country round might find their way to Camdless Bay. But nothing of the sort was to be seen. No prowlers were noticed even on the bank of the river or along the St. John's. The *Shannon*, which passed at ten o'clock, did not stop at the pier, but continued her voyage to Picolata. Neither up stream nor down stream was there anything to alarm the inhabitants of Castle House.

A little before noon Burbank, Stannard, and Carrol repassed the bridge into the enclosure and entered the house The family were waiting for lunch. They seemed less anxious, and talked more at their ease. It seemed as though the course of events had paused for a while. Probably the energy of the Jacksonville magistrates had put a check on the violent spirits of Texar's party. If that state of things continued for a day or so Florida would be occupied by the Federal army, and anti-slavery men, whether Northerners or Southerners, would be in safety.

James Burbank could thus proceed to the ceremony ot

6

emancipation—the first action of the kind that had ever voluntarily taken place in a slave State.

Of all the blacks on the plantation, the one who would be most gratified was evidently a fellow of about twenty, whose name was Pygmalion, or Pyg, as he was more commonly called. He looked after the servants' quarters at Castle House, and so lived there. He did not work in the fields, nor in the factories, nor in the shops. Truth to tell, Pygmalion was a ridiculous, vain, idle fellow, whose faults his master very kindly overlooked. Since the slave question had come up, he had been heard to declaim in sounding phrases about human liberty. On all occasions he indulged in pretentious speeches to his fellow negroes, and was generally laughed down. As they said, he tried to ride the great horse when even a donkey would have thrown him. Many discussions had he had with Mr. Perry when the overseer was in a humour to listen to him ; and we can imagine the enthusiasm with which he would welcome an act of enfranchisement that gave him the dignity of manhood.

The negroes had been told to assemble in the private park in front of Castle House, as an important communication was to be made to them by the planter.

A little before three o'clock--the time fixed for the meeting—the slaves began to assemble. They had not gone to work after the midday meal ; and had tidied themselves up and changed their working clothes as was usual with them when admitted within the palisades. At the barracoons there had been great excitement, and the overseer had walked from one to the other growling to himself,—

"When I think that at this moment we can buy and sell these fellows as if they were merchandise, and in another hour we shall be able to do nothing of the sort ! Yes ! I will say so to the last ! Mr. Burbank, you can do what you like and say what you like, and so can President Lincoln, and so can all the Federals of the North, and all the Liberals of the world !"

And here Pygmalion, who knew nothing as yet, found himself face to face with the overseer.

"Why are we to be called together, please, Mr. Perry?" asked he. "Do you know?"

"Yes, idiot! It is to—"

The overseer stopped, not wishing to betray the secret. An idea occurred to him.

"Come here, Pyg," he said.

Pygmalion approached.

"Have I ever pulled your ear for you, my boy?"

"Yes, Mr. Perry, for contrary to all justice—human or divine—you have a right to do so."

"Well, as it is my right I am going to use it once more!"

And without heeding the cries of Pyg, but without doing him any serious hurt, he pulled the ears which were already of tolerable length. And much did it relieve the overseer to take advantage of his right for the last time.

At three o'clock James Burbank and his people appeared on the terrace at Castle House. Before them stood seven hundred slaves, men, women, and children, among them a score of old negroes, who, when they were past work, found a comfortable retreat for old age in the Camdless Bay barracoons.

Deep silence fell on all. At a gesture from Mr. Burbank the overseer made the negroes form up closer, so that they could distinctly hear what was said to them.

"My friends," said James Burbank, "you know that a civil war has been raging for a long time in the United States. The real cause of that war is the question of slavery. The South is only fighting for slavery, in which it thinks its interests are bound up and which it wishes to maintain. The North, in the name of humanity, desires to put an end to it in America. God has helped the defenders of a righteous cause, and victory has already more than once declared for those who are fighting for the freedom of a race. For some time, as everybody knows, I have shared in the opinions of the North without being able to put them in practice. But now, certain things have happened, and I can lose no time in acting up to my ideas. Listen, then, to what I have to tell you in the name of all my family."

There was a subdued murmur of emotion in the crowd, but it died away almost instantly, and then James Burbank, in a voice that could be heard by all, made the following declaration :—

"From this 28th of February, 1862, henceforth the slaves on this plantation are free. They can leave here or stay here as they please. There are now none but free men at Camdless Bay."

The first greeting from those who had thus ceased to be slaves was a loud cheering. Arms were lifted in sign of thankfulness. The name of Burbank was shouted again and again. The crowd rushed to the terrace. Men, women, and children wished to kiss the hands of their liberator. The enthusiasm was indescribable, and it was all the more vigorous from being unprepared. As to Pygmalion we can imagine how he gesticulated and perorated and attitudinized.

Then an old negro, the oldest on the plantation, advanced to the steps of the terrace. Then he lifted his head, and, speaking with much emotion said,—

"In the name of the old slaves of Camdless Bay, who are now free, I thank you, Mr. Burbank, for having let us hear the first words of freedom ever spoken in the State of Florida."

As he spoke the old negro slowly mounted the steps, and kissed James Burbank's hands ; and then, as little Dy stretched out her arms to him, he lifted her up and held her out to his comrades.

"Hurray ! Hurray for Mr. Burbank !"

The joyous shouts again rent the air, loud enough to carry to Jacksonville, on the other bank of the St. John's, the news of the great deed that had been done.

The family were deeply moved. In vain did they try to quiet these shouts of enthusiasm. It was Zermah who succeeded in procuring silence as she advanced to the edge of the terrace to speak.

"My friends," said she, "we are now free ; thanks to the generosity, to the humanity of him who was our master, the best of masters !"

" Yes ! yes ! " shouted hundreds of voices in one great shout of gratitude.

" We can now go where we please. We can, if we like, avail ourselves of our liberty to leave the plantation. As for me I will follow the instinct of my heart ; and I am sure that most of you will do as I do. For six years I have lived at Camdless Bay. My husband and I have lived here and we wish to die here. I ask Mr. Burbank to keep us now we are free as he kept us when we were slaves. Those who wish him to do so—"

" All ! all ! "

And the words repeated a thousand times showed how much the master of Camdless Bay was appreciated, and proved the bond of friendship and gratitude that united all on the estate.

James Burbank then spoke. He told all those who wished to remain on the plantation that they might do so under new conditions ; all that was to be done was to agree what price should be paid for their labour. It was necessary that the matter should be finished in due form, and consequently each of the negroes would now receive a certificate of liberation.

To issue these was the duty of the assistant overseers. Ever since Mr. Burbank had decided to free his slaves he had had these papers prepared, and as negro after negro came up to receive them, most affecting were the demonstrations of gratitude.

The end of the day was devoted to rejoicing. In the morning the blacks would return to their ordinary work, but to-day must be given over to festivity. The Burbanks, as they walked among the crowd, were greeted with tokens of the sincerest friendship and assurances of boundless devotion.

But among the crowd overseer Perry moved like a lost soul.

" Well, Perry," asked Mr. Burbank, " what say you ? "

" I say, Mr. James, that although they are free, these Africans are none the less Africans and have not changed their colour. They were born black and they will die black."

"But they will live white," said Burbank with a smile, "and that is everything!"

That evening the dinner at Castle House was a happy one; and more confidence was felt as to the future. In a few days the security of Florida would be completely assured. No bad news had come from Jacksonville. It was possible that James Burbank's conduct before the magistrates had had a favourable impression on the majority of the inhabitants.

One of the company at dinner was Mr. Overseer Perry, who had been obliged to help in what he could not hinder. He sat down opposite the old negro who had been invited by Mr. Burbank, in order to show that the freedom given him was not an empty declaration. Outside were heard the sounds of the holiday-making; and the park was illuminated by the reflection of the bonfires lighted in different parts of the plantation. In the middle of dinner a deputation arrived with a magnificent bouquet for the little girl, the finest, certainly, that "Miss Dy Burbank of Castle House" had ever received.

When all had gone, the family went back into the hall, to stay there till bedtime. It seemed as if a day so well begun could not but end as well. About eight o'clock the plantation was quiet. It seemed as though nothing would occur to trouble it, when a voice was heard without.

James Burbank rose and went to the front door.

In front of the terrace a few men were standing and talking in a loud tone.

"What is the matter?" asked James Burbank.

"Mr. Burbank," said one of the overseers, "a boat has just run alongside the pier."

"Where from?"

"The left bank."

"Who is on board?"

"A messenger sent to you from the Jacksonville magistrates."

"And what does he want?"

"He has a letter for you. Shall I let him land?"

"Yes."

Mrs. Burbank came to her husband's side, Alice stepped up to one of the windows, while Stannard and Carrol walked to the door. Zermah, taking little Dy by the hand, stood up. All felt that some serious incident was at hand.

The overseer went back to the landing-place. Ten minutes afterwards he returned with the messenger whom the boat had brought from Jacksonville.

He was in the uniform of the County Militia. He was introduced into the hall, and asked for Mr Burbank.

"I am James Burbank. What is your business?"

"To hand you this letter."

The messenger held out a large envelope which bore the seal of the court.

Burbank broke the seal, and read,—

"By order of the authorities newly constituted at Jacksonville, every slave set free without the permission of the Confederate Government will be immediately expelled the territory.

"The expulsion to take place within the following forty-eight hours ; and, in case of refusal, force will be used.

"TEXAR.

"Done at Jacksonville, 28th February, 1862."

The magistrates had been superseded. Texar had been placed by his partisans in charge of the town.

"What answer shall I take back? " asked the messenger.

"None!" said James Burbank.

The messenger retired, and was escorted back to the boat, which put off towards the other side of the stream.

And so, at the Spaniard's orders, the old slaves of the plantation were to be dispersed! Although they were free men, they were no longer free to live in Florida! Camdless Bay was to be deprived of all the men on whom he had reckoned to defend the plantation.

"Free on those conditions?" said Zermah. "Never! I refuse such freedom ! And if I cannot remain near you I would rather be a slave."

And, taking her certificate of freedom in her hands, Zermah tore it across, and fell at James Burbank's feet.

CHAPTER IX.

WAITING.

SUCH were the first consequences of the generous action of freeing his slaves before the Federals were masters of the territory.

Texar and his partisans were now in power, and could indulge in any deed of violence that their brutal natures suggested. By his vague denunciations the Spaniard had not been able to put James Burbank in prison, but he had gained his end none the less by taking advantage of the excitement of the people at the conduct of the magistrates. After the acquittal of the anti-slavery planter, who was going to proclaim emancipation on the estate, Texar had raised a crowd of malcontents and headed a revolution in the town. He had superseded the old magistrates by the most advanced members of his party, formed a committee of small whites and Floridans of Spanish origin, and assured himself of the co-operation of the militia, with whom he had been in treaty for a long time, and who at once fraternized with the people. The fate of every person in the county was now in his hands.

James Burbank's conduct had not been approved by the majority of the planters on the banks of the St. John's, who feared that their own slaves would compel them to follow his example. Most of them being ardent Southerners, pledged to withstand the pretensions of the Unionists, saw with extreme irritation the advance of the Federal armies, and declared that Florida should resist them as the other Southern States were resisting them. At the outset of the war they had treated the question of enfranchisement with indifference, but they had hastened to range themselves under the flag of Jefferson Davis, and to do their utmost to second the efforts of the rebels against the Government of Abraham Lincoln.

Under such circumstances there was little wonder that Texar, having the same opinions and interests to defend, should have succeeded as he had done, notwithstanding his evil reputation. He had seized his post, however, not so much to organize resistance and repulse Commodore Dupont's flotilla as to gratify his evil instincts ; and that is why, on account of the hatred he bore towards the Burbank family, his first care had been to reply to the liberation at Camdless Bay by the edict which obliged the slaves who had been freed to leave the territory in forty-eight hours.

"In acting thus," he said, "I protect the interests of the planters. They cannot but approve of a measure which will prevent the rising of the slaves in Florida."

The majority had thus applauded without reservation this order of Texar's, arbitrary though it was. It was arbitrary, unique, and indefensible. In freeing his slaves, James Burbank was only acting within his right which he had always possessed. He could have done it before the war had divided the United States on the question of slavery. Nothing had occurred to supersede this right, and Texar's action was neither just nor legal.

But Camdless Bay would be deprived of its natural defenders, and Texar's object would be attained.

This was well understood at Castle House ; and it would perhaps have been better if James Burbank had waited till he could act without danger. But, as we know, he had been charged before the Jacksonville magistrates with acting contrary to his opinions, and so placed that he must conform to them ; and, incapable of mastering his indignation, he had declared himself publicly, and had publicly proceeded before the people of his plantation to give his slaves their freedom. By doing so he had injured his own position and that of his guests, and now it must be decided in all haste what was to be done.

In the first place—and this very evening the discussion was entered upon—could they go back on this act of emancipation ? No. That would make no difference in the state of affairs. Texar would not recognize such a tardy going back. Besides, the negroes, when they learnt what the Jacksonville authorities had decided to do, would unanimously imitate Zermah's example. Rather than leave Camdless Bay and be hunted from the State, they would return to their condition as slaves until the time when they would have the right to be free and live freely where they pleased.

But what would be the good of this ? They would, under their old master, defend the plantation which had become their home, and with all the more ardour now they had been freed. This Zermah guaranteed. James Burbank therefore decided that he would not recall what he had done. All the rest were of his opinion.

And they were not mistaken. In the morning, when the new decree of the Jacksonville Committee was known, marks of devotion and tokens of fidelity came in from all sides. If Texar attempted to put his edict in force they would resist it. If he used force, they would use force to repel him.

"And, besides," said Carrol, "events are hurrying on. In a couple of days, in twenty-four hours perhaps, the slave question in Florida will be settled. To-morrow the Federal flotilla may force the mouths of the St. John's, and then— "

"And if the militia, aided by the Confederate troops, make any resistance ? " asked Mr. Stannard.

"If they resist, their resistance will not last long," said Carrol. "Without ships or gunners, how can they oppose the passage of Commodore Dupont, the landing of Sherman, the occupation of the ports of Fernandina, Jacksonville, and St. Augustine ? When these points are occupied, the Federals will be masters of Florida. Then Texar and his friends will have to run."

"If they could only catch him," said James Burbank, "then we should see if, when he is in the hands of Federal justice, he could substantiate some alibi to escape the punishment he deserves."

The night passed without the security of Castle House

being disturbed. In the morning the rumours that were flying about were inquired into. The plantation was not threatened that day. Texar's decree had ordered the expulsion of the blacks in forty-eight hours. James Burbank had determined to resist the order, and occupied the time in preparing for the defence of his house.

It was, however, important to get at all the reports from the theatre of war. Any moment the state of affairs might be changed ; and James Burbank and his brother-in-law set off on horseback to learn what they could. Descending the right bank of the St. John's, they rode towards the mouth of the river, so as to explore for a dozen miles the widening of the river, which ends at San Pablo, where the lighthouse stands. As they passed Jacksonville they would be able to see if there was any gathering of boats indicating an approaching attack on Camdless Bay. In half an hour they had passed the boundary of the plantation.

Meanwhile Mrs. Burbank and Alice were walking in the park of Castle House. In vain Mr. Stannard tried to calm their apprehensions. They both had a presentiment of a coming catastrophe.

Zermah had been among the barracoons. Although the threat of expulsion was known, the blacks heeded it not. They had returned to their usual work. Like their old master, they had made up their minds to resist. If they were free, by what right were they to be expelled from the country of their adoption ? Nothing could be more satisfactory than Zermah's report—the blacks of Camdless Bay could be trusted.

"Yes," said she, "my companions will all return to slavery, as I have done, rather than leave their master ! And if they are obliged, they will defend their rights."

Nothing more was to be done than to wait for the return of James Burbank and Edward Carrol.

At this date, the 1st of March, it was not impossible that the Federal flotilla had arrived in sight of Pablo lighthouse, ready to occupy the mouth of the St. John's. The Confederates had not too many militia to oppose their passage, and the authorities of Jacksonville would have none to spare to carry out their threats against the former slaves of Camdless Bay.

Mr. Perry made his daily visit to the different workshops and storehouses on the estate. He also could bear witness to the good disposition of the negroes. Although he did not care to admit it, he saw that if they had changed their condition, their assiduity at their work and devotion to the Burbank family had not changed. To resist all that the Jacksonville populace attempted against them they were firmly resolved. But, in Mr. Perry's opinion, these fine feelings would not last. Nature would reclaim her rights. After tasting independence, these enfranchised negroes would return to slavery, and descend to the place that Nature intended for them, between the man and the animal.

As he was thinking of these things, who should he run against but the conceited Pygmalion, strutting like a peacock with his head on high, his hands behind his back, and evidently thinking very much of himself as a free man. One thing was certain, and that was that he was not doing much work.

"Good morning, Mr. Perry!" said he superbly.

"What are you doing, Mr. Idle?"

"I am taking a walk! Have I not the right to do nothing now I am no longer a vile slave, and have the certificate of liberation in my pocket?"

"And who is to feed you, Pyg?"

"I am, Mr. Perry."

"And how?"

"By eating."

"And who is to give you what you eat?"

"My master."

"Your master! Have you forgotten that now you have no master, noodle?"

"No. I had one, and I shall have one; and Mr. Burbank will not send me away from the plantation, where, I can say without boasting, I am of some use."

"But he will send you away?"

"Will he?"

"Certainly. When you belonged to him he could keep you to do nothing. But now you do not belong to him he will show you the door if you do not work, and we shall see what you will do with your liberty, poor lunatic!"

Evidently Pyg had not studied the question from that point of view.

"What, Mr. Perry? Do you think Mr. Burbank would be so cruel—"

"It is not cruel; it is only logical. Besides, whether Mr. James wishes it or no, there is a decree of the Committee at Jacksonville ordering every freed slave out of Florida."

"Then that is true, then?"

"Quite true; and we shall now see how you and your companions will get out of the difficulty now you have lost your master."

"I am not going to leave Camdless Bay even if I am free."

"You are free to go, but not free to stop! You had better pack up."

"And what's to become of me?"

"That is your business."

"But if I am free," said Pygmalion, returning again to that point, "If I am free—"

"That is not enough, it seems!"

"Tell me what I ought to do, Mr. Perry."

"What you ought to do? Well; listen, and follow me, if you can."

"I follow."

"You are free, are you not?"

"Yes, and I have got the certificate in my pocket."

"Well; tear it up."

"Never."

"Then there is only one way I can see for you to stop here."

"What is that?"

"Change your colour, Pyg! When you are white you can live at Camdless Bay; till then you cannot."

The overseer, chuckling at having given Pyg's vanity such a lesson. turned on his heel.

Pyg remained deep in thought. He saw that to be no longer a slave was not enough to keep him his place. He must be white? And how could he become white, when Nature had made him black as ebony? And as he returned to Castle House he scratched his head as if he were tearing the hair from the skin.

A little before noon James Burbank and Edward Carrol returned to Castle House. They had seen nothing alarming at Jacksonville. The boats were in their usual place, some moored to the pier, others anchored out in the stream. A few detachments of Confederates had been seen on the left bank of the river, marching towards the north towards Nassau county. Nothing seemed to threaten Camdless Bay.

When they reached the end of the estuary, Burbank and his companion had looked out over the open sea. There was not a sail in sight. Not a cloud of smoke from some steamer could be traced on the horizon to indicate the presence or approach of a squadron. Preparations for defence there were none. There were no batteries, no earthworks. If the Federal ships appeared either at Nassau Creek or at the mouth of the St. John's, there was nothing to stop them. Only Pablo lighthouse was dismantled; the lantern was unshipped; and the passes were thus unlighted. But that would only prevent the entrance of a flotilla during the night.

Such was the report they brought back with them. There seemed to be nothing doing at Jacksonville to indicate an approaching attack on Camdless Bay.

"That is well," said Mr. Stannard, "but it is unsatisfactory that Dupont's ships are not yet in sight; there is a delay there that I cannot understand!"

"Yes," said Carrol; "if the fleet sailed the day before yesterday from St. Andrew's Bay, it ought now to be off Fernandina."

"It has been very bad weather during these last two or three days," said James Burbank. "It is possible that with these westerly winds Dupont has had to go out to sea.

The wind went down this morning, and I should not be
surprised if this very night—"

"May heaven listen to you, my dear James," said Mrs.
Burbank, "and come to our help."

"If Pablo lighthouse," said Alice, "is not lighted, how
could the flotilla get into the St. John's to-night ?"

"It would be impossible for them to get into the St.
John's," said Burbank. "But before attacking the mouths of
the river the Federals would have to capture Amelia Island
and then Fernandina, so as to command the railway to
Cedar Keys. I do not expect Dupont's vessels up the St.
John's for three or four days."

"That is so, James," said Carrol. "But I hope the capture of Fernandina would force the Confederates to retreat.
The militia might even abandon Jacksonville before the
arrival of the gunboats. Then Camdless Bay would no
longer be threatened by Texar and his accomplices—"

"That is possible," said James Burbank. "Once the
Federals set foot in Florida, our safety will be, to a certain
extent, secured. Is there any news on the plantation ?"

"None," said Alice. "I heard from Zermah that the
blacks had gone to work as usual, and that they are ready
to fight to the last in defence of Camdless Bay."

"Let us hope we shall not have to put their devotion to
the proof ! I shall not be at all surprised if the scoundrels
who have got the upper hand at Jacksonville take themselves off as soon as the Federal fleet is signalled. But we
must be on our guard. After lunch, Stannard, come with
Carrol and me over to the most exposed part of the estate.
I do not want you and Alice to be in as much danger here
as at Jacksonville. In truth, I shall never forgive myself
for bringing you here, if things turn out badly."

"My dear James," said Stannard, "if we had stayed in
our house at Jacksonville we should have been exposed to
the exactions of the authorities, like all the rest who hold
anti-slavery opinions."

"In any case, Mr. Burbank," said Alice, "even if the
danger is greater here, is it not better for us to share it
with you ?"

PART I.

"Yes, my dear girl," said James Burbank. "Come on! I hope and think that Texar will not have time to put his scheme against our men into execution."

During the afternoon Burbank and his friends visited the barracoons with Mr. Perry. They could see for themselves that the feeling among the blacks was excellent. Burbank called the overseer's attention to the zeal with which the newly freed negroes had returned to work. Not one was absent from his post.

"Yes, yes!" answered Perry. "But we have to see how the work will turn out in the end."

"But they did not change their arms when they changed their condition, did they?"

"Not yet; but you will soon see that they have not the same hands at the end of the arms."

"Well, Perry," replied Burbank gaily, "their hands will always have five fingers, I imagine; and we cannot expect them to have more."

As soon as the round had been made, Mr. Burbank and his friends returned to Castle House. The evening passed as quietly as the last. In the absence of all news from Jacksonville there seemed to be ground for hope that Texar had given up his threat, or that he had no time to execute it.

Careful precautions were, however, taken during the night. Perry and the assistant overseers stationed sentries round the estate, and particularly watched the banks of the river. The blacks had been cautioned to retreat on the palisades in case of an alarm, and a sentry was on guard at the gate.

Many times did James Burbank and his friends go out to see that their orders had been attended to. When the sun rose nothing had happened. The night had passed without incident.

CHAPTER X.

THE MORNING OF THE 2ND OF MARCH.

NEXT day, March 2nd, James Burbank had news by one of his assistant overseers, who had crossed the river and returned to Jacksonville without awaking suspicion.

The news was undoubtedly correct and it was important.

Commodore Dupont had anchored at daybreak in St. Andrew's Bay, on the coast of Georgia. The *Wabash*, on which he had hoisted his flag, was at the head of a squadron of twenty-six vessels, of which eighteen were gunboats, one a cutter, one an armed transport, and six were ordinary transports with General Wright's brigade on board. And, as Gilbert had said in his last letter, General Sherman accompanied the expedition.

Commodore Dupont, whom the bad weather had kept back, had at once set to work to take possession of the passes of the St. Mary's. These channels, difficult enough of access, open off the mouth of the river of the same name to the north of Amelia Island on the frontier of Georgia and Florida.

Fernandina, the principal position of the island, was protected by Fort Clinch with a garrison of fifteen hundred men behind its thick stone walls. Would the Southerners hold out against the Federals in this fortress, wherein they might make a lengthened defence? It would be thought so.

Nothing of the kind was done. According to the assistant-overseer's report, a rumour had reached Jacksonville that the Confederates had evacuated Fort Clinch as soon as the squadron appeared in St. Mary's Bay ; and not only had they abandoned Fort Clinch, but they had cleared out of Fernandina, Cumberland Island, and all that part of the Florida coast.

This was all the news that reached Castle House, but there is no need to dwell on its importance with regard to the position at Camdless Bay. Now that the Federals had at last landed in Florida, the whole State would soon be in their power. Obviously a few days would elapse before the gunboats crossed the bar of the St. John's. But their presence would have its effect on the new authorities of Jacksonville, and there was room to hope that, in fear of reprisals, Texar and his supporters would not dare to take action against the plantation of so prominent a Northerner as James Burbank.

This was reassuring for the family, whose fear was suddenly changed to hope. And Alice Stannard and Mrs. Burbank ceased to tremble for Gilbert's safety, with the certainty that he was not far off and the assurance that he would soon return. The young lieutenant at St. Andrew's was within thirty miles of Camdless Bay. He was on board the gunboat *Ottawa*, which had just been distinguished by a feat of arms unexampled in naval annals.

What had happened on the morning of the 2nd of March was this. The assistant-overseer had not ascertained these details during his visit to Jacksonville, but it is important that they should be known on account of the events that followed.

As soon as Commodore Dupont discovered that Fort Clinch had been evacuated by the Confederate garrison, he sent a few vessels of light draught across St. Mary's Channel. Already the white population had retired into the interior of the country with the Southern troops, abandoning the towns, villages, and plantations on the coast. There was a regular panic due to the fear of the reprisals which, the Secessionists falsely stated, were intended by the Federal chief. Not only in Florida, but along the Georgian frontier, along the whole extent of country between the bays of Ossabaw and St. Mary's, the people beat a precipitate retreat so as to escape from the troops landed by General Wright. Under these circumstances, Commodore Dupont did not have to fire a shot to get possession of Fort Clinch and Fernandina. The gunboat *Ottawa*, on which was Gilbert, accompanied by Mars, acted as second, and had to use its guns in the manner following.

The town of Fernandina is connected with the west coast of Florida on the Gulf of Mexico by a branch railway which runs to Cedar Keys. The railway runs along the coast of Amelia Island; then before it reaches the mainland it crosses Nassau Creek on a long bridge of piles.

When the *Ottawa* reached the centre of the creek a train was on the bridge. The garrison of Fernandina was in flight, taking its provisions with it, and followed by many of the more or less important people of the town. Immediately the gunboat started at full speed towards the bridge and fired her bow-chasers at the piles and the train. Gilbert was in charge of the firing, and many good shots were made; among them a shell struck the last carriage of the train and broke the axle and the coupling. The train did not stop for an instant—to do so would have been dangerous—and leaving the carriage to look after itself, steamed off full speed to the south-west. A detachment of Federal troops landed at Fernandina appeared at this moment, and rushed on to the bridge. The carriage was captured with the fugitives it contained, who were chiefly civilians. The prisoners were taken to the superior officer, Colonel Gardner, in command at Fernandina, who took their names, kept them for twenty-four hours on one of the vessels of the squadron, as an example, and then released them.

When the train had run out of sight, the *Ottawa* went off to attack and seize a vessel laden with war material, which had taken refuge in the bay. These events were calculated to spread discouragement among the Confederate troops and the people of the Floridan towns; and this was particularly the case at Jacksonville. The estuary

of the St. John's would be forced as easily as had been
that of the St. Mary's; that was very evident, and probably
the Unionists would meet with no more resistance at
Jacksonville than at St. Augustine and the other coast
towns.

This was good news for James Burbank. He might
well believe that Texar dared not now give effect to his
plans. He and his partisans would be superseded, and in
due course the honest folks would resume the power of
which an outbreak of the mob had deprived them.

There was every reason to think in this way and to
hope; and as soon as the staff at Camdless Bay heard the
important news, which was soon known at Jacksonville,
their joy showed itself in noisy cheering, in which Pygmalion took a prominent part. Nevertheless, it would not
do to abandon the precautions which had been taken to
secure the safety of the estate, at least until the gunboats
appeared in the river.

Unfortunately—and this James Burbank could neither
imagine nor suppose—a whole week was to elapse before
the Federals were ready to enter the St. John's. And
during that time what dangers were to threaten Camdless
Bay!

Commodore Dupont's plan was to show the Federal
flag at every point where vessels could go. He split up
his squadron into detachments. One gunboat was sent
up the St. Mary's River to occupy the little town of that
name, and advance some sixty miles up the country. To
the south were sent three other gunboats, commanded by
Captain Godon, to explore the bays, seize Jekyll and St.
Simon's islands, and take possession of the small towns of
Brunswick and Darien, which had been partly abandoned
by their inhabitants. Six steamers of light draught were
destined, under the orders of Commandant Stevens, to
enter the St. John's and reduce Jacksonville. The rest of
the squadron, under Dupont, was to take care of St.
Augustine's and blockade the coast down to Mosquito
Inlet, the passes of which would be then closed against
contraband of war.

But this series of operations could not be accomplished in twenty-four hours, and twenty-four hours would be enough for the devastation of the country by the Southerners.

About three o'clock in the afternoon James Burbank had his first suspicions of what was being devised against him. Mr. Perry, after a round of inspection on the frontier of the plantation, came hurriedly into Castle House and said,—

"Mr. Burbank, they have reported that some suspicious vagabonds are on their way to Camdless Bay."

"From the north?"

"From the north."

Almost -at the same moment Zermah, returning from the landing-place, told her master that there was a lot of boats crossing the river and approaching the right bank.

"They are coming from Jacksonville?"

"Certainly."

"Go into the house," said Burbank, "and don't go out again, Zermah, on any pretence."

"No, master."

Burbank went off to reconnoitre. When he returned, he could not but tell his friends that matters looked threatening. An attack seemed almost certain, and it was better that all should be forewarned.

"And so," said Mr. Stannard, "these scoundrels, on the eve of being curbed by the Federals, dare—"

"Yes," said Burbank coldly. "Texar could not miss such an opportunity of being revenged when he is free to disappear as soon as his vengeance is satisfied. Then with more animation he resumed, "But will this man's crimes always remain unpunished? Will he always get away? In truth after doubting the justice of man are we to doubt the justice of Heaven—"

"James," said Mrs. Burbank, "at a time when we may only have the help of God to trust to, do not reproach Him—"

"And let us put ourselves under His care," said Alice Stannard.

James Burbank, recovering his coolness, set about giving his orders for the defence of the house.

"Have the blacks been told?" asked Edward Carrol.

"They will be," said Burbank. "My idea is to defend the palisades. We cannot think of defending the whole boundary of Camdless Bay against an armed mob, for it is likely that the assailants will be in large numbers. We must get all the defenders into the inner ring. If, unfortunately, the palisade is forced, Castle House, which once defied the Seminoles, may perhaps be held against Texar's bandits. My wife, Alice, and Dy and Zermah, to whom I entrust them, must not leave the house without my order. If matters become serious, everything is prepared for them to save themselves by the tunnel which communicates with the little Marine Creek of the St. John's; there a boat will be found in charge of two of our men. It is hidden in the bushes; and, Zermah, you must go in it up the river to Cedar Rock."

"But you, James?"

"And you, father?"

Mrs. Burbank had seized the planter by the arm, and Alice had caught hold of Mr. Stannard, as if the time had come for them to escape from Castle House.

"We will do all we can to rejoin you," said Burbank, "when the position is no longer tenable. But you must promise, if the danger becomes too great, to get away to safety at Cedar Rock. We shall want all we have of courage and audacity to keep back the scoundrels, and resist them till our ammunition fails."

Evidently this is what would have to be done if the assailants were too numerous and succeeded in forcing the palisades and invading the park so as to make a direct attack on Castle House.

James Burbank then called together his men, and Perry and his assistants ran off to the barracoons with his orders. In less than an hour the blacks, in fighting trim, were drawn up near the gate in the palisades. Their wives and children had gone off to seek safety in the woods round Camdless Bay.

Unfortunately, the means of organizing a serious defence were limited. Since the beginning of the war it had been almost impossible to procure arms and ammunition in sufficient quantity. Burbank had in vain tried to buy them at Jacksonville ; and he had to be content with what remained in the house after the last siege by the Seminoles.

His plan was to preserve Castle House from being burnt or stormed. He could not dream of protecting the estate, saving the workshops, stores, factories, or barracoons, or preventing the plantation from being devastated. He had hardly four hundred negroes in a state to oppose the assailants, and these were insufficiently armed. A few dozen muskets were distributed to the best men, while the arms of precision were kept in reserve for James Burbank, his friends, Perry, and the assistant-overseers.

The whole force was drawn up at the gate in such a manner as to repulse the threatened assault on the palisades, which were also defended by the creek that ran round them.

Amid the confusion Pygmalion was very busy and excited, bustling hither and thither and doing nothing. He was like one of those circus clowns who pretend to do everything and do nothing, much to the amusement of the audience. Pyg, considering himself as belonging specially to the defenders of the house, did not dream of associating with his comrades outside. Never had he felt himself so devoted to James Burbank.

All was ready in the garrison. On what side was the attack to come? If the assailants appeared on the northern side the defence could be most easily conducted. If, on the contrary, they attacked on the river-front, the defence would be more difficult, owing to Camdless Bay being open on that side. A landing is always a difficult operation, it is true, and, under any circumstances, it would require a good many boats to transport an armed band from one bank of the St. John's to the other. Thus said Burbank, Carrol, and Stannard as they watched the return of the scouts who had been sent to the boundary of the plantation. It would not do to be in the dark as to the manner of attack.

About half-past four in the evening the scouts returned from the northern side of the estate and made their report.

A column of armed men were advancing in that direction. Was this a detachment of the county militia or only a division of the mob, attracted by the hope of pillage, and charged with the execution of Texar's decree concerning the freed slaves ? In any case, the column was a thousand strong, and nothing could be done against it with the force on the plantation. It might perhaps be hoped that, if the palisades were carried by assault, Castle House would offer a longer and more serious resistance.

It was evident that the column had avoided a landing under difficulties in the little harbour of Camdless Bay, and had crossed the river below Jacksonville in some fifty boats three or four journeys being sufficient to ferry it over. And Burbank's precaution of collecting his men within the palisades had been a wise one, for it would have been impossible for him to defend his frontier against such an army.

Who was at the head of the assailants—Texar in person ? Probably not. At the time when the approach of the Federals was threatened the Spaniard might consider it too risky to place himself at the head of his men. If he had done so, it would be because, when his work of vengeance was accomplished, the plantation devastated, the Burbanks massacred or fallen into his hands, he had made up his mind to escape to the south, perhaps even to the Everglades (the backwoods of Southern Florida), where it would be difficult to get at him.

This was the most serious of the possibilities, and Burbank had given it anxious thought. Hence it was that he had decided to put in safety his wife and child, and Alice Stannard, entrusted to the devotion of Zermah, at Cedar Rock, which was about a mile above Camdless Bay. If they had to abandon Castle House to the assailants, he and his friends could there rejoin the family, and wait till safety was assured to the honest people of Florida under the protection of the Federal army.

And so a boat had been hidden in the reeds of the St.

John's, and left to the keeping of two negroes at the end of the tunnel which led from the house to Marine Creek. But before the parting took place, it would be necessary to defend the house for a few hours—at least until nightfall, when, in the darkness, the boat could go up the river in secret, without risk of pursuit from the suspicious-looking canoes that were prowling about in such numbers.

CHAPTER XI.

THE EVENING OF THE 2ND OF MARCH.

JAMES BURBANK, with his companions, and most of the blacks were ready for the fight. He had now nothing to do but to wait. His arrangements were to make his first stand at the palisades round the private park, and then, if driven back, to make another stand behind the walls of Castle House.

About five o'clock the increasing tumult showed that the assailants were not far off. From the shouting it was only too easy to understand that they were in possession of the northern part of the estate. On the right, thick columns of smoke began to rise above the trees. The sawmills had been set on fire, and the barracoons, after being pillaged, were in flames. The poor people had not had time to put in safety the few things that the act of liberation had made their own the evening before; and loud were the cries of despair and anger that answered the shouts of the marauders.

Gradually the shouters approached Castle House. A strange light appeared in the northern horizon, as if the sun was setting in that direction. Occasional puffs of warm smoky air swept up against the house. Violent detonations produced by the burning of the dry wood in the workshops were heard every now and then. Once a louder explosion than the rest showed that the boiler at one of the sawmills had been blown up. Devastation in all its horrors was evidently in progress.

Burbank, Carrol, and Stannard were at the gate in the palisades. There they received and disposed of the last detachment of negroes that were gradually coming in.

The assailants might appear at any moment. The increasing crackle of the musketry showed that they could not be far from the ring, which was easy of assault, for the nearest trees were not fifty yards away. The Confederates could keep in cover to the last moment; and the bullets began to rain on the palisades, while the rifles remained invisible.

After consideration it was thought best to withdraw all the men within the fortress. There the armed negroes would be less exposed, as they could fire between the angles at the top of the timbers; and when the assailants tried to cross the stream and carry the stronghold by storm, they might manage to repulse them.

The negroes were all withdrawn, and the gate was about to be shut, when James Burbank, throwing a last glance around without, caught sight of a man at full run towards him, as if seeking safety amongst the defenders of Castle House. A few shots were aimed at him from the woods close by, but did not hit him. With a bound he jumped on the drawbridge and was in safety within the palisades. The gate was immediately shut and firmly fastened.

"Who are you?" asked James Burbank.

"One of the servants of Mr. Harvey, your correspondent at Jacksonville."

"Did Mr. Harvey send you here with a messager?"

"Yes, and as the river was guarded, I could not cross it hereabouts."

"And you came with the militia without being suspected?"

"Yes. They are followed by a mob of looters. I came with them, and as soon as I was within range, I ran and risked a few shots."

"Good, my friend! Thanks! You have Mr. Harvey's message?"

"Yes, Mr. Burbank. Here it is."

Burbank took the letter and read it. Mr. Harvey said he might put implicit confidence in his messenger, John Bruce, of whose sincerity there could be no doubt. After hearing the news he brought, Mr. Burbank would see what was best to be done.

At this instant a volley was heard from without. There was not a moment to lose.

"What would Mr. Harvey have me understand?" asked Burbank.

"That in the first place," said Bruce, "the armed mob which is attacking Camdless Bay is from fourteen to fifteen hundred strong."

"I did not reckon them at less. What next? Is Texar at their head?"

"Mr. Harvey found it impossible to ascertain. One thing is certain, and that is that Texar has not been at Jacksonville for the last four-and-twenty hours!"

"That ought to indicate some new scheme of the scoundrel's," said Burbank.

"Yes," answered Bruce. "That is what Mr. Harvey thinks. Besides, Texar need not be there to execute the order as to setting adrift the freed slaves—"

"Setting them adrift!" exclaimed Burbank. "Setting them adrift and helping them in incendiarism and robbery—"

"And Mr. Harvey thinks that while there is time, you would do well to put your family in safety by sending them away at once from Castle House."

"Castle House," said Burbank, "can be defended, and we will only leave it when it is untenable. Is there any fresh news from Jacksonville?"

"None."

"Have not the Federal troops made any movement into Florida?"

"None since they occupied Fernandina and the Bay of St. Mary's."

"And what is the chief reason of your being sent?"

"To tell you that the dispersal of the slaves was only a pretext got up by Texar to enable him to lay waste the plantation, and make you his prisoner."

"You do not know if Texar is at the head of these rascals?"

" No, Mr. Burbank.   Mr. Harvey tried to find out, but could not.   And I have tried since I left Jacksonville, but without success."

"Are there many of the militia with this mob?"

"A hundred, at the outside," replied Bruce, "but the mob is composed of the very worst characters.   Texar had them supplied with weapons, and they will not stop at any excess.   I repeat, Mr. Burbank, Mr. Harvey's opinion is that you should abandon Castle House at once.   He ordered me to invite you to his cottage at Hampton Red. It is about a dozen miles up stream on the right bank, and there you would be safe for some days—"

"Yes, I know."

"I could take you and your family there without risk of discovery, if you will go at once, before retreat is impossible."

"I thank Mr. Harvey, and you too, my friend," said Burbank, "but we have not yet come to that."

"As you wish, Mr. Burbank," answered Bruce. "I shall none the less remain until you require my services."

The attack, which now began, required all James Burbank's attention.

A violent fusilade burst out, although the assailants could not be seen owing to the shelter of the trees.   The bullets rained on the palisades, but did little damage. Unfortunately, Burbank and his companions could only reply feebly, having only forty guns amongst them.   Being stationed in the best positions for firing effectively, their shots did more execution than those of the militiamen at the head of the column, a few of whom were hit, though hidden in the wood.

This long-range fight lasted for about half an hour, rather to the advantage of the defenders.   Then the assailants rushed at the palisades to storm them.   As the attack was to be delivered on several sides at once, they brought with them planks and beams from the workshops, now in flames.   In twenty places these beams were thrown across the stream, and over them rushed the Spaniard's men to the foot of the palisades, losing several of their

PART I.   H

number in killed and wounded. And then they climbed
up the planks and hoisted one another up ; but they did
not succeed in getting over. The negroes, infuriated
against the incendiaries, repulsed them with great bravery.
But it was evident that the defenders of Camdless Bay
could not for long hold out at all points, against the
murderous foe. Until nightfall they might keep them at
bay, providing they were not seriously wounded. Burbank
and Stannard had, however, not been touched. Carrol
alone had been hit, by a ball that tore open his shoulder.
He had to retire to the hall, where Mrs. Burbank, Alice,
and Zermah gave him every attention.

But night was coming to the help of the besiegers. Under
cover of the darkness some fifty of the most determined
amongst them ran up to the gate, axe in hand. Probably
they would not have been able to force it had not a breach
been opened by a daring manœuvre.

A part of the outbuildings suddenly took fire, and the
flames, fed by the dry wood, seized on the palisades
against which the building leant.

Burbank rushed towards the fire, if not to put it out, at
least to defend the breach.

By the light of the flames he saw a man run through
the smoke, climb the palisades, and escape over the planks
across the stream.

It was one of the assailants, who had penetrated into
the park on the St. John's side, from among the reeds.
Unseen, he had entered the stables, and at the risk of
perishing in the flames, had set fire to some trusses of
straw.

A breach was thus opened. In vain Burbank and his
companions endeavoured to bar the way. A mass of
assailants threw themselves into it, and the park was
invaded by several hundred men.

Many fell in the hand-to-hand fight. The noise of the
firing was heard on all sides. Soon Castle House was
entirely surrounded, while the negroes, overwhelmed by the
numbers, were forced out of the park to take flight in the
woods of Camdless Bay. They had fought as long as

they could, with courage and devotion ; but if they had resisted longer, they would have been massacred to the last man.

Burbank, Stannard, Perry, the assistant-overseers, John Bruce, who had fought bravely, and a few blacks had to take refuge in Castle House.

It was then nearly eight o'clock in the evening. The night was dark in the west. In the north the sky was ablaze with the glare of the conflagration.

Burbank and Stannard came hurriedly into the house.

"You must escape," said Burbank. "You must go at once. Whether the thieves force their way in, or are kept outside till we are obliged to surrender, there is danger in your remaining. The boat is ready. It is time to part. My wife, Alice, I implore you to follow Zermah with Dy to Cedar Rock. There you will be in safety, and if we are compelled to escape in our turn, we will find you there, we will join you."

"My father," said Alice, "come with us, and you too, Mr. Burbank."

"Yes, James! Yes! Come!" said Mrs. Burbank.

"I!" answered Burbank, "I abandon Castle House to these scoundrels! Never, while resistance is possible! We can hold out for some time yet. And when you are in safety we shall be stronger to defend ourselves!"

"James!"

"It is necessary!"

A terrible tumult was heard as he spoke. The door resounded with the blows dealt on it by the assailants, who were attacking the principal or river front of the house.

"Go!" exclaimed Burbank. "The night is already dark ; they will not see you in the shadow! Go! you are only paralyzing us by remaining here! For God's sake, go!"

Zermah went first, holding little Dy by the hand. Mrs. Burbank tore herself from her husband's arms, Alice left her father's. They disappeared down the staircase which led below the ground into the tunnel to Marine Creek.

"And now," said Burbank, addressing himself to Perry, the assistant-overseers, and the few negroes remaining, "now, my friends, we must resist to the death."

Then they all ascended the grand staircase from the hall, and took up their positions at the windows on the first floor. There, to the hundreds of bullets that honeycombed the front of the house, they answered by fewer but more effective discharges, firing, as they did, into the mass of the assailants, who came on to force their way through the door either by axe or flame. There was no one this time to open a breach into the house. Such an attempt as that against the wooden palisades would have been useless against stone walls.

Nevertheless, a score of men, stealing along in the darkness, which now was profound, gathered on the steps. The door was then attacked furiously. It needed all its solidity to withstand the blows of the picks and axes. The attempt cost many of the assailants their lives, for the position of the loopholes admitted of a cross fire on to the step.

And now something happened to make matters worse. Ammunition began to fail. Burbank, his friends and overseers, and the blacks, armed with guns, had used the greater part during the three hours the assault had lasted. If they had to hold out much longer, how could they do it after the last cartridges had gone? Would they have to abandon Castle House to the mob, who would leave nothing of it but ruins?

And this would certainly have to be done if the assailants broke in the door, which had already begun to shake. Burbank saw this, but he resolved to wait till the last. At any moment might not a diversion take place? There was now nothing to fear for Mrs. Burbank, his daughter, nor Alice Stannard. And as men they could fight to the end against this rabble of murderers, incendiaries, and thieves.

"We have still ammunition for an hour," said Burbank. "Use it all, my friends, and don't let us give up Castle House."

He had hardly finished speaking when a loud report was heard in the distance.

"A cannon-shot!" he exclaimed.

Another report was heard to the westward, on the other side of the river.

"A second shot!" said Stannard.

"Listen!" said Burbank.

A third report was heard, the wind bringing it more distinctly to Castle House.

"Is that a signal to recall the assailants to the right bank?" asked Stannard.

"Perhaps," said Bruce. "It is possible that there has been an alarm over there."

"Yes," said the overseer; "and if these cannon-shots have not been fired from Jacksonville—"

"They have been fired from the Federal fleet!" said Burbank. "Has the flotilla forced the entrance of the St. John's and mounted the river?"

And there was nothing impossible in Commodore Dupont's being now master of the river, at least in the lower part of its course.

But it was not so. The three gunshots had been fired from the battery at Jacksonville; that was quite evident, as no more firing was heard. There had been no engagement between the Northerners and Confederates on the St. John's or in the plains of Duval county.

And there could be no doubt that this had been the signal of recall to the commander of the militia when Perry, who was stationed at one of the side loopholes, exclaimed,—

"They are retiring! They are retiring!"

Burbank and his companions hurried to the central window, which they opened.

The sounds of the axe were no longer heard against the door. Not one of the assailants was in sight. If their shouts and yells were still heard in the air, they were heard further and further away.

Evidently something had happened to oblige the authorities at Jacksonville to recall this mob to the other bank of the St. John's. Doubtless it had been agreed that three gunshots should be fired in case any movement of the squadron should threaten the Confederate position.

So the assailants had abruptly abandoned their final assault, and across the devastated fields of the estate had taken their way, lighted by the fires they had kindled. An hour later they re-crossed the river two miles below Camdless Bay, where the boats were waiting for them.

Soon their shouts died away in the distance. To the uproar succeeded absolute silence. It was as the silence of death over the plantation.

It was then half-past nine o'clock. Burbank and his companions went downstairs to the hall. There lay Edward Carrol, stretched on the sofa, slightly wounded, and somewhat weakened by the loss of blood.

They told him what had happened since the signal from Jacksonville. For the moment, at least, Castle House had nothing to fear from Texar's gang.

"Yes," said James Burbank. "But the scoundrel wished to disperse my liberated slaves, and they are dispersed! He wished to lay waste the plantation in revenge, and only its ruins are left!"

"James," said Walter Stannard, "worse misfortunes might still happen to us. None of us fell in defending Castle House; but your wife, your daughter, and my daughter might have passed into the hands of these rascals, and they are safe."

"You are right, Stannard, and God be praised for it! What has been done by Texar's orders shall not go un-punished, and I will have justice to the last drop of his blood."

"It is a pity," said Carrol, "that Mrs. Burbank, Alice, Dy, and Zermah left us! I know we seemed to be in great danger then; but I would rather know they were here."

"Before the morning," said Burbank, "I will rejoin them. They will be dreadfully anxious, and we must set their minds at rest. I will then see if we can bring them back to Camdless Bay, or leave them for a day or two at Cedar Rock."

" Yes," said Stannard. " We must not be hasty. All
may not be over ; and as long as Jacksonville is under
Texar's control we have something to fear."

" That is why I will act prudently," answered Burbank.
" Perry, you will see that a boat is ready a little before
daybreak. I shall only want one man to go with me—"

A cry of grief, a shout of despair, suddenly interrupted
him.

The cry came from that part of the park where the lawn
lay in front of the house. It was immediately followed
by the words—

" Father ! Father !"

" My daughter's voice !" exclaimed Mr. Stannard.

" What new misfortune !" asked Burbank. And opening the door they rushed out.

Alice was standing a few yards away, and at her feet
lay Mrs. Burbank.

Neither Dy nor Zermah were with them.

" My child !" exclaimed Burbank. At the sound of his
voice his wife rose. She could not speak. She stretched
out her arms towards the river.

" Carried off ?   Carried off ? "

" Yes ! by Texar !" said Alice.

And then she fell senseless by Mrs. Burbank's side.

CHAPTER XII.

THE SIX DAYS THAT FOLLOWED.

WHEN Mrs. Burbank and Alice were in the tunnel leading to Marine Creek, Zermah was in front. The slave held the little girl with one hand; with the other she carried a lantern, by whose feeble light they walked. When she reached the end of the tunnel Zermah asked Mrs. Burbank to wait for her. She intended to make sure that the boat and the two negroes that were to take them to Cedar Rock were at their post. Opening the door at the end of the tunnel she stepped out towards the river.

For a minute—only a minute—Mrs. Burbank and Alice waited for Zermah's return, when Alice noticed that Dy was not with them.

"Dy! Dy!" shouted Mrs. Burbank, at the risk of betraying her presence.

The child did not answer. Accustomed to follow Zermah, she had gone with her out of the tunnel towards the creek before her mother had noticed her.

Suddenly a groaning was heard. Fearing some new danger, and thinking not for a moment of their own safety, they ran out to the bank of the creek, and reached it just in time to see a boat disappearing in the darkness.

"Help! Help! It is Texar!" shouted Zermah.

"Texar! Texar!" shouted Alice in reply. And with her hand she pointed to the Spaniard, revealed by the reflection of the fires at Camdless Bay. He was standing upright in the boat which rapidly shot away.

Then all was silent.

The two negroes with their throats cut lay dead on the ground.

Then Mrs. Burbank, in distraction, followed by Alice who in vain tried to stop her, ran along the bank, calling after her little daughter. No cry answered to hers. The boat had become invisible, either because the gloom had veiled it from her sight, or because it had crossed the river to some point on the left bank.

For an hour this vain pursuit continued. At last Mrs. Burbank fell exhausted. Alice, with extraordinary energy, helped the unfortunate mother to rise, supported her, and almost carried her. In the distance, in the direction of Castle House, rang out the reports of the firearms, mingled every now and then with the terrible yells of the besiegers. But it was necessary to go back in that direction, to try and get back to the house along the tunnel, to open the door which communicated with the underground stairs. When she reached that spot how would Alice make herself heard?

She dragged Mrs. Burbank along, but the mother was unconscious of what she was doing. Twenty times did they stop as they returned along the riverside. At any instant they might fall into the hands of those who were wrecking the plantation. Would it be better to wait till daylight? But how in this place could she give Mrs. Burbank the attention her state required? And so, cost what it might, Alice resolved to get back to Castle House. And as the winding of the river lengthened the way, she thought it would be better to go straight across the fields, guided by the light of the burning barracoons. This she did, and thus it was she came near the house.

There Mrs. Burbank fell motionless at her feet. She could support her no longer.

By this time the detachment of militia, followed by the horde of pillagers, had given up the assault, and were far from the palisades. Not a shout was heard within or without. Alice imagined that the assailants had captured the house and abandoned it without leaving one of its defenders alive. Supreme was her anguish; her strength failed her, and she, too, fell to the ground, while a last groan escaped from her, a last appeal. It had been heard.

Burbank and his friends had rushed out. Now they knew all that had passed at Marine Creek. What mattered it to them that the plunderers had gone? What mattered it to them that there was no fear of falling into their power? A dreadful misfortune had come to them. Little Dy was in the hands of Texar!

This was the story told by Alice, broken with many sobs, and listened to by Mrs. Burbank, who had returned to consciousness and was bathed in tears. This is what was learnt by Burbank, Stannard, Carrol, Perry, and their few companions. The poor child, taken they knew not where, in the hands of her father's cruellest enemy! What could be worse than that? Could the future have greater griefs in store?

All were overwhelmed at the blow. Mrs. Burbank was taken to her room and laid on her bed, and Alice remained with her.

Below, in the hall, Burbank and his friends endeavoured to devise some plan by which they could recover Dy and rescue Zermah from Texar's hands. The devoted half-breed would certainly endeavour to defend the child to the death! But as the prisoner of a scoundrel animated by personal hatred, would she not pay with her life for the curses she hurled at him?

Then James Burbank blamed himself for having forced his wife to leave Castle House, for having arranged such a means of flight which had turned out so badly. Was Texar's presence at Marine Creek to be attributed to chance? Evidently not. Texar, in some way or another, had heard of the existence of the tunnel. He had said to himself that the defenders of Camdless Bay would endeavour to escape by it when they could no longer hold out in the house. And, after leading his men to the right bank of the river, after forcing the palisades, and driving Burbank behind the walls of the house, there could be no doubt he and some of his accomplices had posted themselves near Marine Creek. There he had suddenly surprised the two blacks in charge of the boat, and cut their throats, their cries being unheard amid the tumult

made by the besiegers of the house. The Spaniard had
waited till Zermah appeared with little Dy close behind.
Seeing them alone, he probably thought that neither Mrs.
Burbank, nor her husband, nor her friends were going to
leave Castle House. Then he would have to be content
with this prey, and had seized on the child and the half-
breed to carry them off to some retreat whence it would be
impossible to recover them.

And with what more terrible blow could the scoundrel
have visited the Burbanks ?

A horrible night was passed by the survivors. Was there
not a chance that the assailants might return in greater numbers and better armed ? Fortunately, they did not. When
the day broke there had been no renewal of the attack.

But it was important to know why the three cannon-
shots had been fired the night before, and why the assailants had retired when one effort more—an hour's effort at
the outside—would have given them the house. Was the
recall due to some demonstration of the Federals at the
mouth of the St. John's ? Had Commodore Dupont's
ships become masters of Jacksonville ? Nothing in Burbank's interest could be more desirable. In all safety he
could begin his search to recover Dy and Zermah, and
openly attack Texar—if the Spaniard had not retreated
with his partisans—and prosecute him as the promoter of
the havoc at Camdless Bay and the double abduction of
the half-breed and child.

This time no such *alibi* was possible as that which the
Spaniard had produced at the opening of this history, when
he appeared before the magistrate at Saint Augustine.
If Texar was not at the head of this band of scoundrels
who had invaded Camdless Bay—as Mr. Harvey's messenger had been unable to ascertain—the last cry of
Zermah had only too clearly revealed the part he took in
the abduction. And had not Alice recognized him as the
boat was rowing away ?

Yes ! Federal justice would make the scoundrel confess
where he had taken his victims, and punish the crimes
which he could not deny.

PART I.   I

Unfortunately, nothing happened to confirm this hypothesis concerning the arrival of the Northern flotilla in the waters of the St. John's. At this date, the 3rd of March, no ship had left the bay of St. Mary's, as was only too clearly ascertained by the news which one of the assistant-overseers brought in during the day from the other bank of the river, to which he had gone to inquire. No vessel had appeared off Pablo light. The whole fleet was employed at Fernandina and Fort Clinch. It seemed as though Commodore Dupont could only advance into the centre of Florida with extreme circumspection. At Jacksonville the rioters were still in power. After the expedition to Camdless Bay the Spaniard had again appeared in the town, and was organizing the defence against Stevens's gunboats, should they try to cross the bar. Doubtless some false alarm the evening before had called back the looters. After all, was not Texar's vengeance sufficient, now that the plantation had been wasted, the factories fired, the negroes dispersed in the forests with nothing but the ruins of the barracoons left to them, and little Dy taken away from her father and mother, with no trace as to where she had gone?

Of this James Burbank felt only too certain, when during the morning he and Walter Stannard explored the right bank of the river. In vain they searched the smaller creeks for some clue as to the direction taken by the boat. The search could at the best be but incomplete, unless the left bank was searched as well.

But at this time, was not this impossible? Would it not be necessary to wait till Texar and his partisans were reduced to impotence by the arrival of the Federals? With Mrs. Burbank in such a state, Alice unable to leave her, and Carrol laid up for some days, would it not be imprudent to leave them alone at Castle House, when the return of the assailants was not unlikely?

And what was even more maddening was, that Burbank could not dream of proceeding against Texar, either for the devastation of his estate, nor the abduction of Zermah and his daughter. The only magistrate to whom he could

address himself was the author of the crime. All that
could be done was to wait until regular justice had resumed
its course at Jacksonville.

"James," said Mr. Stannard, "if the dangers which
threaten your child are terrible, at least Zermah is with
her, and you can depend on her devotion—"

"Till death—quite so!" said Burbank. "And when will
Zermah be dead?"

"Listen, my dear James. Consider for a moment. It
is not Texar's interest to proceed to such extremities.
He has not yet left Jacksonville, and until he has I
think his victims have no act of violence to fear. Your
child will be a guarantee, a hostage against the reprisals
which he has to guard against, not only from you, but
from the Federals, for having suspended the regular
authorities of Jacksonville, and devastated a Northener's
plantation. It is his interest to spare them, and wait till
Dupont and Sherman are masters of the territory before
you do anything against him."

"And when will that be?" asked Burbank.

"To-morrow! To-day, perhaps! I tell you, Dy is
Texar's safeguard. It is for that purpose he took the
opportunity of carrying her off, knowing that it would
also break your heart, my poor James; and the scoundrel
has succeeded only too well."

Thus reasoned Mr. Stannard, and he had good grounds
for doing so. Would he convince James Burbank?
Doubtless, no. Would he give him any hope? None. It
was impossible. But Burbank saw that he must force
himself to talk before his wife as Stannard had talked to
him. Otherwise she would not survive the blow. And
when he reached home, he made much use of the arguments which had no effect upon himself.

Meanwhile, Perry and his assistant overseers visited
Camdless Bay. It was a heartrending spectacle which
even made a great impression on Pygmalion, who accompanied them. The "free man" had never dreamt of
following the freed slaves dispersed by Texar. The liberty
to sleep in the woods and suffer cold and hunger seemed

to him excessive. As he preferred to remain at Castle House, he ought, like Zermah, to have torn up his act of enfranchisement to gain the right to live there.

"You see, Pyg!" said Mr. Perry, "the plantation is laid waste, our workshops are in ruins. That is what has been the cost of giving liberty to people of your colour."

"Mr. Perry," replied Pygmalion, "it is not my fault—"

"It is your fault. If fellows like you had not applauded the speechifiers who thundered against slavery, if you had protested against the ideas of the North, if you had taken arms to repulse the Federal troops, Mr. Burbank would never have to think of freeing you, and disaster would never have come to Camdless Bay."

"But what can I do now?" said the disconsolate Pyg. "What can I do, Mr. Perry?"

"I will tell you, Pyg, if you have the least feeling of justice about you. You are free, are you not?"

"It seems so."

"And consequently, you belong to yourself?"

"Certainly."

"And if you belong to yourself, there is nothing to stop you from doing what you like with yourself?"

"Nothing, Mr. Perry."

"Well, in your place, Pyg, I should not hesitate. I would go to the nearest plantation and again become a slave, and the price I realized by my sale I would bring back to my old master, to indemnify him for the wrong I did him when he set me free!"

Did the overseer speak seriously? It was impossible to know what nonsense the witty man might talk once he had mounted his hobby. Pygmalion, the piteous Pygmalion, disconcerted, irresolute, abashed, did not know what to reply.

It was only too evident that James Burbank's act of generosity had brought misfortune and ruin on the plantation. The disaster would cost him a considerable amount of money. There were no barracoons left; they had fallen after they had been sacked. The sawmills and workshops were only heaps of cinders from which grey wreaths of smoke still rose. In place of the stores where the timber was kept, of the factories where the cotton was heckled, of the hydraulic presses where it was squeezed into bales, of the sugar-mills, there were only blackened walls ready to fall, and where the chimney of the factory rose, there was now but a mound of reddened bricks. The fields of coffee and rice, the kitchen garden, the enclosures for the domestic animals, had been completely laid waste, as if a herd of wild beasts had ravaged them for hours. At the sight of this lamentable spectacle, Mr. Perry could hardly contain himself. His anger escaped in threatening words. Pygmalion felt anything but comfortable at the fierce looks the overseer gave him ; and he ended by leaving, to return to Castle House, in order that, as he said, he might reflect more at his ease on the proposition as to selling himself, which the overseer had made. And, doubtless, the day was not long enough for his reflection, for when evening came, he was still undecided.

During the day a few of the old slaves returned in secret to Camdless Bay. It may be imagined what was their distress when they found not a single hut undestroyed. James Burbank gave orders that as much as possible should be done for them. A certain number were lodged within the palisades in the servants' quarters that the fire had not touched. They were, at first, employed in burying their companions who had died in the defence of the house, and also the corpses of the assailants who had fallen in the attack—the wounded had been carried away by their comrades. And they also buried the two negroes who had been killed by Texar and his accomplices when surprised at their post near Marine Creek.

This done, James Burbank could not set about getting his estate again into order until the question between North and South was settled in Florida. Other cares, equally serious but very different, absorbed his attention night and day. All in his power to do to recover some trace of his little daughter he did. Mrs. Burbank's health was in a precarious state, although Alice had not left her

for a moment, and watched over her with filial solicitude ;
and it was necessary to find a doctor for her.

There was one in Jacksonville who possessed the full
confidence of the Burbanks ; and as soon as he was sent
for he did not hesitate to come to Camdless Bay. He
prescribed a few remedies. But would they be efficacious
so long as Dy remained unrestored to her mother ?

Leaving Carrol, who would have to keep to his room for
some days, Burbank and Stannard went out each day to explore both banks of the river. They searched the islands
in the St. John's ; they asked the country people ; they
inquired in the smallest villages in the county ; they
promised a heavy reward to any one who would bring
them any clue. Their efforts remained useless. How
could they learn what was going on in Black Creek where
the Spaniard hid himself ? No one knew of it. And,
besides, to withdraw his victims the better from all search,
had not Texar taken them further up the river ? Was not
the county large enough, were there not enough hiding-
places in the vast forests in the centre, amid the immense
marshes in the South of Florida, in the region of the inaccessible Everglades, for Texar to hide his victims so that
they could not be reached ?

At the same time, through the doctor coming to Camdless Bay, Burbank was kept informed of what was passing
at Jacksonville and in the north of Duval County.

The Federals had made no new demonstration. Had
special instructions arrived from Washington forbidding
them to cross the frontier ? Such a proceeding would be
disastrous for the Unionists in the South, and particularly
so for James Burbank.

Nevertheless, Commodore Dupont's squadron remained
in the estuary of the St. Mary's, and if Texar's men had
been recalled by the three canon-shots fired on the 2nd
of March, it was because the Jacksonville authorities had
been deceived by a false alarm ; and, through the error,
Castle House had escaped from pillage and ruin.

But would not the Spaniard send another expedition to
compiete his work, seeing that James Burbank was not in

his hands ? An unlikely hypothesis !   At present, the
attack on Castle House and the carrying off of Dy and
Zermah were probably enough for him. Besides, some of
the better-class citizens had not hesitated to show their
disapprobation of the affair at Camdless Bay, and their
disgust at the chief of the Jacksonville rioters, although
their opinion might matter little to Texar. The Spaniard
was more powerful than ever in Duval County. His
vagabonds and unscrupulous adventurers were quite at
their ease. Each day they gave themselves up to pleasures
of all sorts, degenerating into orgies. The noise of the
merry-makings even reached the plantation ; and the sky
glowed with the public illuminations, which might be taken
for the light of another incendiary fire Moderate men
were reduced to silence, and had to submit to the yoke of
this faction, which was supported by the populace of the
county.

The temporary inaction of the Federal army oppor-
tunely came in to help the new authorities, who profited
by it to spread the report that the Northerners would not
pass the frontier ; that they had received orders to retreat
into Georgia and the Carolinas ; that Florida would not be
subjected to the invasion of the anti-slavery troops ; that
its position as an old Spanish colony put it outside the
question the United States were seeking to solve by force
of arms, &c., &c. And in all the counties there was produced a certain current favourable rather than contrary to
the ideas which the partizans of violence represented.
This was apparent in many places, particularly in the
north, on the Georgian frontier, where the planters with
Northern sympathies were atrociously treated, their slaves
put to flight, their sawmills and factories destroyed by fire,
their establishments devastated by the Confederate troops,
as Camdless Bay had just been by the populace of Jacksonville.

It did not, however, seem—at present at least—that
there was a chance of the plantation being again invaded.
But much did James Burbank chafe at the delay of the
Federals in making themselves masters of the territory.

As things stood, nothing could be done against Texar ; either to bring him to justice for what could not be denied, or compel him to reveal the hiding-place of Dy and Zermah.

Burbank could not bring himself to believe that the Federals were going to remain quietly on the frontier. Gilbert's last letter had expressly stated that the expedition of Commodore Dupont and Sherman was destined for Florida. Since this letter, had the Federal Government sent different orders to Edisto Bay, where the squadron was waiting ? Had a success of the Confederate troops in Virginia or the Carolinas obliged the army of the Union to halt in its march to the South ?

Thus passed the five days which followed the attack on Camdless Bay. There was no news of a movement of the Federals. No news of Dy and Zermah, although Burbank had done his best to come on their track, and not a day had passed without some fresh effort.

The 9th of March had come. Edward Carrol had completely recovered. He was now fit to join in the work of his friends. Mrs. Burbank continued extremely weak. It seemed as though her life threatened to take flight with her tears. In her delirium she called her little daughter in heartrending tones ; she attempted to go in search of her. These crises were followed by syncopes, which put her life in danger. Often and often Alice feared that the unhappy mother would die in her arms.

A war rumour reached Jacksonville on the morning of the 9th of March. Unfortunately, it was calculated to give new encouragement to the partizans of Secession.

The Confederate general, Van Dorn, had repulsed the soldiers of Curtis on the 6th of March at the battle of Betonville, in Arkansas, and obliged them to retreat. Really this was an engagement with the rear-guard of a small Northern corps ; and the success was more than compensated for a few days afterwards by the victory of Pea Ridge. It, however, provoked an increase of insolence among the Southerners. At Jacksonville, the unimportant action was celebrated as a complete check to the Federal army ; and there were new festivities and new orgies, the murmur of which rolled mournfully over Camdless Bay.

When James Burbank returned, about six o'clock in the evening, from his exploration of the left bank of the river, he had ascertained the following facts.

A native of Putnam county fancied he had discovered some trace of the abduction on an island of the St. John's a few miles above Black Creek. During the preceding night this man thought he had heard a cry of despair, and had come to report the fact to James Burbank. Squambo, the Indian, Texar's confidant, had been seen in the neighbourhood in his skiff. There was no doubt about the Indian's being seen, for the fact was confirmed by a passenger on board the *Shannon*, who, on his return to St. Augustine, had landed during the day at Camdless Bay.

It need not be said how eagerly James Burbank started on the track. Carrol and two negroes accompanied him in the boat with which he started up the river. They speedily reached the island in question, thoroughly searched it, and visited a few fishermen's huts that did not seem to have been recently occupied. Among the almost impenetrable underwood in the interior there was not a vestige of human beings. There was nothing on the bank to show that a boat had put in. Squambo could nowhere be seen, and if he had been prowing round the island he had probably not landed. The expedition was thus without result, like the others. The return had to be made to the plantation with the knowledge that a false track had been followed. In the evening, Burbank, Stannard, and Carrol, as they were together in the hall, talked over this useless search. About nine o'clock, Alice, having left Mrs. Burbank asleep, came to join them, and found that the last attempt had been without result.

The night was to be a dark one. The moon, in its first quarter, had already disappeared below the horizon. A deep silence enveloped Castle House, the plantation, and the river. The few blacks in the servants' apartments were asleep. When the silence was troubled it was by the distant clamour and the reports of the fireworks at

9

Jacksonville, where, with great uproar, the people were celebrating the successes of the Confederates.

Each time the noise was heard in the hall another blow was struck at the Burbanks.

"We ought to find out what it means," said Carrol, "and see if the Federals really have renounced their plans on Florida."

"Yes! It must be done," answered Stannard. "We cannot exist in this uncertainty."

"Well," said Burbank, "I will go to Fernandina to-morrow—and then I will see—"

At this moment there came a gentle tap on the front door of Castle House, on the side facing the river.

A scream escaped from Alice, who rushed to the door. Burbank vainly tried to keep the girl back. And as no reply had come, another knock was heard, this time more distinctly.

CHAPTER XIII.

A FEW HOURS.

JAMES BURBANK stepped to the door. He did not expect anybody. It might be some important news from Jacksonville brought by John Bruce from his correspondent, Mr. Harvey.

A third time there came a knock, and from a more impatient hand.

"Who is there?" asked James Burbank.

"I am," was the reply.

"Gilbert!" exclaimed Alice.

She was not mistaken. Gilbert at Camdless Bay! Gilbert appearing among his people, glad to come and pass a few hours with them, knowing nothing, doubtless, of the disasters that had fallen on them!

In a moment the young lieutenant was in his father's arms; while the man who accompanied him carefully shut the door, after taking a last look round outside.

It was Mars, Zermah's husband, Gilbert Burbank's devoted follower.

After embracing his father, Gilbert turned round. Then, seeing Alice, he took her hand and clasped it with an irresistible movement of affection.

"My mother!" he said. "Where is mother? Is it true that she is dying?"

"You know all, then?" said James Burbank,

"I know all: the plantation laid waste by the Jacksonville ruffians, the attack on Castle House, my mother—dead perhaps!"

The young man's presence in the county where he ran such peril was immediately explained.

This is what had happened :

That evening, some gunboats from Commodore Dupont's squadron had come to the mouth of the St. John's. Ascending the river, they had had to stop at the bar, four miles below Jacksonville. A few hours later, a man, calling himself one of the lighthouse-keepers at Pablo, had boarded Stevens's gunboat, on which Gilbert was second in command. The man had related all that had passed at Jacksonville, including the attack on Camdless Bay, the dispersal of the blacks, and the serious condition of Mrs. Burbank. It may be guessed what were Gilbert's feelings on listening to the story of these deplorable events.

Then he was seized with an irresistible desire to see his mother. With the permission of Commandant Stevens he had left the flotilla in the gig. Accompanied by the faithful Mars, he passed unnoticed in the darkness—by the way he knew so well—and landed half a mile below Camdless Bay, so as to avoid touching at the pier, which would probably be watched.

But what he did not know, and could not know, was that he had fallen into a snare spread by Texar. At any price the Spaniard desired to obtain the proof required by the magistrates—the proof that James Burbank was in correspondence with the enemy. To entice the young lieutenant to Camdless Bay, a lighthouse-keeper at Pablo had been sent to acquaint Gilbert with what had occurred at Castle House, particularly the condition of his mother. The young lieutenant had set out, as we know; and he had been watched as he went up the river. As he glided along by the reeds that bordered the high bank of the St. John's he had, however, thrown the Spaniard's men off the track ; but though the spies had not seen him land below Camdless Bay, they hoped to capture him on his return, particularly as all that part of the river was under their surveillance.

"Mother !" continued Gilbert, "where is she ?"

"Here, my son !" said Mrs. Burbank.

She had just appeared on the landing of the hall staircase ; she descended slowly, holding the rail, and fell on a couch, while Gilbert covered her with kisses.

In her troubled sleep she had heard the knock at the door. Recognizing her son's voice, she had collected sufficient strength to get up and meet Gilbert, to weep with him and the others. The young man clasped her in his arms.

"Mother ! mother !" said he, " I see you again, after all. How you are suffering ! But you live ! Ah ! we will cure you ! Yes ! These evil days will soon end. We shall be re-united—soon ! We will give you back your health. Fear nothing for me, mother No one knows that Mars and I are here." And as he spoke, Gilbert saw his mother was fainting, and tried to revive her by his caresses.

But Mars seemed to understand that he and Gilbert did not know the full extent of the calamity. James Burbank, Carrol, and Stannard stood silent with bowed heads. Alice could not restrain her tears. Dy was not there, nor was Zermah, who ought to have guessed that her husband was at Camdless Bay, that he was in the house, that he was waiting——

So, with his heart torn by anguish, he looked into all the corners of the hall, and then asked Mr. Burbank,—

"Master, what is the matter ? "

At this moment Gilbert rose.

"And Dy ?" he asked. " Has Dy gone to bed ? Where is my little sister ? "

"Where is my wife ? " said Mars.

An instant afterwards the young officer and Mars knew all. In coming from the St. John's, from the place where their canoe was waiting for them, they had seen enough in the darkness of the ruins of the plantation. But they might naturally think that, with the disaster consequent on the enfranchisement of the blacks, the limit had been reached ! Now nothing was hid from them. One did not find his sister at home, the other did not find his wife, and no one could tell them where Texar had hidden them for these seven days.

Gilbert returned to kneel near Mrs. Burbank. His tears

mingled with hers. Mars, with bloodshot face and panting chest, walked to and fro, unable to contain himself.

At last his rage exploded.

"I will kill Texar!" he said. "I will go to Jacksonville —to-morrow—this very night—this very instant——"

"Yes, come, Mars! come!" said Gilbert.

James Burbank stopped them.

"If that was what ought to be done," said he, "I should not have waited for you to come, my son! The scoundrel would already have paid with his life for his evil deeds. But, before that is done, it is necessary that he should say what he alone can say. And when I speak thus, Gilbert —when I advise you and Mars to wait—it is because it is necessary to wait."

"Be it so, father!" said the young man. "But at least I will ransack the country; I will search——"

"And do you think I have not done so? Not a day has passed without our exploring the river-banks and islands which might serve as a refuge for Texar, and not a trace have we found, not a thing to put us on your sister's track. Carrol and Stannard have helped me, and up to now our search has been fruitless."

"Why did you not lodge a complaint at Jacksonville?" asked the young officer. "Why have you not brought an action against Texar for having caused the pillage of Camdless Bay and the abduction——"

"Why?" answered James Burbank. "Because Texar is now the master; because all honest men tremble before the scoundrels who are devoted to him; because the populace is with him, and the county militia is with him."

"I will kill Texar!" said Mars, as if he were possessed by some fixed idea.

"You shall kill him when the time comes," said James Burbank. "At present it would make matters worse."

"And when will the time come?" asked Gilbert.

"When the Federals are masters of Florida—when they have occupied Jacksonville."

"And if it is then too late?"

"My son! my son! I beseech you do not say that!" exclaimed Mrs. Burbank.

"No, Gilbert, do not say that," added Alice.

James Burbank took his son's hand.

"Gilbert, listen to me," he said. "We, like you and Mars, will do instant justice on Texar if he refuses to tell us what he has done with his victims. But for your sister's sake, Gilbert—for your wife's sake, Mars—our anger must give place to our prudence. There is good reason to believe that in Texar's hands Dy and Zermah are hostages for his safety. The scoundrel is afraid of having to answer for turning out the honest magistrates of Jacksonville and letting loose on Camdless Bay the mob of scoundrels to burn and pillage a Northerner's plantation. If I did not believe this, Gilbert, would I speak with such conviction? Would I be strong enough to wait?"

"And would I still be alive?" asked Mrs. Burbank. The unfortunate woman felt that if her son went to Jacksonville he would fall into Texar's power. And what could save an officer of the Federal navy fallen into the power of the Southerners when the Federals were threatening Florida?

Nevertheless, the young officer was not master of himself. He was obstinate in his wish to go; and, like Mars, he repeated, "I will kill Texar!"

"Come, then!" he said.

"You shall not go, Gilbert!"

Mrs. Burbank raised herself from the sofa. She placed herself before the door; but, exhausted by the effort, she could not support herself, and she fainted.

"Mother! mother!" exclaimed the young man.

Mrs. Burbank had to be carried to her room, where Alice remained with her. Then James Burbank rejoined Carrol and Stannard in the hall.

Gilbert was sitting on the sofa with his face in his hands. Mars was standing apart, and silent.

"Now, Gilbert," said James Burbank, "you are in your right senses. Speak! On what you say depends what we shall do. Our only hope is in a prompt arrival of the

Federals in the county. Have they given up their project
of occupying Florida ?"

"No."

"Where are they ?"

"A part of the squadron at this moment is on the way
to Saint Augustine, to blockade the coast."

"But is not the Commodore going to take possession of
the St. John's ?" asked Carrol.

"The lower course of the St. John's is ours. Our
gunboats are anchored in the river under the orders of
Commandant Stevens."

"In the river, and they have not yet endeavoured to
seize on Jacksonville ?" asked Stannard.

"No, for they have had to stop at the bar, four miles
below the town."

"The gunboats stopped," said James Burbank, "and by
an insurmountable obstacle ?"

"Yes, father," answered Gilbert; "stopped by want of
water. The tide must be high for them to pass the bar,
and even then the passage would be difficult. Mars knows
the channel, and he is to be the pilot."

"Waiting! always waiting!" exclaimed James Burbank.
"And for how long ?"

Three days or twenty-four hours—how long the time
would be for the people in Castle House! And if the
Confederates saw that they could not defend the town! If
they abandoned it, as they had abandoned Fernandina,
Fort Clinch, and the other points of Georgia and northern
Florida! If Texar did not run away! Then where would
they search!

Mr. Stannard then asked if it was true that the Federals
had met with a repulse in the North. What was thought
of the defeat at Bentonville?

"The victory of Pea Ridge has enabled Curtis to re-
occupy the ground he for a moment lost. The situation
of the Northerners is excellent; their success is assured in
a delay which it was difficult to foresee. When they have
occupied the principal points in Florida, they will stop
contraband of war from entering through the coast passes;

and arms and ammunition will no longer reach the
Confederates. Then, in a little time, the territory will
resume its calm and security under the protection of our
squadron. Yes, in a few days ! But now—"

The idea of his sister being exposed to such peril returned to him with such force that Mr. Burbank, to divert
his attention, changed the conversation. How did the
belligerents stand ? Could Gilbert give them any news
which had not reached Jacksonville or rather Camdless
Bay?

Several things he could tell them, some of them of great
importance for the Northerners in Florida.

It will be remembered that after the victory of Donelson,
the State of Tennessee had almost entirely fallen under
Federal domination. By a simultaneous combined attack
of army and fleet, the Federals endeavoured to make
themselves masters of the entire course of the Mississippi.
They had descended it to Island 10, where the troops came
in contact with Beauregard's division, which had charge
of the defence of the river. Already, on the 24th of
February, General Pope's brigade, after landing at Com
merce, on the right bank of the Mississippi, had repulsed
J. Thomson's corps. Arrived at Island 10 and the village
of New Madrid, they had, it is true, to halt before a formidable system of redoubts prepared by Beauregard.
Since the fall of Donelson and Nashville, all the positions
on the river above Memphis had been considered as lost
to the Confederates, but those below could still be
defended, and here it was a battle would soon be fought
which might be decisive.

But meanwhile, Hampton Roads, at the entrance of the
James River, had been the scene of a memorable combat.
The battle had been between the first examples of armour-
plated ships, the employment of which has modified the
navies and naval tactics of both the Old and New World.

On the 1st of March the *Monitor*, an armour-plated
vessel built by the Swedish engineer Ericcsen, and the
Virginia, the old *Merrimac* much altered, had been ready
to put to sea, one at New York, the other at Norfolk.

PART I.

At this time a Federal division, under the orders of
Captain Marston, was at anchor in Hampton Roads, near
Newport News. This division was composed of the
Congress, the *Saint Lawrence*, the *Cumberland*, and two
steam frigates.

Suddenly, on the 2nd of March, in the morning, there
appeared the *Virginia*, commanded by the Confederate
Captain Buchanan. Followed by a few other vessels of
minor importance, she attacked the *Congress*, and then the
Cumberland, which latter she rammed and sank with a
hundred and twenty men of her crew. Returning then to
the *Congress*, stranded on the mud, she shelled her and set
her on fire. Only the night stopped her from destroying
the other three vessels of the Federal squadron.

It is difficult to imagine the effect produced by the
victory of a small armour-plated ship over the broadside
ships of the Union. The news was propagated with
marvellous rapidity. Great was the consternation among
the partizans of the North, for the *Virginia* might enter
the Hudson and sink every ship at New York. Great
was the joy of the Southerners, who saw the blockade
raised and trade again untramelled along their coast.

It was this naval success which was being so noisily
celebrated at Jacksonville. The Confederates now fancied
themselves safe from the Federal vessels. Following on
the victory at Hampton Roads, might not Commodore
Dupont's squadron be immediately recalled to the Potomac
or the Chesapeake? No landing would threaten Florida.
The slavery ideas supported by the most violent of the
Southerners would triumph without a contest. And this
would strengthen Texar and his partizans in a position in
which they could do so much evil.

But the Confederates were in too great a hurry. And
the news already known in Florida, Gilbert was able to
supplement with that which was current when he left
Commandant Stevens's gunboat.

The second fight in Hampton Roads had been very
different from the first. On the morning of the 9th of
March, when the *Virginia* was preparing to attack the

Minnesota, one of the two Federal frigates, an enemy whose presence was unsuspected by the Southerners suddenly appeared before her. A strange machine came away from the frigate's side, " a cheese-box on a raft," as the Confederates called it. This " cheese-box " was the *Monitor*, commanded by Lieutenant Warden. He had been sent to destroy the batteries on the Potomac, but on reaching the mouth of the James River, had heard the firing in Hampton Roads, and during the night had brought the *Monitor* on to the scene.

At half a dozen yards from each other these two formidable engines of war fought for four hours, and then the *Virginia*, struck on the water-line and in danger of sinking, took flight in the direction of Norfolk. The *Monitor*, which was to sink nine months later, had completely defeated her rival. Thanks to her, the Federal Government resumed its superiority in Hampton Roads.

" No, father," said Gilbert, as he ended his story, " our squadron has not been recalled to the north. Stevens's six gunboats are anchored in the St. John's in front of the bar. I tell you that in three days, at least, we shall be masters of Jacksonville."

" Then you must see, Gilbert, that you had better wait and return on board ! But on your way to Camdless Bay do you not think you have been followed ? "

" No. Mars and I have escaped all observation."

" And this man who told you what had passed at the plantation, the fire, the robbery, the illness of your mother. Who is he ? "

" He said he was one of the lighthouse-keepers at Pablo, and had come to warn Captain Stevens of the danger run by the Northerners in this part of Florida."

" Did he know of your presence on board ? "

" No, and he seemed much surprised at it. But why these questions ? "

" Because I am afraid it is some plot of Texar's. He more than suspected—he knew that you were in the Federal navy. He learnt that you were under the orders of Commandant Stevens.   If he wished to entice you here —"

" Never fear.   We have got to Camdless Bay without being seen coming up the river, and it will be the same when we go back."

" If you go on board—not otherwise ! "

" I promise you, father, Mars and I shall be on board before daybreak."

" When will you go ? "

" When the tide turns.   That is about half-past two o'clock."

" Who knows ? " said Carrol.   " Perhaps the gunboats will not stop three days at the bar ? "

" The wind must freshen to give enough water on the bar," said the lieutenant.   " May it blow a gale !   And then we can get at the scoundrels !   And then—"

" I will kill Texar," said Mars.

" It was a little after midnight.   Gilbert and Mars would not leave Castle House for two hours, waiting for the ebb to return to the flotilla.   The darkness was great, and there was every chance of their getting away unperceived although several boats were on guard on the St. John's below Camdless Bay.

The young officer went up to his mother.   He found Alice seated at the bedside.   Mrs. Burbank, exhausted by the efforts she had made, had fallen into a deep slumber— a very sorrowful one to judge by the way she sobbed.

Gilbert would not interfere with this state of torpor in which there was more prostration than sleep.   He sat near the bed after Alice had motioned him not to speak.   There in silence they watched together the poor woman whom misfortune had struck so cruelly.   Had they words in which to exchange their thoughts ?   No !   They felt the same suffering, they understood each other and said nothing—it was their hearts that spoke.

At last the time arrived for Gilbert to leave.   He gave his hand to Alice, and both bent over Mrs. Burbank, whose eyes were half-closed and could not see them.

Then Gilbert pressed his lips to his mother's forehead.

which the girl kissed after him. Mrs. Burbank gave a sorrowful sob, but she did not see her son go, nor Alice follow him to bid him a last farewell.

Mars went out to see if the coast was clear. He came back as Gilbert and Alice entered the hall.

"It is time to go," said he.

"Yes, Gilbert," said James Burbank. "Go! we shall meet again at Jacksonville."

"Yes! At Jacksonville, and to-morrow if the tide allows us to cross the bar. As for Texar—"

"We must have him living! Do not forget that!"

"Yes, living!"

The young man embraced his father and shook hands with his uncle Carrol and Stannard.

"Come, Mars," said he.

And following the right bank of the river they kept along for half an hour. They met no one. They reached the place where they had left the gig, and embarked in her to get into the stream, which would take them rapidly to the bar of the St. John's.

CHAPTER XIV.

ON THE ST. JOHN'S.

THEY were alone on the river. Not a light could be seen on the opposite bank. The lights of Jacksonville were hidden by the bend of Camdless Creek, as it rounded towards the north ; but the reflection mounted on high and tinged the lower bank of clouds.

Although the night was dark, the gig could without difficulty make its way down stream to the bar. No vapour, however, rose from the waters of the St. John's, and it could easily be followed and pursued if any Confederate boat was in waiting for it, but this Gilbert and his companion had no reason to expect.

Both were silent. Instead of heading down stream they would much rather have crossed it to seek out Texar in Jacksonville, and meet him face to face. Then ascending the river they could search the forest and the creeks and their banks, and though James Burbank had failed they might succeed. But it was best to wait. When the Federals were masters of Florida, Gilbert and Mars could set to work against the Spaniard with more chances of success. Their duty now was to re-join the flotilla under Commandant Stevens. If the bar became practicable sooner than they hoped, the young lieutenant ought to be at his post ready for action, and Mars should be at his post ready to pilot the gunboats up the channel, the depth of which, at every moment of the rising tide, was so well known to him.

Mars, seated in the stern of the gig, plied his paddle with vigour. In the bow Gilbert kept careful watch down stream, ready to signal any danger that presented itself from boat or drifting tree. Leaving the right bank obliquely, they made for the middle of the channel, so as to take advantage of the full strength of the stream. Once they were there, Mars, by a stroke to port or starboard, could easily keep the gig on its course.

It would have been safer to have kept along by the dark fringe of trees and gigantic reeds which bordered the right bank of the St. John's. In the shadow of the thick branches there was little risk of discovery. But a little below the plantation a sharp elbow of the bank threw the current out to the other side, and formed a wide eddy which made the navigation somewhat difficult. Mars, seeing nothing suspicious ahead, steered the boat out into the current, which was swiftly running to the sea. From the landing-place at Camdless Bay to the anchorage of the flotilla below the bar, the distance was four or five miles, and helped by the ebb and the vigorous strokes of the paddle, this ought to be accomplished within a couple of hours.

A quarter of an hour after their start, Gilbert and Mars were in mid-stream, and approaching Jacksonville. It may be that Mars unconsciously headed towards the town, drawn thither by some irresistible attraction. Nevertheless the hateful place must be avoided, for its neighbourhood was probably better guarded than the middle of the river.

"Starboard, Mars, starboard," said the young officer.

And the gig curved into the line of the current about a quarter of a mile from the left bank.

Jacksonville was now neither dark nor silent. Scores of lights were moving about on the wharves, or swaying in the boats on the water. A few were gliding along from point to point, as if an active guard had been organized.

At the same time songs and shouts showed that scenes of amusement or riot continued to trouble the town. Did, then, Texar and his partizans believe in the defeat of the Northerners in Virginia and the possible retreat of the flotilla? Or were they making the best of the few days that were left to them in launching out into every excess,

10

while the people around them were drunk with whiskey and gin ?

The gig kept on her course in mid-stream. Gilbert had good reason to hope that he would be out of danger as soon as he had passed Jacksonville.

Suddenly he motioned to Mars to stop paddling. Within a mile below the town he had just caught sight of a long line of black objects stretching like a range of reefs from one side of the river to the other.

It was a line of boats broadside on, and guarding the St. John's. Evidently, when the gunboats cleared the bar, these would be powerless to resist them, and would have to retreat, but if any Federal boats attempted to ascend the river they might offer some opposition to their passage. For this reason they had been placed in position during the night. They lay without moving, kept in station either by their grapnels or their oars. Although no men could be seen it was certain that a number were on board and well armed.

Gilbert, of course, remarked that the string of vessels had not barred the river when he came up to Camdless Bay. The precaution had been taken since the passage of the gig, and perhaps, in view of an expected attack from Commandant Stevens. Anyhow, the gig was forced to leave the centre of the stream, and keep as close as possible to the right shore, where it might pass unperceived among the reeds in the shadow of the trees. This was the only chance of passing the barrier.

" Mars, mind you paddle without any noise until we are through the line," said the lieutenant.

" Yes, sir."

" We may get among the eddies, and if you want any help—"

" I shall not want any."

And with a powerful stroke he sent the boat towards the river side some three hundred yards above the guarded line. If she had not been sighted as she crossed the river —and she might have been—she would certainly be safe from discovery under the dark masses along its edge, and if the end of the line of boats did not extend to the bank, it was pretty certain she could get through.

Mars worked her carefully down in the darkness, which the thick curtain of leafage rendered darker. The stumps that here and there showed above the water he dexterously avoided, and with noiseless strokes he advanced, occasionally crossing an eddy or a counter current which, without some trouble, it was not easy to get through. Coasting in this way quite an hour would be lost, though it would matter little if daylight came before the voyage ended, as by that time they would be near enough to the gunboats to fear no danger from Jacksonville.

About four o'clock the gig reached the line of boats. As Gilbert had expected, the shallowness of the river close in shore had caused the passage near the edge to be left unguarded. A few hundred feet beyond, a point jutted out into the St. John's, thickly wooded and crowded with mangroves and bamboos. This point on the up-stream side was as dark and gloomy as could be wished, but on the downstream face the trees and shrubs suddenly came to an end, and the shore was cut up into marshes and creeks, and lay low and exposed, with nothing to cast a shadow. The river there was as light as in the open, and a black moving point like the gig would probably be seen should any vessel be lying off in the neighbourhood.

Beyond it the eddies ended, and the current flowed straight and strong. If the boat could double the point, she would soon be swept down to the bar, and thence to the anchorage.

Cautiously Mars glided by under the bank. Peering into the darkness he intently watched the lower course of the river. Close to the edge as it was safe to go, clearing the eddies which, as the point curved out, grew more troublesome to him, he plied his paddle silently, while Gilbert, forward, kept a steady look-out over the whole surface of the St. John's.

Gradually the gig neared the point. A few minutes more and they would reach the end which ran out as a fine tongue of sand.   They were not more than thirty yards from it when Mars abruptly stopped.

"Are you tired ? " asked the lieutenant.   " Shall I take your place ? "

" Not a word, Mr. Gilbert ! " whispered Mars.

And with two strong strokes of the paddle, he drove the gig towards the land as if to run her on the bank.   Then, instantly, he grasped one of the branches hanging over the river, and under it guided the boat out of sight.   In an instant they were alongside the root of one of the mangrove trees, and motionless in darkness so deep that they could not see each other.

In ten seconds the manœuvre was accomplished.

The lieutenant seized his companion's arm, and was about to demand an explanation, when Mars pointed through the foliage and showed him a moving object just off the spit.

It was a boat with four men in her rowing up-stream, and rounding the point so as to skirt the bank as she passed.

The same thought occurred to Gilbert and Mars. Before everything, and in spite of everything, they must regain their ship.   If the gig was discovered they would not hesitate to climb the bank, run under the trees, and escape along the riverside to the bar.   There at daybreak, whether their signals were answered by the nearest of the gunboats or they had to swim for it, they would do all that was humanly possible to get back to their duty.

But a moment afterwards they found that all retreat by land was cut off.

When the boat arrived at some twenty feet from the spot where they lay hid, a conversation suddenly began between the men in her and half a dozen others who appeared in the gloom among the trees on the top of the bank.

" The worst is over ! " said one from the land.

" Yes," said a man in the boat.   " To double that point against the tide is almost as bad as pulling up a rapid."

" Are you going to anchor here now that we have been landed on the point ? "

"Yes. We shall guard the end of the barrier better."

"Right We will look after the bank, and unless they take to the marshes, the scoundrels will not find it easy to get by us."

"Have they done so, do you think ? "

"No ; they couldn't. They'll try to get back on board before daylight, and as they cannot pass the boat barrier, they will make their attempt along here. And here we are to stop them."

Few as were the phrases, they were sufficient to explain what had happened. The departure of Gilbert and Mars had been observed—there could be no doubt of that. Although they had managed to reach Camdless Bay without falling aboard of the boats ordered to stop them, now that the river was barred, and their return waited for, it would be difficult, if not impossible, to reach the gunboats.

The gig was fairly caught between the men in the boat and the men landed on the point. Flight by the river was impracticable, and none the less so was it impracticable along this narrow bank, with the St. John's on one side and the marshes on the other.

At the same time Gilbert learnt that his presence on the St. John's was known ; and there could be no doubt it was known that he and his companion had landed at Camdless Bay, that one of them was James Burbank's son, an officer in the Federal navy, and the other one of his men. The lieutenant could not well mistake the danger that threatened him when he heard the last words of the conversation.

"Keep your eyes open, then," said one of the men on the land.

"All right," was the reply. "A Yankee officer is a good prize, particularly when the officer is the son of one of our cursed Floridan Federals."

"And they'll pay well for him, for Texar is the paymaster."

"We may not catch them to-night, for they may lay up in some of the creeks. But when day comes we'll search every cranny so well that not a water rat will escape us."

"Don't forget, you are to take them alive."

"All right! Remember, if we get them on the land, we have to hail you to take them over to Jacksonville."

"Unless we have to give chase we shall remain here."

"And we shall stop here across the bank."

"Good luck to you! You had better have spent the night in drinks at Jacksonville."

"Yes, if the rascals outwit us! But never fear, to-morrow we shall take them to Texar bound hand and foot."

The boat then moved off some twenty feet, and then the noise of a chain running out announced that she had dropped anchor. The men above spoke no more, but the sound of their feet was heard as they marched to and fro on the fallen leaves.

By the river as by the land flight was no longer possible.

So thought Gilbert and Mars. Neither of them had made a single movement or uttered a word. There was nothing to betray the presence of the gig under the dark arbour of foliage—an arbour which was a prison. To leave it was impossible. Supposing that they were not discovered during the night, how could they escape when day appeared?

The lieutenant's capture not only meant danger to his own life, but another attack on his father by Texar, and proof of James Burbank's correspondence with the Federals. When Gilbert was in Texar's power, the necessary proof would be to hand. And then what would become of Mrs. Burbank? What would become of Dy and Zermah, when neither father, brother, nor husband could continue the search?

In a moment all these thoughts presented themselves, and Gilbert recognized the inevitable consequences.

If they were taken only one chance was left. The Federals might seize Jacksonville before Texar could injure them. The prisoners might be given enough time for this to take place between the sentence they could not escape and their execution. That was their only hope. But how could they hurry on the arrival of Stevens? How could he clear the bar if the water was still wanting? How could Stevens find his way through the windings of the channel if his pilot, Mars, was in the hands of the Confederates?

Evidently, then, Gilbert must risk even the impossible to get on board before daylight; and he must leave this place at once. But could he do so? Could not Mars, by driving the gig suddenly across the eddy, get clear away? While the men in the boat were losing time by weighing the grapnel or letting out chain, could they not get by out of reach?

That was impossible! The lieutenant knew it only too well. The paddle was no match for four oars. The gig would inevitably be caught. To make such an attempt was to court certain capture.

What was then to be done? Was he to wait? Day would soon appear. It was already half-past four o'clock, and a few streaks of the dawn had risen above the eastern horizon.

It was necessary to do something. Gilbert, bending towards Mars, spoke to him in a whisper.

"We cannot wait much longer. We are both armed with a revolver and a cutlass. In the boat there are only four men. That is only two to one; and we shall have the advantage of the surprise. You can send the gig up to the boat in a stroke or two; she is anchored and cannot stop our boarding. We will fall on the men and settle them before they have time to recognize us, and we can make a dash for it. Before the fellows on the bank have given the alarm we may have got through the barrier and reached the ships. Do you understand?"

Mars replied by drawing his cutlass and slipping it into his belt near his revolver. Then he slacked off the painter of the gig from the mangrove root and grasped his paddle ready for a vigorous stroke.

But as he stooped to begin Gilbert stopped him with a gesture.

Something had come unexpectedly to alter his plans.

With the first streaks of the day, a thick mist began to rise on the water. Like a humid pile of cotton-wool it rolled along the river waves, clinging to them as it came. Formed over the sea, such vapours enter the estuary, and driven before a gentle breeze, ascend the course of the St. John's. In less than a quarter of an hour Jacksonville, on the left bank, and the trees on the right bank had disappeared, wrapped in the yellowish mist whose characteristic odour filled the valley.

Did not this offer a means of safety? Instead of engaging in an unequal struggle in which they might both fall, why should they not try to get by in the fog?

Gilbert saw this, and that is why he stopped Mars from beginning his stroke. Now, instead of dashing out, he was to slip along cautiously and silently, and avoid the boat, which slowly vanished as the mist closed round it.

Then the voices were again heard replying to the bank from the river.

" Look out in the fog."

" Yes. We are getting in the anchor, and coming closer in shore."

" All right. But don't break your communication with the line. If they come near you, keep them back till the fog lifts."

" Yes ! Never fear ; you see that the beggars don't get past you ashore."

Evidently the orders were obeyed. There were certain boats crossing the river from one bank to the other, that also was obvious. But Gilbert did not hesitate. The gig, paddled noiselessly by Mars, glided out from her shelter under the trees, and crossed the eddy in which the boat had been anchored.

The fog seemed to thicken, although it was penetrated by a dim light such as is given by a horn lantern. Nothing could be seen a yard or two away. If the gig passed clear of the boat, there was an excellent chance of her escaping unobserved. And it was not difficult to avoid the boat, for the men in weighing the anchor made enough noise with the chain to leave no doubt as to their exact position.

The gig slipped by unnoticed, and Mars could ply his paddle a little more vigorously.

The difficulty was to keep a proper course without running out into midstream. If possible he would have remained at a little distance from the right bank ; but the only guide was the lapping of the water on the shore. The day was breaking, and the light flooded the mass of vapour although the fog was very thick.

For half an hour the gig, so to speak, wandered about at a venture. Sometimes a vague outline unexpectedly appeared, which might be a boat much magnified by refraction—an instance of a phenomenon commonly observed in sea fogs.

In fact every object appeared with quite fantastic suddenness, and seemed to be of enormous dimensions. Luckily what Gilbert took for a boat would be only a buoy, or rock above water, or a pole with its upper end vanishing in the mist.

A few pairs of birds flew by with measured flap of wing. They could scarcely see them, but they heard their piercing cry. Some came flying along the surface of the water, and turned to flight when the gig approached them. They vanished, but it was impossible to say if they flew to the bank or dived into the water.

From their paddling all the time with the stream Gilbert knew that he must be nearing the anchorage of the gunboats ; but as the ebb had slackened he could not say if he had passed the line, and he was in constant expectation of running aboard one of the boats.

All chance of serious danger was not over. And it soon became evident that the danger was greater than ever. At short intervals Mars had to stop and hold the paddle out

PART I.

of the water. The noise of oars, sometimes far off, sometimes close by, would make itself heard. Shouts would be
exchanged between the boats. Vague masses would loom
and vanish in the fog, and these were evidently the guard
boats it was their object to avoid. Sometimes the mist
would suddenly open as if a puff of wind had penetrated
it. The range of vision would increase to a hundred yards
and more, and Gilbert and Mars would try to make out
their whereabouts; and then the mist would thicken
again, and all they could do was to drop down with the
stream.

It was a little past five o'clock. Gilbert calculated that
he was two miles from the anchorage. As a fact, he had
not yet reached the bar of the river, which would be easily
recognizable by the increase in the sound of the stream,
and by the numerous minor currents intermingling tumul-
tuously in a way no sailor could mistake. Had he crossed
the bar, Gilbert would have thought himself safe. It was
not likely that the boats would venture so far from Jacksonville under the fire of the gunboats.

Gilbert and Mars bent over almost to the level of the
water and listened. They could hear nothing. Perhaps
they had gone astray to the right or left of the river? Had
they not better take an oblique course so as to reach one
of the banks, and wait till the fog grew lighter to get
their proper bearings?

This seemed the best thing to do now that the mist had
begun to rise. The sun, which they knew was now up
was lifting the fog as it warmed it. The surface of the St.
John's would soon come into view for some distance round
before the sky would show itself. Then the curtain would
suddenly collapse, and the horizon appear out of the mist.
A mile perhaps below the bar Gilbert would see the gunboats swinging to the ebb, and he would be able to reach
them.

At this moment a sound of waters rushing together was
heard. Almost immediately the gig began to turn as if
caught in a whirlpool. There could be no mistake.

"The bar!" exclaimed Gilbert.

"Yes; the bar!" said Mars; "and once we are over it we shall be at the anchorage."

Mars seized the paddle, and endeavoured to keep the proper course.

Suddenly Gilbert stopped him. The mist had opened for a moment, and he caught sight of a boat close behind them. Had her men seen them? Were they trying to stop the way?

"Port!" said the young lieutenant.

In went the paddle, and in a few strokes the gig was out of the line.

But again voices were heard. They were hailing noisily. It was evident that in this part of the river many boats were on guard.

Suddenly, as if a powerful gust had cleared the space, the mist fell shattered on the surface of the St. John's.

Gilbert could not restrain a shout of alarm.

The gig was in the centre of a dozen boats. They were on the watch at this part of the winding channel which the bar cut across in a long slanting line.

"There they are! There they are!" came from the boats around them.

"Yes! here we are," said the lieutenant. "Take your cutlass and revolver, Mars, and we will defend ourselves."

Defend themselves! Two against thirty!

In a moment three or four of the boats were alongside. Mars and Gilbert fired their revolvers; the others did not fire, for the prisoners were to be taken alive. Three or four of the sailors were killed or wounded. But in this unequal strife, how could Gilbert and his companion fail to be overpowered?

The lieutenant was throttled in spite of his energetic resistance, and dragged on to one of the boats.

"Escape, Mars! escape!" he shouted for the last time.

With a sweep of his cutlass Mars released himself from

the man who held him, and before they could seize him again he had thrown himself into the river. In vain they sought to recapture him. He had vanished among the whirlpools of the bar, where the tumultuous waters were being lashed into torrents by the return of the rising tide.

CHAPTER XV.

SENTENCE.

An hour later Gilbert was landed at Jacksonville. The reports of the revolvers had been heard up-stream. Did they mean an engagement between the Confederate boats and the Federal flotilla? Was it not to be feared that the gunboats had cleared the channel? No wonder that there was serious excitement among the townspeople! Some of them rushed to the stockades. The civil authorities, represented by Texar and the most determined of his partizans, had followed them. All were looking in the direction of the bar, now free from mist. Field-glasses and telescopes were in constant use. But the distance was too great—about three miles —for them to ascertain the importance of the engagement or its results.

The flotilla evidently remained at the anchorage it occupied the night before, and Jacksonville need not fear an immediate attack from the gunboats. The people who had most deeply committed themselves would have time to escape into the interior of Florida.

If Texar and two or three of his companions had more reason than others to fear for their safety, there appeared to be no cause for anxiety in what had occurred. The Spaniard suspected that it meant the capture of the gig that he wanted at any cost.

"Yes, at any cost," said he, endeavouring to recognize the boat as it neared the quay. "At any cost this son of

Burbank's must fall into the snare I spread for him. Then
I shall hold the proof that James Burbank is in communication with the Federals ! And when I have shot the son,
twenty-four hours shall not slip by before I have shot the
father !"

Although his party were masters of Jacksonville, Texar,
after the discharge of James Burbank, had been waiting
for a propitious occasion of again arresting him. The
opportunity came in the trap laid for Gilbert Burbank.
With Gilbert identified as a Federal officer, arrested in the
enemy's country, condemned as a spy, the Spaniard could
enjoy his revenge to the full.

Circumstances served him well. It was indeed the son
of the Camdless Bay planter whom they were bringing to
Jacksonville. That Gilbert was alone, that his companion
had been drowned or saved made little difference so long
as the young officer was captured. Texar had only to
bring him before a committee composed of his partizans,
where he would preside in person.

Gilbert was received with howls and threats by the
people, who knew him well. He treated the shouts
with disdain. He gave no sign of fear, although a
detachment of soldiers had to be called up to protect
his life against the violence of the crowd. But when
he saw Texar he could not restrain himself, and would
have thrown himself on him had he not been stopped
by the soldiers.

Texar did not move. He did not say a word. He pretended not to see him, and allowed him to be taken away
with the most perfect indifference.

A few minutes afterwards Gilbert Burbank found himself in the Jacksonville prison. There could be no doubt
as to the fate for which the Southerners were keeping
him.

In about an hour Mr. Harvey, James Burbank's correspondent, presented himself at the prison and attempted to
see Gilbert. He was denied admission. By Texar's
orders the lieutenant was kept in solitary confinement.

And the only result of Mr. Harvey's application was that he himself was put under strict surveillance.

His connection with the Burbanks was known, and it was not in accordance with Texar's plans that Gilbert's arrest should immediately be known at Camdless Bay.

When the verdict was given and the sentence pronounced it would be time enough to inform James Burbank of what had passed, and when he was informed of it there would be no time for him to leave Castle House and escape from Texar.

And so Mr. Harvey was unable to send a messenger to Camdless Bay. An embargo had been put on all the boats in the port. All communication was shut off between the left and right banks of the river. While his father thought he was safe on board the gunboat the lieutenant was in prison at Jacksonville.

At Castle House they listened with anxiety for some distant sound of firing to announce the arrival of the Federals above the bar. Jacksonville in the hands of the Northerners meant Texar in the hands of James Burbank.

Not a sound was heard from downstream. Overseer Perry, who went out to explore the St. John's up to the line of boats, Pyg and one of the assistant-overseers sent three miles down the riverside beyond the plantation, came back with the same report. The flotilla was still at the anchorage, and there was no sign of preparation to start for Jacksonville.

And besides, how could they cross the bar ? Admitting that the tide rendered it practicable sooner than they hoped, how could they venture along the intricate channel now that the only pilot who knew the soundings was no longer with them ? For Mars had not reappeared. And if James Burbank had known what had passed after the capture of the gig, would he not have believed that his son's companion had perished in the whirlpools ? And if Mars had been saved, would not his first care have been to return to Camdless Bay as it was impossible for him to return on board?

Mars had not appeared at the plantation.

Next day, the 11th of March, about eleven o'clock, the committee assembled, with Texar as president, in the very Court of Justice where the Spaniard had made his charge against James Burbank. This time, the charges against the young officer were too serious to allow of his escape. He was doomed beforehand. Once this business of the son was settled, Texar could devote himself to the father. With little Dy in his power, Mrs. Burbank would succumb to the successive blows he had dealt her, and he would be avenged. Did it not seem as though everything played into his hands to help him gratify his implacable hatred?

Gilbert was brought from his prison. The crowd accompanied him, groaning and yelling as on the previous evening. When he entered the court, where Texar's partizans were already in force, he was saluted with violent uproar.

"Death to the spy! Death!"

Gilbert took it all very coolly, and even in the Spaniard's presence kept himself well under control.

"Your name is Gilbert Burbank," said Texar. "And you are an officer in the Federal Navy?"

"Yes."

"And you are now a lieutenant on board one of the gunboats under Commandant Stevens?"

"Yes."

"You are the son of James Burbank, a Northerner, the owner of the plantation at Camdless Bay?"

"Yes."

"You admit that you left the flotilla anchored below the bar, during the night of the 10th of March?"

"Yes."

"You admit that you were captured as you were trying to regain the flotilla with one of your men?"

"Yes."

"Will you tell me what your business was on the St. John's?"

"A man came on board the gunboat of which I was second in command, and told me that my father's plantation had been devastated by a horde of scoundrels, that Castle House had been besieged by thieves. I need not tell that to the President of this Committee, who is personally responsible for these crimes."

"I tell Gilbert Burbank," said Texar, "that his father had challenged public opinion by freeing his slaves, that an order had been issued commanding the newly freed slaves to disperse, that this order was executed—"

"With pillage and incendiarism," replied Gilbert, "and rape, of which Texar is personally the author."

"When I am before my judges I will reply," said the Spaniard coldly. "Gilbert Burbank, do not attempt to change our positions. You are the accused, not the accuser."

"Yes, the accused—at this moment, at all events, but the Federal gunboats have only the bar of the St. John's between them and Jacksonville, and then—"

Then the uproar broke out against the young officer, who dared to brave the Southerners to their face.

"Death! Death!" shouted the crowd on all sides.

The Spaniard with difficulty quieted the angry crowd. Then he resumed his questions.

"Will you tell us, Gilbert Burbank, why you left your ship last night?"

"To see my dying mother."

"You admit, then, that you landed at Camdless Bay?"

"I have no reason to hide it."

"And only to see your mother?"

"Only."

"We have reason to believe you had another object?"

"What?"

"To communicate with your father, James Burbank, who

11

has been under suspicion for some time of being in correspondence with the Federal army."

"You know that is not true," replied Gilbert with very natural indignation. "If I came to Camdless Bay, it was not as an officer, but as a son."

"Or a spy?" said Texar.

The shouts began again.

"Death to the spy! Death!"

Gilbert saw that he was lost, and what was a terrible blow to him, that his father was lost with him.

"Yes," said Texar, "the illness of your mother was only a pretext! You came as a spy to Camdless Bay to report to the Federals the state of the defences of the St. John's."

Gilbert rose.

"I came to see my dying mother, as you know well. Never should I have believed that in a civilized country there could be judges who would consider it a crime for a sailor to come to his mother's deathbed, even in the enemy's territory! Let him who blames me and would not do likewise, dare to tell me so!"

Men in whom hatred had not extinguished all feeling, would have applauded a declaration so noble and frank. But this was not the case here.

The declaration was received with renewed uproar; and when the Spaniard remarked that in receiving an officer of the enemy in time of war, James Burbank was as guilty as the officer, his statement was loudly applauded.

Then the committee, making a note of the admissions as to the father, condemned Lieutenant Gilbert Burbank, of the Federal navy, to death.

The doomed man was then taken back to prison amid the shouts of the populace, who followed him with cries of—

"Death to the spy! Death!"

That evening a detachment of the Jacksonville militia arrived at Camdless Bay. The officer in command asked for Mr. Burbank.

James Burbank came forward to meet him, accompanied by Edward Carrol and Walter Stannard.

"What is it they want?" asked James Burbank.

"Read that order!" answered the officer.

The order was to arrest James Burbank, as the accomplice of Gilbert Burbank, condemned to death as a spy by the Committee of Jacksonville, and who was to be shot within twenty-four hours.

END OF PART I.

TEXAR'S REVENGE;

OR,

North Against South.

(NORD CONTRE SUD.)

PART II.

TEXAR, THE SOUTHERNER.

CONTENTS.

CONTENTS.

NORTH AND SOUTH.

Part II.

TEXAR THE SOUTHERNER.

CHAPTER I.

AFTER THE CAPTURE.

"Texar!"—such was the well-hated name that Zermah had shouted into the darkness at the moment Mrs. Burbank and Alice reached the bank of Marine Creek. The girl had recognized the Spaniard. There could be no doubt he was the author of the abduction, of which he now took personal charge.

It was indeed Texar, and with him were half a dozen accomplices.

For some time he had been planning this expedition, which had for its object the devastation of Camdless Bay, the pillage of Castle House, the ruin of the Burbank family, and the capture or death of its head. It was with this in view that he had launched his horde of pillagers on to the plantation. But he had not put himself at their head; he had left the task of leading them to a few of the most violent of his partisans, and hence John Bruce was right when he assured James Burbank that Texar was not among the assailants.

Texar was aware of the existence of the tunnel between Castle House and the Creek. If the house was captured, the defenders would evidently try to escape down the tunnel. Taking a boat from Jacksonville, and followed by another boat with Squambo and two of his slaves, he had come to the creek to watch. He was not mistaken. That he saw at once when he found one of the Camdless Bay boats stationed among the reeds. The blacks in charge of it were surprised, attacked, and strangled. All that had then to be done was to wait. Soon Zermah appeared, and with her the little girl. Fearing that help might come in answer to Zermah's shouts, the Spaniard had thrown her into Squambo's arms; and when Mrs. Burbank and Alice appeared on the bank Zermah was being carried off to the middle of the river in the Indian's boat.

We know the rest.

When the prisoners were secured, Texar did not think it necessary to accompany Squambo, who was entirely devoted to him, and knew where to take Zermah and Dy. and when the three cannon-shots recalled the assailants from storming Castle House he had struck off obliquely across the St. John's and disappeared.

Where had he gone? No one knew. He did not return to Jacksonville during the night of the 3rd and 4th of March, nor for twenty-four hours afterwards. What was the meaning of this strange absence, which he took no trouble to explain? No one could tell. But it would be a somewhat compromising circumstance should he be charged with carrying off Dy and Zermah. The coincidence between the abduction and his disappearance could not but tell against him. Nevertheless, he did not return to Jacksonville till the morning of the 5th to take the necessary measures for the defence of the town—in time enough, however, to lay the snare for Gilbert Burbank, and preside at the committee which sentenced the young officer to death.

One thing was certain, and that was that Texar was not in the boat with Squambo, which was carried off into the gloom by the rising tide.

Zermah, knowing that her shouts would not be heard on the deserted banks of the St. John's, was silent. She sat in the stern with Dy in her arms. The child was quite frightened, and uttered not a single complaint. She clung to the half-breed's breast, and hid herself in the folds of her mantle. Once or twice only did a few words escape her lips.

"Mamma! mamma! Good Zermah, I am afraid! I am afraid! I want to see mamma!"

"Yes, my dear," answered Zermah, "we shall see her. Never fear; I am near you."

At the same moment, Mrs. Burbank had run along the right bank of the stream, and was seeking in vain to follow her daughter as she was borne away to the opposite side.

The darkness was then profound. The fires on the estate had begun to subside, but not without several explosions. From the heavy clouds of smoke in the north the flames shot up but seldom, when they illuminated the river for a second like a flash of lightning. Then all was silent and dark. The boat was in mid-stream, and the banks could not be seen. It could not have been more isolated, more alone, in the open sea.

Whither was Squambo bound? It was important for Zermah to know. To ask the Indian would be useless; and so she tried to make out the position for herself—not an easy thing to do in the darkness while Squambo kept in the middle of the St. John's. The tide was running in, and, paddled by the two blacks, the boat rapidly sped to the south.

And would it not be wise for Zermah to leave some trace of her route, so as to help her master in his search? But on the river that was impossible. On land, a rag torn from her mantle and left on a bush might be the beginning of a trail which, once recovered, might be followed to the end. But what would be the use of entrusting anything to the stream? Could it be hoped that chance would bring it to James Burbank's hands? The idea must be given up, and she must content herself with ascertaining where she landed.

An hour elapsed, and Squambo had not uttered a word. The two slaves paddled in silence. No light appeared on the banks, neither in the houses nor under the trees.

Zermah watched right and left, ready to note the least

indication, and thinking only of the danger which threatened
the girl. Of her own danger she never thought; all her
fears were concentrated on the child. It was Texar who
had stolen her—of that there could be no doubt. She
had recognized the Spaniard, who had been at Marine
Creek either with the intention of entering Castle House
through the tunnel or waiting for the defenders when they
attempted to escape. If Texar had not been in such a
hurry, Mrs. Burbank and Alice Stannard would now have
been in his power. If he had not headed the attack of the
militia and rabble, it was because he felt surer of securing
the Burbank family at Marine Creek.

In any case, Texar could not deny that he had taken part
in the seizure. Zermah had shouted his name, and Mrs.
Burbank and Alice must have heard her. Later on, when
the hour of justice came, when the Spaniard would
have to answer for his crimes, he would not on this occasion
be able to invoke one of those inexplicable *alibis* that had
hitherto succeeded with him.

What fate had he in reserve for his victims? Was he
going to banish them to the marshy Everglades beyond
the sources of the St. John's? Did he look upon Zermah as a
dangerous witness, whose evidence would one day ruin him?

Zermah would willingly have sacrificed her life to save the
child that had been carried away with her. But if she were
dead, what would become of Dy in the hands of Texar
and his companions? The thought was torture to her, and
she clasped the girl more closely to her heart, as if Squambo
had shown some intention of taking her away.

Zermah noticed that the boat was nearing the left
bank of the river. Would that give her any clue? No,
for she did not know that the Spaniard lived in Black
Creek, on one of the islets of the lagoon. Even Texar's
partisans were ignorant of this, for no one had ever been
admitted to the blockhouse which he occupied with
Squambo and the blacks.

It was to Black Creek that Squambo was taking the
prisoners. In that mysterious place they would be safe
from all search. The creek was, so to speak, impenetrable,

for no one knew the plan of its waterways. It offered a thousand retreats where prisoners could be hidden without it being possible to discover any traces of them. If James Burbank tried to explore its tangled thickets, there would be time enough to remove the half-breed and child to the south of the peninsula. There all chance would be lost of recovering them amid the vast regions which the Floridan pioneers rarely visited, and the unhealthy plains where only Indians wandered.

The forty-five miles between Camdless Bay and Black Creek were quickly covered. About eleven o'clock the boat passed the bend which the St. John's makes two hundred yards below the creek. All that had to be done was to find the entrance to the lagoon—not an easy thing to do in the profound darkness which enveloped the left bank of the river. Squambo, though well acquainted with the place, kept off the shore as much as possible. It would have been easier for him to have run close in, but the bank was cut into by a number of small creeks bristling with reeds and other aquatic plants, and he was afraid of running aground. And as the tide had turned he would be in a difficulty were he to do so. He would have to wait nearly eleven hours till the tide came back, and how could he avoid being seen during that time ? There were always a good many boats on the river, and now events necessitated constant communication between Jacksonville and St. Augustine. If the members of the Burbank family had not perished in the attack on Castle House they would be sure to begin an active search in the morning, and Squambo stuck on a shoal at the foot of the bank would inevitably be seen. It would be a dangerous position, and for many reasons it was better for him to remain in the stream, even, if necessary, to anchor and wait for the dawn, when he could be sure of his road.

Suddenly he heard a noise approaching him. It was the sound of paddle-wheels. And almost immediately a moving mass appeared round the bend of the left bank.

A steamboat was advancing at half-speed. In less than a minute it would be upon them.

By a gesture Squambo stopped his men, and with a movement of the rudder turned the boat's head towards the right bank so as to avoid being seen.

But the boat had been sighted by the look-out on board, and she was hailed from the steamer.

Squambo muttered a terrible oath. But he had to obey.

A moment afterwards he ran alongside the steamer, which had stopped to wait for him.

Zermah at once rose from her seat. Here was a chance of safety. Could she not appeal for help, make herself known, and escape from Squambo?

The Indian rose at the same moment, bowie-knife in hand. With the other hand he caught hold of Dy, whom Zermah in vain tried to snatch from him.

"One word," he said, "and I will kill her!"

If it had been her own life that was threatened, Zermah would not have hesitated. But as it was the child's, she was silent.

From the deck of the steamer nothing could be seen of what was taking place in the boat.

The steamer was coming from Picolata, where she had embarked a detachment of militia for Jacksonville, to reinforce the Southern troops defending the mouth of the river.

An officer leaning over the bridge spoke to the Indian:

"Where are you going to?"

"Picolata."

Zermah took note of the name, although she knew that Squambo wished to keep secret his real destination.

"Where do you come from?"

"Jacksonville."

"Any news there?"

"No."

"Nothing about Dupont's flotilla?"

"Nothing."

"No news since the attack on Fernandina and Fort Clinch?"

"No."

"No gunboats in the St. John's?"

" None."

" What was the meaning of the lights we saw, and the reports we heard, while we were at anchor waiting for the tide to turn ? "

" An attack on Camdless Bay plantation."

" By the Northerners ? "

" No. By the Jacksonville Militia. The planter defied the orders of the committee—"

" Right ! Right ! You mean James Burbank, the mad abolitionist ? "

" Just so."

" What was the result ! "

" I do not know. I only saw it as I passed. It looked as though everything was in flames."

At this moment a feeble cry escaped from the child's lips. Zermah put her hand on Dy's mouth, as the Indian's fingers felt for her neck. The officer on the bridge heard nothing.

" Were the guns in action at Camdless Bay ? "

" I do not think so."

" Why the three reports which seemed to come from Jacksonville ? "

" I do not know."

" Is the St. John's clear from Picolata to the bar ? "

" Quite clear, and you need not trouble yourself about the gunboats."

" All right. Sheer off ! "

An order was sent down to the engine-room, and the steamer resumed her way.

" Can you answer me a question ? " asked Squambo.

" What ? " said the officer.

" The night is very dark. I hardly know where I am."

" Off Black Creek."

" Thank you."

The paddle-wheels churned the river face, and gradually the steamer disappeared in the night, leaving behind her a considerable troubling of the waters.

Squambo, left alone in mid-stream, sat down in the canoe and gave the order to resume paddling. He knew his position, and starboarding his helm headed straight for the opening of Black Creek.

That it was to this place of such difficult access that the Indian was taking them, Zermah could no longer doubt, and little good did the knowledge do her. How could she tell her master, and how could he succeed in searching this impenetrable labyrinth ? At the back of the creek were there not the forests of Duval county offering every facility for evading pursuit, in case James Burbank managed to get through the lagoon ? This part of eastern Florida was in those days a lost country, in which it was almost impossible to find a trail. Nor was it prudent to venture on doing so. The Seminoles wandered about the forest and marshlands, and were formidable enemies. They robbed the travellers who fell into their hands, and massacred those who attempted to defend themselves.

A strange affair, much talked of at the time, had happened in the upper part of the country a little to the northwest of Jacksonville.

Twelve Floridans had landed on the coast of the Gulf of Mexico and been surprised by a tribe of Seminoles. They had not been put to death because they had made no resistance, which, as they were one to ten, was not to be thought of. They were stripped, and robbed of all they possessed, even of their clothes. They were forbidden, on pain of instant execution, to again enter the territory, which the Indians claimed as their own ; and, to recognize them in case they disobeyed the order, the chief of the tribe availed himself of a very simple device. He tattooed them on the arm in a curious way with the juice of a dye-plant and a needle-point, so that they could not remove the mark. Without further ill-treatment, they were turned adrift. They reached the northern plantations in a piteous plight, branded, so to speak, with the crest of the Indian tribe, and not at all anxious, as may be imagined, to again fall into the hands of these Seminoles, who would massacre them in order to honour their signature.

At any other time the militia of Duval county would not have allowed such a proceeding to pass with impunity.

They would have gone off in pursuit of the Indians. But at present they had something else to do besides undertaking an expedition against the nomads. The fear of seeing their country invaded by the Northerners overshadowed everything. Their only object was to prevent the Northerners becoming masters of the St. John's and the district it watered, and they could not spare a man from the Southern forces at Jacksonville and on the Georgian frontier. There would be time enough later on to take the field against the Seminoles, when they had been emboldened by the Civil War to the point of invading the enemy's territory. Then they would not be contented to drive them back into the Everglades, but would endeavour to destroy them to the last man.

It was thus dangerous to venture into the territories of Western Florida; and, if James Burbank pushed his researches in that direction, it would be to meet with more than the usual dangers.

The boat had reached the left bank of the river. Squambo, knowing where Black Creek enters the St. John's, had no fear of grounding on a shoal, and in less than five minutes he was under the branching trees in darkness deeper than that extending over the river. Accustomed as he was to the navigation of the network of the lagoon, he could advance without fear, but as he could no longer be seen, why should he not have more light on his path? A resinous branch was cut from one of the trees, and lighted, and stuck in the bow of the boat, so that its smoky light showed the way. In about half an hour Squambo traversed the meanderings of the creek, and at last he reached the island of the blockhouse.

Zermah was there made to land. Overcome with fatigue, the little girl was asleep in her arms. She did not wake when the half-breed entered the door of the fortress and was shut up in one of the rooms communicating with the central redoubt.

Dy, wrapped in a covering which was dragged from one of the corners, was laid on a sort of pallet. Zermah watched by her side.

12

CHAPTER II.

A STRANGE OPERATION.

In the morning, at eight o'clock—it was the 3rd of March —Squambo entered the room where Zermah had passed the night. He brought some food—bread, a piece of cold venison, fruits, a jug of strong beer, a pitcher of water, and the different utensils for the table. At the same time, one of the blacks placed in one of the corners an old piece of furniture with toilet necessaries, towels, and other things for the half-breed's own use and that of the little girl.

Dy was still asleep. By a gesture Zermah had besought Squambo not to wake her.

When the negro had gone out, Zermah asked the Indian in a low voice,—

"What are they going to do with us?"

"I do not know," said Squambo.

"What orders have you had from Texar?"

"Whether they come from Texar or from somebody else they are these, and you would do well to conform to them. So long as you are here, this room will be yours, and you will be kept in it during the night."

"And during the day?"

"You can walk about the enclosure."

"While we are here. But where are we?"

"Where I was told to bring you."

"And are we to remain here?"

"I have said what I had to say," said the Indian. "It is useless to ask me more; I shall not answer."

And Squambo, whose manner gave no hope of further conversation, left the room.

Zermah looked at the girl. A few tears rose to her eyes,

tears which she at once wiped away. It would never do
for Dy, when she awoke, to see that she had been crying.
It was necessary that the child should gradually become
accustomed to her new position, precarious as it might be,
for all depended on the Spaniard.

Zermah thought over what had passed during the night.
She had seen Mrs. Burbank and Alice on the bank while
the boat moved away. Their desperate appeals, their
heartrending cries, had reached her. But had they been
able to get back to Castle House along the tunnel, reach
the besieged, and tell James Burbank and his companions
of the new misfortune that had fallen on them ? Had they
been captured by the Spaniard's men, dragged far from
Camdless Bay, killed perhaps ? If so, James Burbank
would not know that his child had been carried off with
Zermah. He would think that his wife, Alice, his daughter,
and the half-breed had got safe away from Marine Creek
and reached Cedar Rock in safety. He would then make
no immediate seach for their recovery !

Supposing that Mrs. Burbank and Alice had got back to
Castle House, and James Burbank knew everything, was
there not cause to fear that the house had been entered by
the assailants, pillaged, burnt, destroyed ? In that case,
what had become of its defenders ? If they had been made
prisoners or killed in the struggle, Zermah could not hope
for any assistance on their part. Even if the Northerners
had become masters of the St. John's she was lost. Neither
Gilbert Burbank nor Mars would know that the sister of
one and the wife of the other were imprisoned in this islet
in Black Creek.

And although these things were so, and Zermah had
only herself to look to, her energy would not leave her.
She would do all she could to save this child who had
perhaps only her in the world to look to. Her life would
centre in this idea—escape ! Not an hour should pass
without her doing something towards doing so.

But was it possible to escape from the fortress watched
by Squambo and his companions, to get away from the
ferocious bloodhounds that prowled round the enclosure,

to fly from this island lost in the thousand windings of the lagoon ? Yes, it was possible, but only on condition that she was secretly helped by one of the slaves who knew the channels of Black Creek. Why should not the temptation of a large reward induce one of the men to help her in her escape ? That was the direction in which she must work.

Dy had just awoke. The first word she uttered was a call for her mother. Then she looked round the room. The remembrance of last night's events returned to her. She saw the half-breed, and ran to her.

"Good Zermah ! Good Zermah !" she murmured, " I am afraid ! I am afraid !"

"You must not be afraid, my dear."

"Where is mamma ?"

"She will come—soon. We have been obliged to save ourselves—as you know ! We are now in safety. There is nothing to fear. As soon as they have helped your father, he will come to us."

Dy looked at Zermah, as much as to say—

" Is that really true ?"

"Yes," said Zermah, who wished to give the child confidence at any cost. " Yes, Mr. Burbank told us to wait for him here."

" But the men who took us away in the boat ?" said the child, returning to the charge.

"They are the servants of Mr. Harvey, my dear. You know Mr. Harvey, your father's friend who lives at Jacksonville. We are in his cottage at Hampton Red."

" And mamma and Alice, who were with us, why are they not here ?"

"Mr. Burbank called them back as they were going to get into the boat. Do you not remember ? As soon as the naughty men have been hunted from Camdless Bay, they will come and look for you. See now ! Don't cry ! Don't be afraid, my dear, even if we stay here for some days. We are well hidden. And now let me put you straight."

Dy kept her eyes obstinately fixed on Zermah, and notwithstanding what she had been told, a heavy sigh escaped her lips. She had not woke with a smile as she usually did. It was important to keep her busy to distract her attention.

And Zermah tried to do so with the most tender solicitude. She performed her toilet with as much care as if the child were at Castle House, and at the same time tried to amuse her with her stories. Then Dy ate a little, and Zermah shared her first breakfast with her.

"Now, my dear, if you like, we will go out into the enclosure."

"Is Mr. Harvey's cottage very nice ?" asked the child.

"Nice ? No!" said Zermah. "I think it is an old hovel. But there are trees and watercourses, and a place where we can walk. We shall stay here for some days, and if you are not too tired, and are very good, mamma will be pleased."

"Yes, good Zermah, I will be good!" said the little girl.

The door of the room was not locked. Zermah took the child's hand and went out with her. They first found themselves in the central redoubt where it was dark. A moment afterwards they were in full daylight beneath the foliage of the great trees through which the sun shot its rays.

The enclosure was not large ; it was about an acre in extent, and of this the blockhouse occupied the greater portion. The palisade which surrounded it did not allow Zermah to reconnoitre the position of the island in the lagoon. All she could see through the old gateway was a tolerably wide channel, with troubled waters separating it from the neighbouring islands. A woman and a child could not but find it difficult to escape. Even supposing Zermah could get possession of a boat, how could she get out of the interminable labyrinth ? She did not know that Texar and Squambo alone knew the way, for the negroes rarely left the blockhouse. To reach the St. John's, or the marshes to the west of the creek, she would have to trust to chance. And was not that running to certain destruction ?

During the next day or two Zermah, on thinking matters over, saw that no help could be hoped from Texar's slaves. They were for the most part half-brutish negroes of forbidding appearance. The Spaniard did not keep them chained, but they had not more liberty than if he had. With plenty to eat grown on the island, and addicted to strong drink, which Squambo was not at all stingy in giving them, and specially kept for defending the blockhouse, they had no interest in changing their existence for another. The slave question debated a few miles from Black Creek had no interest for them. To gain their freedom? Why? And what would they do with it? Texar assured their existence, and Squambo did not illtreat them, although he would have smashed the head of the first man who advised them to mutiny. They never dreamt of such a thing. They were, indeed, brutes inferior to the hounds prowling round the palisade. And without exaggeration it could be said that the hounds excelled them in intelligence, for they knew all the ins and outs of the creek, and swam its multiple passes, running from islet to islet, guided by a marvellous instinct which never led them astray. Often their bark would be heard along the left bank of the river, and before night they would come back to the blockhouse all by themselves. No boat could enter Black Creek without being at once discovered by these formidable guardians. Except Squambo and Texar, no one would dare to leave the fortress without running the risk of being devoured by these savage Carib dogs.

When Zermah saw how the enclosure was watched, when she saw she could expect no help from those who guarded her, it might be thought that she gave up all thought of escape in despair. But she did not. Help might come from outside, and in that case it would come from James Burbank, if he was free to act, or from Mars when Mars learnt how his wife had disappeared. Failing these she must depend on herself for the child's safety. And she would be equal to the task.

Isolated in this lagoon, she saw herself surrounded only

by brutish men. Sometimes she thought that one of the negroes, who was still young, looked at her with pity. Was there any hope in that? Could she trust him to tell her the way to Camdless Bay, and help her to escape to Castle House? It was doubtful. And Squambo had evidently noticed that the slave was taking an interest in her, for now he was kept away, and Zermah met him no more in her walks about the enclosure.

Several days passed and there was no change in the circumstances. From morning till night Zermah and Dy were at liberty to move about as they chose. When night came, although Squambo did not lock them in their room, yet he did not allow them to leave the central redoubt. He never spoke to them, and Zermah had given up all attempts to question him. Not for a moment did he seem to leave the island. She felt that his watch over them was unceasing. And she employed herself in looking after the child, who constantly asked for her mother.

"She will come!" Zermah would reply. "I have had news of her. Your father will come too, my dear, and with Miss Alice."

And when she had said this she knew not what else to imagine; and then she did her best to amuse the child, who showed more sense than could be expected at her age.

The 4th, 5th, and 6th of March went by. Although Zermah listened for some distant detonation to announce the presence of the Federal flotilla on the waters of the St. John's, no sound reached her. All was silence at Black Creek. It was reasonable to suppose that Florida did not yet belong to the soldiers of the North. And this increased the half-breed's anxiety to the utmost. Failing James Burbank, she must trust to Gilbert and Mars. And what was very strange was that the Spaniard had not once shown himself at the blockhouse, either in the day or the night. At least, Zermah saw nothing to make her think so. And she scarcely slept, passing her long hours of insomnia in listening—always in vain.

What could she do if Texar came to Black Creek?

Would he listen to her prayers or her threats? Was not the Spaniard's presence more to be feared than his absence?

It was the night of the 6th of March, and about eleven o'clock. For the thousandth time Zermah was thinking over these things, as little Dy quietly slept. The room which served them for a cell was in deep darkness. No sound was heard without, except the whistling of the wind along the crumbling planks of the blockhouse.

Suddenly she heard some one walking into the central redoubt. At first she supposed it was the Indian going to his room opposite hers, after making his usual round to see that all was safe.

Then she heard a few words spoken by two voices. She glided to the door, and placed her ear close to it, and listened. She recognized Squambo's voice, and almost immediately afterwards Texar's.

A shudder seized her. What did the Spaniard want at this hour? Was it some new scheme against her and the child? Were they going to take them from their room, carry them to some more unknown retreat, more impenetrable than this of Black Creek? In a moment all these suppositions presented themselves. Then her energy took the upper hand, and she leant against the door and listened.

"Nothing new?" said Texar.

"Nothing, master," said Squambo.

"And Zermah?"

"I refused to answer her questions."

"Have any attempts been made to reach them from Camdless Bay?"

"Yes, but none have succeeded."

From this reply Zermah learnt that people were searching for them. Who could they be?

"How do you know?"

"I have been several times to the river-bank," said the Indian. "And a day or two ago I saw a boat laying off the Creek. The two men in her landed on one of the islands by the bank."

" Who were these two men ? "

" James Burbank and Walter Stannard."

Zermah could hardly restrain her emotion. James Burbank and Walter Stannard! And so the defenders of Castle House had not perished in the attack on the plantation. And if they had begun to search, it was because they knew that she and the child had been carried off. And if they knew that, it must be because Mrs. Burbank and Alice had told them so. So that they were alive, and they must have got back to Castle House after hearing her last shout for help against Texar. James Burbank thus knew what had happened. He knew the scoundrel's name. Perhaps he even suspected where he had hidden his victims. He might even reach them !

This chain of thought linked itself together instantly in Zermah's mind. A great hope took possession of her—a hope that vanished immediately when she heard the Spaniard answer—

" Yes ! Let them search, and they will never find them. In a few days we need have no fear of James Burbank ! "

What these words meant Zermah could not divine ; but, coming from the man whom Jacksonville obeyed, they were a formidable menace.

" And now, Squambo, I want you for an hour," said the Spaniard.

" Right."

" Follow me."

A moment afterwards they had entered the Indian's room.

What were they doing there ? Was it some secret that Zermah ought to know ? In her position she should neglect nothing that might be of use to her.

Her room door, as we know, was not locked during the night. The precaution would have been useless, as the redoubt was locked, and Squambo kept the key. It was impossible to get out of the blockhouse, and consequently to attempt escape.

Zermah could thus open her door and step out. She held her breath as she did so.

The darkness was intense. Only a few streaks of light came from the Indian's room.

Zermah crept to the door, and peeped through the crack between two planks. What she saw was too strange for her to understand its meaning.

Although the room was lighted only by the fag-end of a resinous torch, the light was enough for the Indian, who was occupied in a work of great delicacy.

Texar was seated in front of him, with his leather coat thrown back, and with his left arm bare and stretched out on a little table just under the light of the torch. A piece of paper of curious shape, pierced with little holes, was laid on the inner part of the fore-arm. With a fine needle, Squambo pricked the skin in every place where there was a hole in the paper. The Indian was tattooing, and, as a Seminole, he was an expert at such work. He did it with such skill and lightness of hand that the epidermis was only just touched by the needle-point, and the Spaniard felt not the least discomfort.

When he had done, Squambo lifted the paper ; then, taking a few leaves of a plant Texar had brought with him, he rubbed them over the fore-arm. The sap of the plant rubbed into the needle punctures caused a sharp itching, but the Spaniard was not the man to trouble himself about such small matters.

This part of the operation over, Squambo held the torch close to the tattooed place. A reddish design then appeared on the skin. The design was an exact copy of that formed by the needle-holes in the paper. It was a series of inter-crossed lines, representing one of the symbolic figures of the Seminole religion. The mark could never more be effaced from the arm on which Squambo had put it.

Zermah had seen it all, and, as we have said, could understand nothing of it. What interest could Texar have in being thus tattooed ? Why this "particular sign," as the passports say ? Did he wish to pass as an Indian ? Neither his complexion nor his features would admit of his doing so. Was there any connection between this mark and that which had been put on the Floridans who had been robbed by the Seminoles? And, on account of it, was he going to prove one of those inexplicable *alibis* which had hitherto stood him in such good stead?

Perhaps this was one of the secrets of his life which the future would reveal.

Another question presented itself to Zermah. Had not the Spaniard come to the blockhouse to avail himself of Squambo's cleverness as a tattooer? Was he going back to Jacksonville, where his partisans were still in power? Or was he going to stop at the blockhouse day after day and make fresh arrangements regarding his prisoners?

Zermah's anxiety was not of long duration. She had slipped back to her room as soon as the Spaniard rose to enter the central chamber. Hidden by the door, she heard the few words exchanged between the Indian and his master.

"Watch them with more care than ever," he said.

"Yes," replied Squambo. "But if we are closely pressed by James Burbank—"

"James Burbank, I tell you, will not trouble you after a few days. Besides, you know where to take the half-breed and child—where I shall meet you again."

"Yes, master," said Squambo; "for we must provide against Gilbert Burbank, or Mars, Zermah's husband—"

"Before forty-eight hours they will both be in my power, and when I get them—"

Zermah did not hear the end of the sentence which threatened her husband and Gilbert so seriously.

Texar and Squambo then left the redoubt, and the door shut behind them.

A few minutes later the skiff paddled by the Indian left the island, traversed the sombre sinuosities of the lagoon, and put the Spaniard on board a boat that was waiting for him off the creek. Squambo and his master then separated, Texar going down with the tide to Jacksonville.

He arrived there at dawn, in time to put his plans into execution. And soon afterwards Mars disappeared in the waters of the St. John's, and Gilbert Burbank was condemned to death.

CHAPTER III.

THE DAY BEFORE.

IT was in the morning of the 11th of March that Gilbert Burbank had been tried by the Jacksonville Committee ; and the same evening his father had been arrested. The next day but one the young officer was to be shot, and doubtless James Burbank, charged as being his accomplice, and sentenced to the same penalty, would die with him.

As we know, Texar held the Committee in his hand. His word alone was law. The execution of the father and the son would be the prelude to sanguinary excesses against the Northerners in Florida, and all who shared in their ideas on the slavery question. What an amount of personal vengeance would be gratified under the cloak of civil war ! Nothing but the presence of the Federal troops could put a stop to this. But would they come, and, above all, would they come before the first victims had been sacrificed to the Spaniard's hatred ?

Unfortunately it seemed to be doubtful.

One can fancy the anguish at Castle House at this prolonged delay.

It seemed as though the plan of ascending the St. John's had been temporarily abandoned by Stevens. The gunboats made no movement to leave their anchorage. Did they not dare to clear the bar now that Mars was not with them to pilot them along the channel ? Had they given up the idea of taking Jacksonville, and by the capture assuring safety to the plantations on the St. John's ? What new events of the war had modified the projects of Commodore Dupont ?

Such were the questions that Mr. Stannard and Overseer

Perry asked themselves during this interminable day of the 12th of March.

From the news then current it seemed that the Federal efforts in this part of Florida, between the river and the sea, were confined to the coast. Commodore Dupont, in the *Wabash*, with the heaviest gunboats of the squadron, had just appeared in the Bay of St. Augustine. It was even reported that the militia were preparing to abandon the town without attempting to defend Fort Marion any more than Fort Church had been defended at the surrender of Fernandina.

Such, at least, was the news brought by the overseer during the morning to Castle House; and he at once reported it to Mr. Stannard and Edward Carrol, who, his wound not having healed, was obliged to recline on one of the sofas in the hall.

"The Federals at St. Augustine!" said the latter; "and why do they not come to Jacksonville?"

"Perhaps they wish only to blockade the river without taking possession," answered Perry.

"James and Gilbert are lost if Jacksonville remains in Texar's hands," said Mr. Stannard.

"Could I not go," said Perry, "and tell Commodore Dupont that Mr. Burbank and his son are in such danger?"

"It would take a day to reach St. Augustine," said Carrol, "even supposing that you were not stopped by the retreating militia. And before Dupont could order Stevens to occupy Jacksonville, too much time would have gone! Besides, there is this bar—this river bar, which the gunboats cannot pass. How can they save our poor Gilbert, who is to die to-morrow? No! it is not to St. Augustine you should go, but to Jacksonville! It is not to Commodore Dupont you should appeal, but to—Texar!"

"Mr. Carrol is right, father, and I will go!" said Alice, who had heard the few last words.

The brave girl was ready to risk everything for Gilbert's safety.

The evening before, when he left Camdless Bay, James

Burbank had particularly enjoined that his wife should **not** be told of his departure to Jacksonville. It was better to hide from her that the Committee had ordered his arrest. Mrs. Burbank was thus unaware of his having gone, as she was unaware of the fate of her son, whom she believed to be on board the flotilla. How could the unhappy woman bear up under the double blow that had fallen on her? Her husband in the power of Texar, her son on the eve of being executed! She would never survive it. When she had asked to see James Burbank, Alice had replied that he had left Castle House in resumption of his search after Dy and Zermah, and that he would be away forty-eight hours. So that all Mrs. Burbank's thoughts were concentrated on her stolen child.

Alice knew all the dangers that threatened James and Gilbert Burbank. She knew that the young officer was to be shot in the morning, and that the same fate was in store for his father. But though she knew all this, she resolved to see Texar, and asked Mr. Carrol to take her across the river.

"You—Alice—at Jacksonville!" exclaimed Mr. Stannard.

"Father, it is necessary!"

Mr. Stannard's very natural hesitation suddenly ceased before the necessity of acting without delay. If Gilbert could be saved, it was only by the way Alice wished to try. Perhaps by casting herself at Texar's knees she could shake his resolution! Perhaps she might obtain a respite! Perhaps she might find support among the better citizens who might be induced to rise against the intolerable tyranny of the Committee! In short, she must go to Jacksonville whatever danger she might run.

"Perry," she said, "will you take me to Mr. Harvey's house?"

"Immediately," said the overseer.

"No, Alice; I will go with you," said Mr. Stannard. "Yes, I will! Let us start—"

"You, Stannard?" asked Carrol. "You are exposing your life. They know your opinions."

" What does it matter ?" said Mr. Stannard. " I will not
let my daughter go alone amongst those vagabonds.
Perry can stay at Castle House, as you cannot walk yet,
for we must prepare in case we are detained—"

" If Mrs. Burbank asks for you," said Carrol, " if she asks
for Alice, what am I to say ?"

" Say that we have gone with James in his search on the
other side of the river. Tell her, if necessary, that we have
had to go to Jacksonville—in fact anything you like to keep
her quiet, but nothing to lead her to suspect the dangers
that surround her husband and son. Perry, get a boat
ready."

The overseer retired at once, leaving Mr. Stannard to
prepare for his journey.

It would be better for Alice not to leave Castle House
without telling Mrs. Burbank that she and her father had
been obliged to go to Jacksonville. If need be she could
even say that Texar's party had been superseded, that the
Federals were masters of the river, that to-morrow Gilbert
would be at Camdless Bay. But would the girl have
sufficient self-command, would her voice not betray her
when she asserted as facts what now seemed impossible ?

When she arrived in the invalid's room Mrs. Burbank
was asleep, or rather deep in sorrowful slumber, in profound
torpor, from which Alice had not the courage to wake her.
Perhaps it was better that the girl had no need to speak
and soothe her.

One of the women of the house watched near the bed.
Alice told her not to leave for a moment, and to ask Mr.
Carrol to answer Mrs. Burbank's questions. Then she
bent over the unhappy mother, almost till their lips met,
and then she went out and joined her father.

As soon as she saw him, " Let us go," she said.

They clasped Carrol's hand and went out from the hall.
In the middle of the bamboo-path to the landing-path they
met the overseer.

" The boat is ready," said he.

" Good," said Mr. Stannard. " Keep careful guard over
the house, my friend."

PART II.

"Never fear, Mr. Stannard, our blacks are coming back to the plantation, and that means much. What would they do with a freedom for which nature has not created them ? Bring us back Mr. Burbank, and they will all be found at their post."

Mr. Stannard and his daughter took their places in the boat with four of the Camdless Bay men. The sail was hoisted, and under a light easterly breeze they speedily left the shore.

Mr. Stannard thought it best not to land at the wharf at Jacksonville, where he would inevitably be recognized, but to run into a little creek a short distance above. From there it would be easy to reach Mr. Harvey's house, which was on this side and well out in the suburbs. Once there they could consult over matters and act accordingly

The river at this time was deserted. Nothing above stream ; nothing below. There had been no fight between the Floridan vessels and the gunboats under Commandant Stevens, whose anchorage could not even be seen, owing to a bend in the St. John's closing the horizon below Jacksonville.

After a quick passage, Mr. Stannard and his daughter reached the left bank. Without being noticed they were able to land in the creek, which was not watched, and in a few minutes they found themselves in the house of James Burbank's correspondent.

Mr. Harvey was much surprised and much alarmed to see them. Their presence could not be without danger among a mob more and more excited and quite devoted to Texar. It was known that Stannard shared in the anti-slavery ideas adopted at Camdless Bay. The pillage of his house at Jacksonville was a warning that could not be disregarded.

Assuredly he was running a great risk. The least that could happen to him, if he was discovered, was to be imprisoned as an accomplice of James Burbank's.

"We must save Gilbert !" was all that Miss Alice could answer to Mr. Harvey's observations.

"Yes," he said. "We must try ! But Mr. Stannard

must not go out of this house! He must stay here while we act."

"Will they let me into the prison?" asked Alice.

"I do not think so, Miss Stannard."

"Shall I get to see Texar?"

"We will try."

"Will you not let me go with you?" said Mr. Stannard.

"No! that would do harm with Texar and his Committee."

"Come, then, Mr. Harvey," said Alice.

Before they left, however, Mr. Stannard asked if there had been any war news which had not yet reached Camdless Bay.

"None," said Mr. Harvey; "at least none that concerns Jacksonville. The Federal flotilla has appeared in the Bay of St. Augustine, and the town has been surrendered. At the St. John's nothing has been done; the gunboats are still at anchor below the bar."

"The water is too low for them to get over."

"Yes, Mr. Stannard; but to-day we are to have one of the highest tides of the equinox. It will be high water for three hours, and perhaps the gunboats will clear it—"

"Clear it without a pilot, now that Mars is no longer there to guide them through the channels!" said Alice in a tone which showed that she thought little of this hope. "No! It is impossible! Mr. Harvey, I must see Texar, and if he repulses me, we must sacrifice everything to help Gilbert escape—"

"And we will do so, Miss Stannard."

"Feeling has not changed in Jacksonville?" asked Mr. Stannard.

"No," replied Mr. Harvey. "The roughs are the masters, and Texar leads them. But owing to the exactions and menaces of the Committee the respectable people are growling with indignation, and it only wants a movement of the Federals on the river to bring about an immediate change. The mob is a cowardly mob; and if they have cause to fear, Texar and his partisans will be upset. I hope still that Commandant Stevens will be able to clear the bar—"

13

"We will wait for that," said Alice resolutely; "and before then I shall have seen Texar."

It was then agreed that Mr. Stannard should remain in the house, so that his presence in Jacksonville should not be known. Mr. Harvey was to help Alice in all her plans, the success of which, it was well understood, was problematical. If Texar refused to give Gilbert his life, if Alice could not get to see him, they would try even at the cost of a fortune to procure the escape of the prisoners.

It was about eleven o'clock when Alice and Mr. Harvey left the house for the Courts of Justice, where the Committee under Texar's presidency was in permanent session.

The town was still in a state of great excitement. The militia, reinforced by the detachments arrived from the South, were constantly on the move. Those set free by the surrender of St. Augustine were expected during the day, either by the St. John's or by the road through the forests on its right bank. The people thronged the streets. A thousand rumours were afloat, contradictory as usual, and provoking a tumult akin to disorder. It was easy to see that if the Federals did arrive there would be no unity of action in the defence; there would be no serious resistance. Fernandina had surrendered nine days before to the troops landed under General Wright; St. Augustine had received Dupont's flotilla without even attempting to bar his passage; and so would it be at Jacksonville. The Florida Militia would give place to the Northern troops, and would retire into the interior of the country. There was only one thing to save Jacksonville from capture, to prolong the powers of the Committee and allow them to accomplish their sanguinary plans; that was, that for want of water or want of a pilot the gunboats kept outside the bar. And in a few hours it would be seen if this were to be the case.

Through a crowd which grew closer at every step, Alice and Mr. Harvey made their way to the principal square. How were they to get into the court? They could not imagine. Once there, how could they get to see Texar? They did not know. Who could tell if the Spaniard, when he heard that Alice Stannard demanded to see him, would not arrest her and imprison her until after the lieutenant's execution? But she would not think of such things. To see Texar, to compel him to have mercy on Gilbert, no personal danger would be too great for her to run.

When she and Mr. Harvey reached the square, they found there a still more tumultuous crowd. Shouts rent the air, and these words of menace were yelled from one group to another: "Death! Death!"

Mr. Harvey ascertained that the Committee had been sitting as a court of justice for an hour. A dreadful presentiment seized on him, and the presentiment was only too well justified. The Committee were trying James Burbank for being the accomplice of his son Gilbert, and holding communication with the Federal army. The same crime, the same sentence, there could be no doubt, and the crowning of Texar's work against the Burbank family.

Mr. Harvey would have gone no further. He tried to lead Alice away. He would not subject her to the sight of the violence which the people threatened when the condemned men came out of the court after sentence was pronounced. This was hardly the time to seek an interview with the Spaniard.

"Come away, Miss Stannard," said Mr. Harvey. "Come away! We will come back when the Committee—"

"No!" answered Alice. "I will throw myself between the accused and their judges—"

The girl's resolution was such that Mr. Harvey despaired of overcoming it. Alice led the way. He was bound to follow her. The crowd was quiet—some of them recognized her, perhaps, and yet it opened to let her pass. The cries of "Death!" sounded horribly in her ears. Nothing could stop her. She reached the doors of the court. Here the crowd was rougher than ever,—not the roughness that follows the storm, but that which precedes it. The most terrible excesses were to be feared.

Suddenly a tumultuous wave burst from the court. The shouts redoubled. Sentence had been given.

James Burbank, like Gilbert, had been condemned for

the same pretended crime to the same penalty. Father
and son would fall before the same firing platoon.

"Death! Death!" yelled the crowd of roughs.

James Burbank appeared on the steps. He was calm
and collected. A look of scorn was all he had for the
shouting crowd.

A detachment of militia surrounded him, with orders to
take him back to prison.

He was not alone.

Gilbert was by his side.

Taken from the cell where he awaited the hour of execution, the young officer had been brought into the Committee's presence to be confronted with James Burbank,
who could only confirm what his son had said. Gilbert
had come to Castle House to see his dying mother for the
last time. On the evidence the charge would have collapsed,
had not the trial been settled beforehand. The same doom
awaited both innocent men—a doom imposed by personal
vengeance, and pronounced by iniquitous judges.

The crowd closed on the prisoners. It was with great
difficulty that the militia could clear the way.

There was a sudden movement in the crowd. Alice
rushed towards the father and son.

Involuntarily the mob recoiled, surprised by this unexpected attempt.

"Alice!" exclaimed Gilbert.

"Gilbert! Gilbert!" murmured Alice as she fell into
his arms.

"Alice! why are you here?" asked James Burbank.

"To ask mercy for you. To beg it from your judges.
Mercy! mercy for them!"

The girl's cries were heart-breaking. She clung to the
clothes of the doomed men, who had for a moment
stopped.

Could they hope for pity from the wild crowd that surrounded them? No! But her intervention for a moment
prevented them from proceeding to violence, in defiance of
the militia guard.

Texar, informed of what was happening, appeared at the

threshold of the Courts of Justice. A gesture from him silenced the crowd. The order he gave was to take the Burbanks back to prison.

The detachment resumed its march.

"Mercy! mercy!" sobbed Alice, throwing herself at Texar's knees.

The Spaniard's reply was a gesture of refusal.

The girl stood up.

"Scoundrel!" she said.

She would have rejoined the prisoners, followed them to the prison, and spent with them the last hours left them to live.

They were already out of the square, the crowd escorting them with yells and insults.

It was more than Alice could bear. Her strength abandoned her. She staggered and fell. She had neither feeling nor consciousness when Mrs. Harvey received her in her arms.

She did not come to herself till she was with her father in Mr. Harvey's house.

"To the prison! To the prison!" she murmured. "Both of them must escape."

"Yes," said Mr. Stannard. "That is all we can try! Wait till night comes!"

Nothing could be done during the day. When darkness enabled them to act with more safety, without fear of being surprised, Mr. Stannard and Mr. Harvey would endeavour to help the prisoners escape, with the connivance of their guard. They would take money with them, so much—so they hoped—that the man would be unable to resist them; particularly as a single shot from Stevens's gunboats might end the Spaniard's power.

But night came, and they had to give up all thought of their scheme. The prison was guarded by a detachment of militia, and all idea of flight was in vain.

CHAPTER IV.

A GALE FROM THE NORTH-EAST.

THERE was now only one chance for the doomed men—that before a dozen hours had elapsed the Federals were masters of the town. At sunrise James and Gilbert Burbank would be shot. Their prison was watched, so was Mr. Harvey's house ; how could they escape ?

The capture of Jacksonville could not be made by the troops landed at Fernandina, who could not abandon that important position in the north of Florida. The task must be that of the gunboats : to accomplish it the bar must be crossed. Then when the line of boats was driven back, the flotilla could anchor opposite the town. Once they had the town under their guns, the militia would beat a retreat to the marshes. Texar and his partisans would certainly follow them, to avoid the well-deserved reprisals. The respectable citizens would then resume the place from which they had been hunted with such indignity, and negotiate with the Federal representatives for the surrender.

Was it possible to effect this passage of the bar, and within the time ? Was there any way of overcoming the obstacle which the want of water put in the way of the gunboats ? It was very doubtful, as we shall see.

After sentence was pronounced Texar and the commander of the militia went down to the wharf to inspect the lower course of the river. Their attention was fixed on the bar.

"Nothing fresh has been reported ? " asked Texar, as he stopped at the end of the stockade.

"Nothing," said the officer. "A reconnaissance I sent out to the north tells me that the Federals have not left

Fernandina for Jacksonville. Probably they are kept in observation on the Georgian frontier until their flotilla has forced the channel."

"Have any troops come from the south, from St. Augustine, and crossed the St. John's at Picolata?"

"I think not. Dupont has only troops enough to occupy the town, and his object is to blockade the whole coast from the St. John's to the furthest inlets of Florida. We have nothing to fear from that side, Texar!"

"Then the only danger is from the flotilla if it clears the bar, below which it has been at anchor for three days."

"That is so. And the question will be decided in a few hours. Perhaps, after all, the enemy's object is to close the river so as to cut off the communication between St. Augustine and Fernandina! It is most to his interest not to occupy Florida at present, but to stop the contraband of war coming in from the south. The expedition has no other object—at least I think not. If it had, the troops at Amelia Island would have been on the march to Jacksonville."

"You may be right," said Texar. "It doesn't matter! But I wish this question of the bar was over."

"It will be settled this very day."

"If the gunboats do come, what will you do?"

"Act according to my orders, and take the militia into the interior, so as to avoid all contact with the Federals. If they can occupy the towns, let them. They cannot keep them long, for they will be cut off from their communications with Georgia and the Carolinas, and we shall soon retake them."

"But," said Texar, "if they are masters of Jacksonville only for a day, we must expect reprisals. All these pretended honest men, these rich planters, and abolitionists will return to power, and then— But it shall not be! No! and rather than abandon the town—"

The Spaniard did not finish his thought, but it was easy to see his meaning. He would not surrender the town to the Federals, who would place it in the hands of the magistrates he had supplanted. He would give it to the flames; and perhaps his measures were taken with a view to this work of destruction. Then he and his followers would retire after the militia, and in the marshes of the south find an inaccessible retreat, where they could await events.

But there was nothing of this to be feared if the gunboats could not clear the bar, and the time had come to settle the question.

The people came crowding on to the wharves. A moment was enough to show why they had come. Deafening shouts arose.

"The gunboats are coming!"

"No! they have not moved."

"The sea is open!"

"They are going to try it at full speed!"

"Look! look!"

"So they are!" said the commander of the militia. "There is something! Look, Texar!"

The Spaniard did not reply. He never took his eyes from where the horizon was closed by the line of boats drawn across the stream. Half a mile below were the spars and funnels of the gun-vessels. A thick smoke was rising, and driven by the wind came floating up to Jacksonville.

Evidently Stevens, taking advantage of the full tide, was trying to cross the bar at all costs. Would he do so? Would he find enough water, even if he scraped his keels as he came? No wonder there was violent excitement among the crowds on the bank of the St. John's.

And the excitement increased as some thought they saw something, and others thought they did not.

"They have gained half a cable!"

"No! they have not moved further than if their anchor was still down."

"There is one moving."

"Yes; but she is swinging on a pivot because she has not got water enough."

"What a smoke!"

"They may burn all the coal in the States, but they won't get over."

" And now the tide is slackening ! "

" Hurrah for the South ! "

" Hurrah ! "

The flotilla's attempt lasted about ten minutes—ten minutes which appeared long to Texar, to his partisans, and to all there whose liberty or life would be endangered by the capture of Jacksonville. What had really happened they did not know ; the distance was too great for them to be sure. Had the channel been forced or not ? By discharging all useless weight to lighten his draught, had Stevens been able to clear the narrow shoal that kept him out of the deep water, by which the passage up to the town would be easy ? So long as the tide was on the turn there was a chance that he might.

But as the people said, the tide had begun to run out. Once the ebb began, the level of the St. John's would soon sink.

Suddenly arms were stretched towards the bar, and there was a shout that was heard over all,—

" A boat ! a boat ! "

A little boat was sighted coming along the left bank, where the flow of the tide was still perceptible, while the ebb appeared in mid-channel. The boat rowed up rapidly. In the stern sat an officer in the uniform of the Florida Militia. He soon reached the stockade, and, running up the ladder, landed on the wharf. Perceiving Texar he came towards him, followed by a crowd almost choking with anxiety to see and hear.

" What is it ? " asked the Spaniard.

" Nothing, and there will be nothing ! " said the officer.

" Who sent you ? "

" The commander of the boats, who will soon be back here."

" And why ? "

" Because the gunboats have failed in crossing the bar, although they were lightened for draught and were driven at full speed. There is now nothing to fear—"

" For this tide ? " asked Texar

" Nor for any other—at least for some months."

"Hurrah ! Hurrah !"

The cheers spread over the town. And as the roughs more than ever cheered the Spaniard, in whom all their detestable instincts were incarnate, the respectable people saw with despair that for some time yet they would be under the iniquitous rule of the Committee and its chief.

The officer's report was true. From that day the tide would decrease each day. The tide of the 12th of March was one of the highest of the year, and several months would elapse before it again reached the same level. The bar being impassable, Jacksonville would escape Stevens's guns. Texar would remain in power ; the scoundrel would accomplish his work of vengeance. Even if General Sherman sent Wright to occupy the town with the troops landed at Fernandina, the march would take several days. As far as the Burbanks were concerned, their execution being fixed for the next morning, nothing could save them.

The news spread to the suburbs. We can imagine its effect on the riotous portion of the community. Decent people prepared to leave a town in which they could not be safe.

The cheering and shouting reached the prisoners, and told them that all hope of life had vanished, and they were heard in Mr. Harvey's house. We need not dwell on the despair with which they filled Mr. Stannard and his daughter. What could they do now to save James Burbank and his son ? Corrupt the gaoler ? They could not now leave the house in which they had taken refuge ! A troop of desperadoes kept them in sight, whose curses could be heard at the door.

Night came on. The weather, which had been threatening for some hours, changed rapidly ; the wind had gone round to the north-east. Great masses of grey, broken clouds came racing past, too hurriedly to dissolve in rain, and almost low enough to sweep the surface of the sea. A frigate's masts would certainly have reached into the mass of vapour. The barometer suddenly fell, and there was every sign of a storm over the distant Atlantic.

From its position the storm would strike full into the

estuary of the St. John's. It would raise the waters and drive them back like the bores of large rivers, and the flood would rise over the lands by the river-side.

During this night of trouble Jacksonville was swept with terrible violence. A part of the stockade succumbed to the fury of the surf against the stockades ; the water came over the wharf, and dashed to pieces on it several dogger-boats, whose cables broke like threads. It was impossible to remain in the streets or squares owing to the shower of fragments that rained down from the roofs. People took refuge in the public-houses, and the noise therein con-tended, not without advantage, with the roar of the storm.

It was not only over the land that the gale raged. In the St. John's, the agitation of the waters produced quite a furious sea. The boats moored above the bar were caught in the storm before they could get into safety ; their grap-nels broke, and their cables parted. The night's tide, increased by the gale, carried them up the river resistlessly. Some were stove against the piles, others were swept past Jacksonville and lost on the islands and points miles up the St. John's. Many of the sailors lost their lives in the storm, which came on so suddenly as to render useless the measures usually taken under such circumstances.

Had the gunboats weighed anchor and steamed off to shelter in the creeks at the mouth ? Had they, thanks to this precaution, escaped complete destruction ? Had they gone out of the river ? That they had remained at their anchors Jacksonville could not believe, for the bar would now be impassable.

Darkness enveloped the valley of the St. John's, while the air and the water mingled together as if some chemical action was trying to combine them into one element. It was one of those cataclysms which are so frequent at the equinox, but in violence it exceeded all that this part of Florida had experienced.

Owing to its violence the storm lasted but a few hours. Before the sun rose the storm had passed over into the Gulf of Mexico.

About four o'clock, as the first streaks of dawn were

tinting the horizon, a calm succeeded to the tumult of the
night, and the people began to crowd into the streets from
the drinking-bars where they had taken refuge. The
militia reappeared at their deserted posts. The damages
caused by the tempest began to be taken in hand, particularly along the river front, where they were considerable,
the tide bringing down with it many of the drifted boats
that had been wrecked and carried up the river.

But these wrecks could only be seen for a few yards out
from the bank, as a dense fog had accumulated over the
river, and was rising towards the higher zones that had
been cooled by the tempest. At five o'clock the centre of
the stream was still invisible, although but a few moments
would elapse before it would be dissipated in the rays of
the sun.

Suddenly, just after five o'clock, loud reports broke
through the mist. There could be no mistake. It was
not the long roll of thunder, but the formidable detonations
of artillery ! Something whistled characteristically over-
head ; a shout of terror rose from the crowd, who rushed
towards the wharf.

The fog began to open ; it was pierced by bang after
bang. Its wreaths mingled with the smoke from the guns
and fell to the river.

There lay Stevens's gunboats in line before Jacksonville, which they commanded completely within short
range !

"The gunboats ! The gunboats !"

The words, repeated from mouth to mouth, soon spread
to the outskirts. In a few minutes the respectable population with extreme satisfaction, the disreputable population with extreme alarm, learnt that Stevens was master
of the St. John's.

What had happened ? Had the Northerners found the
storm of unexpected assistance ? Yes. The gunboats
had not sought shelter in the lower creeks of the estuary.
Notwithstanding the violence of the wind and sea, they
had held to their anchors. While the enemy cleared off
with his small craft, Stevens rode out the hurricane at the

risk of disaster, so as to attempt the passage, which circumstances had made practicable.

The storm, by driving back the waters up the estuary, had raised the level of the stream above the normal height, and the gunboats being driven at full speed at the bar, had safely got over, although they had scraped the sand with their keels.

About four o'clock in the morning, Stevens, coming up in the fog, calculated that he was off Jacksonville. There he had anchored. And when all was ready he had rent the mists by the discharge of his heavy guns, and hurled his first projectiles at the left bank of the St. John's.

The effect was instantaneous. In a few minutes the militia had evacuated the town, following the example of the Southern troops at Fernandina and St. Augustine. Stevens, seeing the wharves deserted, began at once to slacken fire, his object being not to destroy Jacksonville, but to occupy it.

Almost immediately a white flag was displayed on the Courts of Justice.

When the guns were first heard in Mr. Harvey's house, great was the anxiety. The town was certainly attacked. The attack could only come from the Federals. Either they had ascended the St. John's, or come from the north of Florida. Was this the unhoped-for chance of safety— the only one that could save James and Gilbert Burbank ?

Mr. Harvey and Alice rushed to the door of the house. Texar's men who were on guard had taken flight and followed the militia.

Alice and her companion rushed to the riverside. The fog was just vanishing and the other bank of the river could be seen.

The gunboats were silent, for already Jacksonville had abandoned its resistance.

A number of boats had put off from the flotilla, and were landing on the quay a detachment armed with rifles, revolvers, and axes.

Suddenly a shout was heard among the sailors.

The man who had shouted rushed towards Alice.

"Mars! Mars!" she exclaimed, stupefied to find herself in the presence of Zermah's husband, who she thought had been drowned.

"Mr. Gilbert! Mr. Gilbert!" asked Mars. "Where is he?"

"Prisoner with Mr. Burbank! Save him, Mars! Save him! and save his father!"

"To the prison!" shouted Mars, turning and joining his companions.

And then all set off at a run to prevent a last crime being committed by Texar.

Mr. Harvey and Alice followed them.

So that, after jumping into the water, Mars had escaped the eddies on the bar? Yes! And the brave half-breed had prudently refrained from letting his safety be known at Castle House. To have sought there for shelter would have been to risk his safety, and to accomplish his work he must be free. Having swum to the right bank of the river, he had been able, by creeping through the reeds, to get down opposite the flotilla. There his signals had been noticed, and a boat had been sent to bring him on board Stevens's vessel. Stevens was fully informed of what had occurred, and on account of Gilbert's imminent danger efforts were made to get through the channel. But they were useless, as we know, and the operation was about to be abandoned when, during the night, the storm raised the river level. But without knowledge of the difficult waterway the flotilla might have grounded on the shoals. Fortunately Mars was there. He had skilfully piloted the commandant's gunboat, and the others followed, notwithstanding the storm. And before the fog had risen on the St. John's, they were anchored with the town under their guns.

It was time, for the two men were to be executed at daylight. But already all cause for fear had been removed. The magistrates had resumed the authority usurped by Texar. And when Mars and his companions reached the prison, James and Gilbert Burbank were coming out, free at last.

In a moment the young lieutenant had clasped Alice to his breast, while Stannard and James Burbank fell into each other's arms.

" My mother ? " asked Gilbert.

" She lives ! she lives ! " answered Alice.

" Well, let us go to Castle House ! " said Gilbert.

" Not before justice is done ! " answered James Burbank.

Mars understood his master. He rushed towards the main square, in the hope of finding Texar.

Would not the Spaniard have already taken flight, so as to avoid reprisals ? Would he not have withdrawn himself from public vengeance with all those concerned with him in the late period of excess ? Would he not have followed the militia, who were in full retreat ?

It would have been thought so.

But, without waiting for the intervention of the Federals, a number of the inhabitants had run to the Courts of Justice. Texar was arrested at the moment he was about to escape. He was put under a guard ; and very resigned to his fate did he appear. But when Mars came towards him, he saw that his life was in danger.

The half-breed threw himself on him. In spite of the efforts of those who guarded him, he seized him by the throat, and would have strangled him there and then, if James Burbank and his son had not appeared.

" No ! no ! Living ! " shouted James Burbank. " He must live ! he must speak ! "

" Yes, he must ! " said Mars.

A few minutes later Texar was locked up in the very cell where his victims had awaited the hour of execution.

CHAPTER V.

A PRISONER.

AT last the Federals were masters of Jacksonville, and consequently of the St. John's. The troops brought by Commandant Stevens immediately occupied the chief points of the city. The usurping authorities had fled. Of the old committee only Texar had been captured.

Whether owing to weariness at the exactions of the last few days, or to indifference on the slavery question, the people did not give at all a bad reception to the officers of the flotilla, who represented the government of Washington.

Meanwhile, Commodore Dupont at St. Augustine busied himself in closing the Floridan coast against contraband of war. The passes of Mosquito inlet were all seized. That at once cut off the trade in arms and munitions with the Bahamas. It was evident that henceforth Florida would be subject to the Federal Government.

The same day as the surrender of Jacksonville, James and Gilbert Burbank and Mr. Stannard and his daughter crossed the St. John's to Camdless Bay.

Perry and the assistant-overseers were waiting for them at the little landing-place with a few of the blacks who had returned to the plantation. It can be imagined how they were received, and with what demonstrations they were welcomed.

Soon James Burbank and his companions were at his wife's bedside.

It was when she thus again beheld her son that for the first time she learnt what had passed. The young officer clasped her in his arms. Her people would never leave her again. Alice could give her all her attention. She would soon recover her strength. There was nothing now to fear from Texar's schemings. The Spaniard was in the hands of the Federals, and the Federals were masters of Jacksonville.

But if she had to tremble no more for her husband and son, her whole thought was on her daughter. She wanted Dy; and Mars must find Zermah.

"We shall find them!" exclaimed James Burbank. "Mars and Gilbert will help in the search."

"Yes, father, and without losing a day!"

"As we have got hold of Texar," said Mr. Burbank, "Texar must speak."

"And if he refuses to speak?" asked Mr. Stannard. "If he pretends he knows nothing about the disappearance of Dy and Zermah?"

"And how can he?" said Gilbert. "Did not Zermah recognize him at Marine Creek? Did not Alice and mother hear Zermah shout his name as the boat moved off? Can you doubt that he was the author of the outrage, and was in command there?"

"It was Texar!" said Mrs. Burbank, rising as if she would have thrown herself out of bed.

"Yes," said Alice, "I recognized him! He was standing up in the stern of the boat, which he was steering into mid-stream."

"Be it so," said Mr. Stannard. "It was Texar. There is no doubt! But if he refuses to say where he has hidden them, where are we to look?—for we have searched in vain along the river for miles."

To this question, so clearly put, there was no reply. All depended on what the Spaniard said. Was it his interest to speak or be silent?

"Do you not know where the scoundrel usually lives?" asked Gilbert.

"No one knows; no one has ever known," said James Burbank. "In the south of the country there are so many huge forests and inaccessible marshes where he could hide himself. To explore that country would be in vain. The

14

Federals themselves could not there pursue the retreating militia. It would be trouble thrown away."

" I must have my daughter ! " exclaimed Mr. Burbank

" My wife ! I will find my wife ! " said Mars ; " and I will force the rascal to tell me where she is."

" Yes," said James Burbank, " when the man sees he may save his life by speaking, he will speak. If he were in flight we might despair. With him in Federal hands, we can get his secret out of him. Have confidence, my poor wife ! We are on the track, and we will give you back your child."

Mrs. Burbank fainted and fell back on her bed. Alice remained with her, while Mr. Stannard, James Burbank, Gilbert and Mars went down into the hall to talk matters over with Edward Carrol.

It was agreed to wait till the Federals had organized their capture, and that Commodore Dupont should be informed of the facts relative not only to Jacksonville, but to Camdless Bay. Perhaps he would decide to bring Texar at once before a military tribunal ?

Gilbert and Mars would not let the day pass without starting on their search. While James Burbank and Stannard and Carrol were thinking over the first steps, they would be off up the St. John's, in the hope of discovering a clue.

Was it not to be feared that Texar would refuse to speak, and in his hatred prefer to undergo the last penalty, rather than surrender his victims ? Better to do without him. Let them discover where it was he lived. But that was a vain search. They knew nothing of Black Creek. They thought the lagoon was inaccessible. And they passed along by the thicket on the bank without discovering the narrow entrance.

During the 13th of March there was no change in the situation. At Camdless Bay the reorganization of the estate proceeded slowly. From all parts of the district, from the neighbouring forests, into which they had been forced to disperse, the blacks were returning in great numbers. Although set at liberty by the generous act of

James Burbank, they did not think that all obligation to him was at an end. They would be his servants if they could not be his slaves. They longed to get back on the plantation, to rebuild the barracoons destroyed by Texar's roughs, to set up the factories and refit the workshops, and resume the work which for so many years had been the welfare and happiness of their families.

The routine of the plantation was first taken in hand. Edward Carrol, almost cured of his wound, resumed his accustomed work. There was plenty of zeal on the part of Perry and the assistant-overseers. Even Pyg bestirred himself, although he did not do much. The poor creature had rather come down in his ideas. He called himself free, but he acted like a platonic freedman, much embarrassed to use the liberty which he had the right to enjoy. When the men had returned to Camdless Bay, and rebuilt the houses that had suffered, the plantation would soon resume its accustomed aspect. Whatever might be the issue of the war, there was every reason to hope that security was assured to the Florida planters.

Order was re-established at Jacksonville. The Federals did not attempt to interfere with the municipal administration. They occupied the town for military purposes, and left the civic authority to the magistrates whom the outbreak had for a time suspended. It was enough that the stars and stripes floated over the buildings. If the majority of the inhabitants were not indifferent to the question which divided the States, they at least showed no repugnance at submitting to the victorious party. The unionist cause would meet with no opposition. The doctrine of " state's right" dear to Georgia and the Carolinas was not held in Florida with anything like the same ardour, nor would it be, even if the Federals withdrew their troops.

The events of the war up to this had been as follows :— The Confederates, in order to support Beauregard, had sent six gunboats, under Commodore Hollins, who had taken up his position on the Mississippi, between New Madrid and Is and Ten. A struggle began, in which he was vigorously withstood by Admiral Foote, with the

object of holding the upper river. The day that Jacksonville fell to Stevens, the Federal artillery opened against
Hollins's gunboats. The advantage rested with the Northerners, who took Island Ten and New Madrid, and thus
occupied the course of the Mississippi for a hundred and
twenty-four miles, reckoning the windings of the stream.

At this time much hesitation showed itself in the plans
of the Federal government. General MacClellan had to
submit his ideas to a council of war, and although they
were approved by the majority of the council, President
Lincoln's yielding to regrettable influences postponed their
execution. The army of the Potomac was divided so as to
assure the safety of Washington. Fortunately the victory
of the *Monitor* and the flight of the *Virginia* had opened
the navigation on the Chesapeake; and the precipitate
retreat of the Confederates, after the evacuation of Manassas,
had allowed the army to go into cantonments in that town.
In this way the question of the blockade of the Potomac
was settled.

Politics have always a disastrous effect on military affairs,
and the interests of the North now suffered severely from a
decision come to for political purposes. General MacClellan
was deprived of the command-in-chief of the Federal
armies. His command was reduced to that of the army of
the Potomac, and the other corps, now become independent,
passed under the sole direction of President Lincoln.

It was a mistake. MacClellan keenly resented the
affront of his undeserved dismissal. But like a soldier who
thought only of his duty, he resigned himself to his fate.
The very next day he formed a plan the object of which
was to land troops on the beach of Fort Monroe. The
plan was adopted by the chiefs of the corps and approved
by the president. The war minister sent orders to New
York, Philadelphia, and Baltimore, and vessels of all kinds
arrived in the Potomac to take on board General MacClellan's
army and its baggage. The threats which so long had
made Washington tremble would cease, and Richmond, the
Southern capital, would in its turn be threatened.

Such was the situation of the belligerents when Florida

submitted to General Sherman and Commodore Dupont. At the same time that their squadron completed the blockade of the Floridan coast, they had become masters of the St. John's, and assured themselves of the complete possession of the peninsula.

In vain had Gilbert and Mars explored the banks and islands up to Picolata. And all that could be done was to deal with Texar. From the day when the doors of the prison shut on him he had had no communication with his accomplices. And it seemed to follow that Dy and Zermah would be found wherever they might have been before the Federal occupation.

The state of things at Jacksonville was now such that justice could safely be left to take its course against the Spaniard, if he refused to give information. But before proceeding to extremes it was hoped he would make certain confessions on condition of being set at liberty.

On the 14th it was decided to try what could be done, the military authorities having previously signified their approval.

Mrs. Burbank had recovered her strength. The return of her son, the hope of soon seeing her child, the peace which had settled down on the country, and the safety now guaranteed to Camdless Bay had all united in restoring to her the energy she had lost. There was no more to fear from the partisans of Texar, who had terrorized over Jacksonville. The militia had retired into the interior of Putnam county. If, later on, the St. Augustine militia, after passing the river farther up, joined hands with them in attempting an expedition against the Federals, the peril would be distant, and need cause no anxiety while Dupont and Sherman remained in Florida.

It was agreed that James and Gilbert Burbank should go to Jacksonville this very day, and go alone. Carrol, Stannard, and Mars would remain at the plantation ; Alice could not leave Mrs. Burbank. The young officer and his father thought they would be back before night, and with good news. As soon as Texar had told them where he was keeping Dy and Zermah, they would see about their deliverance, which would doubtless be accomplished in a few hours or a day at the outside.

Just as they were going away, Alice took the young officer apart.

"Gilbert," she said, "you are going to see a man who has done much evil to your family. He is a scoundrel who would have killed both you and your father. Gilbert, you must promise me to keep your temper when you are with Texar."

"Keep my temper!" exclaimed Gilbert, who grew pale with anger at the mere mention of the Spaniard's name.

"It is necessary for you to do so. You will gain nothing by being angry. Forget all idea of vengeance to secure the safety of your sister, who will soon be mine! For that you must sacrifice everything. You must make Texar feel sure that he has nothing to fear in the future."

"Nothing! Do you forget that owing to him my mother might have died, my father might have been shot?"

"And so might you, Gilbert; you whom I never thought to see again! Yes, he did all that, and we must not think of it any more! I tell you, because I am afraid that your father will not control himself, and if you do not do so you will fail. Why did you decide to go to Jacksonville without me? I might have gained by kindness—"

"And if this man refuses to answer?" asked Gilbert, who felt the justice of Alice's advice.

"If he refuses, you must leave the magistrates to compel him. He risks his life, and when he sees he can save it by speaking, he will speak. Gilbert, promise me, in the name of our love, promise me—"

"Yes, my dear Alice; yes! Whatever he may have done, if he gives us back my sister, I will forget it."

"Good, Gilbert. We have passed through a terrible trial, which will soon be at an end. For the sad days we have been through God will give us years of happiness."

Gilbert clasped the hands of his sweetheart, who could not restrain a few tears, and they parted

At ten o'clock James Burbank and his son took leave

of their friends, and entered a boat at the little landing-place.

The river was being speedily crossed when, at an observation of Gilbert's, the boat, instead of running straight to Jacksonville, was steered for Captain Stevens's gunboat.

Stevens was in military charge of the town. It was therefore best that James Burbank's undertaking should be first of all submitted to him for approval. His communications with the authorities were frequent. He knew what Texar had done when in power, what was his share of the responsibility in the events that had laid the plantation waste, and why and how he had been arrested when the militia had begun to retreat. He knew of the reaction which had taken place against Texar, and how the whole respectable population of Jacksonville were asking that he should be punished for his crimes.

Stevens gave a willing reception to the Burbanks. For the young officer he had particular esteem, having been able to appreciate his character and courage while Gilbert was under his orders. After the return of Mars to the flotilla, when he learnt that Gilbert had fallen into the hands of the enemy, he did his utmost to save him. But stopped before the bar of the St. John's, how could he reach him in time? We know under what circumstances the safety of the prisoners had been obtained.

In a few words Gilbert told him what had passed, confirming what had already been reported by Mars. There could be no doubt that Texar was personally responsible for the outrage at Marine Creek, and that he alone could say where Dy and Zermah were now detained by his accomplices. That their fate was in the Spaniard's hands was only too evident, and Stevens saw this at once. Would he allow the Burbanks to take the matter in hand and act as they thought fit? He approved of all that had been done; and if it was necessary to set Texar free, he would do so, and take the responsibility with the Jacksonville magistrates.

James and Gilbert Burbank, having obtained full permission, thanked the captain, and received from him a written permission to communicate with the Spaniard. They then resumed their voyage to Jacksonville.

There they met Mr. Harvey, by appointment. The three then went to the court, where they received from the magistrates an order to enter the prison.

A physiologist would have been much interested in Texar's bearing and conduct since his incarceration. There could be no doubt that he was very angry at the arrival of the Federal troops, which put an end to his being first magistrate of the town. Although he had held the power to do what he liked, and had every facility for gratifying his personal hatred, yet a delay of a few hours had prevented him from shooting James and Gilbert Burbank! But his regret went no further. That he was in the hands of his enemies, imprisoned on the most serious charges, responsible for all the violent deeds that could be so justly laid to his charge, seemed to be a matter of perfect indifference to him. His only trouble was that he had not brought to completion his plans against the Burbanks. He seemed to take no interest whatever in the proceedings against him. Would he now render futile the attempts about to be made to get a word from him ?

The door of the cell opened. James and Gilbert Burbank were in the prisoner's presence.

"Ah! the father and the son," said Texar in the insolent tone that was habitual to him. "I ought to be much obliged to the Federals! Without them I should not have had the honour of this visit. The mercy you no longer ask for yourselves you have doubtless come to offer me ?"

The tone was so provoking that James Burbank would have exploded had not his son restrained him.

"Father, let me speak. Texar would like to meet us on ground where we cannot follow him—that of recrimination. It is useless to talk about the past. It is with the present we are concerned—the present alone."

"The present !" exclaimed Texar ; " or rather the present situation ! It seems to me that is clear enough ! Three days ago you were in this cell, which you would never have left but to meet your death. To-day I am in your place, and I feel much more comfortable than you think."

The reply was disconcerting, for the Burbanks had come to offer him his freedom in exchange for his secret.

"Texar," said Gilbert, "listen to me. We will act frankly with you. What you have done at Jacksonville is no concern of ours. What you have done at Camdless Bay we are willing to forget. We are interested in only one thing. My sister and Zermah disappeared the night your partisans invaded the plantation and laid siege to Castle House. It is certain that both were carried off—"

"Carried off?" answered Texar, mechanically. "I am delighted to hear it."

"To hear it!" exclaimed James Burbank. "Do you deny, you scoundrel, dare you deny—"

"Father," said the lieutenant, "keep cool—you must. Yes, Texar, they were carried off during the attack on the plantation. Do you admit that you did it?"

"I have nothing to answer."

"Do you refuse to tell us where my sister and Zermah have been taken under your orders?"

"I repeat, I have nothing to answer."

"Not even if by speaking we could set you free?"

"I do not want to be free."

"And who will open the gates of this prison for you?" exclaimed James Burbank, whom so much impudence had completely astounded.

"The judges I ask for."

"The judges! They will condemn you without mercy."

"Then I shall see what is to be done."

"So you definitely refuse to reply?" asked Gilbert, for the last time.

"I refuse."

"Even at the price of the liberty I offer?"

"I do not want your liberty."

"Even at the price of the fortune I offer you?"

"I do not want your fortune. And now, gentlemen, leave me alone."

It must be admitted that the Burbanks were completely

bewildered at such assurance. On what could it rest?
How dare Texar expose himself to a trial which could only
have one result? Neither liberty nor all the gold they
had offered could tempt him to answer. Was his inex-
tinguishable hatred forcing him to act against his own
interests?

"Come, father, come!" said the young officer; and he
led James Burbank out of the prison. At the door they
rejoined Mr. Harvey, and the three went off to Captain
Stevens to report their want of success.

Meanwhile a proclamation from Commodore Dupont
had arrived on board the flotilla. It was addressed to the
inhabitants of Jacksonville, and stated that no notice would
be taken of political opinions, nor of what had happened
in Florida since the outbreak of the civil war. Submission
to the flag covered all responsibilities in a public point of
view.

Evidently this measure, a very wise one in itself, and in
accordance with President Lincoln's policy in all similar
circumstances, could not apply to private affairs as in
Texar's case. He had usurped the powers of the regular
authorities, and used them to organize resistance. Be it
so! That was a question between Southerners and
Southerners in which the Federals did not wish to be
concerned. But attempts on persons, the invasion of
Camdless Bay directed against a Northerner, the destruction of James Burbank's property, the capture of his
daughter and a woman in his service, were crimes against
ordinary law, and for them redress could be had in the
regular course of justice.

Such was the advice of Commandant Stevens. Such
was the advice of Commodore Dupont as soon as the complaint was made to him, and permission asked to proceed
against the Spaniard.

In the morning of the 15th of March an order was issued
for Texar to appear before the military tribunal on the
double charge of pillage and abduction. It was before
the court-martial sitting at St. Augustine that the accused
would have to answer for his crimes.

CHAPTER VI.

ST. AUGUSTINE.

ST. AUGUSTINE is one of the oldest towns in North America, and dates from the fifteenth century. It is the capital of St. John's county, which, large as it is, contains less than 3000 inhabitants.

Spanish in origin, St. Augustine remains very much as it was. It rises near the end of one of the islands on the coast. Its harbour is a safe refuge for ships of war or commerce ; it is well protected against the winds which unceasingly sweep in from the sea along the dangerous shore. But to enter it vessels have to cross the bar which the eddies of the Gulf Stream heap back at its mouth.

The streets of St. Augustine are narrow, like those of all cities beneath the direct rays of the sun. Owing to their position, and to the sea-breezes which night and morning freshen the atmosphere, the climate is a mild one, and the town is to the United States what Nice and Mentone are to Provence.

The population is thickest about the harbour and the neighbouring streets. The suburbs, with their few huts covered with palm-leaves, would be completely deserted were it not for the dogs, pigs, and cows allowed to wander where they please.

The city, properly so-called, has a very Spanish look. The houses have strongly-barred windows, and in the interior they have the traditional patio, or central court, surrounded by slender colonnades, fantastic gables, and carved balconies. Sometimes, on Sundays or holidays, the houses pour forth their inhabitants into the town. Then there is the strangest mixture of senoras, negresses, mulattoes, half-breeds, Indians, thoroughbred blacks, English

PART II.

ladies, gentlemen, clergymen, monks, and Catholic priests, all with a cigarette in their lips, even when they are going to the Calvary, which is the parish church of St. Augustine, whose bells have rung their peal almost without interruption since the middle of the seventeenth century.

We must not forget the markets, richly stored with vegetables, fish, poultry, pigs, lambs—slaughtered as required by the buyers—eggs, rice, boiled bananas, frijoles—a sort of small cooked bean—in short, all the tropical fruits, pineapples, dates, olives, pomegranates, oranges, guavas, peaches, figs, marañons—all in the best condition to make life agreeable and easy in this part of Florida.

The highways are not cleansed by paid scavengers, but by flocks of vultures, which the law protects, and forbids being killed under very strong penalties. The birds eat everything, even snakes, which are in considerable numbers, notwithstanding the voracity of the feathered scavengers.

There is no want of green among the chief houses of the town. Where the roads cross, a glance will show many a group of trees with its branches above the roofs of the houses, and alive with its noisy crowd of wild parrots. Often there are huge palms waving their foliage in the air, like huge fans or Indian punkahs. Here and there are large oaks garlanded with lianas and glycenas, and bouquets of gigantic cactuses, which at their base form an impenetrable hedge. Everything is cheering and attractive, and would be more so if the vultures only did their work more conscientiously. Decidedly they are not as good as mechanical sweepers.

At St. Augustine there are but one or two steam sawmills, a cigar factory, and a turpentine distillery. The town is more commercial than industrial, and exports or imports molasses, cereals, cotton, indigo, gums, timber, fish, and salt. At ordinary times the harbour is busy enough with the arrival or departure of steamers employed in the trade and passenger service to the different ports of the ocean and the Gulf of Mexico.

St. Augustine is the seat of one of the six courts of justice existing in Florida. Its only means of defence are a solitary fort—Fort Marion, or St. Mark—built in the Castilian style in the seventeenth century. Vauban or Cormontaigne would doubtless have made very little of it, but it is admired by archæologists and antiquaries for its towers and bastions, and demilune and machicolations, and its old guns and mortars, which would be more dangerous for those that fire them than those they are fired against.

It was this fort which the Confederate garrison had hurriedly abandoned at the approach of the Federal flotilla, although the Government, a few years before the war, had improved its means of defence. After the militia had left, the inhabitants of St. Augustine had voluntarily submitted to Commodore Dupont, who occupied the town without a blow.

The proceedings against the Spaniard, Texar, had made much noise in the county. It seemed as though there was at last to be an end to the strife between this suspicious individual and the Burbank family. The abduction of the little girl and Zermah was calculated to intensify the public opinion, which had pronounced emphatically in favour of the planter of Camdless Bay. There could be no doubt that Texar was the author of the crime. But it would be curious to see how he would get out of the charge, and whether he would get off, as he had always done before.

Excitement threatened to be great at St. Augustine The proprietors of the neighbouring plantations crowded in. The matter was of great interest to them personally, as one of the charges referred to the overrunning and pillage of Camdless Bay. Other plantations had also been ravaged by the Southerners, and it was important to know how the Federal Government would look upon such crimes against the common welfare, though perpetrated under cover of politics.

The chief hotel in St. Augustine, the City, had accommodated a goodly number of visitors whose sympathy was entirely with the Burbank family, and it could accommodate a great many more. And, for a hotel, there could be no more appropriate building than this huge sixteenth-

century house, the old home of the corregidor, with its
puerta, or principal door, covered with carvings, its sola or
room of honour, its interior court with the columns garlanded with passion-flowers, its verandah, on to which
opened the most comfortable rooms with their wainscoting
hidden under the brightest colours of emerald and golden
yellow, its miradors on the walls in Spanish fashion, its
leaping fountains and smiling grass plats, all in a vast
enclosure, the high-walled patio.

There it was that James and Gilbert Burbank, and Mr.
Stannard and his daughter, accompanied by Mars, had
taken up their abode the evening before.

After their fruitless journey to the prison at Jacksonville,
James Burbank and his son had returned to Castle House.
When they learnt that Texar refused to answer any question about Dy or Zermah, the family felt their last hope
vanish, although the news that Texar would have to answer
to military justice for his doings at Camdless Bay was some
consolation. In view of a sentence which he could not
escape, the Spaniard would doubtless break silence when
it was necessary for him to treat for his liberty or his life.

In this matter Alice Stannard would be the principal
witness. She had been at Marine Creek when Zermah
had shouted Texar's name, and she had recognized the
scoundrel in the boat which bore him away. She had come
to St. Augustine, and her father and his friends had accompanied her. After dinner, on the 16th, they had bidden
farewell to Mrs. Burbank and Edward Carrol. One of the
steamboats had embarked them at Camdless Bay, and
landed them at Picolata, and thence a stage-coach had
brought them along the winding road, through the oaks,
and cypresses, and plantains, which here abound. Before
midnight comfortable hospitality had received them in the
apartments of the City Hotel.

Texar had not been abandoned by his friends, as might
be imagined. His partisans were chiefly among the
smaller planters, all of them embittered slaveholders.
Knowing that they would not have to answer for any of
the troubles at Jacksonville, his companions resolved to

rally round their old chief. Many of them had come to St. Augustine. It is true that it was not in the patio of the City Hotel that one would look for them; but there were many of them in the inns in the town, in the tiendas where the half-bred Spaniards and Creeks sell everything that can be eaten, drunk, or smoked. There these individuals of low origin and equivocal reputation lost no opportunity of protesting in Texar's favour.

Commodore Dupont was not now at St. Augustine. He was away on the blockade. But the troops landed after the surrender of Fort Marion were in firm possession of the city. There was no movement to be feared on the part of the Southerners or of the militia, who were retreating on the other side of the river. If the partisans of Texar attempted any rescue, they would be immediately put down.

One of the gunboats had brought the Spaniard to Picolata, and thence he had been brought under a strong escort, and placed in one of the cells in the fort, from which escape was impossible. As he had demanded a trial, he was not likely to attempt an escape. His partisans were aware of this. If he were condemned this time, they would see what they could do to help him, but till then they would be quiet.

In the absence of the Commodore, Colonel Gardner was in military command. He was the president of the court-martial appointed to try Texar in one of the rooms of Fort Marion. This was the colonel who had assisted at the capture of Fernandina, and it was at his orders that the prisoners captured from the train by the *Ottawa* had been detained for forty-eight hours, a fact which it is here important to notice.

The court-martial opened at eleven o'clock in the morning. A numerous public filled the room. Amongst the noisiest of the crowd were the friends and partisans of the accused.

James and Gilbert Burbank, Mr. Stannard, his daughter, and Mars occupied the place reserved for the witnesses. There seemed to be no defence. No witnesses were apparently to be called. Did the Spaniard scorn all evidence,

or had he found it impossible to bring any to his help ?
It would soon be known. Anyhow, there seemed to be
no doubt as to the issue of the affair.

An indefinable presentiment had seized upon James
Burbank. Was it not in this very town that he had before
prosecuted Texar ? Had not he, then, by an incontestable
alibi, escaped from justice ?

As soon as the court-martial was seated Texar was
brought in. He sat down coolly and quietly. Nothing
seemed to be able to disturb his natural impudence. A
smile of disdain for his judges, a look full of assurance for
the friends he recognized in the room, a look of hatred for
James Burbank, and then he settled himself and waited
for Colonel Gardner to begin.

The interrogatories began in the usual way.

"Your name ? " asked Colonel Gardner.

"Texar."

"Your age ? "

"Thirty-five."

"Where do you live."

"At Jacksonville ; at Torillo's tienda."

"I want to know your usual abode."

"I have none."

James Burbank felt his heart beat as he heard this reply,
given in a tone which plainly denoted a firm resolve to
keep secret the real place of residence.

The president again tried to get at the facts, but Texar
persisted that he had no fixed abode. He gave himself
out to be a nomad, a backwoodsman, a hunter in the vast
forests, a dweller in the cypress-groves, living by his rifle
and his decoys. That was all that could be got from him.

"Be it so," said Colonel Gardner. "It does not matter
much."

"It does not matter much," said Texar impudently.
"Put down, if you like, Colonel, that my domicile is now
Fort Marion, in St. Augustine, where I am detained contrary to all justice. Of what am I accused, if you please ? "
he asked, as if he wished to take the management of his
own trial.

"You are not called upon to answer for anything that took place at Jacksonville. A proclamation from Commodore Dupont has been issued announcing that the Government will not interfere in the local revolution which substituted for the regular authorities of the county certain new magistrates, whoever they may have been. Florida is now under the Federal flag, and the Government of Washington will soon proceed with its reorganization."

"If I am not charged with the change in the municipality of Jacksonville, and that with the support of the majority of the people, why am I brought before this court-martial?"

"I will tell you what you pretend not to know. Crimes against the common welfare have been committed while you were exercising the functions of chief magistrate of the town. You are accused of having excited the violent part of the population to commit them."

"What are these crimes?"

"In the first place, there is the outrage at Camdless Bay plantation, where a horde of thieves was set loose."

"And a detachment of soldiers, commanded by an officer of the militia," added the Spaniard quickly.

"Be it so. But there was robbery, incendiarism, and armed attack against a house, which it was right to repel —as was done."

"Right?" answered Texar. "Right was not on the side of him who refused to obey the orders of a properly constituted Committee. James Burbank—for he it was— had given his slaves their freedom in defiance of public opinion, which, in Florida, as in most of the southern states of the Union, is in favour of slavery. That act might have been the cause of much disaster on the neighbouring plantations by exciting the blacks to revolt. The Committee of Jacksonville decided that under the circumstances it was their duty to interfere. They did not annul the act of enfranchisement, but they thought fit to expel the newly freed slaves from the district. James Burbank refused to obey the order, and the Committee had to use force. That is why the militia, accompanied by some of

15

the inhabitants, proceeded to disperse the former slaves at
Camdless Bay."

"Texar," replied Colonel Gardner, "the court-martial
cannot admit that the view you take of the outrage is the
correct one.   James Burbank is a Northerner by birth, and
was quite within his rights in freeing his slaves.   Nothing
can excuse the excess which took place on his plantation."

"I consider that I am losing time in discussing matters
of opinion with the court-martial.   The Committee of
Jacksonville considered it their duty to act as they did.
Am I accused as president of that Committee ?   Is it your
intention to make me alone responsible for its acts ?

"Yes.   You were not only the president of the Committee, but you in person led the thieves."

"Prove it," said Texar coolly.   "Have you a single
witness who saw me among either the citizens or the
soldiers of the militia who carried out the Committee's
orders ? "

At this reply Colonel Gardner called on James Burbank
to give his evidence.

James Burbank related what had happened since Texar
and his partisans had superseded the regular authorities
of Jacksonville.   He laid stress on the attitude of the
accused in inciting the people to attack his estate.   But to
Colonel Gardner's question as to the presence of Texar
among the assailants, he could only reply that he had not
himself seen him.   We know in fact that when John
Bruce, Mr. Harvey's messenger, had been asked if the
Spaniard was one of the mob, the reply was he could not
say.

"In any case no one can doubt," added James Burbank,
"that this man is solely responsible for the crime.   He it
was who incited the people to attack me, and had he had
his way my house would have been given to the flames,
and destroyed with its last defenders.   His hand was in
all this, as it will be found to have been in a still more
criminal act."

The witness offered no further evidence.   Before dealing

with the abduction it was best to finish with the first charge.

"And so," continued Colonel Gardner, "you say that you only had a share in the responsibility which lay on the Committee in executing their order?"

"That is so."

"And you adhere to your statement that you were not at the head of those who attacked the plantation?"

"I do. You have not a single witness who can swear he saw me. No; I was not among the brave citizens who executed the Committee's orders. And I may add that on that day I was absent from Jacksonville."

"Yes; that is possible after all," said James Burbank, who considered that it would be better to rely on the second charge.

"It is true," said Texar.

"But if you were not amongst the thieves at Camdless Bay," continued James Burbank, "you were at Marine Creek, waiting for the opportunity of committing another crime."

"I was not at Marine Creek," coolly answered Texar. "I was not at Jacksonville during that day."

It will not have been forgotten that John Bruce had told James Burbank that Texar had not been seen at Jacksonville during the forty eight hours from the 2nd to the 4th of March.

After this statement of the Spaniard's, the president of the court-martial put to him the following question:—

"If you were not at Jacksonville, where were you?"

"I will tell you when the time comes," said Texar. "It is enough for me now to have proved that I was not on the plantation during the attack. And now, colonel, what is the next charge?"

And, with his arms crossed, he glared impudently at his accusers, and defied them to their face.

The charge was not long in coming, and Colonel Gardner put it in a way that made it difficult to meet.

"If you were not at Jacksonville, the charge is that you were at Marine Creek."

"At Marine Creek?   And what did I do there?"

"You carried away a child, Diana Burbank, the daughter of James Burbank, and Zermah, the wife of a half-breed named Mars, here present, who was with the child."

"Ah!   I am charged with this carrying away!" said Texar, in a tone of profound irony.

"Yes, you!" exclaimed James Burbank, Gilbert, and Mars, all at once.

"And why am I accused, if you please, and not somebody else?"

"Because you alone were interested in committing this crime."

"How interested?"

"As an act of revenge on the Burbank family.   More than once before James Burbank had prosecuted you.   By pleading an alibi you escaped from justice; but you on many occasions proclaimed an intention of being revenged on those who accused you."

"Be it so," said Texar.   "That between me and James Burbank there is an implacable hatred I do not deny; that I had an interest in making him break his heart over his child I do not deny; but that I did what you say is another matter.   Have you any witnesses who saw me?"

"Yes," said Colonel Gardner; and he called on Alice Stannard to be sworn.

Miss Stannard related what had passed at Marine Creek. She was absolutely certain as to the facts.   In coming from the tunnel she and Mrs. Burbank had heard the name shouted by Zermah, and that name was Texar's.

After stumbling over the corpses of the murdered negroes, she had run along the river bank.   Two boats were pushing off.   In one were the victims; in the other was Texar, standing upright in the stern.   And by the light of the fires of the burning plantation she had recognized the Spaniard.

"You swear that?" asked Colonel Gardner.

"I swear it," answered Alice.

After this precise declaration there could be no doubt of Texar's guilt.   But James Burbank and the entire audience could not help observing that the accused had not for a moment lost his coolness.

"What have you to say to the charge?" asked the president of the court-martial.

"This," said the Spaniard. "I do not wish to accuse Miss Stannard of perjury. Nor do I accuse her of serving the hatred of the Burbank family against me, by affirming on oath that I am the author of a crime of which I never heard till after my arrest. All I say is that she is mistaken when she says she saw me in one of the boats."

"But if Miss Stannard was mistaken on that point," said Colonel Gardner, "she cannot be mistaken when she says that she heard Zermah cry, 'Help! It is Texar!'"

"Well," said the Spaniard, "then if Miss Stannard was not mistaken, Zermah was, that is all."

"Would Zermah have shouted your name if you were not there?"

"Very likely, for I was not there, and I was not even at Marine Creek."

"That you must prove."

"That is easy enough."

"Another alibi?" asked Colonel Gardner.

"Another!" said Texar.

At this there was a movement of voices amongst the audience, a murmur of doubt that was not in favour of the accused.

"Texar," said the colonel, "if you plead another alibi, can you prove it?"

"Easily, for I have only to ask you a question."

"What is that?"

"Were you not in command of the troops landed to capture Fernandina and Fort Clinch?"

"Yes."

"You remember the train for Cedar Keys that was attacked by the *Ottawa* on the bridge between Amelia Island and the mainland?"

"Yes."

"Well, the rear carriage was knocked off and stopped on the bridge, and a detachment of Federal troops captured the fugitives, and the prisoners had their names taken, and did not receive their liberty for forty-eight hours afterwards."

"I know that."

"Well, I was one of those prisoners."

"You?"

"Yes, I!"

A fresh murmur still more unfavourable to the accused greeted this declaration.

"Then," continued Texar, "as these prisoners were in your custody from the 2nd to the 4th of March, and the attack on this plantation took place on the night of the 3rd of March, it is simply impossible that I could have been at Marine Creek. Alice Stannard could not have heard Zermah shout my name. She could not have seen me in the boat, for I was then a Federal prisoner."

"That is false!" exclaimed James Burbank. "It cannot be!"

"I swear I saw that man," said Alice, "and I recognized him there as I do now."

"Look at the papers?" said Texar.

Colonel Gardner searched among the papers that had been sent to Commodore Dupont after the capture of Fernandina, and in the list of prisoners there appeared the name of Texar, with his description.

There could be no room for further doubt. The Spaniard was innocent of the abduction. Miss Stannard must have been mistaken. He could not have been at Marine Creek. His absence from Jacksonville for forty-eight hours was fully accounted for; he was then a prisoner on one of the gunboats. And, again, an indisputable alibi, proved by official evidence, had come to clear him of the charge.

James Burbank, Gilbert, Mars, and Miss Stannard were overwhelmed at the result. Texar had again escaped them, and with them all chance had gone of ascertaining what had become of Dy and Zermah.

The decision of the court-martial could not be in doubt for an instant. Texar was discharged, and walked out of the room amid the enthusiastic cheers of his friends.

Before night he had left St. Augustine, and no one knew to what part of Florida he had gone to resume his mysterious life of adventure.

CHAPTER VII.

LAST WORDS AND A LAST SIGH.

THE same day, the 17th of March, James and Gilbert Burbank, Mr. Stannard and his daughter, and Zermah's husband returned to Camdless Bay.

They could not hide the truth from Mrs. Burbank. The unfortunate mother received a fresh blow which, in the weak state she was, might prove fatal.

The last attempt to discover the fate of her child had failed. Texar had refused to answer. And how could he be obliged to do so when he asserted that he was not the author of the abduction? By an alibi more unintelligible than those that had preceded it, he had proved that he was not at Marine Creek when the crime took place. Had he been found guilty, they could have given him his choice between suffering the consequences or revealing the where-abouts of his victims.

"But if it was not Texar," asked Gilbert, "who was it?"

"It must have been some of his people," said Mr. Stannard.

"That is the only explanation," said Edward Carrol.

"No, father, no, Mr. Carrol!" said Alice. "Texar was in the boat. I saw him. I recognized him when Zermah shouted his name! I saw him! I saw him!"

What could be the answer to this? Alice adhered to her statement that it was impossible for her to have been mistaken. And if she was not mistaken, how could the Spaniard have been at Fernandina, in one of Dupont's gunboats at the time?

It was inexplicable. But if the others had any doubt, Mars had none. He made no effort to comprehend the incomprehensible. All he did was to make up his mind to follow after Texar and to wring from him the secret even if it became necessary to torture him.

"You are right, Mars," said Gilbert. "But we may have to do without the scoundrel if we do not know what has become of him. We must start on our search again ! I have orders to remain on leave as long as is needful, and to morrow—"

"Yes, Mr. Gilbert, to-morrow ! "

And the half-breed went to his room, where he could give free vent to his sorrow and his anger.

In the morning Gilbert and Mars completed their preparations for departure. They were going to devote the day to a careful search among the minor creeks and small islets on both banks of the St. John's above Camd-less Bay.

During their absence James Burbank and Edward Carrol would prepare for a more extended campaign. Provisions, ammunition, means of transport, men—nothing would be neglected. If they had to go to the wild regions of Lower Florida, to the southern marshes, and through the Ever-glades, they would go. That Texar had left Florida was impossible. To the north he would have found the Fede-ral troops on the Georgian frontier. By sea he would have to make for the Bahamas, and Commodore Dupont's flotilla had closed all the passes. He must be in Florida, hidden where his victims had been hidden for a fortnight, and the expedition would seek for his traces over the whole territory.

There was peace at Jacksonville. The old magistrates had resumed their position in the municipality. There were no more citizens in prison for their opinions. Texar's partisans had all fled.

The war continued in the central states much to the advantage of the Federals. On the 18th and 19th the first division of the army of the Potomac landed at Fortress Monroe. On the 22nd the second division prepared to leave Alexandria for the same destination. In spite of the military genius of the old professor of chemistry, Stonewall Jackson, the Southerners were beaten at Kerns-

PART II.   F

town. There was thus no rising to be feared in Florida, which always remained somewhat indifferent to the heated passions of North and South.

The Camdless Bay men gradually came back. After the capture of Jacksonville, the orders of Texar and his Committee relative to the expulsion of the freed men were of no effect. On the 17th of March the greater part of the blacks had returned, and were busy rebuilding the barracoons, while many were at work clearing the ruins of the stores and saw-mills. Under the direction of Edward Carrol, Perry and the assistant overseers were very busy. To him James Burbank left the whole task of reorganization. The father's whole time was devoted to the search for his child. A dozen of the freed negroes were chosen to help in the expedition, who, with heart and soul, entered on their work.

Where was the expedition to go? There was much reason for hesitation. But an unhoped-for circumstance fortunately gave a clue.

On the 19th Gilbert and Mars left Castle House, and set off up the St. John's. None of the negroes of the plantation accompanied them. It was necessary to act as secretly as possible, so as not to awake the suspicion of the spies, who might be watching Castle House.

Gilbert and Mars were coasting along the left bank. Among the masses of foliage and floating islands detached by the high tides of the equinox, the boat ran no risk of discovery.

Up to the village of Mandarin the river is almost a marsh. At high water the stream overflows the low banks, and it is not till half-tide that the ebb is enough to reduce the St. John's to its normal level. The right bank is higher; the fields of maize are above the level of the periodical floods, which prevent any tillage being attempted. It might even be called a ridge, along which rise the few houses of Mandarin; and the ridge ends in a cape projecting into the stream.

Below numerous islands occupy the bend of the river, and, reflecting the white canopies of their magnificent

magnolia-trees, the river divided into these channels runs
in or out with the tide.

After examining the western arm, Gilbert and Mars were
making their way along the main bank; they were assuring
themselves that no creek opened up beneath the branches
of the tulip-trees. Up to the present they had seen nothing
but the wide marshes of the lower river, valleys bristling
with tree-ferns and liquidambars, whose early blossoms,
mingling with the garlands of serpentarias and aristolochias,
impregnated the air with their penetrating perfumes. But
the water was of no depth; it was running off in tiny
streams, and the ebb would soon leave the ground quite
dry. Among the streams were a few huts, which did not
seem to have been recently occupied, although it seemed
as though a good many animals had made it their home.
There were dogs barking, and cats mewing, and frogs
croaking, and snakes hissing, but there were neither dogs
nor cats, nor frogs nor snakes, for the cries were the call of the
cat-bird, a sort of thrush with a black head and orange throat.

It was about three o'clock in the afternoon. The boat
was alongside a thick clump of reeds, when a powerful
stroke of the gaff from Mars cleared away a heap of verdure that had seemed to be impenetrable. Beyond was a
sort of backwater some half-acre in extent, where the sun
never penetrated through the dome of tulip-trees.

"I did not know of this pond," said Mars, rising so as to
look round the banks.

"Let us explore it then," said Gilbert. "It ought to
communicate with that row of lagoons, which may be fed
by some creek up which we may find our way."

"That is so," said Mars, "and I see an opening over
there to the north-west."

"Do you know where we are?"

"Not exactly, unless this is what they call Black Creek;
but I thought, like everybody else, that it was impossible to
get into it, and that it had no communication with the
St. John's."

"Had there not used to be a blockhouse here, to keep
the Seminoles in check?"

"Somewhere, yes. But that was years ago, and the entrance to the creek is shut and the fortress abandoned. I have never been there, but it is all in ruins."

"Let us get there," said Gilbert.

"We'll try," said Mars, "although it will be difficult to do so. The water will soon be off, and the marsh will not give very good footing."

"Well, if there is not enough water, we'll stop in the boat."

"We must not lose any time ; it is three o'clock, and the night soon makes under these trees."

It was indeed Black Creek into which, by a lucky stroke of the boat-hook, Gilbert and Mars had found an entrance. The lagoon was, as we know, only practicable for light skiffs such as that used by Squambo when he and his master ventured on the St. John's. To reach the block-house in the middle of the creek, a knowledge of the thousand twists and turns was necessary, and for many years no one had ventured to attempt such a thing. The existence of the fortress had dropped out of recollection, and hence its security for the strange malignant personage who had made it his home.

To steer up the labyrinth required the thread of Ariadne, for it was always in darkness, even when the sun was on the meridian. Without the thread, chance alone could reveal the central island ; and it was to chance that Gilbert and Mars had to trust. When they were out of the first pond they entered a series of channels, and paddled on, urged by some secret presentiment. As they were going to explore the whole country, it would never do to leave this lagoon unknown.

In about half an hour the boat had gone a mile. More than once some bank had blocked the way, and they had had to paddle back and try another channel. Strong as he was, the half-breed felt that he wanted a rest after his efforts. But he would not stop until he had reached a larger island than the rest, where a few rays of the sun found their way through the trees.

"That is queer," said he.

" What is the matter ? " asked Gilbert.

" There are signs of cultivation on that island."

Soon they landed on a less marshy bank than most of the others.

Mars was not mistaken. There were traces of culture. A few yams were visible here and there ; there were four or five furrows in the soil; a pick was sticking in the ground.

" The creek is inhabited ! " said Gilbert.

" It looks like it. At any rate, it is known to some backwoodsmen or Indians who grow vegetables."

" Then they may have built houses, cabins—"

" If there is one to be found we shall find it."

It was of great interest to discover what sort of people lived at Black Creek. Were they hunters from the lower country, or were they Seminoles, who still live in the marshy parts of Florida ?

Without thinking of returning, Gilbert and Mars got back into the boat, and followed up the curves of the creek, peering into the thick of the bushes in every direction. Sometimes they thought they saw a house, but it was only a curtain of verdure stretching from tree to tree. Sometimes they thought a man was looking at them, but it was only a twisted root with an outline in the shape of a human figure. Perhaps what was hidden from their eyes would reveal itself to their ears ? The least noise in this deserted place would reveal a man's presence.

Half an hour after their first halt they reached the central island. The blockhouse was so completely hidden in the trees that nothing could be seen of it. It seemed as though the creek ended, and that further passage was impracticable.

" I do not think we can go further," said Mars ; " there is no water."

" But," said the officer, " we cannot have been wrong about that cultivated patch. People come to this creek. They may have been here recently ? Perhaps they are here now ? "

" Perhaps ; but we must make the best of the daylight

to get back to the St. John's. Night is coming on. The darkness will soon be thick, and how can we then make out the way ? I think we had better return and come back first thing to-morrow morning. Let us go back, as usual, to Castle House. We can tell them what we have seen, and prepare to explore Black Creek with better chance of success—"

"Yes ; that is best. But before we go I should like—"

Gilbert was standing motionless, taking a last look under the trees, and he was about to give the order to put off when he stopped Mars by a gesture.

The half-breed stood up and listened.

A cry, or rather a sort of groan, was heard which could not be confounded with that of a beast of the forest. It was a cry of despair and lamentation, the appeal of a human being in great pain, the last appeal of a voice about to be silent for ever.

"That is a man !" said Gilbert. "He wants help ! Perhaps he is dying."

"Yes," said Mars. "We must go to him. We must find out who he is. Jump ashore !"

This was done in a moment. The painter was hitched on to a stump, and they were up the bank and under the trees and looking at the footprints of men as revealed by the last rays of the sun. They followed these up. Now and then they stopped and listened. Could they hear the noise ? They listened again. They heard it close by, very near them now ; the darkness was growing deeper, but they would reach the spot from which the sounds came.

Suddenly a more doleful cry was heard. There was no mistake about the direction. In a few steps Gilbert and Mars were through a thicket and in the presence of a man stretched on the ground near a palisade.

Stabbed in the chest the blood was flowing from him, and formed a pool around. The last breath was on his lips. He had but a few moments to live.

Gilbert and Mars stooped over him. He opened his eyes and vainly tried to answer the questions put to him.

"We must see this man !" said Gilbert.   "Get a torch ;
set a knot on fire ! "

Mars had already snapped off a resinous bough from
one of the trees that grew in such numbers on the island.
He lighted it with a match, and its smoky flame illuminated
the gloom.

Gilbert knelt near the dying man.   He was a negro, a
slave, and still young.   His shirt lay open and showed the
gash made by the knife.   The wound was mortal, for the
lung was pierced.

"Who are you?   Who are you ? " asked Gilbert.

No reply.

"Who stabbed you ? "

The slave could not utter a word.

Mars swung round the torch to recognize the place where
the murder had been committed.

He then saw the palisade, and through the open door
caught sight of the dim outline of the blockhouse.

"The fortress ! " he exclaimed.

And leaving his master near the dying slave, he rushed
through the door.

In an instant he had entered the blockhouse, been in the
central redoubt, and into all the rooms.   In one he found
the remains of a fire.   The fortress had therefore been
recently occupied ; but by whom ? Floridans or Seminoles ?
That must be ascertained immediately, and from the
wounded man.   Who were his murderers ?   They had fled
within the last hour or so.

Mars ran out of the blockhouse and round the palisade
in the enclosure.   But no one did he find.   If he and
Gilbert had come earlier in the day, they might have discovered the inhabitants of this fortress, but now they were
too late.

The half-breed returned to his master, and told him they
were at the blockhouse of Black Creek.

"Can the man speak ? " he asked.

"No ; he has lost consciousness, and I don't think he
will regain it."

"Try and make him," said Mars.   "There is a secret

here we must know, and no one can tell us when that unfortunate man is dead."

"Yes! Let us take him into the blockhouse. He may come to himself there. We cannot let him die out here."

"You hold the torch, Mr. Gilbert; I can carry him."

Gilbert held the burning bough. The half-breed lifted the inert body in his arms, mounted the steps of the postern, entered the embrasure, and laid down his burden in one of the rooms of the redoubt.

The dying man was laid on a bed of herbs, and Mars put his flask to his mouth.

The heart still beat but feebly, and at long intervals. Life was failing. Would his secret escape him with his last sigh?

The few drops of brandy seemed to give him new life, His eyes opened. He fixed them on Mars and Gilbert, and strove to fight with death. He would speak! Some vague sounds escaped from his lips—a name, perhaps!

"Speak! Speak!" said Mars.

The excitement of the half-breed was truly inexplicable. It seemed as though the task to which he had devoted his life depended on the last words of this dying man.

The young slave in vain endeavoured to utter a word. He had not the strength.

At this moment Mars noticed a slip of paper in his waistcoat pocket.

To seize this paper, open it, read it by the light of the torch, was the work of an instant.

There were a few words on it.

"Carried off by Texar from Marine Creek—taken to the Everglades—to Carneral Island—message given to the young slave—for Mr. Burbank."

The handwriting Mars knew well.

"Zermah!" he exclaimed.

At this name the dying man opened his eyes, and his head fell in sign of affirmation.

Gilbert raised him a little, and asked,—

"Zermah?"

"Yes."

" And Dy ? "

" Yes."

" Who stabbed you ? "

" Texar."

And that was the poor slave's last word.   He fell back dead.

16

CHAPTER VIII.

FROM CAMDLESS BAY TO LAKE WASHINGTON.

IT was not till just upon midnight that Gilbert and Mars returned to Castle House. Great had been their difficulty in getting out of Black Creek. When they left the block-house night had begun to fall in the valley of the St. John's, and beneath the trees of the lagoon the darkness was complete.

Mars took the boat back among the shoals and islets, guided by a sort of instinct, without which he would never have reached the river. Twenty times and more had he to stop before a barrier he could not pass, and return by the way he had come in search of a practicable channel. He had to light resinous pine-knots, and stick them in the bow of the boat, so as to throw some light on his course. The difficulty was greatest where he had to find the only mouth by which the waters joined the St. John's. The gap in the reeds by which they had entered a few hours before proved unrecognizable ; but luckily the tide was ebbing, and the boat floated out with the stream. Three hours afterwards they were at Camdless Bay.

At Castle House neither James Burbank nor his people had gone to bed. They were waiting anxiously for their long-delayed return. Gilbert and Mars came back every night, why had they not come now? Had they found a clue ?

At last they arrived, and, as they entered, all in the room rushed towards them.

" Well, Gilbert ? " said James Burbank.

" Father, Alice was not mistaken. It was Texar who carried off my sister and Zermah."

" You have the proof ? "

" Read ! "

And Gilbert held out the scrap of paper with the few words in the half-breed's writing.

" Yes," continued he. " Doubt is no longer possible. It was the Spaniard ! And he took or caused to be taken his two victims to the blockhouse at Black Creek. There they have been living isolated from all. A poor slave to whom Zermah had trusted this paper, that it might reach Castle House, and from whom she doubtless learnt that Texar was taking them to Carneral Island, has paid with his life for his devotion. We found him dying, stabbed by Texar, and now he is dead. But if Dy and Zermah are not at Black Creek we know at least where they have gone. They are in the Everglades, and there we must find them. To-morrow we must start."

" We are ready, Gilbert."

" Then to-morrow let it be."

Hope had returned. There would now be no fruitless endeavours. Mrs. Burbank, being told of what had happened, began to revive ; and she had strength enough to rise from her bed and kneel and thank Heaven.

According to Zermah, it was Texar in person who had been in command at the capture at Marine Creek. He it really was whom Alice had seen. But how could this be reconciled with the Spaniard's alibi ? How could he have been a Federal prisoner at the time the crime was committed ? Evidently the alibi was false like the others. But how could it be explained ? What was the secret of Texar's ubiquity ?

It mattered little after all. It had now been ascertained that the half-breed and child had been taken first to the blockhouse at Black Creek, and that now they had gone to Carneral Island. There they must seek for them ; there they must take Texar by surprise. This time nothing must hinder them from visiting him with the just punishment of his crimes which he had so long deserved.

And there was not a day to lose. From Camdless Bay to the Everglades the distance was considerable. The

voyage would take many days.   Fortunately the expedition had been organized carefully and was ready.

Carneral Island was shown by the maps to be on Lake
Okee-cho-bee.

The Everglades are in a marshy region bordering on
Lake Okee-cho-bee, a little below the twenty-seventh
parallel, in the southern part of Florida.   From Jacksonville to the lake was about four hundred miles.   And it
was a rarely visited district; in fact, at this epoch it was
almost unknown.

If the St. John's had been navigable to its source the
journey would not have been a difficult one, but there was
every chance that they would only be able to sail up it for
one hundred and seven miles; that is to Lake George.
Beyond that the road would be choked with islands and
shoals, the channel might even sometimes at ebb tide be
dry, and a heavily-laden boat would under any circumstances find it difficult to pass.   If it were possible to
reach Lake Washington, in about the twenty-eighth degree
of latitude, the end would be near.   But it was only wise to
prepare for a journey of two hundred and fifty miles across
an almost deserted region, where there were no means of
transport and no likelihood of provision.

On the 20th of March the expedition mustered at the
landing-place.   James Burbank and his son had said good-
bye to Mrs. Burbank, who was not able to leave her room.
Mr. Stannard and his daughter and the assistant overseers
were there, and Pyg had come to bid farewell to Mr. Perry,
for whom he, strange to say, had a great regard.   He
remembered the lessons he had received as to the incon-
veniences of a liberty for which he was not ready.

The expedition consisted of James Burbank and his
brother-in-law, now cured of his wound, his son, Mr. Perry
the overseer, Mars, and a dozen negroes chosen from the
most devoted of those on the estate—in all, seventeen.
Mars knew enough of the St. John's to serve as pilot below
as well as above Lake George.   The blacks were all experienced boatmen, and, when the current or the wind
failed, could handle the oars to good purpose.

The boat, one of the largest on the plantation, would be worked under sail whenever the wind was favourable She carried arms and ammunition sufficient for James Burbank and his companions to fear nothing from either the Seminole bands or Texar's companions.

Gilbert embraced Alice, and James Burbank clasped her to his arms as if she were already his daughter.

" Father—Gilbert," she said, " bring back to us little Dy ! Bring me back my sister."

" Yes, dearest Alice, yes ! we will bring her back. May heaven protect us ! "

Mrs. Stannard and Alice and the assistant overseers and Pyg remained at the landing-place till the boat put off. They signalled their last adieux as before the north-east wind and served by the flowing tide she disappeared behind the little point at Marine Creek.

It was about six o'clock in the morning. An hour afterwards the boat passed the village of Mandarin, and it was nearly ten o'clock when, without having had to take to the oars, she was off Black Creek.

All hearts beat as they ran by the left bank of the river through which its waters flowed. It was behind those clumps of reeds and canes and mangroves that Dy and Zermah had first been hid. It was there that for more than a fortnight Texar and his companions had so closely concealed them that all trace of them had been lost. Ten times had James Burbank and Stannard and Gilbert and Mars passed by that lagoon without thinking for an instant that the old blockhouse might be their prison.

This time there was no reason for stopping. Their search took them now hundreds of miles to the south, and the boat passed Black Creek without even stopping.

The first meal was taken together. The boxes contained twenty days' provisions, and there were a number o packages ready to be carried when the journey had to be continued overland. And there were the necessaries for camping, either by day or night, in the thick woods with which the river-banks are clothed.

At eleven o'clock, when the tide turned, the wind

remained favourable, but the oars had to be taken to
keep up the speed. The blacks bent cheerily to their
work, and propelled by ten vigorous pairs the boat rapidly
ascended the river.

Mars sat silently at the helm, taking the boat without
hesitation through the channels among the islands and
islets with which the river is dotted. Where the stream was
weakest he took his way without hesitation. Never did he
enter an impracticable channel ; never did he risk grounding on any of the shoals which the ebb would soon leave
dry. He knew the river up to Lake George as well as he
knew it below Jacksonville, and he piloted the boat with as
much certainty as he had piloted Stevens's flotilla over the
bar.

Hereabouts the St. John's was deserted. Since the
capture of Jacksonville the trading-boats on the river had
been stopped, and there was no vessel on the river except
for the use of the troops or under the orders of Commandant Stevens. Above Picolata even these would
probably have disappeared.

About six o'clock in the evening Picolata was reached.
A detachment of Northerners occupied the pier. The
boat was hailed, and had to run alongside. Gilbert
Burbank made himself known to the commanding
officer, and showing the pass with which he had been
furnished by Commandant Stevens, was allowed to
proceed.

The halt lasted but a minute or so. The tide began to
turn, the oarsmen stopped, and the boat under sail sped on
between the woods that fringed the stream. On the left
bank the forest soon ended in a marsh. On the right, the
forest remained thick and interminable, and they would
have it with them all the way to Lake George. At times
it ran back a little, and fields of rice and indigo and cotton
filled up the stretches in front, and bore witness to the
fertility of the Floridan peninsula.

A little after six o'clock a bend of the river shut out the
view of the red tower of the old Spanish fort, which for a
century and more had been abandoned.

"Mars," asked James Burbank, "you are not afraid to keep to the river during the night?"

"No, sir," said Mars. "I can answer for myself all the way to Lake George. Beyond that we shall see. We have not a moment to lose, and as long as the tide serves we had better take advantage of it. I think we might as well carry on night and day."

There was no occasion to regret this decision. All night the boat kept on her way; when the tide failed the oars were got out. Neither that night nor the following, nor the day of the 22nd of March, nor the next twelve hours, were marked by any adventure. The upper course of the river seemed to be quite deserted. The route lay through a long forest of ancient cedars, whose leafy masses again and again came close to the bank and formed a thick bower of verdure. Villages they saw none. Plantations or isolated habitations there were none. The banks of the river showed no trace of cultivation. On the 23rd, at daybreak, the river broadened out into a wide stretch of water, bordered, as usual, by the interminable forest. The country became very flat, and opened out till the horizon was miles away.

They had reached the lake which the St. John's traverses from south to north, and from which it drains a part of its waters.

"Yes," said Mars, "this is Lake George, which I came to when I was with the expedition to the upper river."

"And how far are we from Camdless Bay?" asked James Burbank.

"A hundred miles," said Mars.

"That is not a third of the distance to the Everglades," said Carrol.

"Mars," said Gilbert, "what are we to do now? Are we to leave the boat and take to the bank? That will be a slow, laborious affair. When we are through the lake, cannot we keep to the water as long as it is navigable? Shall we try it, keeping ready, of course, to take to the shore as soon as we run aground? We might as well try it. What do you think?"

PART II.

"We will try it, Mr. Gilbert."

And they could not have done better.

There would be time enough to take to the land. To keep to the water meant the saving of much fatigue and delay. And the boat headed out across the lake, keeping the eastern bank well in view.

Round the lake the vegetation is not so luxuriant as by the river-side. Extensive marshes stretch away almost out of sight. Some portions of the soil, less exposed to the invasion of the waters, are carpeted with black mosses, from which spring violet clouds of tiny fungi growing in millions. Only the waterfowl could venture across these marshes, and they were alive with infinite numbers of teal and duck and snipe. If the expedition ran short of provisions, here was enough to fill the vacancy without difficulty. But to follow the game on land they would have to risk meeting with armies of dangerous snakes, whose hissings could be even heard in the boat, and whose ravenous enemies, the white pelicans, rose in flocks along the margin of the lake.

The boat slipped along rapidly under sail with the wind from the north. The breeze was so fresh that the oars were not needed throughout the day, and when evening came the thirty miles which Lake George measures from north to south had been traversed without fatigue.

About six o'clock James Burbank and his men had reached the lower angle by which the St. John's enters the lake.

If they stopped—and the stoppage was only to take breath for half an hour at the outside—it was because three or four houses formed a village at this place. These were occupied by some of those nomadic Floridans who devote themselves chiefly to hunting and fishing at the beginning of the season. At Carrol's suggestion it seemed opportune to ask for information relative to the passage of Texar.

One of the inhabitants was questioned. During the last few days had he seen a boat crossing Lake George towards Lake Washington; a boat with seven or eight people, one a woman of colour, and a little child of white birth?

"Yes," said the man. " Two days ago I saw a boat like that."

" Did it stop here ? " asked Gilbert.

"No! It kept on as hard as it could go to the upper river. I distinctly saw a woman with a child in her arms."

" My friends," said Gilbert, "there is hope for us! We are really on the traces of Texar ! "

"Yes," answered James Burbank, "he is only forty-eight hours in front of us ; and if we can keep to the boat we shall gain on him."

" Do you know the river about Lake George ? " asked Carrol.

"Yes, sir ; I have been up it more than a hundred miles."

" Do you think it is navigable for a boat like ours ? "

" What does she draw ? "

" About three feet," said Mars.

"Three feet," said the man " That may do. If you take soundings as you go, you will get into Lake Washington."

"And then," said Carrol, "how far shall we be from Lake Okee-cho-bee ? "

" About a hundred and fifty miles."

" Thanks, my friend."

" Let us get on board, and keep to the boat till the water fails us."

The men took their places. The wind had fallen as evening closed ; the oars were got out and pulled with vigour. The narrowing banks began to disappear. At nightfall the boat had made many miles to the south. There was no need to stop, as they could sleep on board. The moon was almost full. The light was enough to steer by. Gilbert was at the helm ; Mars was in front with a long pole in his hand, sounding all the time, and ordering the boat to starboard or port as occasion required. He touched ground only five or six times, and each time got off without effort. About four o'clock in the morning. when the sun rose, Gilbert estimated that at least fifteen miles had been rowed during the night.

If the river continued navigable for a few more days, James Burbank's chances of success would be much improved. But several serious difficulties arose during the day On account of the windings of the river, there were many projecting points in its course where the accumulated sands increased the number of shoals that had to be avoided. The wide sweeps necessary to avoid these made the journey so much longer, and caused delay. The wind, although it did not shift, was brought round so by the windings of the stream that the sail could not always be used, but the blacks bent to their oars and did their best to make up for lost time.

And many obstacles were met with peculiar to the St. John's. There were the floating islands formed by a prodigious accumulation of that exuberant plant, the "pistia," which certain explorers have justly compared to a gigantic lettuce spread on the top of the water. This herbaceous carpet is solid enough for otters and herons to disport themselves on; but it would never do to run into such vegetable masses, as withdrawal would not be easy, and so Mars did his best to avoid them.

On the river-banks the thick forest again had appeared. But now there were none of those innumerable cedars with their roots bathed by the river. There were, in their stead, quantities of pines, a hundred and fifty feet high, belonging to the southern species, which found a favourable soil amid the inundated tracts known as "barrens." The mould there has a peculiar elasticity, so much so as to throw a man off his balance should he attempt to walk over it. Fortunately James Burbank's men did not make the experiment.

The St. John's continued to carry them through the regions of Lower Florida. The day passed without adventure. So did the night. The river continued to be completely deserted. Not a boat appeared on the waters. In this there was nothing to complain of. Better to find nobody in this distant country than to risk disaster, for the backwoodsmen and professional hunters of these parts are people to be treated with suspicion.

And there were the militia from Jacksonville or St. Augustine, whom Dupont and Stevens had driven to the south, who might be met with, and the meeting would have been still more undesirable.   Among them Texar certainly had many partisans, who might attempt to avenge him on James and Gilbert Burbank.   It was the object of the expedition to avoid fighting with every one except the Spaniard, and only to fight with him should he attempt to carry off his prisoners by force.

Fortunately, James Burbank was so well served by circumstances that on the evening of the 25th of March he reached Lake Washington.   There the narrowness and shallowness of the river brought the boat to a stop.   Two-thirds of the distance had, however, been sailed or rowed, and James Burbank was now only a hundred and forty miles from the Everglades.

CHAPTER IX.

THE GREAT CYPRESS FOREST.

LAKE WASHINGTON is about a dozen miles long. It is one of the least important lakes in this part of southern Florida. Its waters are not deep, and they are crowded with bushes and branches brought down by the stream from the floating fields, where the snakes are in such numbers as even to render the navigation dangerous. Like its banks, its surface is almost deserted, and seldom indeed is it that a boat from the St. John's ventures so far.

At the southern end of the lake the river resumes its course, bending more towards the middle of the peninsula. It is then little more than a shallow brook, its source being some thirty miles further south, between the twenty-eighth and twenty-seventh degrees of latitude.

Below Lake Washington the St. John's is not navigable. Much to the regret of James Burbank, the stream had to be abandoned, and the land-road taken through a very difficult country, often no better than a marsh, through endless forests with the ground so cut up with rivulets and quagmires as to be almost impassable.

The expedition landed. The weapons and bales of provisions were divided amongst the blacks. Every one knew his place, and there would be no cause for delay. All had been thought out in advance, and when a halt was called the camp could be pitched in a few minutes.

Gilbert and Mars occupied themselves in hiding the boat, so that it might escape the observation of any Seminoles or Floridans who might pass that way. Under the drooping branches of the trees by the bank, and among the gigantic reeds, it was easy to find a fitting place of concealment.

There was another boat which Gilbert would have been glad to find—that which had brought Dy and Zermah to Lake Washington. Evidently Texar must have abandoned it somewhere in the neighbourhood. What James Burbank had been obliged to do the Spaniard must have done. And for some hours in the afternoon a search for this boat was made, in order to procure positive proof that Texar had reached Lake Washington.

The search was in vain. The boat could not be found. Perhaps the Spaniard had destroyed it, thinking it would be of no further use to him.

How painful must the journey now have become ! There was no longer the river to save the woman and child from fatigue. Dy, carried in Zermah's arms, forced to follow the men who were used to such marches through this difficult country; the half-breed subject to insults and violence, and beaten to hasten her steps, and falling often to save the child when thinking nothing of herself—all this was pictured to the minds of those in pursuit. As Mars thought of all this he grew pale with anger, and muttered to himself—

" I will kill Texar ! "

Would he were at Carneral Island face to face with the villain whose abominable machinations had caused such suffering to the Burbanks, and injured him more deeply by taking away Zermah his wife !

The camp was formed at the extremity of a small cape projecting northwards into the lake. It had not been thought wise to risk travelling in the forest during the night, and it was decided to wait for the dawn before the start was made. At four o'clock the signal to move was given. The bales and packages were distributed amongst half the crew, it being intended to work in relays. All, masters and men, were armed with Minie rifles, loaded with a bullet and four buckshot, and Colt revolvers, which came into general use during the war of Secession.

Armed in this way they were equal to attacking Texar even at the head of sixty of his men.

It had been decided to keep to the course of the river as closely as possible. This would take them to the south in the direction of Lake Okee-cho-bee. It was a thread through the forest labyrinth, and it was followed easily enough. Along the right bank was a sort of footpath, a towing-path, in fact, used by those who had dragged their light canoes up stream. Gilbert and Mars went first; James Burbank and Edward Carrol brought up the rear; Perry was in the middle and every hour saw that the loads were changed. Before the start a rapid breakfast had been taken, a stoppage was to be made at noon for dinner, and another at six o'clock for supper and camping, if matters did not look promising for a night-march. That was the programme, and it was punctually adhered to.

At first the road lay along the eastern shore of Lake Washington, low and flat, and almost on the move. Then the forest came on, but of slight extent compared to what it was to be. This forest was chiefly composed of thickets of logwood with small leaves and yellow clusters, and with the brownish heart-wood so well known to dyers; then there were Mexican elms, guazumas with white bouquets, used in so many ways, and with a shade giving, it is said, a most obstinate cold. Dotted about were a few groups of cinchonas, here mere shrubs instead of magnificent trees as in Peru. Everywhere rose large masses of bright-coloured plants, such as gentians, amaryllides, and asclepias; all plants and flowers yellow or white in Europe being here of different shades of red and purple.

Towards evening the thickets disappeared, to give place to the great cypress forest, which extends to the Everglades.

During the day they had walked twenty miles. Gilbert asked of the negroes if they were tired.

"We are ready to go on, sir," said one of them, answering for the rest.

"Are we not likely to go astray during the night?" asked Edward Carrol.

"No," said Mars. "We have only got to keep to the river."

"And the night is clear," said the young officer, "the sky is cloudless; the moon will rise at nine and last till day. Besides, the foliage of the cypresses is not very thick, and the darkness is not as great as in any other forest."

So they made a fresh start. The next morning, after travelling part of the night, they stopped to breakfast at the foot of one of those huge cypress-trees which can be counted in millions in this region of Florida.

He who has not explored these natural marvels can hardly figure them to himself. Imagine a stretch of green more than a hundred feet above the river, with tree-trunks straight as towers, on whose tops it seems almost possible to walk. Below the ground is wet and marshy; the water in pools on the impermeable soil, round which and in which are crowds of frogs and toads, and lizards and scorpions, and spiders, turtles, snakes, and aquatic birds. Above the pools flash, like shooting stars, bright-plumaged orioles; in the trees leap squirrels and gather parrots, who fill the forest with their noisy screeches. A curious country it is, and difficult to penetrate. The ground must be carefully studied, for a foot-passenger may sink to his armpits in the many quagmires. But keeping a sharp look-out in the clear night, the expedition advanced without accident.

The river still gave them their true course. And this was fortunate, for the cypresses all resembled each other, with their twisted, spiral trunks, hollow below, and throwing out their long roots that ridged the soil, and rose for twenty feet or more in cylindrical stems, huge ribs with knotty handle supporting an immense green umbrella that gave but little protection from either rain or sun.

It was beneath these trees that James Burbank and his companions were journeying a little before daybreak. The weather was magnificent. There was no storm to fear, which might make the ground an impracticable marsh, although a constant look-out was necessary to keep clear of the never-drying bogs.

During the day no trace was met with of either Southerners or Seminoles. It might be that the Spaniard had gone down the left bank, which was clear of obstacles ; but by either bank the road lay direct to the country mentioned in Zermah's letter.

The night came. James Burbank halted for six hours ; then the rest of the night speedily slipped away. The road lay in silence through the sleeping cypress-grove. Not a breath of wind troubled the dome of foliage. The moon outlined on the ground a light network of shadow. The river murmured in its almost level bed ; many shoals appeared above its surface, and showed that it could be easily crossed, if necessary.

After a halt of two hours, the march was resumed, but during this day the guiding-thread occasionally gave out, as though the end of the skein would soon be reached. The river was a mere streak, diving every now and then under a clump of cinchonas, while beyond the cypress-forest shut in three-quarters of the horizon. At last it gave out altogether ; they had passed its source.

And now they reached a cemetery reserved, according to native custom, for the blacks who had become Christians and died in the faith. Here and there were humble crosses, some of stone, some of wood, rising from the little mounds and marking the graves between the trees. Two or three aerial burials had taken place, and the skeletons were gently swaying in the wind on their cradle of boughs.

"The existence of a cemetery," said Carrol, "ought to show that we are near a village—"

"Which need not exist," said Gilbert, "for it is not on our map ; and villages often disappear in these parts, owing to the inhabitants abandoning them or their being destroyed by Indians."

"Gilbert," said James Burbank, "what shall we do now the St. John's has gone out ? "

"We must follow the compass. However thick the

forest may be, it will be impossible for us to lose ourselves."

" Well, let us get on," said Mars, who could hardly keep still during these stoppages. " Let us get on, and trust to Providence."

Half a mile beyond the negro cemetery they came out on to a green plain, and, compass in hand, struck off due south.

During the first part of the day no incident occurred. Up to then nothing had been found to give a clue ; would it be so to the end ? Would they attain their object, or would the end be despair ?

At noon they stopped. Gilbert, taking account of the distance from Lake Washington, estimated that they were still fifty miles from Okee-cho-bee. Eight days had elapsed since they left Camdless Bay, and more than three hundred miles had been traversed with exceptional rapidity. In the absence of heavy rain, which would have made the course of the St. John's unnavigable, and flooded the country, and in the clearness of the moon, everything had been favourable for the journey.

A comparatively short distance now separated them from Carneral Island, and they expected to reach it during the next two days. What was to happen then it was impossible to foresee.

But if hitherto good fortune had been theirs, it seemed as though they were now to meet with insurmountable difficulties.

The journey had been resumed as usual after the noonday meal. The character of the road had not changed. There were still large sheets of water and quagmire to avoid, and tiny streams to be crossed knee-deep.

About four o'clock Mars suddenly stopped. When his companions came up with him he pointed out the print of feet on the ground.

" There can be no doubt," said James Burbank, " that a body of men have recently passed here."

" And a large body," said Edward Carrol.

" Where do the footsteps come from ? Where do they
17

go to ?" asked Gilbert. "We must find that out before we do anything else."

And they set to work to do so.

For five hundred yards to the east they traced the footsteps, and it seemed useless to go further. It was clearly shown that a band of from a hundred and fifty to two hundred men had come from the Atlantic coast into the cypress grove. The footprints were continued westward towards the Gulf of Mexico, and thus seemed to lead across the peninsula, which is here only two hundred miles wide. It was apparent that these men had camped on the very spot that the Burbanks were now examining; and Gilbert and Mars went off to follow the westward trail for a little. To their astonishment, they found that it soon turned to the south. When they returned, Gilbert explained.

"We are preceded by a body of men who are going the same road as we are. They are armed, for we found the bits of the cartridges they used to light their fires with. Who they are I know not. All I can say is that they are numerous, and are going to the Everglades."

"Are they not a band of wandering Seminoles ?" asked Edward Carrol.

"No," answered Mars ; "the footprints show they are Americans."

"Perhaps soldiers of the Floridan militia," said James Burbank.

"That is to be feared," said Perry. "They seem to me to be too many of them to belong to Texar."

"Unless he has been joined by some of his partisans, who must have come to him in hundreds," said Carrol.

"We are only seventeen," said the overseer.

"What does that matter ?" exclaimed Gilbert. "If they attack us, not one of us will run."

"No ! no !" said all his companions.

Their courage was the same as it had been ; but it seemed hard to meet with an obstacle when so near their object. And what an obstacle ! A detachment of Southerners, come to join the Spaniard in the Everglades until the time came for them to appear again in the north of Florida. Therein was the danger. All felt it to be so. And after the first display of enthusiasm, they stood silent, looking at their chief, and asking what orders he would give. Even Gilbert shared in the common impression, but notwithstanding, he gave the word—

"Forward !"

CHAPTER X.

A MEETING.

YES ; forward they must go. But under these serious circumstances every precaution was taken. It was indispensable to clear the march, to reconnoitre the thickets on the road, to be ready for anything.

The weapons were carefully examined and held ready for immediate service. At the least alarm the packages were to be dropped on the ground and the men would fight behind them. The order of march remained as before. Gilbert and Mars formed the vanguard, but they kept further ahead to guard against surprise. The rate of progress was the same, but it seemed better not to follow in the same track as the others had gone. Better would it be if they did not meet with the detachment in advance of them on the road to the Everglades. But this did not seem to be easy, for the detachment had not moved in a straight line, but had diverged to the right and left, showing a certain amount of hesitation, though the general advance was unmistakably southwards.

A day passed. Nothing happened to bring James Burbank to a standstill. He had kept on at a good pace, and had evidently gained on those in front of him. Hour by hour the traces of their passage became more recent. It became easy so see how often they had halted either to camp or take counsel.

Gilbert and Mars studied the trail with great care; almost as if they had been Seminole trackers.

"We are certain," said Gilbert, "that neither Zermah nor Dy are with this party. There are no footprints of a horse, and if Zermah was with them it is obvious that with Dy in her arms her footprints would be easily recognizable,

and we should see Dy's footsteps at the halting-places.
But there is no mark of woman's foot or girl's foot. The
detachment carries firearms. We can see the marks of the
stocks on the ground. But I notice that the stocks are
like those on the rifles carried by sailors. Probably the
Florida militia has such arms ; if not, I cannot understand
it. One thing is certain, and that is that the band is ten
times as numerous as ours, and we must be very careful as
we get nearer to them."

And everything was done to carry out his suggestion.
His deductions from the evidence of the footprints were
correct. It was obvious that neither Dy nor Zermah were
with the detachment, and it seemed from this certain that
they were not on the track of the Spaniard. The men
from Black Creek could not be so numerous or so well
armed. And there could be little doubt that a strong
body of militia were on the march to the Everglades,
where Texar had probably arrived a day or two before.
And these militiamen might make matters serious for
James Burbank.

That evening they halted on the edge of a narrow
clearing, which had been occupied an hour or two beforehand, to judge from the heap of scarcely cold cinders
and the traces of the camp. When this was ascertained,
it was decided not to resume the march till after nightfall.
The night was dark. The sky was cloudy. The moon
did not rise till late. They could approach the detachment under the most favourable conditions. Could they
reconnoitre the camp without being perceived ? Could
they get round it during the night, and hurry on in
front so as to be first at Lake Okee-cho-bee and Carneral
Island ?

The expedition, with Mars and Gilbert ahead as scouts,
started about half-past eight, and silently entered into the
darkness under the trees. For two hours they kept on,
making as little noise as possible.

A little after ten o'clock James Burbank stopped with a
word the group of blacks at whose head he and the overseer were walking. His son and Mars were coming back

towards him, and he waited anxiously for an explanation of their rapid retreat.

The explanation was soon given.

"What is it?" he asked. "What do you see?"

"A camp under the trees, and the fires alight."

"Far off?" asked Carrol.

"About a hundred yards."

"Did you see who they were?"

"No; the fires are dying down," said Gilbert. "But I do not think we are wrong in saying there are two hundred men."

"Are they asleep?"

"Most of them, but they have got men on the watch. We saw the sentinels with their rifles on their shoulders pacing backwards and forwards under the cypresses."

"What are we to do?" asked Carrol.

"We must first of all reconnoitre them," said Gilbert, "and see who they are, if possible."

"I am ready," said Mars.

"I'll go with you," said Perry.

"No; I'll go," said Gilbert; "I would rather see for myself."

"Gilbert," said James Burbank, "there is not one of us who would not risk his life for the good of us all; but to make this reconnaissance with some chance of not being seen, only one ought to go."

"I'll go alone."

"No, my son. I would rather you stayed with us."

"I am ready, master!"

And Mars, without another word, disappeared in the darkness.

While he was gone James Burbank prepared for an attack. The bales and packages were laid down in a circle; the bearers took to their weapons, and with the others went into hiding among the trees, awaiting further orders.

From where James Burbank stood he could not see the camp. He had to go about fifty yards before the fires were visible; and he resolved to wait till the half-breed returned before he took any further measures. The lieutenant was more impatient, and went forward a few yards.

Mars approached the camp, gliding silently from trunk to trunk, hoping to get near enough to see how the men were placed and who they were, and how many they were. This did not seem to be difficult. The night was dark, and the fires gave but little light. But to succeed he must get almost inside the camp.

To have the free use of his limbs as much as possible he had taken with him neither rifle nor revolver. It would be necessary to defend himself in silence, and his only weapon was his axe.

Soon the brave half-breed was close to one of the sentries, who was only seven or eight yards from the fires. All was still. Evidently the men were tired after their long march, and were asleep. The sentinels alone were watching at their posts with more or less vigilance.

For a moment or so he looked at the man who was nearest him. He was standing upright against a cypress-trunk, and gave no sign of moving. His gun was resting on the ground, and he seemed half-asleep. Was it possible to slip round him ?

Mars crept stealthily towards him. Suddenly the crackling of a dry branch revealed his presence.

Instantly the man raised his head and looked to the right and left.

Doubtless he saw something suspicious, for he brought his gun to his shoulder.

Before he could fire Mars had knocked his gun up against him and sent him flying to the ground, and at the same time clapped his large hand on his mouth so that he could utter no cry. A moment afterwards the man was gagged, and carried hurriedly to James Burbank.

The other sentinels took no notice of what had passed. Evidently their watch was a negligent one.

Mars laid his burden at his young master's feet. The blacks crowded up. The man was half-suffocated, and when the gag was removed he could not for a moment or

PART II.

so say a word.   The darkness was too great for his uniform
to be seen.

"Help !" he shouted.

"Not a word !" said James Burbank, stopping him.
"You have nothing to fear from us."

"What do you want with me ? "

"To answer truthfully to our questions."

"That will depend on your questions," said the man.
"Are you for the South or the North ? "

"For the North."

"I am ready to reply."

Gilbert took up the examination.

"How many men are there in that camp ? "

"Nearly two hundred."

"Where are they going ? "

"To the Everglades."

"Who is in command ? "

"Captain Howick."

"What, Captain Howick of the *Wabash* ? "

"Yes."

"Is it a detachment of seamen from Commodore Dupont's squadron ? "

"Yes ;   Federals, Northerners, Anti-slavery men,
Unionists !" said the man, apparently quite proud at announcing the different titles of the followers of the good
cause.

And so, instead of a body of Florida militia, of Texar's
partisans, James Burbank had met with friends, with
companions in arms, whose reinforcement was most welcome.

"Hurrah !" they shouted with such vigour that the
whole camp was instantly afoot.

Suddenly torches flared up in the darkness.   Burbank's
men rushed into the clearing, and Captain Howick, without
a word of explanation, held out his hand to the young
lieutenant, whom he never expected to meet on the road to
the Everglades.   Explanations did not take long, nor were
they difficult.

"What are you doing in Lower Florida, captain?" asked Gilbert.

"My dear Burbank," said the captain, "we have been sent on an expedition by the commodore."

"Where do you come from?"

"From Mosquito Inlet, and we have been to capture New Smyrna in the interior of the county."

"And where are you going now?"

"To punish a band of Southerners who took a couple of our boats in an ambuscade, and to avenge the deaths of our brave comrades."

And Captain Howick related what James Burbank could not know, for it took place two days after he left Camdless Bay.

Commodore Dupont was, it will be remembered, organizing the effective blockade of the coast. In doing this his flotilla was stationed off Anastasia Island, above St. Augustine, at the mouth of the channel separating the Bahamas from Cape Sable at the southern end of Florida. But this did not seem enough to him, and he resolved to give chase to the Southern vessels in the smaller rivers of the peninsula. One of the expeditions on this service consisted of a detachment of seamen and two boats. The Southerners kept a careful watch on their proceedings, and allowed the boats to get well up into the wild part of Florida. To advance so far was certainly imprudent, for the Indians and militia were in great force in the neighbourhood, and the result was that they fell into an ambuscade on the shore of Lake Kissimmee, about eighty miles westward of Cape Malabar. They were attacked by a numerous body of the enemy, and the two officers in command and many of the men were killed. The survivors regained Mosquito Inlet by a miracle, and Commodore Dupont at once sent off an expedition to avenge the massacre of the Federals.

A detachment of two hundred men was placed under command of Captain Howick, and landed near Mosquito Inlet. It soon reached New Smyrna, some miles from the

coast, and, after taking such measures as were necessary,
Captain Howick struck off to the south-west in chase of
the party who were responsible for the Kissimmee massacre,
and this party had fled to the Everglades.

"We are also going to the Everglades," said Gilbert.

"You!" said the officer. "What are you going to do
there?"

"Catch a few scoundrels and chastise them, as you are
going to do, captain!"

"Who are these scoundrels?"

"Before I answer that, answer me one question. When
did you leave New Smyrna?"

"Eight days ago."

"And you have not met any party of Southerners on
your way?"

"No, but we know from a sure source that detachments
of militia are hiding in Lower Florida."

"Who is in command of the detachment you are after?
Do you know him?"

"Oh, yes! And if we catch him Mr. Burbank will not
be sorry."

"Why not?" asked James Burbank.

"Because he is the Spaniard the court-martial at St.
Augustine acquitted for want of evidence."

"Texar!"

"What!" exclaimed Gilbert, "Texar chief of the partisans you are after?"

"Himself! He was the author of the Kissimmee massacre, at the head of some fifty fellows like him; and we
ascertained at New Smyrna that he had taken himself off
o the Everglades."

"And if you catch him what are you going to do?"
asked Carrol.

"Shoot him on the spot," said Captain Howick. "That
is the commodore's order, and rest assured we shall execute
it without delay."

It will easily be imagined what an effect this revelation
produced on James Burbank. This reinforcement meant
the almost certain deliverance of Dy and Zermah, the

assured capture of the Spaniard and his accomplices, and the inevitable punishment for his crimes.

Gilbert then told Captain Howick the object of their expedition to Southern Florida, which, in the first place, meant the deliverance of Zermah and the girl, carried off to Carneral Island, as the half-breed's letter showed. The captain also learnt that the alibi invoked by the Spaniard at the court-martial could not be true, although they could not at present disprove it. But with this massacre at Kissimmee there seemed to be no chance of Texar again escaping.

An unexpected observation of James Burbank's, however, led to somewhat different thoughts.

" Can you tell me," he asked Captain Howick, " when the Federal boats were attacked ? "

" The massacre took place on the 22nd of March."

" But on the 22nd of March Texar was at Black Creek ! How could he have taken part in the massacre at Kissimmee, two hundred miles away ? "

" What do you mean ? " asked the captain.

" I mean that Texar could not have been at the head of the Southerners who attacked your men."

" You are mistaken, Mr. Burbank. The Spaniard was seen by some of the men who escaped. I examined them myself, and they recognized Texar from having seen him at St. Augustine."

" That cannot be, captain. The letter written by Zermah proves that on the 22nd of March Texar was at Black Creek "

Gilbert had listened without a word. He saw that his father must be right. The Spaniard could not have been near Kissimmee on the day of the massacre.

" What does it matter ? " he said. " There is something about the man which at present we cannot understand, and why should we try to do so ? On the 22nd of March he was at Black Creek, as Zermah says. On the 22nd he was at the head of a party of Floridans, two hundred miles away, so you say. Well, be it so. We are agreed that he is now in the Everglades. Let us catch him as soon as we can ! "

"Yes, Gilbert, that's it," said Captain Howick. "And we'll shoot him anyhow! Let us be off."

The fact, like the others, was none the less incomprehensible. It seemed as though the Spaniard had a double.

Would the mystery be cleared up? In any case, the only thing to do was to make sure of Texar; and Howick's seamen and Burbank's negroes fell in together, and resumed their way to the south.

CHAPTER XI.

THE EVERGLADES.

A HORRIBLE district is that of the Everglades, and yet it is superb. Situated in the southern part of Florida, it extends right down to Cape Sable, the extreme point of the peninsula, and it is simply an immense marsh. The waters of the sea flood it in wide stretches, when the storms of the Atlantic or the Mexican Gulf beat on to its shores, and mingle with the waters from the clouds that the winter season pours down in cataracts. And in consequence it is a country half liquid and half solid, and almost uninhabitable.

But let it not be supposed that it is barren. On the contrary, it is on the surface of the islands in the marsh that nature asserts her rights. The malaria is, so to speak, conquered by the perfumes of the wonderful flowers ; the islands are steeped in the fragrance of a thousand plants, blooming in such splendour as to justify the peninsula's poetic name. And it is in these healthy oases that the Indians take refuge, though not for long at a time.

A few miles beyond the frontier of this territory is the wide sheet of water known as Lake Okee-cho-bee, which is just a little below the twenty-seventh parallel. In one of the angles of this lake lies Carneral Island, where Texar fancied he had an unknown retreat in which he could defy pursuit.

The country was worthy of him and his companions. When Florida belonged to the Spaniards, it was thither that all the white scoundrels fled from justice. Mixing with the native population, among whom there still were traces of Carib blood, they made common cause with the Creeks and Seminoles and nomadic Indians who were

only subdued after the long bloody war that ended in
1845.

Carneral Island seemed safe from all attack. On the
eastern side it is separated from the mainland by a narrow
channel about a hundred feet across, and the only means
of communication was a heavy boat. To escape by
swimming was impossible, for no one would dare to enter
the slimy water which bristled with long interlacing plants
and swarmed with reptiles.

Beyond was the cypress forest with the ground half
under water and traversed but by narrow paths which were
by no means easy to trace. A clayey soil sticking to the
feet like glue, enormous trunks of fallen trees barring the
way, and a suffocating odour of mouldiness were among
the other obstacles to be overcome in the approach, And
there were masses of formidable plants, such as the
phylacias, and millions of pezizas, gigantic mushrooms,
as explosive as if they were charged with gun-cotton or
dynamite, going off with a violent report at the slightest
shock and filling the air with a choking cloud of tawny
spores that give the human skin an eruption of painful
pustules, so that the spiteful vegetables have to be avoided
as carefully as the most dangerous animals of the teratologic
world.

Texar's dwelling was an old Indian wigwam built on
piles under the branches of the large trees in the eastern
end of the island. Hidden amid the foliage, it was invisible even from the nearest bank. The two hounds
guarded it with as much vigilance as they did the blockhouse at Black Creek, and trained to the chase of men
would tear in pieces any one attempting to approach the
wigwam.

Two days had passed since Zermah and little Dy had
arrived. The journey had been easy enough till they
reached Lake Washington, but after entering the cypress
forest it had been exceedingly painful, even for the vigorous men who were used to the unhealthy climate and the
long wearisome advance through the marsh. What the
woman and child had suffered can be imagined ! But

Zermah was strong, brave, and devoted, and throughout
the journey had carried little Dy whose legs would soon
have failed her ; and when she reached Carneral Island she
was almost exhausted.

And after what had passed when Texar and Squambo
had dragged her from Black Creek, is it not a wonder that
she still held out ? She had no means of knowing that
the letter she had given to the young slave had fallen into
James Burbank's hands, but she knew that he had paid
with his life for the act of devotion by which he had
attempted to save her. He had been surprised at the
moment he was starting for Camdless Bay, and had been
mortally wounded ; and the half-breed had said to herself
that now James Burbank would never know that the
Spaniard was going to Carneral Island, and how could he
get any clue to her whereabouts ? How then could she
retain the shadow of a hope ? Every chance of safety
seemed to have vanished in this region whose horrors she
knew too well. And no escape was possible !

The little girl was in a state of great weakness ; and in
spite of Zermah's constant care, the fatigue had made her
ill. Pale and emaciated as if she had been poisoned by
the emanations from the marshes, she was no longer strong
enough to remain upright, and could with difficulty utter
but a few words, which were always an inquiry for her
mother. Zermah could no longer tell her, as she had done
for the first few days after her arrival at Black Creek, that
she would soon see Mrs. Burbank, and that her father,
brother, Miss Stannard, and Mars, would soon come to her.
With her precocious intelligence rendered more acute since
the dreadful scenes at the plantation, Dy saw that she
had been torn from her home and was in the hands of a
wicked man, and unless some one came to her rescue she
would never again see Camdless Bay. And so Zermah
knew not what to answer, and in spite of all she could do,
saw the child gradually wasting away.

The wigwam was only a huge hut which in the winter
season afforded no adequate protection. The wind and
the rain penetrated it on all sides. But in the hot season

which was now coming on in this latitude, it at least provided shelter from the heat of the sun. It was divided into two rooms of unequal size. One was narrow and badly lighted and did not communicate with the open air, but with the other room, which obtained its light from a door that opened on to the bank of the narrow channel. Zermah and Dy had been lodged in the small room, where a litter of herbs served them for a bed.

The other room was occupied by Texar and the Indian Squambo, who never left his master. For furniture, they had a table with many jars of brandy, and glasses and a few plates, a sort of cupboard for provisions, a half-squared tree-trunk for a seat and two bundles of herbs for beds. The fire necessary to cook the meals was made on the stone hearth outside, in one of the angles of the wigwam, and it proved sufficient for the preparation of the dried meat and venison that a hunter could find on the island, and the fruits and vegetables in an almost wild state, just enough, in fact, to keep them from dying of hunger.

The half-dozen slaves Texar had brought with him from Black Creek slept out of doors like the dogs, and like them served as guards on the approaches.

From the first day Dy and Zermah were allowed to go out and in as they pleased. They were no longer imprisoned in their rooms. But they were watched. The precaution was superfluous, for no one could cross the channel without using the boat that was always in the safe keeping of the blacks. And as she walked about Zermah took careful notice of the difficulties of escape.

The first day the half-breed was never out of sight of Squambo ; but she did not see Texar. When night came she, however, heard the Spaniard talking to the Seminole, and ordering him to keep a strict watch. And soon all but Zermah were asleep in the wigwam.

Up to then Zermah, it should be said, had not had a single word spoken to her by Texar. As she ascended the river towards Lake Washington, she had in vain asked him what he was going to do with her and the child. And **while she spoke the Spaniard contented himself with** shrugging his shoulders and fixing his cruel eyes on her, and looking as if he scorned to answer. But Zermah had no intention of giving in. When she reached Carneral Island, she resolved to attack Texar so as to excite his pity, if not for herself, at least for the unfortunate child, and if his pity failed her to appeal to his self-interest.

An opportunity offered. The day after her arrival, while the little girl was asleep, Zermah walked out towards the channel by the side of which Texar was then standing and giving orders with Squambo to the slaves, who were at work weeding, for the water was so choked that the barge could hardly pass. While this was being done two of the negroes were striking the surface of the water with long poles so as to frighten away the reptiles whose heads appeared every now and then above the surface.

A moment afterwards Squambo left his master, and Texar was also going away when Zermah came up.

"Texar," said Zermah firmly, "I wish to speak to you. This will be the last time, doubtless, and I beg you to hear me."

The Spaniard, who had just lighted his cigarette, did not answer, and Zermah having waited a few seconds continued,—

"Will you tell me what you are going to do with Dy Burbank?"

No reply.

"I say nothing about my own fate. All I have to do with now is that of this child, whose life is in danger, and who will soon escape you."

At this Texar made a gesture of the most absolute incredulity.

"Yes, very soon," continued Zermah. "If not by flight it will be by death."

The Spaniard took a long whiff at his cigarette, and replied,—

"Bah! The little girl will be all right after a few days' rest, and I reckon on your care, Zermah, to retain its precious existence for us."

18

"No, I repeat. Before very long, the child will be dead, and dead without any profit to you."

"Without profit!" replied Texar, "when I have her far from her dying mother, her father and her brother reduced to despair?"

"Be it so," said Zermah. "You have your revenge, Texar, but believe me, it would be more to your advantage to give up the child than to keep her here."

"What is that you say?"

"I say that you have made James Burbank suffer enough; that now it is your interest to speak."

"My interest?"

"Certainly. The plantation of Camdless Bay has been laid waste. Mrs. Burbank is dying, perhaps dead at this moment; her daughter has disappeared, and her father is vainly endeavouring to find her. All this has been done by you, Texar. I know it! and I have the right to tell you so to your face. But take care! Your crimes will be discovered some day, and think of the punishment that will come to you! Your best interest now is to show pity. I do not speak for myself, though my husband will not find me when he returns. No, I speak only for the little girl who is dying. Keep me if you like, but send the child back to Camdless Bay to her mother; then they will never ask you about the past and if you want it they will even pay you well for the girl's liberty. If I take upon myself to speak like this, and propose this exchange, it is because I know James Burbank and his people to the bottom of their hearts; because I know they would sacrifice all their fortune to save the child, and I call God to witness they will keep the promise their slave has made."

"Their slave?" exclaimed Texar ironically. "There are now no slaves at Camdless Bay."

"There are; for in order to stay with my master I refused to be set free."

"Indeed, Zermah, indeed!" answered the Spaniard. "Well, since you do not mind being a slave we can understand each other. Six or seven years ago I wished to buy you of my friend Tickborn. I offered for you, for you alone, a considerable sum, and you would have belonged to me ever since if James Burbank had not got hold of you. Now I have you, and I will keep you."

"Be it so, Texar," said Zermah. "I will be your slave. But the child! Will you not give her up?"

"The child of James Burbank!" answered Texar in a tone of the deepest hatred. "Give her up to her father? Never!"

"Villain!" exclaimed Zermah in anger. "If her father does not take her from you, God will!"

A grin, a shrug of the shoulders, and that was all the Spaniard's answer. He had rolled up a second cigarette and lighted it calmly with the end of the last, and strolled off up the bank of the channel without another look at Zermah, who would have struck him as if he had been a wild beast, at the risk of being massacred by Squambo and his companions, had she only had a weapon. But she could do nothing. Motionless she stood and watched the blacks at work. Nowhere a friendly face; nothing but the faces of brutes hardly seeming to be human. And she went back to the wigwam to resume her part of mother to the child who in a feeble voice was calling her. She tried to console the poor little creature, whom she took in her arms and animated with her kisses; and then she brought the child outside and gave her a warm drink made on the hearth. All she could do in her state of destitution she did. Dy thanked her with a smile—and such a smile—sadder than if it had been tears.

Zermah did not see the Spaniard again all that day. And she did not seek to see him. What good would it do? He would not change his sentiments, and by these recriminations things might become worse. For though up to then, during her stay at Black Creek, and since her arrival at Carneral Island, the worst treatment had been spared her and the child, there was everything to be feared from such a man. A fit of anger might drive him to the greatest violence. No pity could be expected from him, and as his interest did not stand in the way of his hate, Zermah had given up all hope in the future. As to the Spaniard's

companions, Squambo and the slaves, how could **they be**
expected to be more human than their master? They
knew the fate that awaited them if they showed the slightest
sympathy. From them nothing was to be hoped. Zermah
must trust to herself. Her resolution was taken. She
would try and escape during the night.

But how? The ring of water that surrounded the island
must be crossed, and though near the wigwam the channel
was narrow, yet it could not be swum. There was only
one chance, and that was to seize on the barge.

The night fell dark and gloomy, for the rain had come
on, and the wind swept fiercely across the marsh.

If it was impossible for Zermah to quit the wigwam by
the door of the large room, perhaps it would not be difficult
for her to make a hole in the wall, and so get through.

Ten o'clock came, and nothing was heard outside but the
moaning of the storm. Texar and Squambo were asleep.
The hounds hiding under one of the thickets no longer
prowled round the dwelling.

The moment was favourable.

While Dy lay sleeping on the couch of herbs, Zermah
began to pull away quietly the straw and reeds in the side
wall of the wigwam.

At the end of an hour the hole was only large enough
for the girl to get through, and she was making it larger
when a noise suddenly stopped her.

The noise came from far out in the darkness, and was
the barking of the hounds announcing some arrival. Texar
and Squambo suddenly awakened, got up, and hurriedly
went out.

Voices were heard. Evidently a troop of men had
reached the opposite bank of the channel. Zermah must
for the present give up her attempt at flight.

Soon, in spite of the tumult of the storm, it was easy to
distinguish the sound of many footsteps. Zermah listened.
What was happening? Had Providence taken pity on
her? Had the help come on which she had not dared to
reckon?

No, and she knew it could not be so, for there was no

sound of a struggle as the channel was crossed, no reports of firearms. It was a reinforcement that had arrived at Carneral Island.

A minute afterwards Zermah saw two persons enter the wigwam. The Spaniard was accompanied by another man who could not be Squambo, for the Indian's voice could be heard outside on the bank of the channel.

Two men were, however, in the room. They had begun to talk in a low voice, when they suddenly stopped. One of them, lantern in hand, came towards Zermah's room, and she had only just time to throw herself on the bed so as to hide the hole in the wall.

Texar, for it was he, opened the door, looked round the room, saw the half-breed apparently asleep by the side of the child, and retired.

Zermah then took her place behind the door he had shut. If she could not see or recognize the strange man, she could hear all that passed.

And this is what she heard.

CHAPTER XII.

WHAT ZERMAH OVERHEARD.

" You, at Carneral Island ? "

" Yes.   I have been here for some hours."

" I thought you were at Adamsville, near Lake Apopka ? "

" I was there a week ago."

" And why have you come here ? "

" Because I had to do so."

" We ought never to meet, you know, except in the marsh at Black Creek, and then only after you have written to tell me ! "

" But I had to beat a hurried retreat, and escape to the Everglades."

" Why ? "

" I am going to tell you."

" But is there no risk of our being found out ? "

" No ! I came in the dark, and none of your slaves saw me."

Zermah listened, but she could not up to this point make out the meaning of the conversation, nor could she imagine who was the wigwam's unexpected guest.   There were certainly two men talking ; and yet it seemed as though it was only one man who questioned and answered.   The voice was the same ; the accent was the same ; the words seemed to come from the same mouth.   In vain Zermah tried to look through a crack in the door.   The room was lighted but feebly, and remained in a half-shadow which prevented the least object from being distinguished.   The half-breed had therefore to content herself with listening as intently as possible to a conversation which might be of extreme importance for her.

After a moment's silence the two men had continued as

follows. Evidently it was Texar who asked the first question.

"You have not come alone?"

"No; some of our men came with me to the Everglades."

"How many?"

"Forty."

"Are you not afraid that they will find out what we have kept secret from them for so long?"

"No. They will never see us together. When they leave Carneral Island they will have learnt nothing, and the plan of our life will in no way be changed."

And Zermah thought she could hear the clasp of the hands as they met in token of continued friendship.

Then the conversation was resumed.

"What has happened since Jacksonville was taken?"

"A serious business. You know that Dupont took possession of St. Augustine?"

"Yes, I know; and you, I suppose, know why I know?"

"Yes! The story of the Fernandina train came in handy to allow you to establish the *alibi* that forced the court to acquit you."

"Which did not quite suit them! Bah! It is not the first time we have got off like that."

"And it won't be the last. But do you know what the Federals are after in occupying St. Augustine? It was not so much to hold the capital of St. John's county as to organize the blockade of the Atlantic coast."

"So l heard."

"Well, to watch the coast from the mouth of the St. John's to the Bahamas did not seem to be enough for Dupont, and he resolved to follow up contraband of war into the interior of Florida. So he sent off two boats' crews. Have you heard of this?"

"No."

"But when did you leave Black Creek? Some days after you were acquitted?"

"Yes! The 22nd of this month."

"This took place on the 22nd."

PART II.

It should be remembered that Zermah knew nothing of the ambuscade at Kissimmee, of which Captain Howick had spoken to Gilbert at their meeting in the forest. So she, like the Spaniard, heard for the first time how the boats had been burnt, and hardly a dozen survivors had found their way back to the Commodore with news of the disaster.

"Well! well!" exclaimed Texar. "That is a happy revenge for the capture of Jacksonville, and if we can lure those infernal Northerners into the thick of Florida, not one of them will get back."

"Not one. If we can get them among the marshes of the Everglades. And we shall have them there before long."

"What do you mean?"

"Dupont has sworn to avenge the death of his officers and sailors, and a new expedition has been sent out to the south of St. John's county."

"The Federals are coming from that quarter?"

"Yes, but more numerous and better armed, and well on their guard against ambuscades."

"Have you met them?"

"No, for our people are not in force now, and we have had to retreat. But, as we retired we drew them on after us. When we have been joined by the militia who are somewhere about, we will fall on them, and not one shall escape."

"Where did they come from?"

"Mosquito Inlet."

"Which way did they come?"

"Through the cypress grove."

"Where are they now?"

"About forty miles from Carneral Island."

"Good," said Texar. "We must get them further south, for there is not a day to lose in concentrating the militia. If necessary, we must be off to-morrow to the shore of the Bahama Channel."

"And from there, if we are pressed before we can collect our friends, we will find a safe retreat in the English islands."

The different matters alluded to in this conversation were of the greatest interest to Zermah. If Texar decided to leave the island, would he take the prisoners with him, or would he leave them at the wigwam in charge of Squambo? In that case it would be better not to attempt to escape until after the Spaniard's departure. Then she might, perhaps, have a better chance of success. And perhaps the Federal expedition then in Lower Florida might reach Lake Okee-cho-bee, in sight of Carneral Island?

But these hopes vanished almost as soon as they rose. For the next question that was asked was, what was to be done with the half-breed and child, and to it Texar answered, without hesitation,—

" I shall take them with me, if necessary, to the Bahamas."

" But will the little girl bear the discomforts of the voyage ? "

" Yes! I will answer for that ; and besides, Zermah knows how she can avoid them ! "

" But if the child were to die ? "

" I had rather have her dead than give her back to her father ! "

" Ah ! you are a good hater of these Burbanks ! "

" As good as you are ! "

Zermah could hardly contain herself, and was on the point of throwing open the door and meeting face to face these two men, who were so like to each other, not only in voice, but in evil instinct and want of conscience and heart. But she controlled herself. Better hear to the end what Texar and his accomplice had to say. When their talk was at an end perhaps they would sleep ! Then there might be time to escape before they left the island.

Evidently the Spaniard was in the position of one who had everything to learn from him he was talking to. And so he continued to question him.

" What news is there from the north ? "

" Nothing of much importance. Unfortunately, it seems

as though the Federals were getting the best of it, and that the slave cause is done for."

" Bah ! " said Texar, in a tone of indifference.

"Well, we are neither for South or North, really, are we ? "

" No. The only thing is, while they are at each other's throats to be always on the side where most is to be gained."

In this remark Texar revealed his true character. The two men fished in the troubled water of civil war only for what they could catch.

"But," said Texar, "what has happened in Florida during the last week ? "

"Nothing that you do not know. Stevens remains master of the St. John's up to Picolata."

" And he does not seem to care to come further down ? "

" No ; the gunboats have not been sent to the south of the county. And 1 fancy the occupation of this river will soon end, and that the Confederates will get back the command of the whole stream."

" How ? "

"There is a rumour that Dupont intends to abandon Florida, and leave two or three ships to blockade the coast."

" Can that be possible ? "

"They are talking about it ; and if so, St. Augustine will soon be evacuated."

" And Jacksonville ? "

" Jacksonville, too."

" Then I can go back, get the committee together again, and resume the place the Federals pushed me from ! Ah ! my Northerners, if I come back, you will see how I will treat you ! "

" That is so."

" And if James Burbank and his people have not cleared out of Camdless Bay they will not again escape me."

" That is right. All that you have suffered from them I have suffered with you. What you wish, I wish ! what you hate, I hate ! The two of us are but as one."

"Yes! as one!" replied Texar.

The conversation stopped for an instant. The clink of the glasses told Zermah that the Spaniard and the other man were drinking together. Zermah was thunderstruck. To listen to them, it seemed as though these two men had had an equal hand in every crime committed during the last few years in Florida, and more particularly in those against the Burbank family. She learnt much as she listened to them for another half-hour, and all the time the same voice gave question and answer, as if Texar were alone and talking to himself. Here was a mystery which the half-breed had the greatest interest in discovering. But if the villains knew that Zermah had heard some of their secrets would they not settle the danger by killing her? And what would become of the child when Zermah was dead?

It was about eleven o'clock. The weather continued terrible ; wind and rain blew and fell without ceasing. Assuredly Texar and his companion would not leave their shelter. They would pass the night in the wigwam, and do nothing till the morning.

And Zermah's doubts ended when Texar's accomplice— who ought to have been Texar himself—asked,—

"Well, what shall we do?"

"This," said the Spaniard. "To-morrow morning we will go with our men and reconnoitre round the lake. We will explore the cypress grove for three or four miles, after sending on in advance those who know it best, particularly Squambo. If there are no signs of the approach of the Federal detachment, we will return and wait till it is time to retreat. If there is danger, we will get together our partisans and my slaves, and I will take Zermah off to the Bahama Channel while you concentrate the militia in Lower Florida."

"Agreed," said the other ; "while you reconnoitre I will hide in the woods on the island. It will not do for us to be seen together."

"No! certainly not!" said Texar. "We must keep from any imprudence that would reveal our secret. Do not come back here till to-morrow night; and, if I am obliged to go off during the day, do not leave the island till I have got clear away. Meet me, then, at Cape Sable."

Zermah then saw that she could not be rescued by the Federals. If in the morning their approach was discovered, the Spaniard would not leave the island without her. She could only be saved by her own efforts, great as was the danger. Escape under such difficult circumstances was almost impossible.

But with what courage would she have attempted it had she known that James Burbank, Gilbert, Mars and his companions at the plantation were on their way to deliver her from Texar; that her letter had told them where to look for her; that already Mr. Burbank was up the St. John's, beyond Lake Washington; that the greater part of the cypress grove had been crossed; that the little band from Camdless Bay had been joined by the detachment under Captain Howick; that it was Texar whom they looked upon as the author of the ambuscade at Kissimmee; that the scoundrel was to be hunted to death, and that he would be shot on the spot if they could only get hold of him!

But Zermah knew nothing of this. She could wait for help no longer. And she resolved to risk everything to get away from Carneral Island.

But she must wait for twenty-four hours before she made her attempt, although the night was very dark and favourable for her chance of escape. The men, who had not even taken shelter under the trees, were all round the wigwam. She could hear them walking about on the bank, smoking and talking. If her attempt failed, if her plan was discovered, she would be worse off than she was, and Texar would have an excuse for his violence.

Would the chance of escape be better to-morrow? Had not the Spaniard said that his companions, his slaves, even the Indian, Squambo, would accompany him to reconnoitre the Federal advance? Would something come out of this to increase her chance of getting away? If she could get across the channel without being seen, and reach the forest, she did not doubt that she would be safe. She could hide, and need not again fall into Texar's hands. Captain Howick could not be far off.   If he was advancing towards Lake Okee-cho-bee, was there not a chance that she might meet with him ?

Better, therefore, wait for to-morrow ! But hardly had she so decided, than something happened, that at once swept away the scaffold on which her last hopes were built.

There came a knock at the wigwam door. It was Squambo, who made himself known to his master.

" Enter ! " said the Spaniard.

Squambo came in.

" Have you any orders for the night ? " he asked.

" Keep careful watch, and let me know at the least alarm."

" I will do so," said Squambo.

" To-morrow morning we will reconnoitre for some miles in the forest."

" The half-breed and Dy ? "

" Will be under guard as usual.   See that no one disturbs us here."

" Right."

" What are the men doing ? "

" Walking about.   None of them seem to care to rest."

" See that none get far away."

" None shall go."

" What is the weather like ? "

" Not so bad as it was.   The rain has stopped, and the wind will soon drop."

" Good."

Zermah had listened to all this.   The conversation was evidently nearing its end, when a stifled sigh, a sort of rattle, made itself heard.

Zermah's blood flowed back to her heart.   She rose, rushed to the bed of herbs, and bent over the little girl.

Dy had just awoke, and in what a state ! A choking, husky breath was escaping from her lips.   Her little hands were beating the air, as if she sought to drag it into her mouth. Zermah could just hear the words,—

" Drink ! water ! "

The child was being suffocated. She must be taken into the air at once. In the darkness Zermah, distracted, took her in her arms to revive her with her own breath. She felt her struggle in a convulsion. She uttered a cry—she burst open the door of the room.

Two men were there, standing before Squambo. But so like were they in face and build that Zermah could not tell which of them was Texar.

CHAPTER XIII.

A DOUBLE LIFE.

A FEW words will suffice to explain that which has hitherto seemed inexplicable in this story.

The men before whom Zermah had suddenly appeared were twins

Where they were born they themselves did not know. Probably their birthplace was some village of Texas— whence the name of Texar by merely changing a letter.

Texas, it will be remembered, is an extensive territory, situated in the south of the United States, and on the Gulf of Mexico. After revolting against the Mexicans, Texas assisted by the United States in its work of independence was annexed to the Union in 1845, under the presidency of John Tyler.

It was about fifteen years before this annexation that two children were found abandoned in a village on the Texan coast, and were taken care of and brought up by public charity.

Attention was first directed to the children on account of their marvellous resemblance. They had the same gestures, the same voice, the same attitudes, the same physiognomy, and it may be added the same instincts testifying to a precocious perversity. We know not how they were educated, nor what instruction they received, nor to what family they belonged unless it was to one of those who roamed about the country after the declaration of independence.

As soon as the brothers Texar thought they could support themselves, they disappeared. This was when they were about twelve years old. They then took to a life of thieving among the fields and farms, stealing bread in one place, fruit in another, ending at length in highway robbery. Then they ceased to be seen in the Texan villages in the company of lawbreakers, who, even in those early days had put their strange resemblance to account. Years rolled by. The Texar brothers were soon forgotten even by name. And although the name became notorious enough in Florida, nothing happened to show that they had passed their early years in the coast districts of Texas.

But how was it that after their disappearance no one knew that there were two Texars? It was on this ignorance that their plans had been built. As was ascertained later on when the duality was discovered and proved, the brothers for twenty or thirty years lived apart. Fortune they sought in all ways; but they did not meet again except at rare intervals away from observation, either in America, or wherever their search after fortune led them.

One of them—which it was not known, though it was probably both—engaged in the slave trade. They brought cargoes of slaves from the coasts of Africa to the Southern States of the Union, acting as intermediaries between the merchants on the coast and the captains of the ships employed in the inhuman traffic.

Did their trade prosper? We do not know. But probably not; for it diminished rapidly, and was finally put a stop to when the slave trade was denounced as a barbarism, and gradually abolished by the civilized world.

The brothers had not made their fortune, and they resolved to do so at any price. It was then they resolved to avail themselves of their extraordinary resemblance.

It often happens that such a resemblance dies away as the children grow to manhood. But this was not the case with the Texars. The older they got, the more their physical and moral resemblance increased. It was impossible to distinguish one from the other either by his face or his figure or his gestures or voice. And resolving to take advantage of this natural peculiarity, they entered upon a hateful career of crime, intending if one was caught to establish an *alibi* by means of the other. When one went off to commit some act that would bring him within reach of the law, the other would show himself in public, so that all criminating evidence would fail. Of course, they never allowed themselves to be taken in the act, for then no *alibi* could have been pleaded.

Having drawn up their programme the twins came to Florida, where neither of them was known, the attraction being the numerous opportunities offered in a state where the Indians still carried on a struggle against the Americans and the Spaniards.

It was about 1850 or 1851 that Texar appeared in the Floridan peninsula—Texar, not the Texars, be it understood, for it was their intention never to be seen together, never to be on the same day in the same place.

Hiding themselves thus under a complete incognito, they found a retreat that was quite as mysterious. This was in Black Creek, which they discovered in one of their explorations of the St. John's. There they brought a few slaves, to whom their secret was not revealed. Squambo alone knew the mystery of their double existence. The confidant was worthy of his masters, whom he served with unequalled devotion and discretion, and pitilessly executed their commands.

Never, it need scarcely be said, did they appear together at Black Creek. When they wished to consult on any matter they wrote to each other. We have, in fact, seen their post-office. A letter was slipped into the stalk of a leaf, and the leaf was fixed to the branch of a tulip-tree in the neighbouring marsh. This means never failed them. Every day Squambo cautiously visited the tree. If he was the bearer of a letter from the Texar then at Black Creek he fixed it to the branch of the tulip-tree. If the letter had been written by the other brother the Indian found it in the usual place and took it back to the block-house.

After their arrival in Florida the Texars leagued themselves with all that was bad among the population. Many of the criminal classes became their accomplices in the numerous robberies that then took place, and these

became their accomplices later on when the war brought
them to the front in political matters. But although sometimes one and sometimes another took the lead in these
matters, their companions never knew that there were two
Texars. Thus it was that an *alibi* was always forthcoming
when a Texar was brought to answer for his crimes. Thus
it was that although James Burbank and Zermah had
positively recognized the Spaniard as the author of the
fire, he had been acquitted by the tribunal at St. Augustine,
for numerous witnesses swore that at the time of the crime
he was in Torillo's tienda at Jacksonville. And so it was
regarding the attack on Camdless Bay. How could Texar
be leading the assault at Castle House, or carrying away
Zermah and Dy when he was one of the prisoners made
by the Federals at Fernandina, and then in safe keeping
on one of the gunboats?

And even admitting that the duality of Texar was
known, how could they tell which of them was the culprit?
Were there not in fact two who were guilty? Should not
the justly-merited punishment fall on both?

At Jacksonville it was probable that both brothers had
in turn played the same part after the outbreak. When
Texar No. 1 absented himself on some agreed expedition,
Texar No. 2 would take his place without the people being
aware of the change. They thus took an equal part in the
excesses then committed against the colonists of Northern
birth and the Southern planters holding anti-slavery
opinions.

Both were aware of what passed in the Central States
of the Union, where, as in Florida, civil war underwent
such unexpected changes in fortune; both had acquired
great influence over the lower class of whites, and over
the Spaniards, and even the American slave partisans.
Their correspondence was considerable, and their meet-
ings in out-of-the-way places were many, to enable them
to conduct their operations and prepare their future
alibis.

It was while one was in the hands of the Federals that
the other organized the expedition at Camdless Bay.

And we know how they had turned this to account at the court-martial at St. Augustine.

Age, as it has been said, confirmed and increased the resemblance between the brothers ; but it was possible that an accident or a wound might alter that resemblance. For instance, in a night-attack some time after their arrival in Florida, one of the Texars had his beard burnt by a rifle fired at him point blank. Immediately the other shaved his beard so as to be like his brother, a fact that was mentioned in the early part of this history.

Another fact requires explanation. It will not have been forgotten that one night while she was at Black Creek Zermah saw the Spaniard's arm tattooed. The reason was that his brother had been captured by a band of Seminoles, and had been so indelibly marked on his left arm. Immediately a tracing of the device was sent to the fortress and Squambo set to work, so that the identity continued absolute.

In fact if Texar No. 1 had happened to lose a limb, Texar No. 2 would have submitted to amputation to resemble him.

For twelve years the Texar brothers lived this double life, but with such skill and prudence that justice was set at defiance.

Had the twins grown rich at this trade ? Yes, in a certain measure. A considerable sum of money saved from the proceeds of pillage and theft had been hidden in a secret redoubt of the blockhouse at Black Creek, but as a precaution it had been taken away by the Spaniard when he started for Carneral Island, and we may rest assured he would not leave it behind him if he went to the Bahamas.

When the twins learnt that Commodore Dupont contemplated an early evacuation of Florida, they saw that there would be a chance of further enriching themselves, and the Northern planters could be made to pay dearly for the Federal occupation. They had therefore resolved to keep on the watch. Once they were back at Jacksonville, with the help of their partisans and the Southerners in league with them, they could resume the position which a riot had given them once and could give them again.

And besides this they had a means of acquiring wealth almost beyond their desires. They had only to listen to the proposition Zermah had made to one of them; they had only to return Dy to her parents. James Burbank would have given his fortune as his child's ransom. He would have undertaken to make no complaint or instigate any pursuit against the Spaniard. But among the Texars hate was stronger than self-interest. They wished to be revenged on the Burbanks before they left Florida.

Such is all that need be said about the history of the brothers Texar. We can now resume our story.

When Zermah suddenly found herself in their presence, she understood all. The past instantly rushed back through her mind. In astonishment she looked at the men—motionless as if rooted in the ground, holding the little girl in her arms. Fortunately the air in the room was abundant, and all fear of the child's suffocation had gone.

Her appearance before the brothers, her discovery of the secret of their lives, meant, she well knew, sentence of death.

CHAPTER XIV.

ZERMAH AT WORK.

THE Texars were furious at Zermah's interruption.

With the exception of Squambo, never before since their childhood had a third person seen them together. And this person was their mortal enemy. Their first impulse was to hurl themselves at her and murder her, so as to save the secret of their double life.

The child raised herself in Zermah's arms; and holding out her little hands, she cried,—

"I am afraid! I am afraid!"

At a gesture from the two brothers Squambo stepped roughly up to the half-breed, took her by the shoulder, and pushed her back into her room and shut the door.

Then Squambo returned to the brothers. His attitude told them they had only to command for him to obey. But the interruption had been so unexpected that it had troubled them more than might be supposed. They seemed to consult each other with a look.

Zermah had thrown herself into a corner of the room, after laying the little girl on one of the beds. Her self-possession returned to her; and she went to the door to hear what was passing. In a moment her fate would probably be decided. But the Texars and Squambo had just gone out of the hut, and were no longer within ear-shot.

And this is what they were saying,—

"Zermah must die."

"She must! If she escapes, or if the Federals get hold of her, we are lost! She must die!"

"This moment!" said Squambo.

And knife in hand he had turned to go to the hut, when one of the Texars stopped him.

"Wait," said he. "It will always be time enough to put Zermah out of the way ; and we have need of her to take care of the youngster. Let us first see how we stand. A detachment of Northerners is now in the cypress grove. Let us take a careful look-out round the lake, for there is no proof as yet that the detachment is coming this way. If it is coming we shall have time to get away ; if it is not coming we can stop here and let it get deeper into the wilds of Florida when it will be at our mercy. We shall have time to muster the militia and cut off the Federal retreat. Some escaped from Kissimmee, but none will escape here."

This was obviously the best thing to do under the circumstances. A large number of Southerners were in the neighbourhood only waiting for an opportunity to try a stroke at the Federals. One of the Texars could go out and reconnoitre, and then they could decide either to remain at Carneral Island or move off to Cape Sable. That could be done to-morrow, and Squambo could be trusted to take care of Zermah whatever might be the result of the exploration.

"As for the child," said one of the brothers, "it is our interest to keep her alive. She cannot have understood as Zermah did, and she may be the price of our ransom should one of us fall into the hands of Captain Howick. To get back his daughter, James Burbank would accept any condition we like to impose."

"If Zermah dies," said the Indian, "are you not afraid that the child will die too ?"

"No, she will be well looked after, and I can easily find an Indian woman to take the place of the half-breed."

"Do so then ! We must not have anything to fear from Zermah."

"Well, whatever happens, we shall soon put her out of the way."

And Zermah heard the brothers come back into the wigwam.

What a night it was for the unhappy woman! She knew she was doomed, and yet she had no thought for herself, but for Dy, who would thus be abandoned to the cruelty of these pitiless men. It was to their interest that the child should live, but when Zermah was gone would she survive? And the thought of this returned to her so often and took such obstinate possession of her that she resolved to escape before Texar could separate her from the child.

In the conversation she had overheard, she had learnt that one of the Texars and his companions was going to reconnoitre round the lake, evidently with the object of fighting the Federal detachment should opportunity offer. Texar would therefore be away with all his men, and his brother would remain on the island so as in the first place not to be recognized, and in the second to watch the hut. Then was the time for Zermah to attempt her escape. Perhaps she might find a weapon of some sort, and in case of surprise she would not hesitate to use it.

The night went by. Vainly did Zermah listen for some sign among the sounds on the island of the arrival of Captain Howick and the capture of the Texars.

A few minutes before daybreak the little girl awoke. Zermah gave her a few drops of water. Then looking at her as if she would never see her again, she clasped her in her arms. At that moment had any one entered to tear her away from her charge she would have defended herself with the fury of a wild beast being taken from her little ones.

" What is the matter, Zermah ? " asked the child.

" Nothing—nothing! " said the half-breed.

" And mamma—when shall we see her again ? "

"Soon," said Zermah ; "to-day, perhaps! Yes, my dear! to-day I hope we are near her—"

" And the men I saw to-night ? "

" The men ! Did you see them ? "

" Yes, and they made me afraid."

" But did you notice them ? Did you see how much they were alike ? "

PART II.

" Yes."

" Well, remember to tell your father, and your brother, that there are two brothers—do you understand ? there are two brothers Texar, so alike that you cannot tell one from the other."

" Will you tell them that too ?" asked the child.

" Yes. I'll tell them so. But if I am not there, you must not forget it."

" And why will you not be there ?" asked Dy, putting her arms round the half-breed's neck.

" I shall be there, my dear, I shall be there ! But if we go out, as we have a long way to go, we must get something to eat. I will get you something."

" And you ? "

" I had something while you were asleep, and I am not hungry."

The truth was, that Zermah could not have eaten had she tried, owing to the state of excitement she was in. As soon as the child had finished, Zermah put her back on the herb couch, and went to a gap among the reeds in a corner of the room ; and thence she watched for an hour the scene outside.

Preparations were being made for departure. One of the brothers, only one, was mustering the men that were to go into the cypress grove. The other, whom none of the men had seen, was concealed, either in the wigwam or in some corner of the island.

At least, so thought Zermah, who knew how careful they were to hide the secret of their lives. And she thought to herself that this other one had been told off to keep watch on Dy and herself.

And Zermah was not mistaken, as we shall soon see.

And now the men, to the number of about fifty, were all mustered ready before the hut waiting for orders. By about nine o'clock they had all entered the forest, the barge being only able to take some five or six at a time. Zermah saw them go off in small groups, and walk up the other bank ; but she could not see the surface of the water.

Texar remained till the last, and then went off, followed by one of the dogs, whose instinct was to be made use of during the expedition. At a sign from his master the other hound returned to the hut, as if he was to be the only guard.

A minute afterwards Zermah saw Texar move up the opposite bank, and stop for an instant to arrange his men. Then, with Squambo at their head, and accompanied by the dog, the men disappeared among the trees. Doubtless one of the negroes had brought back the barge, so that no one could cross over to the island. But the half-breed did not see this.

She, however, hesitated no longer.

Dy had just awoke.

"Come, darling," said Zermah.

"Where?" asked the child.

"There! Into the forest! Perhaps we shall find your father—your brother! You are not afraid?"

"Not when you are with me."

Then the half-breed opened the door carefully. As she had heard no noise in the hut, she supposed that Texar was not there.

And she was right.

She sought about for some weapon of defence. On the table was one of those large knives used by the Indians when hunting. She picked it up and hid it under her clothes; and she took a little dry meat to last her for a few hours.

But the time came for her to leave the wigwam. She looked out through the palisade in the direction of the channel. There was not a living creature in sight.

The half-breed tried to open the outer door.

The door was shut from the outside, and would not give way.

Then Zermah went back to the hut. There was only one thing to be done. That was to make use of the hole she had already half made in the wall of her sleeping-room.

The work was easy. She had only to use her knife to

cut into the reeds—and this she did with as little noise as possible.

But if the hound that had not gone with Texar were to appear? Would he not throw himself on her and the child?

There was, however, no time to hesitate. The hole was made large enough, and through it Zermah drew the child, whom she passionately embraced as she did so. Dy gave back kiss for kiss; she had understood. It was necessary to escape through this hole.

Zermah glided through and looked to the left, to the right, and listened. Not a sound could she hear.

But soon she heard the bark of a hound It seemed to come from the west of the island. She picked up the child. Her heart beat ready to burst. She could not think she was safe until she was through the reeds on the opposite river-bank.

But to cross the hundred yards between the wigwam and the stream was the most critical part of the escape. There was a chance of her being seen either by Texar or by the slaves.

Luckily, to the right of the hut was a thicket of arborescent plants and reeds, extending to the bank of the channel, a few yards only from the barge.

Zermah entered the thicket. The plants opened to give passage to the fugitives, and closed behind them. The barking of the dog was heard no longer.

The way through the thicket was not easy. There was but a narrow path between the interlacing shrubs. Zermah's dress was in rags, and her hands were torn. Little did it matter so long as the child was unharmed!

The brave half-breed uttered no complaint, and although Dy often made acquaintance with the thorns, not a cry did she utter.

Although the distance was short, about sixty yards at the outside, it took quite half an hour before the channel was reached.

Zermah then stopped, and through the reeds she looked first at the wigwam, then at the forest.

There was no one to be seen. On the other bank was no sign of Texar and his companions, who were a couple of miles or so away. Unless they met the Northerners they would not be back for some hours.

But Zermah did not believe she had been left alone in the hut. It was not likely that one of the Texars had gone off unseen and taken the dog with him. Besides, had not the half-breed heard the barking—a proof that the hound was still prowling under the trees? Any moment she might see one or the other appear. But if she made haste she might reach the cypress grove.

While she watched the Spaniard's men in their journey from bank to bank she had not been able to see the surface of the stream, and she supposed that the barge had been brought back by one of the slaves. This was necessary for the safety of the wigwam, in case Captain Howick and his men defeated the Southerners.

But if the barge was on the other side, so as to be ready to help in Texar's retreat, should he have to retreat? If it were not there, would he not have to find another hiding-place?

But Zermah must have the barge to get across. She could not see it. Where could it be? For half a dozen yards she glided through the reeds. Then she stopped.

The barge was on the other side of the channel.

CHAPTER XV.

THE TWO BROTHERS.

THE position was critical. How could she cross? The boldest swimmer could not do it without risking his life a score of times. There were but a hundred feet from bank to bank, but without the boat it was impossible to cross them. Triangular heads appeared every now and then above the surface of the water, and the weeds waved to let the reptiles pass.

Little Dy, almost dead with fright, clung close to Zermah. If she could have saved the child by throwing herself into the thick of this crowd of snakes, who would have closed on to her like the arms of some giant octopus, the half-breed would not have hesitated for a moment!

But only some special intervention of Providence could save her. And Zermah knelt and prayed for help.

Any moment some of Texar's companions might appear on the edge of the forest. If the Texar remaining on the island went back to the wigwam and missed her, would he not come in pursuit?

"Oh God! have pity on me!"

And as she prayed she looked to the right of the channel.

A gentle current was running through towards the north of the lake, where a few affluents of the small river Calaooschatches flow out to the Gulf of Mexico. It is this river which feeds Lake Okee-cho-bee at the great monthly tides.

A trunk of a tree came drifting along from the right, and had just struck against the bank. Would not this tree afford the means of crossing the channel? Evidently.

In any case if the tree drifted back to the island the fugitives would be no worse off than they were now.

Without stopping to think, Zermah, as if by instinct, ran to the floating tree. If she had stopped she might have hesitated at the hundreds of reptiles swarming in the water, and the chance that the weeds would keep the trunk motionless in mid-channel! But anything would be better than remaining on the island! And so Zermah, with Dy in her arms, climbed along into the branches and pushed off the tree, which immediately began to move with the current.

She tried to hide among the foliage which partly covered it. The banks were deserted. There was no sound from the island or the cypress grove. Once across the channel the half-breed would hide away till night-time, and then enter the forest without being seen. Hope returned to her. She scarcely gave a thought to the reptiles who swam open-mouthed round the tree and glided over its lower branches. The little girl kept her eyes shut as Zermah clasped her to her breast with one hand, while she held the knife in the other ready to defend herself. But whether it was that the monsters feared the sight of the knife, or were only dangerous in the water, they made no attempt to attack her.

At length the tree reached the middle of the stream, and was being steadily borne towards the forest. In a quarter of an hour if it did not get caught in the weeds it would ground on the other bank. And then, great as were the dangers she had to face, Zermah thought herself safe from Texar.

Suddenly she clasped the child more tightly to her.

There was a furious barking on the island. And soon afterwards a dog came bounding along the river-side.

Zermah recognized the hound that the Spaniard had left to guard the wigwam.

With coat bristling with anger and eyes flashing fire, he stood ready to leap among the reptiles that crowded the surface of the water.

At the same moment a man appeared on the bank.

It was the Texar who had stopped on the island. Warned by the dog's bark, he had run up to see what had happened. His rage at finding Zermah and Dy on the drifting tree may be imagined. He could not follow them, for the barge was on the other side of the stream. Only one thing could he do to stop them, and that was to shoot Zermah at the risk of killing the child.

He had brought his gun with him, and he did not hesitate to use it. He took careful aim at the half-breed, who tried to cover the child with her body.

Suddenly the dog in its mad excitement jumped into the water. Texar thought he had better wait to see what it could do.

The hound swam swiftly towards the tree, and Zermah, knife in hand, was ready. But it was not necessary.

In a moment the snakes had twisted themselves on to their prey, and with a few bites from its teeth in answer to those from their venomous fangs the dog had sunk among the weeds.

Texar saw the dog die before he could help it, and now Zermah was escaping him.

" Die then ! " he exclaimed.

But the drifting tree had now reached the opposite bank, and the bullet only grazed the half-breed's shoulder.

Next moment the tree grounded. Zermah carrying the child stepped ashore and vanished into a clump of reeds. Texar fired again, but missed.

She had escaped from the Texar on the island, but she was now in danger of falling into the hands of his brother. Her first endeavour was to get as far from Carneral Island as possible. When night came she would make for Lake Washington. Calling up all her strength and energy, she fled along, running rather than walking, and carrying the child in her arms. Dy's little legs refused to run on the irregular ground amid the quagmires that sunk like traps, and the roots that grew in such tangled masses as to be impassable for her.

She did not seem to feel the weight of her burden. Sometimes she stopped, less to take breath than to listen to the sounds of the forest. Sometimes she thought she could hear the bark of the other dog that Texar had taken with him. Sometimes she thought she could hear the report of firing in the distance. And she wondered if the Southerners had come up with the Federal detachment. Then, when she had recognized that the noises were but the cries of a bird, or the breaking of some dry branch, she would resume her flight, and full of hope, think nothing of the dangers that threatened her until she reached the sources of the St. John's.

For an hour she continued to leave Lake Okee-cho-bee, making towards the east, so as to approach the Atlantic shore. It appeared probable to her that ships of the squadron would be cruising off the coast in support of the detachment under Captain Howick.

Suddenly she stopped. This time there could be no mistake. A furious barking was heard under the trees, and it was coming quickly towards her. Zermah recognized the baik as one she had often heard while the dogs kept watch round the Black Creek blockhouse.

"The dog is on our track," thought she, "and Texar cannot be far off."

She looked round in search of a thicket, in which she and the child could hide. But the dog was as intelligent as he was fierce, and had been trained to slave-hunting, would he not scent her out?

The barking came nearer and nearer, and shouts could be heard in the distance.

A few yards away stood an old cypress-tree, hollow with age, round which serpentarias and lianas had thrown a thick network of branchlets.

Zermah ran to the hollow, which was just large enough to hold her and the child, while the network of lianas concealed them.

But the dog was on their track. A minute afterwards Zermah saw him in front of the tree. He barked with renewed fury and sprang at the cypress.

A stab with the knife made him retreat ; and he began to bark more furiously than ever.

A minute or so afterwards voices were heard—those of
Texar and Squambo, among others.   It was the Spaniard
and his companions who were running to the lake in
an endeavour to escape from the Federal detachment
which they had unexpectedly met in the cypress grove,
and found too strong to resist.   Texar's object was to
get back to Carneral Island by the shortest way, so as to
put a ring of water between the Federals and himself.
The Federals would not be able to cross it without a boat.
After a few hours of respite the Southerners could reach
the other side of the island, and when night came make
use of the barge to land on the southern side of the
lake.

When Texar and Squambo reached the cypress-tree in
front of which the dog continued to bark, they saw that
the ground was red with the blood that flowed from an
open wound in the flank.

"Look! look!" exclaimed the Indian.

"Is the dog wounded?" asked Texar.

"Yes! wounded by a knife, and not a minute ago.   The
blood is still smoking."

"Who could have done it?"

And here the dog again jumped at the network of foliage
which Squambo lifted aside with the butt end of his gun.

"Zermah!" he exclaimed.

"And the child!" said Texar.

"Yes.   How did they get away?"

"Kill her!   Kill Zermah!"

The half-breed stabbed at the Spaniard, but Squambo
snatched away the knife and drew her out from the tree so
roughly that the child fell and rolled among a lot of the
giant pezizas, which abound under the cypress-trees.

At the shock, one of the mushrooms exploded like a gun,
and a luminous dust crackled in the air.   At the same
moment other pezizas went off, and there was a noise all
round as if the forest were filled with fireworks.

Blinded by the myriad spores, Texar had to leave go of
Zermah, and the burning dust in Squambo's eyes for a
moment rendered the Indian powerless.   Fortunately **the**

half-breed and child were stretched on the ground, and lay unharmed while the spores crackled above them.

But Zermah could not escape from Texar. Already the air, after a few more explosions, had become breathable. . . . Then a new series of reports began, but this time they were the reports of firearms.

It was the Federal detachment come up with the Southerners, whom they surrounded in an instant and ordered to lay down their arms. As the order was given, Texar seized hold of the half-breed and stabbed her in the breast.

" The child! Carry off the child !" shouted the Spaniard to Squambo.

The Indian caught up the girl and had run a stride or two towards the lake, when a gun was fired. He fell dead, shot through the heart by Gilbert Burbank.

For all had come up, James Burbank and Gilbert, and Carrol, and Perry, and Mars, and the blacks from Camdless Bay, and Captain Howick's seamen, who had made prisoners of the Southerners. Among the prisoners was Texar standing upright by Squambo's corpse. Only a few of the men had escaped towards Carneral Island.

Dy was in her father's arms and he was clasping her as tightly as if he feared she was to be again taken away from him. Gilbert and Mars were leaning over Zermah endeavouring to revive her. She still breathed, but she could not speak. Mars held up her head, called to her, kissed her.

She opened her eyes. She saw the child in Mr. Burbank's arms, recognized Mars covering her with kisses, and smiled. Then her eyelids fell.

Mars stood up, and catching sight of Texar jumped towards him shouting, " Kill Texar ! Kill Texar ! "

" Stop, Mars," said Captain Howick, "and let us deal with the scoundrel."

"Now," said he, turning towards the Spaniard, "you are Texar of Black Creek."

" I have nothing to say," replied Texar.

" James Burbank, Lieutenant Burbank, Edward Carrol, and Mars, all know you and recognize you."

20

"Be it so!"

"You are to be shot."

"Well, shoot!"

Then, to the surprise of all who heard her, Dy said to her father,—

"Father, there are two brothers, two wicked men, who are so much alike—"

"Two men?"

"Yes! Zermah told me to tell you so."

It would, perhaps, have been difficult to understand the meaning of these strange words had not the explanation been almost immediately given, and in a very unexpected fashion.

Texar had been taken to the foot of a tree. There, looking James Burbank in the face, he stood smoking a cigarette he had just lighted, when, suddenly, as the firing-party formed up, a man leaped past them and stood by the Spaniard's side.

It was the second Texar, whom the men who had reached Carneral Island had told of his brother's arrest.

The sight of these two men, so like to each other, explained the child's meaning. Here at last was the explanation of the life of crime and the inexplicable *alibis*.

But the brother's intervention could not but cause a certain amount of hesitation in carrying out the commodore's orders.

The order for immediate execution only referred to the author of the ambuscade in which the officers and men of the Federal boats had perished. The author of the robbery at Camdless Bay and the seizure of the child ought certainly to be taken back to be re-tried at St. Augustine.

But could not both brothers be considered equally responsible for the long series of crimes they had been able to commit with impunity?

Certainly! But out of respect to the law Captain Howick thought it best to put the following question,—

"Which of you was guilty of the massacre at Kissimmee?"

There was no reply.

Evidently the Texars intended to say nothing in reply to the questions put to them.

Zermah alone could tell which was which. The brother who was at Black Creek on the 22nd of March could not be the author of the massacre committed a hundred miles off the same day. Zermah had a means of identifying the man who carried her off. But was she not dead now?

No. Supported by her husband she was seen to come forward. In a voice that could hardly be heard, she said,—

"The man who carried me off is tattooed on the left arm."

At these words a smile of disdain appeared on the lips of the brothers, who folded up their sleeves and showed on the left arm of each a similar tattoo mark.

At this new impossibility of distinguishing one from the other, Captain Howick thought it was time to bring the scene to a close.

"The author of the massacre at Kissimmee is to be shot. Which of you was it?"

"I was," said both the brothers together.

That was enough. At the words the firing-party took aim.

There was a flash and a report, and hand in hand the Texars fell.

That was the end of these two men, whose extraordinary resemblance had enabled them for so many years to commit crime with impunity. The only human sentiment they could be credited with was this savage friendship of brother to brother which had been theirs till death.

CHAPTER XVI.

CONCLUSION.

THE civil war continued with varying fortune. Some things had recently happened of which James Burbank had not heard since his departure from Camdless Bay, and which he only knew when he got back.

During this time it seemed as though the advantage rested with the Confederates round Corinth, while the Federals occupied the position of Pittsburg Landing. The Southern army had Johnston as general-in-chief, and under him were Beauregard, Harder, Braxton-Wragg, and Bishop Polk, an old pupil at West Point; and these cleverly profited by the shortsightedness of the Northerners, who, on the 5th of April, were surprised at Shiloh. The result of that surprise was the dispersal of Peabody's brigade and the retreat of Sherman. The Confederates, however, paid cruelly for their success, the heroic Johnston being killed as he repulsed the Federal army.

Such was the first day of the battle of the 5th of April. The day but one after there was another fight along the whole line, and Sherman retook Shiloh. In their turn the Confederates had to retreat before the soldiers of Grant. The struggle was a sanguinary one ; out of eighty thousand men engaged, twenty thousand were wounded or killed.

This was the last news of the war that James Burbank and his companions heard the morning after their return to Castle House, on the 7th of April.

After the execution of the Texars they had accompanied Captain Howick and his prisoners to the coast. At Cape Malabar one of the vessels of the flotilla had been stationed to cruise off the coast, and in her they were taken to St

Augustine. Thence a gunboat took them from Picolata to Camdless Bay.

And so all got back to Castle House—even Zermah, who had recovered from her wounds. Carried to the Federal vessel by Mars and his companions, she had had every attention, and in her happiness at having saved little Dy, and restored her to those who loved her, how could she die?

Mrs. Burbank, with her child near her, gradually recovered her health. With her had she not her husband, her son, Alice (soon to become her daughter), Zermah, and Mars? And she had nothing to fear henceforth from the scoundrel, or rather, two scoundrels, whose chief accomplices were in Federal hands.

But a rumour was abroad which, it will be remembered, was mentioned by the brothers at their interview at Carneral Island. It was said that the Northerners were to abandon Jacksonville; that Dupont, confining himself to the blockade of the coast, was to withdraw the gunboats that assured the safety of the St. John's. This plan would evidently jeopardize the safety of the planters who held anti-slavery notions, and especially James Burbank.

The rumour was well founded. On the 8th of April, the day after that on which the family returned to Castle House, the Federals began the evacuation of Jacksonville. A few of the inhabitants, who were favourable to the Unionist cause, thought it better to leave the town, some for Port Royal, others for New York.

James Burbank did not think it necessary to follow their example. The negroes had returned to the plantation, not as slaves, but as free men, and their presence would assure the safety of Camdless Bay. The war had entered on a favourable phase for the North, and this allowed of Gilbert remaining on leave at Castle House to celebrate his marriage with Alice Stannard.

The work on the plantation was recommenced. There was no question of putting in force against Mr. Burbank the order expelling the freed slaves from Floridan territory. Texar and his companions were no longer at hand to raise the populace, and the gunboats on the coast would promptly re-establish order at Jacksonville.

The war dragged on for three more years, and even Florida was destined to receive a few more of its counter-effects. In the month of September of this same year Dupont's flotilla appeared at St. John's Bluffs, near the mouth of the river, and Jacksonville was occupied for the second time. Later on it was occupied by General Seymour for a third time, after a trifling resistance.

On the 1st of January, 1863, a proclamation by President Lincoln abolished slavery in all the States of the Union. But the war did not end till the 9th of April, 1865. On that day, at Appomattox Court House, General Lee surrendered with his whole army to General Grant, under a capitulation which did honour to both parties.

The sanguinary struggle of North against South had lasted four years. It had cost two thousand seven hundred millions of dollars, and killed more than half a million of men ; but slavery was abolished throughout North America. And by it was assured the indivisibility of the Republic of the United States, thanks to the efforts of those Americans whose ancestors a century before had freed their country in the War of Independence.

END OF THE SECOND AND LAST PART.